About the Author

Alex Gardiner served as an officer in the Royal Greenjackets, and as a troop and squadron commander in 22 SAS before leaving the British Army to command 1st Regiment The Sultan's Special Force in Southern Oman. Since then, he has covered conflict in Bosnia, Kosovo, Iraq, Afghanistan and Yemen. He is married to the fashion designer Beatrice von Tresckow and is working on his next novel from their home in Gloucestershire.

*To Steve,
Thanks for having
me on your excellent
show.
Alex.*

The
DEVIL'S
MAGISTRATE

Alex Gardiner

NINE
ELMS

The Devil's Magistrate

This edition published in 2022 by
Nine Elms Books
Unit 6B, Clapham North Arts Centre
26–32 Voltaire Road
London SW4 6DH

Email: info@nineelmsbooks.co.uk
www.nineelmsbooks.co.uk

ISBN: 978-1-910533-65-9
Epub: 978-1-910533-66-6

First edition published as The Good Muslim in 2018 by Brown Dog Books and
The Self-Publishing Partnership.

Cover design and typesetting: Tony Hannaford
Printed in the UK.

For Beatrice, Max and Frederike

Acknowlegements

Alex I am hugely indebted to my patient, tenacious agent Harry Bucknall who brought his focus and energy to the challenge of getting my literary efforts noticed. It was he who persuaded Anthony Weldon to give this story a chance.

I wish to thank Anthony whose faith in the tale and his suggestions have proven crucial to maturing the story…it always takes Guardsmen to see the possibilities.

It has been a privilege to work with Peta Broadfoot, my indefatigable editor, whose enthusiasm for the novel has been inspirational. She set the bar high, kept me on track and rightly deserves the lioness's share of credit for the stunning result.

To the team at Nine Elms and in particular Tony Hannaford who designed the cover and typeset the book, I say a special thank you.

And to the soldier-adventurers I have journeyed with, courageous men and women who had my back, faced fear, hunger and uncertainty with me, who placed selflessness, trust and friendship above religious difference, you are the inspiration for this story.

COUNTY TYRONE, ULSTER. 1987

I the grey half-light of dawn, he felt the fury of the storm as it
flailed at the scrawny treeline. Curtains of rain, driven sideways by a howling wind, lashed down at the line of men. His
borrowed cap and clothes were soaked, and the water gathering at his collar began to snake down his spine. Looking down
he could see ruts gouged in the mud where his rubber boots
had slid away from under him as he knelt against the side of
the ditch. Mush in his socks told him rain had seeped in or
the boots were leaking, probably both. A freezing cold he'd
never experienced before sliced into his bones; when he com-
manded his fingers to move over the metal of his weapon, he
saw twitches of movement but felt nothing. Maybe he wouldn't
be able to trust them when the time came.

In the distance, a faint speck of yellow light in an isolated
farmstead pricked the gloom, signalling that a household was
stirring to meet its day. His companions, lined out along the
ditch, all noticed it at the same time. Two men on his left

pointed, shouting above the wind, in their bizarre mix of English and profanity. Even in ideal conditions he could barely understand them. Disgorged by a churning, filthy trawler a few days earlier and still homesick for Libya, he had found himself entrusted to these people. They were rough but not unkind; one moment he was treated as an exotic guest, the next an encumbrance, all the while subjected to a constant barrage of friendly insults.

One of the two stepped in close and clapped him on the shoulder, 'Ok, Darky, mate? We're not often this lucky with the fucking weather. You should see it when it's bad.' The other man laughed and fumbled inside his jacket pocket, extracting a bottle. He waved the others into a tight circle, every man bunching in, bringing his weapon.

'The fucker's up and about.' He jerked a thumb in the direction of the light. 'Remember lads, he's a fucking tout. We top him and get the hell away.'

It was like being in a film, he thought, as he watched his man take the cork out with his teeth and hold the bottle up in salute before taking a long pull. It made its way round the five men, reaching him last. They watched, nodding encouragement. One yelled, 'Sláinte, Darky! Put some lead in your pencil.'

The glass rim rattled against his chattering teeth as he tipped and swallowed, eyes closed, rain beating off his upturned face. Liquid fire tore at his throat, convulsing him. His eyes goggled as the breath left him, and even the wind could not drown out the explosion of laughter from his companions. The man reached out to claim the bottle back. 'Masks on, lads!' he shouted, 'into your positions, safety catches off.'

After a minute, a tingling warmth kindled in his gut. A surge of confidence started to build, and he began to work blood back into his frozen fingers by taking one hand at a time off the Kalashnikov and stuffing it into his trouser pocket, pushing it to his crotch for warmth. He rolled his shoulders vigorously inside the oversize jacket, and the man next to him called over, 'Ease up on the rain dance, Tonto, or we'll all fucking drown.' He thought maybe the wind was dropping, had lost some of its bite.

Headlights from the farm hit the scudding clouds and drew a sharp whistle from the lookout. Each man hefted his weapon, getting ready.

'He's leaving…just one car,' the lookout called.

'You sure?' the man with the bottle called back.

'For fuck's sake, take a look yourself.'

He was extraordinarily alert now, no sense of cold. He thumbed the safety lever of the Kalashnikov, clacking it down: no problem with his fingers, but his mouth had gone bone dry.

'At the junction. It's turning our way.'

Twin beams, juddering over rough ground, turned the raindrops into a shower of crystal as the car eased off the rough farm track and onto the main road.

The wool of his balaclava was itching, and he realised he was sweating. The eye and mouth holes at least let in some air and he licked his lips, craving a long drink of cool water. His gut was churning now. He wondered if this was fear.

'He's past the marker. Three hundred yards and coming on fast,' the lookout shouted.

'Drop the fucker!' the leader yelled. The man at the extreme right of the line pulled a cord and a length of telegraph pole, hidden in the tree line, began to move. It spun in slow motion, then pitched forward across the narrow road, catching in the stunted tree opposite and stopping a foot above the tarmac.

Even as the car slewed to a shrieking halt, bullets were slamming into it. Cracking blasts stabbed his eardrums and long muzzle flashes seared his eyes. Spent cases from a Kalashnikov on his left hit him on the cheek and temple. He felt his own weapon bucking, its butt hammering his shoulder. The car rocked with the impact, its windshield puckering with rosettes and side windows showering glass from the exiting bullets.

Then he became aware of screaming, maybe from inside the vehicle, certainly from his companions. 'Stop! Enough! For fuck's sake, stop!' The man with the bottle was now on the road, steam rising off his weapon as he stalked warily towards the car. The storm had quietened, and they all watched as he craned his head at the results of the ambush. Abruptly, he jerked back, lowering his weapon, pleading 'Jesus, Jesus…aah no, Jesus! Please not this.'

One of the others strode in to look, and then turned away without a word. Even the wind and rain had paused, as if silenced by the shock. All five men, now gathered at the vehicle, could see a man sitting in the driver's seat, leaning back, hands down, blood spattered over his torso, the top half of his skull scooped off above the right ear. A mess of tissue, bone, cartilage and flesh sat like a topping above the victim's nose.

Moving spasmodically in the passenger's seat was another figure, a young boy, his jacket and jeans sprayed with blood. He was still alive but appallingly hurt. His blood-soaked right hand lifted towards the men, pleading, then jerked back to his face.

'For the love of Christ,' someone said, 'the wee lad…one of you…put him out of it.'

'You fucking do it,' someone else said. 'I'm out of ammo.'

'He'll talk if he lives.'

The man with the bottle said, 'We stay here a second longer, he won't need to.'

Another voice said, 'Darky, step up, mate. Welcome to the struggle for a united Ireland. Don't think, just finish it, for God's sake.'

1

CHELTENHAM, ENGLAND. MONDAY 2ND MARCH

The court building on St Georges Road reminded Hash that in Britain crime did pay and here was the proof; six-ties architects had robbed Cheltenham of its Georgian perfection and never been brought to book. The courthouse was an abortion of grey concrete fronted by a pair of cantilevered steps offering the choice to go up left or right. Either route, he had long decided, led to flabby, lenient justice.

The balcony at the head of the stairs afforded a spot for people to smoke and chatter. By the time Hash arrived, a haze of smoke and nervous bravado hung in the sharp March air. Anyone watching him coming up the steps would have had no difficulty singling Tariq Hashmi out from the shell suits. He was clearly a member of the establishment, a posh bastard, one of them…not one of us.

Once in court, Hash, in unison with the two other magistrates, one the Bench Chairman and the other a winger like himself, bowed and sat.

Standing alone in the glass-screened dock, a lanky young

man struck a pose somewhere between self-consciousness and nonchalance. He looked uncomfortable in a suit which Hash guessed had been in mothballs since its last court appearance. A fresh haircut revealed scrolling tattoos on his neck and a hand crept up now and then to rub his raw skin. He glanced up at the Bench, and around the court before darting a conspiratorial smirk to his crew of supporters sitting at the back. His rolling eyes and 'here we are again' look drew a rash of grins from his mates. A reporter, making a late entrance, took a seat halfway down the court. The clerk's request for identity commenced proceedings, and Hash automatically scribbled a name and address.

The defendant's every utterance was accompanied by a 'sir' and his ready responses to court procedure hinted at coaching from his lawyer, although four consecutive words without swearing was pushing it for him. In fairness, Hash reflected, a complete sentence with verbs at the same time as standing up wasn't obligatory. The clerk read out the charge, 'Burglary of a dwelling whilst the occupant was present'. A custodial sentence with the thug behind bars by the end of the day was guaranteed, Hash knew.

There was an early recess. Catching sight of the balding man with the tired brown eyes in the Gents' mirror, Hash grimaced and gave himself a quick pep talk: 'Cheer up, old scout! Things could be worse. Chin up, chest out!' He could hear his Dad's voice, the black and white movie buff. The lines were probably originally uttered by David Niven or Kenneth More, a cheery face above a blood-soaked uniform anyway, dying a valiant death somewhere on the North-West Frontier. Hash aped the commanding stare of one of those old actors; head cocked, hyper-attentive, one eyebrow raised, his best courtroom face in place, before flicking at a speck of dust on his blue suit, perfecting the knot in his silk tie and heading back.

The court resumed to hear the only prosecution witness, an

elderly widow, occupant of the burgled flat. She got straight to the point, 'That is the man who was in my flat,' but her voice was so faint the clerk had to coax her to repeat it. She paused, visibly trembling, and Hash could see she was terrified. She took a deep breath, pulled herself together and said much more firmly, looking straight at the defendant, 'He's the one who robbed my flat.'

Seeing her distress, the Chairman offered her the chance to sit and she stayed there, looking at her hands, dabbing her eyes with a handkerchief while the thug in the dock stared at her aggressively until his lawyer coughed.

'What was he doing at the time you saw him?' the prosecution service lawyer asked.

'He was holding my stuff.'

'What stuff was that?

'My personal things. My silver photo frames,' she whispered. 'It's the photos I want back. My late husband, my mother and father.' Her voice faltered. 'They've all passed away.'

'You are quite sure the man who stole your possessions is the man you can see in the dock?' the lawyer repeated.

'And he had a knife, one of them Stanley things,' she said.

Hash guessed the old girl's photos would be lying in a bin somewhere or just tossed into the mud wherever the thug happened to be after ripping them out of the frames. He'd have swapped them for drugs and moved on.

A whispered conversation between the man and his lawyer followed and Hash's mind strayed to the photographs he kept at home. The favourite black and white of his own family hanging in the kitchen was irreplaceable: the one he had smuggled out when they'd sent him to the UK, all those years ago. And later, when the anguish of his wife's death had begun to ease, he had taken a favourite snap out of their album, framed it in silver and kept it permanently at his bedside. Taken on a windy hillside in Tyrone on the eve of parting, the lens had captured a wistful expression in Tara's dark eyes, her delicate hand holding back strands of long, dark hair. If anyone ever destroyed those two photographs, he would be capable of murder.

The lawyer looked up at the bench and announced that his man now wished to plead guilty, while the defendant shot the 'shit happens' look at his crew and the elderly victim sat on in the witness box, quivering with strain. The clerk looked up for the Bench's decision. The Chairman nodded at Hash and the other winger and announced, 'The Bench accepts the defendant's plea.'

Defence counsel took his cue. 'Your Worships will be mindful of the need to obtain reports before passing sentence,' he began smoothly, 'and the matter of bail now arises.' He viewed his client with pride. 'In acknowledging guilt, your Worships will give credit to my client for taking responsibility for his actions. A small step but an important one you'll agree.'

Hash doodled a concentric pattern in biro around the yob's address as he listened to the lawyer advance the notion that, in actual fact, his client was the victim. Back home in Libya, theft from a defenceless old lady would've earned the perpetrator an enthusiastic battering from prison staff before being delivered as a titbit to the sex-starved inmates.

'Denying bail will put my client at risk from the very influences, associations and temptations he is struggling to break away from,' the legal aid lawyer continued. 'Granting bail, if your Worships were so generously minded as to approve, with strict reporting conditions of course, may appear lenient but is a far-sighted option.' His protegee tried hard to look contrite.

Once in the retiring room, as the junior winger, Hash was asked to speak first.

'No bail,' he said.

The Bench Chairman said nothing, nodding to the other winger, a woman in her sixties. 'Bail to be granted,' she said. The casting vote rested with the chairman who stalled a moment. Without waiting, she pressed on with her argument, 'He'll be banged up with the low-life.'

'He is low-life', Hash interrupted but she carried on.

'Screws will turn a blind eye, he'll get all the gear he wants,' she shrugged, rolling her eyes. 'I mean, come on, folks. We all know what Gloucester Prison's like.' Hash watched her work it up. 'He'll be a wreck when he comes out and we'll start right back at the bottom again. Someone else will get robbed and,' she spread her hands, 'hey-ho and on we go...'

'Surely, we're not here to discuss the shortcomings of Gloucester Prison,' Hash said. The Chairman, still neutral, said nothing so Hash continued. 'We're being asked if our friend in the dock is a bail risk. I think he is.' He tapped his notes. 'He's a violent thug who robs old ladies and waves knives in their faces.'

'Is he going to run away?' the woman asked. 'And if he does, are we saying we can't catch him?'

'It's not just about him reporting to the police every so often,' Hash countered. 'It's what he does with his time, who else he threatens with his Stanley knife. Think victim?' This silenced the woman.

'I'm not worried about your friend, the screws and...the "gear".' Hash waggled his fingers in inverted commas and saw her stiffen. 'I'm worried about the old lady. What if he goes after her? Doesn't she deserve a break, especially now she's given evidence?'

'To be precise,' she said, 'he didn't go after her...just after her belongings.'

'Perhaps we should give him a medal, then,' Hash said. 'He threatened her after breaking into her flat. Acting responsibly is not part of his make-up. He's a thug.'

'We give him bail and tie him up with strict reporting conditions,' the woman said. 'He reports twice a day, stays away from her home. If he threatens her or breaks any of the conditions, then he falls even harder.' She folded her hands on the table. 'Simple.'

'He won't threaten her,' Hash shot back. 'He's not completely stupid. His mates will do that. I say he stays inside,' Hash said. 'We take all those 'ifs' off the table.' He looked across at the Chairman. 'It sends a signal to the community.' He pointed through the wall to the courtroom, 'You saw the reporter taking notes.'

The Chairman's decision when they returned to the courtroom brought fist pumps from the gaggle of supporters at the back of the court. Afterwards, as they collected their coats in the retiring room, he appeared at Hash's elbow.

'Hard luck, Hash. It's the system. Doesn't always work the way it seems it should.' Hash inwardly cursed the man's feebleness, but his mind was already on getting to school in time to pick up Jim.

'We'll get him when he breaks his bail conditions,' Hash said, dropping his folders into his briefcase.

'Harrow man, I see,' the Chairman said. 'Which house?'

'Sorry?'

'Your house? I was in Rendalls, well before your time probably. Who was the housemaster?' Hash realised he meant the school tie.

'This?' He flipped it. 'It belonged to an old uncle who knew I was coming to England. Back in Jordan everyone wears one because of the King. I was never at Harrow.'

The Chairman's head went back in surprise. 'Why do you wear it, then?' His attempt at fence-mending was turning sour.

'It was a gift.'

'You shouldn't be wearing it in court anyway,' the Chairman continued, his smile strained. 'No school, club or regimental ties, remember.'

'I'll bear that in mind,' Hash said drily, and excused himself.

Out through the rear entrance, and striding fast to warm up, he imagined the yob already celebrating in the pub with his mates and the Echo's next headline reading, 'Offender robs OAP at knifepoint. Court sets him free.'

2

AFTERNOON – MONDAY 2ND MARCH

Behind him, further back on Cheltenham Racecourse's vast parking area, Hash could hear the chainsaw buzz of a tiny motor. Amazing just how far that piercing whine could reach, Hash thought. His son Jim, easily a hundred yards away, his face turned to a cold, clear sky, manipulated the radio controls while a model Spitfire soared and swooped hundreds of feet above him. Small for his fifteen years, he concentrated hard on the aircraft, turning his torso slowly into the path he wanted the aircraft to follow, a free-dance artist transmitting his moves. Hash's heart lurched as he saw Jim's intense concentration, the pursed lips and determined jut of his chin: all so characteristic of the boy's mother. Tara died when Jim was still tiny, and Hash often wondered how much he really remembered of her.

He whistled to the boy, teasing, to break his concentration.

'Bandits! Ten o'clock!' he called out, like a Spitfire pilot in the Battle of Britain.

Jim, familiar with the ploy, flashed a smile, but didn't take his eyes off the model. 'No, please…Dad.'

'Achtung! Engländer! Spitfeuer,' Hash hammed his stock of

comic German from old second world war films.

'Don't, Dad! Give me a break!' the boy yelled back, laughing now, eyes locked on the plane.

But a challenge was a challenge and the Spitfire banked, its tiny motor rasping in protest at the command to swing round in search of prey. It dived, lining up on Hash and the dog, flying fast straight at them for a few seconds before Jim pulled it up, and executing a victory roll as it powered past its targets. Hash applauded, and the dog barked.

'Twenty minutes,' Hash called. He knew Jim had heard and turned away towards the vast meadow, whistling for the dog.

As he walked, he considered the request he'd received earlier that afternoon. His son's favourite teacher had broken away from talking with another parent and waved him over, more a command than a greeting. The young teacher had been Jim's form mistress two years ago and still taught him English. Seeing Susan Pine always made Hash feel good about life.

'Got a minute, Mr Hashmi?' Her expression hinted at conspiracy. 'I was going to ask you a favour.'

'Hash to you. And, as it's you asking, please, take all the time in the world.'

'It's the headmaster,' she began.

'What's he done this time?'

'He wants a favour.' She put a hand on his arm, 'I said you were perfect.'

The headmaster rose behind a wide desk covered in paperwork. Fifteen years Hash's junior, dressed in a dark blue suit and crisp white shirt, he looked more businessman than academic. Hash was offered a surprisingly clammy handshake.

'Kind of you to drop by, Mr Hashmi,' he began. 'A request. I was wondering if you could spare an hour to join our sixth form debating society, talk about your background and give them some of your life experience.'

Hash looked at Susan then back at the headmaster. 'What has Miss Pine set me up for?'

'The society always holds a debate at the end of term, and we wondered if you would make a guest appearance,' he said. 'Susan runs it.'

'What's the debate about?'

'Religious tolerance, essentially.' The headmaster looked out of the window, as if seeking inspiration. 'But not too heavy if we can keep the Chaplain under control. I'll introduce the motion. We have a Jewish mum, but...' he held both palms out to Hash, 'we need a Muslim parent to balance it up.'

'You're the prime candidate,' Susan added.

'Aaah,' Hash said, 'possibly the only candidate. But you should know that I'm not a perfect Muslim. I've been known to drink beer, I bet on horses.' He put on a helpless expression. 'Often at the same time.'

The headmaster smiled. 'Not everyone's perfect. Muslim-lite works better, for me at least. You come from Jordan, don't you?'

'Originally, of course, but I've not been back for years.'

'Where Arabs, Jews and Christians live side by side.'

'Well,' Hash canted his head, 'up to a point. I can see why you might need help.'

'With a name like Hashmi, you're obviously connected to the royal family?'

'If you're looking for an endowment, sorry to disappoint you. We're an old family from Amman.' Hash had heard himself tell this lie so many times he almost believed it himself. 'A family of lawyers. Always in court, just not the royal court.'

'But you are actually someone who, for our purposes has, um,' he searched for the word, 'integrated here. I hope that doesn't sound patronising?' He observed Hash for signs of offence. 'And you also serve as a Justice of the Peace if my source is correct?' He turned to Susan for confirmation. 'There can't be many Muslim JPs in Gloucestershire,' he continued. 'In fact, you're the only one, aren't you?'

'Maybe,' Hash hedged.

'Susan and I want this debate to zoom in on Britain's religious tolerance, or lack of it.' He looked at Hash. 'You won't have to participate in the discussion, of course. You introduce yourself, tell them about your home in Jordan, give some cultural and religious insights. Five minutes at the most, with a bit of extra time for some questions.'

'When are we talking about?' Hash asked.

'Friday next week, mid-morning. We break for the Easter holidays straight afterwards,' Susan said.

'Actually, that puts me in the middle of the races, the Gold Cup,' Hash said doubtfully.

'Apologies for the short notice, so many things to think about.' He gestured at his desk. 'Of course, if it's too much…'

'I'd be absolutely delighted,' Hash said.

'That's really good of you,' Susan said as they walked back to his car.

'So… now you owe me,' Hash said. 'You do,' he insisted, smiling at the wary look on her face.

'Owe you what?'

'Let me take you out for dinner afterwards?'

As he walked on the racecourse Hash found himself looking forward to the debate, pleased that Susan had agreed to the dinner date. He'd sometimes wondered what his chances might be; with her he experienced the almost forgotten tingle of pleasure when real attraction sparks. And Susan connected with Jim in a way no one else had managed before or since. She was young but, in reality, she and Tara wouldn't be so very far apart in age. There'd been a few brief relationships since Tara's death but bringing another woman into their lives had always seemed too big a step. He couldn't imagine how Jim would react to someone new joining their life together and hadn't ever had the courage to find out.

Their rescue dog, a Weimaraner bitch called Shamsa, streaked ahead of him as he descended the grassy slope. He watched her muscled flanks ripple as she accelerated, her undocked tail acting as a rudder as she swerved and turned. She'd certainly settled in fast enough in the six months since they'd taken her in. Along with what the re-homing agency had coyly described as 'a strong personality', she'd brought exuberant affection into their lopsided little household, and she and Jim had bonded quickly, each fulfilling a need in the other.

A huge sea of meadow dressed in winter green rolled away in front of him, heading north, finally breaking against the brown shoulder of Cleeve Hill a mile distant. A church spire, slate roofs and ribbons of tree lines stood out in the middle distance. This was England and, even at its post winter weariest, Hash simply loved it. He saw beauty in this Cotswold landscape in all seasons: whether fine or filthy weather, something in the scenery always pleased him, and he thanked whatever God there was for hoisting him out of murderous Ulster and dropping him here.

He glanced at his watch. Five-thirty, with evenings getting longer by a noticeable fraction. Scents of wood smoke drifting across on the early evening chill raised the temptation of a pub meal in front of a warm fire before getting Jim back for homework. As he walked down the gentle slope, Shamsa looked for his approval to cross the footbridge and begin the next leg of the walk. He waved his arm forward and the dog leapt away ahead of him.

Noises of construction, clanking and drilling, floated across from the racecourse where last-minute preparations for the racing festival were hitting deadlines. Crews were probably working through the night at this stage, Hash thought. When they'd driven in, their first walk on the racecourse for a week or more, all the boards and signs to guide cars and punters to the entrance gates were already up.

Shamsa was barking an alert somewhere beyond the tiny footbridge and he called her name several times. Behind a sparse screen of trees, Hash recognised the friendly face of a fellow dog walker, a middle-aged woman fussing at her three whippets, leads taut as they hauled her down onto the bridge.

'They know it's dinner time,' he called across, raising his tweed cap.

The three dogs pulled towards him and he spent a few moments patting them. 'Got your hands full here.'

The woman smiled as Shamsa trotted back to check on the hold-up.

'Friend of mine had one of these.' She pointed at the Wei-maraner. 'Mad, she was. Nutty as a fruit cake.'

'The friend or the dog?'

'I couldn't have one. Never be able to pronounce the name,' she said.

'We've only had her for a few months. Still waiting for her to find her feet.'

'Shamsa,' the woman said, and the dog cocked her head. 'Strange name for a dog.'

'Arabic for sun,' Hash said, 'our new ray of sunshine.' The dogs pushed and shoved around Hash's legs.

'Getting a bit crowded here.' Hash eased past her and got to the end of the bridge. He was looking down at the muddy pool there, when his eyes snagged on a detail on the bridge structure at boot level. He steadied himself with one hand on the rail and waved a farewell to the woman.

'This place'll be too busy for walking in a week or so,' she called, returning a friendly wave. Hash hopped over the puddle and moved on, barely registering her reply.

She was right, from the middle of next week, thousands of happy punters would swarm onto the racecourse. There would be Irish chums from the old days, the days of the struggle. Pint after pint and tales of daring deeds, memories of others best never mentioned. The prospect both thrilled and scared him because, contrary to his bravado with the headmaster, his hard-drinking days were long over.

Barking up ahead made him step out after Shamsa again. She could be stirring up trouble with another dog. He walked fast, crossing the road, unbolting the steel gate, and letting himself into the huge meadow. He found Shamsa searching thickets along the stream. Hash saw she had disturbed the old hare who was streaking off, out of sight to the dog. The wily old animal, the highlight of many a dog's walk, must have spent most of its life running from predators and Hash prayed it would never be caught. Walking away from the little copse, urging Shamsa across the road, he felt a sudden twinge of unease, acute, almost physical and very unwelcome.

With the chase long abandoned, and both master and dog at the highest point on the meadow, the sound of a motor sputtering and revving signalled Jim had landed his Spitfire and was burning off fuel, clearing the tubes as part of the shutdown drills. As Hash turned to look back down at the sparse copse by the bridge, the stab of anxiety flared again.

Reaching the wicket gate before re-crossing the road, Hash stopped and waited, bracing himself, sucking cold, clean air into his lungs so fast it froze his throat and sinuses. As he moved towards the little footbridge, the handrail came into focus and a jolt of adrenaline stopped him dead.

Down at ground level, wound around one of the scaffold uprights, four bands of brown tape held his gaze in a vice. A few millimetres apart, one on top of the other, they formed a collar, almost unnoticeable in the weakening daylight. But Hash had been meant to see them. The shock kept him rooted to the spot, his eyes screwed tight shut hoping it was his imagination, but when he opened them the tape was still there. Shamsa heard her master's low groan and came straight to him.

He checked Jim was still in the distance, absorbed in his

aircraft. Whoever had put the tape there had smeared mud over it and let raindrops splashing off the concrete do the blending in.

There'd been only one heavy shower four days earlier, before the dry spell had set in. He worked out he'd probably walked the dog on the racecourse a week back, crossing the bridge as usual, so he knew the marker was between five and six days old. In his mind's eye, he saw someone on the bridge, crouching down with a roll of tape.

Why was he thinking singular? They'd have been operating as a pair, maybe with a third man in a car nearby for backup; those were the procedures he and his Tripoli classmates had learned. It would have taken less than a minute; the other job, hiding the package, a few seconds more.

Hash knelt and scraped off the sticky brown tape with his car keys. Shamsa came in, splashing muddy sludge over Hash's legs. It was electrical, he saw, but no other great forensic 'eureka' leapt at him on his way back to the car. Rolling it into a ball, and calling to Jim, he tossed the scrap away.

Jim was there, on his knees, doing his final checks to the model aircraft. Fending off Shamsa as she pushed her nose at his face, he looked up, catching his father's dark mood and the damp stains on his trousers.

'I see you've wet yourself again,' Jim said.

Hash forced a smile. He'd made a mistake scraping off the tape, he now realised. Had he left it alone he could maybe have gained some time. He pulled himself together. 'How about something to eat next, before we go home?' he asked. Jim would be hungry, and he needed the distraction of a bright, relaxed atmosphere himself.

'Something hot…maybe curry?' Jim said.

'Pub?' Hash offered.

'Too cold and draughty.'

'Pub with a roaring fire?'

'Curry?' Jim countered again.

'Tell you what,' Hash held up a finger, 'a brilliant idea has just occurred. How about curry?'

'I was just about to suggest that,' said Jim.

They were given a booth at the rear of the restaurant and the owner, Siddiq, carried their drinks to the table; a Coke with ice and lemon in front of Hash, while Jim got the litre bottle of Cobra.

'On the house,' Siddiq said with irony, 'because your father is a good Muslim.'

'If he is,' Jim said, 'he's keeping it pretty quiet.'

'How about saying thanks, Jimbo?' Hash said.

'Your father will be in the mosque with me tomorrow.' Siddiq shot a sideways glance at Hash. 'You'll see. The imam likes him very much.'

'Does he?' Jim said quietly, looking at the Coke, wanting to start.

'Maybe he will bring you.' Siddiq was smiling.

Hash reached for the beer and pushed the Coke across to Jim.

'School, exams, pressure…you know,' Jim said. 'But if I change my mind, I'll let you know.'

Siddiq gave a short chuckle and sat down with the pair, shoving Jim along the cushioned bench.

'You play cricket?' Siddiq asked, 'I think you are a bowler. A spinner, yes, you look like a spinner. Over the wicket?'

'I play quidditch,' Jim replied, straight faced.

'Rubbish sport, for girls only,' Siddiq snorted. 'Better you play cricket, like your father.'

'If I played cricket like my father, I'd be too embarrassed to admit it.'

Siddiq smiled at Jim before his eyes flitted automatically to his squad of waiters. He ran several restaurants, from Cheltenham across to Gloucester and up to Birmingham, but this one, on Cheltenham's Bath Road, was his flagship and business headquarters. Short, fussy and always dressed in the full regalia of charcoal grey suit, shirt, tie and cufflinks, Siddiq liked to greet his guests personally. He and Hash had been friends for a long time. Siddiq had been one of the privileged few at Tara's funeral. Hash remembered that gathering at St Gregory's. Bella, the Old Boy and Sean his brother-in-law, all over from the 'strife-torn province,' standing with Bangladeshi Muslim Siddiq and his wife in a hijab. Tara, he knew, would have relished the quirkiness of it.

When Siddiq rose to attend to other customers, Jim said, 'If he's always so smart, I mean so smartly dressed, why does he have such a scruffy beard?' He sucked at his drink. 'It's all long and straggly. Like some old wizard.'

Hash knew the reason, though looking around at the rest of the clientele in the restaurant he doubted if Cheltenham's finest either knew or cared.

'It's a Muslim sign of being devout. It means he's a religious man,' Hash said. 'All this talk of religion reminds me. I'm giving a talk to your sixth form next week.'

'Cool, Dad. What about?'

'Religious tolerance.'

'Ouch! Not as cool as I thought. How come you've been asked?'

'I suspect they needed a Muslim parent and they only have me.'

'But do you go to the mosque?'

'Not very often.'

'Do you pray in a row, on your knees, bum up in the air?' Jim took another pull at his Coke.

'That's the traditional way Muslims pray,' Hash protested.

'Why am I not a Muslim, then?'

'Your mum and I agreed we would let you choose when

you're ready. That's religious tolerance, by the way.'

Jim was silent while a waiter laid a dish in front of them.

'Why is Siddiq so nice to you, Dad?' Jim asked when the waiter had left.

'That's Mr Siddiq, to you,' Hash said, 'and it's because I helped him in the old days.' He took a sip of his beer. 'I helped him set up his businesses when he was just starting out. And then he helped me.'

'What sort of help?'

'Buying up restaurants. He's an accountant, I'm a lawyer. That sort of business.'

'Boring stuff, then,' Jim said.

'That's nice, thank you.'

'You really a Muslim, Dad?' Jim persisted. 'You're not supposed to drink alcohol, but you drink like a fish.'

'As we're being so open with each other,' Hash said. 'I drink to ease the pain.'

'What pain?' Jim was looking at him, curious about this turn of the conversation.

'The pain of paying your school fees, and then watching you do so badly.'

'I knew that was coming, Dad,' Jim sighed. 'Bit lame, but I'll let you have half-marks.'

MONDAY NIGHT

Just before ten that evening, a call from a tenant put Hash back on the road. The time of night was unusual but the urgency in the Portuguese's voice told Hash that whatever the problem was, it was serious. The man had run the chippy for fifteen years, a safe pair of hands who'd never missed a rent payment. Hash could make out the words, 'trouble…bastards, and police' in a torrent of accented English.

'Going out for half an hour!' Hash called up the stairs. There was no reply from Jim's room and he had to climb the stairs, knock on the door and prise one headphone off his boy's head before he could deliver the message.

It would take him at least ten minutes to get his ageing Discovery across town to the right housing estate, he knew. It was almost a relief to have something to do to stop him dwelling on the bridge and its disturbing message. A light drizzle covered the windscreen and the wiper blades scraped on his nerves as he drove. He left behind the red-brick terraces and passed The Suffolks heading into Tivoli, watching for some of his favourite houses. One day soon, when there were no more school fees, he and Jim would move. Not to something big and showy, just big enough, detached, probably Georgian, definitely someplace elegant. He reached the turnoff at the big roundabout before GCHQ.

The chippy came into sight at the end of the long approach into Princess Elizabeth Way, and Hash pulled over to dial the place. He could see two staff, the Portuguese and his wife. They were bustling about behind the counter and food display but there were no customers and he assumed they were closing. He saw the man pick up.

'Mr Hash?'

'How are you? All ok?'

'These young bastards!' the tenant spat. 'They come in drunk tonight, they fighting, call names, make order then no pay. Bastards.'

'I'm coming now.'

'Too late now. They gone, the bastards!'

'How many?'

'Three guys. Always the same ones, always the same tricks.'

'I'm looking for them.' Hash accelerated past the chippy, turning the Discovery off the main road and into the housing estate, slowing to a crawl when he saw people ahead. He was not hopeful. The culprits could be sitting in a car, or have disappeared into one of the hulking, sixties tenement blocks in the immediate area. He gave up after ten minutes, returning and parking outside the chippy.

'Young guys,' the man began before a burst of Portuguese from his wife at the back of the shop halted him. He listened to her then pointed to his throat and side of his neck, tracing with his finger. 'Tattoos…flowers.' The wife nodded confirmation then looked over to Hash.

'Look at the TV.' His stubby finger jabbed at the CCTV lens high up on the back wall of the shop. The three of them crowded together at the small monitor as the husband hit the play button. Hash watched a grainy black and white pantomime of three men, one with smudges on his neck. The Portuguese stabbed the screen, 'Pretty boy. My best friend,' he said. 'Wants to look after my business, be my partner.'

Hash was looking at the man from the morning's court case; the man they'd given bail a matter of hours ago was already back in business.

The figures jerked around on the screen, play-fighting, the tattooed ringleader turning to the Portuguese in a mock appeal for help. Hash caught a sense of escalating menace in the exchange of waving arms and the flicking of V signs. Then the ringleader shed his protective persona, taking cans of drink from the fridge cabinet and tossing them to his friends, stuffing others in his pockets. At one point, one of the trio hurled a can towards the back of the shop and another held out a Stanley knife. 'This when they tell me to open the till. Bastards!'

'How much?' Hash said. 'How much did you lose tonight?'

The man counted on his fingers. 'One hundred sixty-six pound then.' He pointed at the drinks fridge. 'Twenty-four pound for drinks. Maybe I lose customers too. They don't come if they see trouble.'

Hash pulled out his wallet, counted out ten twenties, and held them out to the man. The Portuguese shook his head. 'Not necessary, Mr Hash. Normally business is good. But tonight…'

His voice trailed off.

'Yes necessary,' Hash countered. Placing the money in the man's hand, he added, 'Next time we go to the police.'

'You joking? Police bastards,' the man said, 'fucking useless. They do nothing.'

Hash found Jim downstairs slumped on the sofa, Shamsa beside him, and a news programme on the television. He looked up as Hash came in.

'That dog's getting too lazy to bark with you spoiling her,' Hash said. 'What's this?' He was looking at footage of men wearing Arab headdress, riding in pickup trucks waving black ISIS flags and firing weapons into the air. The narrator was talking about the death of Muammar Gaddafi as the camera cut to scenes of the dictator's swollen and bloody face, jowls shaking as men pushed him forward roughly. Knowing exactly what came next, Hash seized the channel selector and switched the television off.

'Dad!' Jim protested.

'You'd have nightmares for weeks. Why on earth are you watching that stuff?'

'It's interesting!'

Hash ruffled Jim's hair. 'So, we're interested in Middle Eastern politics all of a sudden? Why is that?'

'Because they want democracy,' Jim said, 'like us.'

'So not because you want to stay up a bit longer?'

'Seriously, Dad,' Jim said. 'I can watch it just as easily on my phone if I want. It'll be on the net.'

'You need to put that rubbish out of your mind and get some sleep.'

For Hash, sleep was an impossibility; his churning mind refused to leave the day's events behind. The fracas in the chippy was pure poetic justice, the direct result of releasing the scum back into the wild. But that was kids' play compared to the tape on the footbridge. The shock had been like hearing a doctor deliver an ominous diagnosis, something terminal. And scraping off the brown tape, that had been a basic blunder: a huge mistake and being out of practice by a few decades was no excuse for such sloppiness. If he had left the tape, he could have won time. Instead, he had signalled Tripoli that Tariq Hashmi, class of '86, had received and was back in the game. He wondered if Jim had already seen the gory images of Gaddafi's death on the internet. Maybe it was an omen, the dead-letterbox marker on the bridge and then images of Gaddafi's execution, all on the same day. For the first time in years his gut instinct was firing up, preparing him for the danger he knew was ahead.

3

EARLY MORNING – TUESDAY 3RD MARCH

Hash always slowed to look at the vintage Victorian railway station on the east side of the racecourse. The promise of another fine spring day lifted his mood and he remembered Jim's excitement at being taken on the hissing, chuffing steam engine when he was small. The quaint building with its fretted magnolia woodwork always evoked childhood memories too, of scenes from his father's vast collection of black and white films. Hash and his sisters had loved the elaborate English and pretended to be the Victorian dandies and their ladies, trading extravagant courtesies.

'Got to be a quick one,' he urged Shamsa, swinging the rear door open and watching the dog dash out. He walked steadily in her wake as she tore ahead, zigzagging to the lure of fresh scents. Even before they reached the footbridge, his eyes were sweeping the area. He had to remind himself he wasn't on a battlefield strewn with booby-traps or mines, just a parking area with nothing more threatening than a scruffy copse and some dog shit. The footprints in the congealed mud at the beginning of the bridge were too numerous to tell if any were fresh.

There was no new tape on the steel upright, and as he softly whistled for the dog, he saw where his key had left bright scratches on the metalwork the day before. Shamsa reappeared, hovering impatiently as Hash stood on the bridge. He took one more glance around, checking for other dog walkers or anyone else: nothing, nobody anywhere in sight, but he doubted that would last. Snapping off a dried twig he held it to Shamsa for a second, then threw it hard towards the railway embankment, aiming for the culvert. The dog watched his arm jerk then dived after the stick. For a few seconds, he could hear splashing movement and caught a glimpse of her grey coat. She was back within less than a minute, the stick clamped in her jaws. Hash repeated the move and followed her in. She'd have been barking like crazy if there'd been anyone in there.

Hash stepped into the stream bed, feeling the water wrap its cold grip around his Hunters. A few careful strides, edging his way over slabs of stone slick with algae, brought him to the mouth of the culvert. The red and black brickwork must have been at least a hundred years old, but had stayed clean, no moss or creepers. He crouched down to look inside with Shamsa beside him, her nose pointing along the tunnel. Light at the other end told Hash there was nobody inside it.

Standing up again, Hash drew his phone and keyed the torch, holding its beam to a small, circular slot for drainage on the culvert wall set at waist level. He turned the torch and looked along the shaft. Lodged about eighteen inches further in, Hash could see a package wrapped in black plastic, the second part of his Tripoli classmates' task that night. His heart thumped as he gently eased his fist inside to grip on the package. It came out smoothly, light and dry to his touch.

Back home, with Shamsa fed and dozing in the warmth of the kitchen, he called up to Jim to make sure he was awake, shoving the plastic-wrapped package into a sideboard drawer. He flicked on the kettle, put two slices of bread into the toaster, and paused to take stock.

His eyes lit upon the old black and white family photograph, which he had had enlarged and framed, and kept on the dresser shelf. Young faces returned his gaze: his father stern, unsmiling but proud, his mother beaming, his two sisters, one putting on her most alluring look and the other unable to take her eyes off the bundle in her arms, her firstborn and Hash's infant nephew. He was there, too: a version of himself thirty years younger, leaner, with long sideburns and an arrogance he now remembered with a shudder. That was the last time they'd been together and maybe why the old man had commissioned the photo; he knew that once Hash was gone, he would stay away forever. He had planned it that way, after all. The photo was his father's way of saying of saying, 'goodbye, my son, good luck.'

The toaster popped, and Hash reached for the butter, yelling up to Jim once more. He sighed, left the tea and toast on the table and headed upstairs for a shower. Next, his wardrobe. Getting it right was important to him, and today his persona would be 'successful businessman who still makes time to serve his community'. He had to attend a meeting at the Magistrates' Court and afterwards would walk the short distance to his office on the Promenade. There, Thelma, his Filipina bookkeeper, unfailingly loyal and ever efficient, would be waiting with letters for his approval. She ran his property portfolio, checking the rents, filing the returns and paying the bills and had seen his rise from owning nothing to holding the deeds to fifteen freeholds in town. Thelma was, he frequently thought, pretty much the mainstay of the whole enterprise.

By the time he appeared downstairs a few minutes later, he'd achieved his objective; tailored grey suit, blush pink shirt with cutaway collar, double cuffs and a light blue tie, completed by highly polished black brogues. 'A gentleman is judged by the shoes he wears,' someone had once said to him. He loved the Britishness of it all. It still gave him a thrill of pleasure when he looked at the passport that officially recognised his status as a naturalised Brit.

Jim was at the kitchen table checking his mobile phone when Hash came down.

'Ok for my court appearance, Jim?' he asked.

The fifteen-year-old looked up from his phone long enough to allow an appraisal of the outfit.

'What's the charge, this time? You been pimping? Again?'

Hash tipped him back in his chair and caught him midway to the floor. Jim laughed up at him and Hash set him upright again.

'Eat, eat, eat!' said Hash, taking the phone out of Jim's hands. 'How about going to stay with Grandma and Grandpa for a bit? This week.'

'Now?' Jim looked up in surprise. 'Holidays don't start until next week.'

'How about I speak to Miss Pine and get you released early? Today even.'

'Any excuse and you're talking to Miss Pine,' Jim said. 'Isn't it working?'

'Isn't what working?'

'I told her you have a massive crush on her but you're incredibly shy.'

'You did what?'

'And she said,' Jim poured more cornflakes and reached for the milk, enjoying the moment. He slowly spooned food into his mouth and chewed. 'She said she never does it on the first date, especially not with balding...'

'Who teaches you that stuff for God's sake? I hope you said

no such thing.'

'Chillax, Dad,' Jim said. 'I made that up.'

'All of it, I hope?'

'No, just the bit about the balding middle-aged man.'

'Actually,' Hash said, 'she's the one who's invited me to talk on religious tolerance.'

'Fine by me if you fancy Miss Pine, Dad,' Jim grinned. 'Besides, if pretending to be religious gets you where you want to go with girls, I need to know.'

'My God! Silence! But listen,' Hash pressed, 'I need an answer. How do you feel about an emergency dash to the sickest grandfather in Ireland?'

'Is it an emergency?' Jim asked, suddenly serious.

'Well, your granddad has had a stroke and he is getting worse,' Hash said. 'That's a fact.'

'How about I go and stay with Uncle Sean then?' Jim said. 'He's so cool.'

Hash shook his head. 'The last time he had you drinking.'

'Uncle Sean's magic,' Jim said. 'He's an absolute legend.'

'A legend in his own lunchtime perhaps. Also, a certified psycho,' Hash said.

'But you like him, too?'

'That's different.' Hash clipped the lid on the sandwich box and placed it on the table. 'Sandwiches, apple, juice, crisps and KitKat. Maybe I'll speak to Sean,' he added. 'You start off with Granny and Grandpa and then, when you've put a bit of work in, maybe, just maybe,' he stressed, 'Sean will drive over and take you on trips.'

'What sort of trips?' Jim asked, picking up his phone.

'Like you always enjoy. You could take one of your models, one that would fit in a suitcase.'

'My little quadcopter?'

'Why not? Plenty of space to fly it when you're not helping out on the farm, earning incredible pocket money.'

'Cleaning out the pigsties. Hammering a nail through my hand could be more fun,' Jim said.

Hash bent to whisper in his ear, 'Incredible pocket money.'

'Why such a rush to get rid of me? That farm's in the middle of nowhere, nobody even comes to visit. Out there they trap strangers and drink their blood.'

'Precisely what I was thinking,' Hash said. 'Actually, I have to go away for a few days, do some stuff with some colleagues.'

'I could come along, too.'

'It's boring stuff. Accounting, numbers, meetings, long days in offices.'

'Then I could stay here and look after Shamsa instead,' Jim countered.

'You mean stay in bed all day, not walk her and leave her to crap in the garden?'

'I'd clean the crap up.'

'Last time I only left you for two days and Mrs Hamilton never stopped phoning me.' He mimicked the voice of their elderly neighbour, ''Ere, 'Ash, your bloody dog was barking for two days.'

'Nosy old bag,' Jim said.

'She's a very kind lady and don't you forget it.' Hash shot back. But Jim's face clouded, and he quickly added, 'Anyway, I'll be joining you after I've taken care of the dull business.' He turned to Shamsa and murmured. 'How does a new quadcopter sound to you?' He turned back to Jim. 'Grandma really wants you to go and stay. She was on the phone to me this morning,' he lied.

'What was that about a quadcopter, Dad?'

'Aaah,' Hash smiled, 'might we be a tiny bit interested?' He held out his hand. 'Deal?'

'What sort of budget are we talking here?' Jim cautiously extended his. 'I'm well past the toy stage, Dad. I fly with the professionals, you know.'

'Yes, of course you do,' Hash said. 'All negotiable but totally dependent on your smiling cooperation.'

'How much, Dad?'

Hash made a fist and flicked up one, two and finally three fingers. 'Shall we say three hundred quid?'

'Wow! That gets me a Phantom 3 Professional,' Jim said. 'Top of the range, all the pros have them.'

'Deal?' Hash repeated.

Jim looked into his father's face, checking for the catch, then slowly shook hands. 'Deal.'

'What will you tell Miss Pine?' Jim asked. 'She's not my form teacher anymore remember.'

'Not to worry. I'll find her this afternoon, work it through her, tell her it's urgent family stuff, something like that.'

Hash waited until Jim was well on his way, heading for the college, before he retrieved the package and cut away the plastic. He found himself in possession of three items. The first was an old model BlackBerry phone with half of its QWERTY keyboard in Arabic. The Mukhabarat lecture room at Ben Gashir in Tripoli floated before him, students learning spy tradecraft, spouting Gaddafi's maxims, desperate to impress instructors. There was a charger with a three-point plug. The third item was a car key with a Citroën fob. He powered up the phone and seconds later it told him it was on an Etisalat UK contract, probably an attempt to disguise the phone's Libyan provenance.

He needed the password but knew too many failed attempts to unlock it could provoke a shutdown. This task needed calm, logic and a pen and paper. He had half the password in his mind already, an unforgettable, simple but unique number etched on his memory decades ago by those same instructors. Whoever had sent the phone would have inserted that number as part of the password; the rest he had to crack himself. Hash picked up the phone and slowly, as if giving the device time to follow, he typed in his birth date; 12021960, the twelfth of February 1960. The phone told him it was incorrect: only half complete. Close, but no cigar yet.

He shook his head to clear it for another attempt. There had to be a key to it, but this was not the time to test the old phone's patience and he was already running late. Leaving it on charge, he paused at the hallway mirror to make a final check on his appearance. It was neither cold nor wet enough for a coat, but his scruffy Barbour jacket, part of the Brit uniform, slipped over his suit easily. His tweed cap was already tucked into one of the pockets. Shamsa, bought off with a rawhide chew, ignored him as he closed the door.

It took him fifteen minutes at a brisk walk across the north-south grain of Cheltenham's streets and past the first of the Ladies' College boarding houses. He used the exercise to sharpen up his mind, searching through the cobwebs and recalling lessons on codes as he strode towards his day's work.

LATER
Home once more, Hash calculated he had about an hour before Jim would be walking in through the door. He picked up the Arab BlackBerry, tuning his mind as he did so. He was still stung by his uncomfortable encounter with the not so cute or amenable, as it turned out, Miss Pine. His chat with her had started well and then gone rapidly downhill. Her shy smile and hint of a blush had vanished at the first suggestion of his taking Jim away early. She'd heard out the classic gambit of a favourite grandparent at death's door and could hardly refuse but she'd been curt, and it soon became clear she felt insulted. Their dinner date was probably at best on hold, he thought wryly.

The display on the mobile told him he now had a full battery and an SMS waiting. Whoever had prepared the phone had pegged the date at January 26th.

He rummaged in the bin to retrieve the packaging and, taking a pen and pencil, slumped into a kitchen chair with the device, the charger, bubble wrap and liner in front of him, and cursed himself again for clearing the letter box down at the bridge too early. He could've left the tape and still cleared the box, checked the contents, got the gist of things and then run like hell with Jim. But he was stuck now, and anyway he had no way of knowing if there was another team close by, tracking his movements. He checked the wrapping for clues. None. Next, he looked at the Citroën key on the fob: nothing except the tiny brand name with the chevrons and the symbols for lock and unlock. Just then a clue hit him, validating his freshness of mind theory. He keyed in his special number and the letters spelling Citroën, but only to be rejected. He reversed the sequence and was rejected again.

There would be a limited number of tries before the phone closed him out, and he momentarily considered deliberately fluffing his lines. Maybe he could disqualify himself from this particular game, or at least get a bye to the next round. Maybe he could feed a message back into the letter box saying, 'Phone damaged, send replacement'. Then he remembered the instructors at Ben Gashir casually showing photographs of an agent somewhere in Europe, sprawled on the boulevard in a pool of blood, an agent who had tried to evade a mission. 'We always know where to find you,' they'd said.

A glance at the kitchen clock told him four-thirty. Jim would be back in forty-five minutes. Concentrating his mind on what he knew he could achieve, he put the Blackberry down and dialled his mother- in-law on the landline. This met with more success. Precious minutes were taken up listening to Bella's old age aches and pains, then his father in law's ailments and the problems on the farm, complete with the weather and the prices. Hash was almost hopping with impatience when she finally said, in her country drawl, 'Aye. I suppose we could take wee Lord Jim for few days. It wouldn't be the end of the world,' which Hash knew was Irish for 'Send him now!' They'd be over the moon.

And Hash trusted them, was fond of them. When he'd first appeared in their world, it was as a fugitive from the hated Brits, an Arab with a Kalashnikov, not easy to hide on a farm in Tyrone but they'd stepped up. First it was because their son Sean was a fighter in the struggle. And later, when things had gone wrong with Sean and he, Hash, had asked for their daughter Tara's hand in marriage, they'd miraculously agreed, even if only in the hope they'd have grandchildren at last. A little patience was the least the old girl deserved.

'I'll get Sean to meet him off the plane,' he said.

'You'll do no such thing,' Bella said. 'He'll be drunk.'

'He'll be fine,' Hash reassured her. 'It's too long a drive for you, and Sean's on the doorstep. The plane will be arriving late, might even be delayed. I'll call him well before opening time. He's looking forward to it, too. He'll feed him and drive him over to you.'

'Aye, ok, then.' Her tone was heavy with scepticism.

'Relax. And remember,' he lied again, 'I'll be over, in a few days.'

Hash knew the mention of Sean would open wounds that were still raw even after all these years. The uncomfortable truth was that he, Hash, had been there too.

He spent fifteen more vital minutes booking a seat on the Birmingham to Aldergrove Easyjet, scheduled for departure at nine that evening. He sent a warning SMS to Sean while the printer chugged out a boarding pass and tore up the stairs, taking them three at a time. Minutes later he came down with a roll-on case stuffed with the basics Jim would need for an extended stay on the farm. Warm clothes to travel with were laid on the bed. It would still be cold in Tyrone for weeks to come.

He quickly checked the clock and sat down with the Black-

Berry and the car key again and noticed for the first time that the key blade had, in tiny lower-case letters, the name 'Valeo' stamped on it, high up near the plastic. From the depths of his memory, his law training told him this was Latin and had something to do with strength. He keyed in his code and date of birth followed by the five letters on the blade. The phone almost heaved a sigh of relief and immediately pinged an SMS at him. The Libyan number alone was proof of who was playing, and he knew that by releasing the SMS from its limbo its sender would see delivery had been made. Hash read 'BHXLS5C15', an instruction to wade deeper into the swamp. Birmingham Airport, long-stay car park five; somewhere in area C15 something, or someone, was waiting.

The doorbell triggered excited barking from Shamsa. Hash moved from the kitchen and saw a hunched figure on the other side of the glass. Mouthing a silent expletive, he fixed on his best smile and opened the door.

'Mrs Hamilton, how nice. What can I do for you?' The way she looked past him so hopefully told him she was hunting Jim. When she wanted something, she rarely wasted time on pleasantries. 'Jim's going away,' Hash said, 'Actually, I was just packing his suitcase.' Her face fell. 'But if there's anything I can do?' He let it hang in the air, in an agony of impatience.

Shamsa had come wriggling to the door and she tousled the dog's ears.

'Where's he going?' she asked, and then answered her own question, sounding disappointed. 'Granny in Ireland, I expect.'

'I mean anything you need,' Hash insisted.

'Just wanted some wood chopped.' She sighed. 'I'd do it myself, but…'

'No problem, I'll do it. But it'll have to be tomorrow,' Hash said. As he started to close the door, he caught sight of Jim approaching. Jim read the situation instantly and tried a theatrical backtrack, mouthing an exaggerated 'No!' at his father.

Mrs Hamilton turned, seeing Jim. 'Just the man. Got some wood needs chopping. It'll only take a few minutes.'

Normally, Hash would have been on the old lady's side, and today was surely the right day to intervene on behalf of every old lady. But the message on the Arab BlackBerry had started the clock ticking.

'He's got a plane to catch and we're running late,' Hash said with firmness. 'And he's still got to change.'

Shamsa had joined the small gathering, trying to jump up at Jim as he squeezed past.

'Jim's got to get changed, Mrs Hamilton,' Hash repeated gently.

'Or I'll be late,' Jim called from the sanctuary of the hall-way.

'And he's got to be down in five minutes. Or else.'

'Sometimes I think you spoil that boy,' Mrs Hamilton grumbled as she turned on the pathway. Only Mrs Hamilton was allowed to talk to Hash like that. When Tara'd died, she'd pitched in, caring for the two of them equally with solid advice and much needed practical support and she'd been the first ever outsider in Jim's fan club, showering affection on him in her own particular eccentric way. Hash listened to her muttering as she made her way back up the path. Another one he'd have to make it up to when this was all over.

He ran full tilt into the kitchen, scooping up the Arab Black-Berry and the Citroën key, yelling up the stairs to Jim. 'Two minutes!'

'Ok, ok! What's the hurry, Dad?'

'One minute,' Hash called back.

He dropped the items into his Barbour pocket.

'Thirty seconds!' he yelled, getting a muffled shout back. He dashed into the sitting room, opened a desk drawer and picked up Jim's passport. From another drawer he took a wad of banknotes and peeled off three hundred pounds. Crossing to the printer he whipped off the boarding pass and double-checked the name and flight number.

'Now! Or the plane will leave without you!' he shouted and blew a sigh of relief when he heard the thud of Jim's feet on the stairs.

4

CHELTENHAM. TUESDAY 3RD MARCH

Hash pushed at the wheel of the Discovery, then pounded it in frustration. Rush hour traffic in town was costing vital minutes and he was beginning to worry about conditions on the motorway.

'Got to get through,' he growled.

'Music, Dad,' Jim soothed, reaching forward. His finger pushed one of the numbers on the console and got a local DJ finishing off a traffic report.

'Yes…no!' Hash thumped the wheel. 'Find another channel, find Radio 2.'

'Dad, if you used your satnav, you'd see the jams.'

Hash forced a smile.

'How did you swing it with Miss Pine?'

'I'm in her bad books.'

'But she gave permission?' Jim asked.

'She said she'd pass it on with her support. But she wasn't happy.'

'You've blown it, Dad.' Jim shook his head in commiseration.

'We'll blow it again, if we're not careful,' Hash muttered,

hauling the Discovery over to the right, circling on the flyover roundabout, heading back to Cheltenham.

Jim looked up from his phone. 'Dad?'

'Train,' Hash said. 'Otherwise, you won't make it. You sure you're ok with the train?'

'I've only done it, like, a hundred times, Dad.'

The boy's confidence relaxed Hash a little. 'Uncle Sean's going to meet you,' he said.

'Yesss!' Jim punched the air.

'Don't let him take you to a pub.'

At the railway station, Hash made Jim hold up one item after the other. 'Phone?'

'Check.'

'Passport and ticket?' Jim held them up. Hash bought the rail ticket and handed over an envelope with the money inside.

'Wow,' Jim said. 'You must really want to get rid of me.'

'Can't bloody wait,' Hash smiled. 'Three hundred,' he said, holding a finger to his lips. 'Keep it in your pocket and don't open it until you see Granny.' He slipped a twenty-pound note into Jim's back pocket. 'That's for a sandwich and a Coke on the journey. You'll be in Birmingham at seven. Don't dawdle, get the first train to the airport.'

'I take it,' Jim cocked a quizzical eyebrow, 'this is not a down payment on the quadcopter?'

Father and son looked at each other. 'One day, you'll be a first-class businessman,' Hash said.

'What I'm saying is,' Jim held up the envelope, 'this is just to get me through the next weeks on a muddy farm.'

'Maybe we should make it performance-related.' Hash made to snatch the money back. Jim retreated towards the ticket barrier, holding up the money.

'Not the down payment...right?'

'Why don't you just wave it around until someone mugs you?'

Jim hoisted his daysack onto his shoulder and made for the ticket barrier.

'What time do you have to check in by?' Hash asked, one last test.

'Eight o'clock, Dad.'

'Safe trip,' Hash said, pulling the boy back for a moment. 'Give your old man a hug. Catch up with you next week.'

'Ok.'

'Call me when you get there and give my love to your Gran and Grandpa. And don't let Uncle Sean take you drinking.' Jim waved back once more before trotting down to the platform. When Hash returned to the Discovery, Shamsa was staring past him, straining for a last glimpse of Jim.

He arranged his own phone and the Arab BlackBerry on the dashboard tray, side by side, then buckled himself in, comforting the dog until he saw the train leave the station. Getting the lad away before things moved beyond his control had been his smartest move so far, and it won him some headspace. Light was fading under leaden skies as he took the Discovery back onto the northbound M5, and he was struck by the irony of setting off for Birmingham Airport again...twice in one day. This time there was no urgency, nobody to drop off or meet, no reason for speed; if anything, this was a time for caution. True, he told himself, if it had not been for the traffic jams, a combined trip might have been better. He could have seen Jim through the system, waved him off, and then moved to the next task. But no matter; the train would make sure Jim made it on time.

Pelting rain slowed traffic to a crawl, and he used the time to try Sean. His mobile was off, and Hash had to think for a minute. It was early in the pubs, but not for Sean: chances were, his brother-in-law was in some drinking den. His favourite place, Kelly's Bar on the Whiterock Road, in Belfast's Republican wild west, had always been a hang-out for Sean in his heyday. Now, with those days long gone, it was almost the only place that tolerated him. When the phone rang the handset was lifted immediately. The silence at the other end reminded Hash that suspicion was always close to the surface even years after the troubles. In the background Hash could hear accordion music and the buzz of conversation. After a few seconds, a voice simply said, 'Kelly's'.

'Is Sean there?' Hash asked.

'Mate,' the voice said quietly, 'we have a thousand fucking Seans in here.'

'Just tell Sean it's Darky.'

The man at the other end muffled the receiver but Hash could just make out, 'Tell Sean there's a Darky after him!' and caught the gust of laughter before the phone was muffled again as it was passed to another pair of hands.

'Darky! See you?' The accent was exaggerated Belfast. Hash could hear rebel music and laughter and Sean's voice, raised to cut across the babble.

'See me!' Hash said. 'What about ye?'

'Oh the best, the very best.'

'Your mobile was off.'

'Never trust the thing,' Sean said. 'Been taking tea at the Palace, old chap?' Hash wondered how much Sean had already drunk.

'Away and fock yerself,' he mimicked, already weary of the exchange.

Sean's change of tone at the other end of the line signalled a truce. 'Sorry about the mobile,' he said. 'I was in confession.'

'Like hell,' Hash said. 'Sorry about the short notice, can you do it?'

'Why not?'

'Good man. You'll look after him?'

'Aye, but you'll want me to drop him down at the farm with the folks, surely?'

'I need you here too, mate. Can you make it over next week?'

'Mate? Nice to be needed, mate.' Bitten by the sarcasm, Hash looked at the phone. Sean had definitely been drinking. The question was, how much?

'I'm serious now,' Hash said. 'I've got a problem and I need help.'

'Ok, ok. Jim'll be fine over with the old folks,' Sean said.

'He still has his nightmares,' Hash said.

'Him and me too. Why the panic?'

'I might have a bit of a problem.'

'Who with?'

'Tell you next week.' Hash paused then added, 'I'll make it a business expense. Cover your costs.'

'This is family. I don't want your money,' Sean mumbled.

Hash swallowed his irritation. 'Promise me you'll be there for Jim? And keep your mobile on.'

'No problem.'

'Then get him down to the farm?'

There was a pause on the line. Since his conviction for killing the tout and his little boy, Sean was shunned by his catholic community back home. Bella and the old boy had borne the brunt of the shame and he'd never been forgiven. There had been no hero's welcome for him, not even after the years in Brit concentration camps.

'I've told your mother and she's expecting you both.' There was still silence. 'Mate?' Hash said. 'You still there?'

'Aye, Darky. All under control...mate.'

'This means a lot to me. Speak later when he's landed. And see you next week.'

He laid the phone beside the Arab BlackBerry and exhaled long and slow. He could do without Sean on one of his downswings. The years in Long Kesh prison had destroyed the Sean he'd known. In his thirties Sean Barr had been every inch the handsome, swashbuckling rebel freedom fighter. But a British court saw him in a different light, more as a brutal killer who could turn his gun against children. Ten years into a life sentence, the Good Friday Agreement opened the prison doors and waved him out, but there was nowhere for Sean to go. The new era of peace cast him as yesterday's hero, redundant, an embarrassment in the changing world of Northern Ireland. So now he found his comfort in the drinking dens along the Falls and Whiterock, scooping beer with the remaining diehard Republicans.

But Hash knew that the real Sean, or what was left of him, was a loyal friend and a devoted uncle, bloodied but unbowed. Even by the exceptionally high standards of West Belfast thuggery, Sean Barr still ranked as a hard bastard. Nobody would get near his boy on Sean's watch. Of that he was absolutely sure.

5

By the time he pulled off the motorway for the airport it was past eight o'clock. Darkness had fallen and it was raining heavily, which suited Hash fine. He nosed the vehicle through the barrier of the 'Drop and Go' parking area and found the nearest parking space. Jim would be through the system and sitting at the departure gate by now, he guessed. He put his cap on, whispering to Shamsa to guard the vehicle. He didn't lock it; if anyone wanted to steal it, they'd have to deal with her first. He made the Long Stay 5 car park in ten minutes. Zone C, row 15 was long, empty of people but full of cars. A security camera operator, with a bank of screens to monitor, would simply see a shadow traipsing along rows of cars; a soaked driver returning from a long trip, tired and trying to remember where he'd left his car.

He sought out Citroëns and offered the electronic fob, pressing the 'unlock' as he approached. After five rejections, a small bright red C3 flashed a welcome. He glanced back to make sure he was alone then looked inside to see if there were any packages on the seats. None in sight. He went for the hatch, releasing a smell of old, worn upholstery and sickly air freshener; a mid-size trolley suitcase lay in the boot space. He quickly checked the front and rear of the car, and the glove compartment. There was no paper, no object to identify the car in any way. It was all about the suitcase.

Hoisting it out, judging its weight at around fifteen kilos, he looked around again then, as the rain danced off every surface, locked up and put the keys on top of the back left wheel. Stepping back, he fished out his own mobile and snapped the car and its registration.

Tugging the suitcase back to the Discovery, he diverted into the departure terminal to check the desks and the departures screen. Jim's flight to Aldergrove displayed 'Closed', and there were no staff on duty.

He was back on the M42 fifty minutes after arriving at the airport. Jim's plane would be in the air. Unwrapping a pack of sandwiches with his free hand, he pondered the reason for the suitcase's weight. An hour if the traffic was good, he calculated, would see him unlocking its secrets. He wolfed down the sandwiches, feeding the crusts to Shamsa, as he drove on.

Nose-to-tail congestion in the rain soon wrecked his estimate. The flashing of brake lights and the scraping of his windshield wipers grated on his already raw nerves, and weariness began to catch up with him.

He blinked his tired eyes and wondered if he should make a clean breast to the British authorities, a plea bargain perhaps. It would guarantee immediate safety for them both but at a high cost: personal ruin and almost certainly time in prison. He could imagine the Echo reporter grinning as he tapped out, 'Cheltenham Magistrate unmasked as sleeper in our midst'. He wound the window down, letting freezing air into the car, then shook his head vigorously to refresh himself. He tried Jim's mobile. No luck. Probably still on inflight mode

It was just after ten when he reached the first turn off for

Cheltenham. Jim would have landed by now. He pictured the boy advancing, slightly bashful, towards his Uncle Sean who would start off gruff and then give him a rapturous bear hug before marching him to the nearest McDonald's, conveniently delaying the long drive across Ulster to Tyrone and the border farmhouse at Clady. Bella would be waiting up, but the old Badger would have been put to bed so he'd be fresh in the morning. The nickname still made him smile; his father-in-law had apparently been known far and wide for his grumpiness in the early mornings, so was 'best seen at night' like a badger, and it had stuck. At least Sean wouldn't have to confront both parents, although his mother would be sure to remind him that he'd been the cause of his father's stroke. He'd drop Jim as quickly as possible, Hash knew, and retreat to the Falls.

Hash tried Jim again, and again there was no reply. The boy'd forgotten to turn his phone back on. Unheard of for a teenager. He checked for signal strength on his phone; sometimes the atmospherics played with the signals, but trying Sean's number, the purring ringtone kicked in. A series of clicks and rustles told him Sean was on the line.

'I'm waiting on him. The sign says baggage is in the hall.'

'He'll be a few minutes yet. I'll ring back,' Hash said.

'What did Bella say?' Sean asked, apprehensive.

'Looking forward to seeing you both,' Hash lied. 'Said the Badger has his good days and bad days and misses a man on the farm. They reckon they'll have to give the job to Jim if you don't get there soon.'

'Bollocks,' Sean snorted. 'You know she'll go mad at me.'

'Jim wants to do some shooting.'

'Not so easy in Belfast these days.'

'Don't change your mind at the last minute.'

'Wouldn't miss the craic, don't you fret' Sean said.

'Call me when Jim's with you.'

'Aye, Ok.' Sean hung up. In contrast to his earlier mood,

Sean's spirits seemed to have lifted and his speech was clear. Killing time, Hash pulled over at a pump and filled up. On his way out, he rang Jim again but got no answer. After another wait of five minutes, Sean rang. 'No sign of him. Still a few people off that flight coming through, though.'

'Can't understand it,' Hash said. 'He should've been well through by now.'

'Give him a ring, then'

'He's not picking up.'

'Maybe forgot to turn his phone on,' Sean said.

'He's a teenager,' Hash said. 'He breathes through that damn phone.'

'Two other flights have landed after his,' Sean said. 'There are folk coming through in shorts and suntans. Don't think it's that hot in Brum.'

'You sure you're at Aldergrove?'

'For fuck's sake,' Sean growled. 'You sure you sent him to the right fucking country? I'm standing here for an hour and I'm not blind.'

'He took off at nine. Maybe there was a delay.'

'The plane's fucking landed, and all the passengers got off.'

'Maybe you can ask at the desk, ask for a passenger list?' The phone went dead.

Blinking on the dashboard caught his eye. He was holding his own phone, so it was the BlackBerry that had pulsed another SMS. He steered across into the empty car park of a retail estate and sat there, engine running. He keyed in the unlock code, fumbling it the first time and having to redo it.

The message read, 'I am OK father...James.'

A wave of nausea hit Hash and he dropped the phone on the seat, opened the car door, hung out and vomited. He could feel the veins in his neck and temple throbbing as he heaved. He got out, and leaned against the vehicle, sucking in air.

Shamsa watched.

'How soon can you get here?' Hash walked a short distance from the Discovery, pulling at the bottled water, rinsing and spitting. He felt sweat on his face, with the drizzle cooling him. He was climbing back in as Sean growled, 'Well, I'm still at the airport if that helps. He been in touch yet?'

'He's not coming.' Hash's voice was hard, unemotional. He stared down at the puke, steam rising off it. 'Has Bella called you?'

'What the fuck are you talking about?'

'Has Bella rung you?'

'No.'

'Thank fuck,' Hash said. 'If she does, tell her I pulled the plug on the trip.'

'You're a bit short on detail, mate.'

'I'll have to tell her he's had one of his turns.'

'I didn't realise he was bad,' Sean said.

'It's much worse than that,' Hash said. 'How soon can you get here? Something's happened.'

'So you just said. What?'

'He just sent me an SMS telling me he's OK.'

'That's a result,' Sean said. 'Where is he, then?'

'That's the problem. The SMS came from his phone, but it maybe wasn't him sending.'

'What the fuck are you talking about?'

'That's not the bad news,' Hash said. 'The really bad news is that the message came through to,' he took another swig of water, 'another phone, one I've just been lent.'

'Someone stole his phone, then,' Sean said.

'And then made him send a message to a stranger's phone. That's why I need you here. How soon can you get here? Also… he signed off as James, he never calls himself James.'

'You've fucking lost me, mate. Listen, I see my licence guy on Friday, he signs me off to come to the mainland on Monday.

Got a hospital appointment on Monday, too and can't miss that.'

'You're the only one who'll understand, the only person who'll get this fucking mess,' Hash broke in desperately. 'But we have to talk face to face.'

'Jesus,' Sean breathed. 'How bad is this?'

'When do you get in on Monday and how long can you stay?'

'They'll only let me come for the races. Out on Monday but back Saturday. If I come back a minute
later, they'll pull my privileges.'

Bella's voice was breezy when she picked up. She couldn't see Hash, sitting in the driver's seat, his mouth sour with his own vomit, bracing himself.

'So, the young lord's on his way to us his humble servants?' The country drawl would normally have brought a smile to Hash's face. 'The wee soul must be dead beat.'

'Bad news, Bella, I'm afraid,' he said. She didn't hear him. 'Bella?' Hash was gritting his teeth.

'Aye? We're waiting for Lord Jim. His room's ready, the one his poor mother used…' Her voice went silent for a second or two. '…Wee Lord Jim, the spitting image of his mum.'

'He's not coming, Bella.' Hash screwed his eyes, waiting in the charged silence.

'Dear God, tell me you're joking. Please.'

'Bella, he's not at his best.'

'Has that idiot Sean crashed the car?'

'Nothing to do with Sean,' Hash said hastily. 'I've just told him, too. He's been waiting at Aldergrove.'

'What's going on then?'

'I think he's had a turn,' Hash said.

'A turn?'

'You know how he gets too worked up about things some-times,' Hash said.

'What things?'

'I don't know, Bella. Could be something at school, some pressure, growing pains, teenage worries. Maybe someone said something.'

'Is he ok? Where do you have him?'

'It happened at the check-in,' Hash looked towards the empty car park. 'He just fainted on me,' he said. 'He came to and I brought him straight back home.'

'I'll have a word with him,' she said.

'He's fast asleep. He'll call you tomorrow.'

'Are you sure he's ok?'

'We'll both be over by the end of next week.' It was a lie he desperately wanted to believe.

'I'll speak to you both tomorrow then,' she said. 'Oh, Lord above, what am I going to tell the poor old boy sitting here?'

Immediately after putting the phone down on Bella, he dialled Jim's mobile and waited. A digitised voice told him to leave a message. He looked at the BlackBerry to double check it really was Jim's number and tried to itemise the sequence of events. Jim had been waved off at the station at around six in the evening. He would have made it from New Street to the airport in half an hour, checked in no later than eight, due to fly around nine. He would have called if there had been a delay, surely? But Sean had told him the flight landed on schedule and all the passengers were gone.

'For fuck's sake, Hash, get a grip,' he moaned. Shamsa flinched at the distress in his voice.

Whoever was out there had read all their movements. He began to seethe with self-loathing. If only Jim had been mugged, merely lost his money and phone. It was just a stupid joke at the station, but it would have been a thousand times better than him being caught up in this horror.

The first SMS, the one telling him about the Long-Stay car park, had come from a Libyan number, so the sender could be in the UK or even in Libya. His mind jumped to the suitcase sitting in the back of the Discovery. The second SMS had come through at twenty past ten, from Jim's own phone. They wanted Hash to join the dots and Jim would never use 'father' unless he was taking the mickey, or 'James,' unless he was in trouble.

A new SMS pulsed, two words only. As he read it tears began to sting his eyes. He rocked from side to side in the driver's seat, jamming his fist against his teeth and choking back a scream of anguished rage.

6

NIGHT - TUESDAY 3RD MARCH

The second SMS read 'Dafe coming. Jim couldn't possibly have sent this one, but it had come from his phone. Hash knew there was nobody in Jim's address book with the name Dafe. Someone was either dictating to Jim or using it himself. He looked at the keyboard on the Arab BlackBerry, where the 'f' and 'v' buttons were close. Maybe the fingers sending the message had made a typo, straying from 'Dave' to 'Dafe'. He told himself to try kidding someone else. The word 'dafe' came all the way from Ben Gashir and Jim was just the messenger, shanghaied into passing it on.

His brain was racing. First out of the window was any notion of going to the authorities. He was on his own with this and he had to catch up and overtake somehow, get an advantage over the bastards. Jim's absence from school needed to be prolonged; he needed a more plausible excuse. He thanked God for the school holidays coming up; his clumsy assumptions where Susan was concerned had been a salutary shock, but he'd need her help again. She was probably key to keeping the school quiet. He'd have to patch things up with her, tell her Jim was down with some virus or other and staying put with his grand-parents. They could be fed the line that Jim was in hospital in Cheltenham, under observation for a few days; the same virus would do. He could spin it out for a while, tell them later their wee lad was at home, confined to bed.

Sean would need to get the full picture, but only when he came over and they were face to face. Maybe Siddiq could be used, too. At last, Hash felt a flicker of hope. He could safely open up, just a little, to Siddiq; he knew he could trust him to keep his mouth shut. On an impulse, he keyed a return SMS to the Libyan number: 'Confirm my son ok'. It was just possible they'd want to reassure him, keep him on board.

The engine was idling, and he was still sitting in a deserted car park with a puddle of vomit at his feet. He revved up and nosed out into almost empty streets, keeping the driver's window down. The rain had stopped; the air was fresher for the earlier downpour, clearing his head a little as he drove.

The 'dafe' SMS had been another order. In English, the word meant 'guest'. They could have sent it in Arabic but would have known that Cheltenham was the world centre of eavesdrop-ping software. Instead, someone with a sharp brain had mashed the languages so the word would look like an innocent typo on a teenager's phone. Soon, Hash thought, and maybe the sod was already on the way, an unwanted guest would cross his threshold.

Twenty-seven years ago, in early December 1988, a simi-lar cryptic instruction had brought a "dafe" to his doorstep. The man, a fellow Libyan by his accent, had spent hours at various telephone kiosks, revealed nothing about his mission and moved on after four days. A week later, Pan Am Flight 103 exploded over the Scottish town of Lockerbie. When Gaddafi's hand was detected in the catastrophe, Hash instinctively knew he and his guest had been part of it and that he, Hash, had yet more blood on his hands. The man's name subsequently came out in the press as Megrahi, and he often wondered if he'd been the same 'McGraw' Sean had occasionally mentioned back in the days of the attacks on the Brits in Tyrone; Sean enjoyed having trouble with Arab names. The Pan Am flight was not a military target and the losses had disgusted Hash. Gaddafi was quick to throw his Megrahi under a bus as soon as the international outcry had started turning up the heat. And Hash knew, beyond any possible doubt, that his own fate, and Jim's, would hang on the whims of his masters back in Libya in just the same way.

Whoever was out there calling the shots, they were the heirs to the Gaddafi regime. But who were they exactly, and how had they got through to him so quickly? The people who had Jim were professionals, no question, and had read Hash all too easily. He needed to steel his nerves and get his edge back. The bargaining chip that Jim had become would need to be played both ways. The first thing was to get a guarantee Jim was safe. They needed his cooperation, could only get it if he knew Jim was alive and unharmed.

As soon as he was home, he flicked on the laptop. Jim's phone had been a two-for-one deal on his business account. It also allowed him to monitor Jim's usage and he had downloaded a find-my-phone app to locate the phone if it was left on a bus.

Jim's iPhone had transmitted the 'ok' message at 22:21 from the junction of Stratford Road and Henley Street in the Sparkbrook area of South Birmingham, only a few miles from the airport and even less from New Street Station. How had they grabbed Jim? Almost certainly, they'd followed him, but from where? Home? The train?

The 'dafe' message had come through at 23:05, forty-four minutes later and from roughly the same area as the first. Had Jim been driven around in a holding pattern, made to send the first message, maybe rewarded in some way and then made to send the second?

He could be on those dark wet streets within the hour, he realised, could walk around them with a photo of Jim, asking people if they had seen him. On the other hand, whoever had the phone could simply be throwing him off the scent. Maybe they'd moved the phone to Sparkbrook as a decoy, with Jim being held somewhere else entirely. He tried him again, but the iPhone was switched off.

If he drove there and set up, he considered, and they switched it back on and let Jim send another message, that would put him right on the spot. Maybe he would get lucky and zero in on the exact location. Or maybe they were waiting for him to try so they could teach him a lesson about who was in control. Another transmission could get him dummied into a wild goose chase, or an ambush. Maybe they were waiting to see if the BlackBerry would move, and where to. Hash massaged his aching temples and closed his eyes

Most of the people living in Sparkbrook would be Asians. He knew it would be smarter to be looking for Jim with a team who knew the area but sitting around at home was out of the question. And once his uninvited guest arrived, he'd have even less freedom of movement. He had to act.

SPARKBROOK. DAWN – WEDNESDAY MARCH 4TH

At the first hint of light, Hash was pulling into a pay-and-display car park off the Stratford Road. The approaching dawn kindled some small hope he might get near enough to see and grab Jim. The Arab BlackBerry was sitting on the kitchen table, bleeping to anyone counter-monitoring that he was still in Cheltenham.

Walking the streets between the sites of the phone emissions,

Hash looked for likely places Jim could have been sitting the previous evening. He saw drab two-storey red-brick parades of Asian restaurants, halal produce and convenience stores all with their signs in English, Arabic and what he guessed was Sanskrit. Windows were screened with adverts or stacked with produce ready to go back out on the pavement when the awnings were unfurled. Most restaurant windows were draped with heavy curtains. As he walked, he looked up at the first-floor windows. A young lad too terrified to sleep might just spot his father.

As the working day gathered momentum, Hash began to feel conspicuous and headed back to watch from the Discovery; Jim might even find a way to break free if he recognised the vehicle. He switched on his laptop, connected to the net and kept vigil, dialling Jim's number every half-hour.

Shamsa's low growl woke him, and he realised he must have dropped off. Her explosion of barking brought him bolt upright. Following the dog's gaze, he saw a traffic warden approaching. The man had a full Islamic beard and walked slowly, methodically stopping to look at vehicles. He clocked the Discovery, incensing Shamsa who barked even more fiercely. The man had passed in less than a minute, but she continued to bark until Hash rapped her on the nose. An Islamic fundamentalist traffic warden wasn't just a Christian's nightmare, Hash reflected grimly.

Bella rang soon after nine.

'How's our little lord? He any better yet?'

'Still under the weather,' Hash replied, 'some sort of flu bug. It's been doing the rounds at school, apparently. It's put a few of the other kids out of action, so Jim's not the only one.'

'You had us all worried there,' she said. 'Is he up to a chat with his granny?'

'I'm out of the house. He's in bed. At least he was when I left him. But you could try his mobile.'

'I haven't got the number,' Bella said. 'Never mind, it'll wait.'

'I'll give it to you,' said Hash, 'I'm sure he'd like a chat. Got a pen?'

'Doesn't matter, Hash,' she said. 'I'll call him later, maybe he'll be feeling better.'

'How's Badger doing?' Hash asked. He was looking out of the Discovery windscreen, not listening to her. Eventually her silence at the other end of the phone warned him she was expecting an answer.

'Sorry, Bella, I got distracted. His lordship just texted me. I think he wants pizza.'

'For breakfast? Tell him he shouldn't eat that rubbish,' she said. 'And tell him his old gran sends her love.'

Around eleven the battery on his laptop start to fade and going to the rear door to plug in a charging cable, he saw the suitcase. He'd forgotten about it in the stress of the last twelve hours. He pulled the case to him and checked the two outside pockets, finding nothing. He unzipped the main compartment and the cover fell back. The contents had been wrapped in a large, blue plastic shopping bag. He needed two hands to get the bag out and upend it onto the boot space. Two items slid out, both wrapped in blue plastic, bound tight with strips of masking-tape.

The first was rectangular and light, like a pack of printing paper. Easing it out, he found himself looking at a vacuum-sealed block of images of The Queen, wads of them, rubber-banded and each about an inch thick. The face notes had the £50 denomination. He flipped the block, end over end, to look at it from all angles and, walking his fingers across the whole package, came up with twenty wads. Someone wanted him to look after a hundred thousand pounds. He dropped the block back into the suitcase, threw in the second sealed object, zipped it up and slammed the vehicle door.

Jim shoved his knuckles hard into his temples, desperate to work out what was going on, make sense of all this weirdness. But his head was too fuzzy to think properly. Had he been ill again? It didn't feel like that though. He could hardly remember anything about how he'd ended up here. There was the woman at Birmingham station, he remembered her. Really pretty, and she'd put her arm round his shoulders, looked concerned, saying something about Dad? There was a man there too, silent type, bit rough.

He felt around the bedding. Where the fuck was his phone? A blurred memory of the grouchy bloke telling him to send a message on it, to his Dad. Well, he could bloody well give it back. He really wanted his Dad, badly...He'd soon sort him out. Where was he, why wasn't he here, why did he have to tell him he was OK? Tears suddenly pricked in his eyes. Pathetic, stupid...

He should have been with Uncle Sean by now. His Granny would be asking where he was. His Dad would be thinking about him too, wherever he was.

He forced himself to stand and crossed unsteadily to the curtains. They smelt of cigarette smoke too, felt sticky as he pulled one back. The window was fogged up with smears and condensation and he tried to open it, but it was screwed down. He rubbed at the glass, hard enough to clear a good patch, and looked down onto the street below where a traffic warden was walking slowly along a line of cars. He thought he could hear a dog barking somewhere. The warden looked back as if he could hear it too. The urge to pee became too strong and the basin in the corner of the room was the obvious answer. He needed to sleep...

7

MORNING.

Hash looked at Siddiq's name on the phone and answered 'I was thinking of calling you'.

'Now you have me,' Siddiq's voice was quiet but friendly. 'Where are you, my friend?'

Hash looked out of the window at the red-brick buildings, the people on the streets all heavily clothed against the cold, grey morning.

'I'm on my way to the mosque,' Hash lied.

'You're too late or too early, my friend.'

'Not your mosque,' Hash said. 'I'm going to one in Birmingham.'

'What's wrong with ours in Cheltenham?'

'I've got a problem,' Hash said.

'And the solution is in a mosque in Birmingham?' Siddiq sounded surprised. 'I also have a problem.'

'What sort of problem?'

'But my problem is not in the mosque.' Siddiq cleared his throat and his voice dropped. 'I am bringing you someone. A guest but not a guest. If you follow me?'

'You're not making it easy, Siddiq,' said Hash.

'That's why it's better we talk face to face.'

Had Siddiq become involved? He had a network of Bang-ladeshi relations stretching across the Midlands: restaurants, import-export, immigration agencies and others, all inter-twined in a web of marriage and relatives. So why else would he need Hash's help all of a sudden?

'I also have a problem,' he'd said. He felt a stab of hope, and fear. If Siddiq was involved with the dafe he knew what was going on. He could also be involved with Jim's disappearance.

'I'm having a bit of trouble with Jim,' Hash tried.

'I'm sorry to hear that,' said Siddiq. 'Is he at home?'

'Why do you ask?'.

'Because you are driving to a mosque in Birmingham for the first time in your life.'

'He's at school,' Hash lied. 'I'm doing a charity thing up here.'

'Who with?' Siddiq asked. 'Charity begins at home.'

There was an awkward silence between the two men. Siddiq broke it. 'Please come and sit with me, it'll be easier to talk.'

As he drove, Hash thought about his relationship with Siddiq, a business arrangement that had developed into a firm friendship and went back over twenty years. They were two foreigners in an English town and had met in a small mosque north of the High Street. In the beginning, and with only a handshake as security, Hash had lent Libyan cash to the ambitious Bangladeshi, interest free. The loan had been repaid promptly with Siddiq setting up the properties and Hash doing the legal work. The formula had repeated itself and they'd become tried and trusted colleagues, both wealthy: Siddiq with his chain of restaurants, and Hash with a property empire.

He wondered again if he should just go to the police and hold his hands up. He'd have to hide the money before he surrendered. Maybe leave it with Sean, or better with Siddiq who could at least take a small commission. A hundred thousand working for him over the coming years would be a tidy pension pot when he was finally released from jail. The flaw in that idea was having to explain the beginning; Tripoli to Eire with a shipload of weapons, then the attacks in Ulster where people had been murdered and lives shattered. It would take a miracle, and a lot of time, to convince the police that although he wasn't exactly on their side, he was definitely one of the "good guys." He wasn't sure about miracles, but he knew he was fast running out of time.

The second package had not felt as regular as the block of money, and he needed to check it when he got home. The stash of money was a hallmark of old-school methods; cash for everything, use small amounts and leave no electronic trail. Hash knew it was his to grease wheels with; the Libyan auditors were the least of his worries.

Jim, his precious boy. What were the chances of the Brits getting the picture and working fast enough to save him? Probably nil; more likely they'd begin a game of cat and mouse with Jim as bait. They'd use him exactly as he was being used now, just another bargaining chip. Hash thought of Jim, tired, worried, afraid and maybe hurt and cursed himself for being so stupidly slow off the mark, for not having understood straightaway and moved faster. He had to turn the tables somehow and do it quickly.

At home, he pulled out the money block and laid it to one side. The second bag, the heavier of the two, was also vacuum-sealed and through the blue plastic he saw what looked like an angler's vest, its khaki fabric stained with dirt or oil. Hash ran his fingers over the pockets feeling lumps of solid material that gave slightly to his pinching touch, as if chunks of kids' plasticine were packed into every pocket. Eventually he came to the top right pocket and felt two small, cylindrical objects; batteries, or plastic tubes to hold batteries. His fingers found the wires beneath the tubes that would lead to a detonator tucked into the nearest block of explosive.

Holding the waistcoat up, he judged the weight at around twelve kilos of explosive, enough to scatter his house across Cheltenham with a bang that would be heard ten miles away. There'd be nothing but a hole in the ground where he stood, or where old Mrs H next door was probably sitting at this moment enjoying a cuppa. He turned it over again. The bomber could set it off himself, or the aerial inside the fabric could receive the detonating signal from an obliging third party.

Sitting opposite Siddiq, in one of the corner booths of his restaurant, Hash could see his friend was nervous. He leant forward conspiratorially. 'We need to hide someone,' he said.

'We?'

'You need to hide someone,' Siddiq corrected. 'I'm asking you.'

'Why me?'

Siddiq checked left and right for anybody within earshot, looking shifty.

'If it's for you,' Hash cut in, 'I'll do it.'

Siddiq's face cleared, and he sat back against the booth seat. 'Just one person,' he said. 'I know you have places.'

'But you have places too,' Hash pointed out.

'I'm sure yours are better than mine.' Siddiq sat back against the seat, moving his gaze to his staff. 'Can't use my places,' he said.

'How soon?'

'Very soon.'

'I've only got one place empty just now,' Hash said. 'A nice little place behind GCHQ. It'll need a bit of a clean though. Have you got someone who could do it?'

Siddiq sucked his teeth and shook his head. 'Can't use my staff,' he said. 'Too risky.'

'Today, tonight, tomorrow?' Hash leaned back. 'Give me a clue.'

'Tonight, tomorrow most probably.' Siddiq canted his head one way then the other. 'Depends when I'm told.'

Hash searched his face, his friend of so many years, usually so suave and courteous but now an odd mixture of nerves and embarrassment. 'Let me know,' he said. 'I'll get Thelma to have the place freshened up.'

'What about Jim?' Siddiq looked across at Hash. 'How can I help?'

It was Hash's turn to be evasive. At Ben Gashir, the instructors had drummed into the class how a cell on the ground in enemy territory operated more securely the less each member knew collectively about the activities and responsibilities of the others.

'He's run away,' he said. Siddiq's eyebrows shot up. 'I took him to the station last night, but he didn't go where I sent him.'

'What is wrong with the boy?' Siddiq looked shocked.

'I need to find him.' Hash patted his pocket. 'I tracked his phone location to Sparkbrook.'

'Sparkbrook!' Siddiq exclaimed. 'That's why you were driving there today. You were looking for him?'

Hash nodded slowly. 'What else could I do?'

'Go to the police?' Siddiq said.

'That's delicate, wouldn't be my first choice.'

'What would be?'

'I don't know, to be honest.' Hash shrugged. 'Maybe he'll phone when he's tired.'

'Is he sick, needing medication, a doctor?' Siddiq seemed genuinely concerned.

'There's his epilepsy, and he's especially vulnerable when he's stressed. We always keep the medication close by, just in case.' This was bullshit; Jim was physically disgustingly robust but if Siddiq was passing on information to Libya, it was worth inserting a medical complication as a test.

'If he doesn't come home, you should go to the police, check the hospitals. Surely?' Siddiq was becoming animated.

'I need to know he's ok, or at least have some communication with him,' Hash said.

'And you were going to the mosque in Sparkbrook?' Siddiq's brow shot up. 'Which mosque, my friend?'

'Of course not. I was going to check the streets and cafés where the signal came from.'

'Maybe that's not a bad idea,' Siddiq said.

'It's my only idea, so far.'

'I meant the mosques,' Siddiq said. 'Going to a mosque is better than going to the police. Especially in Sparkbrook.'

'We both know I can't go to the police.' Hash watched Siddiq's face for any hint of agreement.

'If you say so,' was all he got.

'Depends on the mosque, of course,' Siddiq continued. 'Do one thing, now. SMS me a good photo of him, a good one of his face.'

'Why?'

'I can pass the photo on to imams in Birmingham, to the right mosques.'

Hash scrolled through his pictures looking for the most recent snap of Jim and they agreed on one of him kneeling with Shamsa, smiling Tara's pursed smile.

'Like his mother,' Siddiq said. 'Do you have any money?'

Hash nodded.

'You are sure you don't want to go to the police?'

'Sure. How much?'

'Come to my mosque tomorrow and we'll sit with a friend.'

'I'm in a real hurry, Siddiq.'

Siddiq held up his right hand, fingertips pinched. 'Better to listen and think. Barge into any mosque in a rush, and you will make it worse.'

In the pitch-dark, with Shamsa standing guard, he checked the footbridge with his hands. There was no fresh tape so no new message in the dead letter box. The gentle incline, as he trudged back to the Discovery, sapped the last remnants of his strength. He'd been awake for twenty-eight straight hours.

8

MORNING - THURSDAY 5TH MARCH

His dreams had taken him back to Ireland looking at little Jim sitting in a car, covered in blood, reaching for his father, calling out in terror…and Hash helpless, mute, pinioned by strong arms, desperate to run to the boy. He had woken, shaken and with dread churning in his gut.   He could only hope that whatever lay in store for him at the meeting with Siddiq and this unknown helper was the beginning of his counter-attack and not a well-meant but misguided red herring. He was aware of putting off leaving the house, doing things that could well have waited, in the end screwing up the courage to make the move. He was in the car before he remembered he hadn't done anything about the trouble at the chippy, but the clock was running; he couldn't spare time or attention for his tenant now. He put a call through to Thelma in the office, asking her to contact the Portuguese, get a list of his repair costs and send flowers to the man's wife.

A small sign above the door proclaimed the house a 'Masjid', a mosque for the Muslim community. An internal wall had been knocked through to enlarge the space for worshippers where Hash counted twelve other men in two lines, bowing in unison for midday prayers. He saw faces from Siddiq's crew of waiters as well as young men in smart leisure clothes, probably students from the nearby language school. Hash prayed silently, his lips moving in time to the observances. He hadn't forgotten the words but was grateful to Siddiq, upfront and speaking clearly, for leading the way. His mind was on Jim. He'd had his second night away from home; he must be exhausted, bewildered, terrified.

Siddiq held him back as the others dispersed then led him into a sparse, gloomy kitchen. A pine table shoved against the wall made space for four chairs. The only decoration was an Islamic calendar for the year 1436 with a picture of the Kaaba at Mecca. They were joined by a short, wiry man. Hash had seen him among the worshippers. Mid-forties, dressed in grey trousers and a brown bomber jacket zipped to the neck. His beard, grey and mid-length and shaved to leave no moustache, showed traces of henna. He offered the Arabic greeting, 'Salaam-Alaikum", without a smile but with a handshake as strong as hell. Hash could feel the unblinking owl-like stare boring into him from behind the rimless glasses.

'This gentleman is Mr Hakim, and he may be able to assist you,' was all Siddiq said, pulling the chairs round the table. They sat, and a silence set in, prolonged, tense. The stranger glared down at a spot on the table and when Siddiq flicked a nervous smile in his direction, Hash took his cue to pull an envelope from his pocket, placing it on the smudge where the man's eyes seemed to be focused.

'This is for the mosque,' he said. 'Five thousand pounds.' He had no qualms about using his recently acquired wealth.

The silence continued with neither Siddiq nor Hakim making a move to take the envelope. Finally, Siddiq eased forward on his chair, clearing his throat. 'A very generous gift, my brother.'

Hakim nodded but otherwise said nothing, then lifted his gaze from the table to Hash. After a further moment of silence, he said one word, 'And?'

'My son...' Hash began but was immediately interrupted.

'The boy who has run away from home?' Hakim jutted his chin at Siddiq. 'He told me.' Hash was stunned by the brutality of his words, his bluntness. 'Is he a Muslim?' Hakim continued.

Siddiq stepped in, 'He is the son of a good Muslim.'

Hakim looked at Hash. 'I want his answer.'

'My son is not a Muslim and,' Hash said, 'he has not run away from home.' He was wondering if this was some sort of test, a trial with Siddiq as a witness. It was possible this fierce, taut man was behind the Libyan messages, and here to assess Hash's state of mind, his willingness to comply.

'But maybe he is and maybe he has,' Hakim countered. 'You say he is not.' The stress was placed on 'you', with a sneer. 'How sure are you? How do you know he's not a Muslim? How well do you even know your son? Do you know what he watches on the internet?' A boxer could not have rained a more devastating flurry of punches. 'Maybe your son ran away and is now on his way to join the jihad.'

Hash shook his head, and was about to protest angrily, when Hakim added, 'Maybe your son knows exactly what he is doing.' He stalled Hash with a raised hand. 'Do you know how many young people in South Birmingham have already gone to the jihad?'

'My son isn't an adult,' Hash began to explain, 'and he has...,' he groped for right the words, 'issues.'

'Issues are perfect,' Hakim interjected. 'A lot of young men with issues have gone. Around two hundred so far. And none of the parents saw it coming.'

'My son has difficulties,' Hash began again. 'He still suffers from his mother's death.'

Hakim said nothing as he watched Hash struggle.

'I put him on the train to Birmingham on Tuesday evening,' Hash said. 'I've had two messages from his phone, and I traced the calls to Sparkbrook.' He told the two men about his vigil in the streets the previous day.

'And you were going there to look for him? Why didn't you go to the police instead?'

Hash wondered why Siddiq hadn't briefed the man, on this at least. 'Maybe I will go to the police.' Hash leaned forward. 'If nobody else can help me.'

Hakim understood but was unfazed by Hash's barely veiled threat. 'I told him not to,' Siddiq offered.

'I thought I might see him on the street,' Hash said. 'I thought maybe he'd been mugged, his phone stolen, something like that.'

'Why not go to the church, instead of the mosques?' Hakim said.

'There don't seem to be many there.' Hash raised his hands. 'To be honest, I didn't know what the hell I was doing.'

'I told him the imams would think he was an undercover policeman, like those immigration cops,' Siddiq tried again. Hash couldn't remember hearing that but was grateful for his friend's support.

'I told him we could get the boy's photograph around our imams and friends in a few minutes,' Siddiq added.

'Maybe the boy is on his way to jihad, thanks to' Hakim held up his fingers in inverted commas, 'an imam.'

'He's never shown any interest in Islam, or any religion,' Hash said.

'So why are you here, giving money to the mosque.' The man looked down at the envelope.

'Are you a father?' Hash asked. 'Put yourself in my position and tell me what you'd do.' Hakim nodded, in agreement for the first time, but didn't reply.

'He could have called the police into Sparkbrook,' Siddiq said. 'Mr Hash did not want that to happen.' He looked directly at the rigid figure across the table. 'Now it's a question of helping a friend, not letting him rush into a bad decision.'

Hakim looked at his watch, preparing to leave. 'We'll be in touch,' he said, holding out his hand to Siddiq.

'Tell me what to do?' Hash said.

'We'll be in touch,' the man repeated. ''Insh'Allah. God willing.'

Hash felt the crushing handshake again and pointed to the envelope. 'You're forgetting the money.'

'You gave it to the mosque,' Hakim said.

In the car park, Siddiq calmed Hash. 'Don't worry, my friend.'

'Such nonsense about Jim,' Hash said. 'Who is that man? Do you trust him? Did you hear him say Jim had run away?'

'You have to trust him.'

'Where does he come from?'

'He's an imam.'

'And he's from Sparkbrook,' Hash said.

'He's a very important businessman,' Siddiq added.

'He didn't like me.'

'Maybe he is suspicious of strangers who don't pray but offer money to buy help. He is very cautious.'

'What happens now?' Hash asked. 'I just wait for him. What about the money, was that a mistake? Or too much?'

'You gave enough. Tomorrow is Friday and he will be seeing many people at his mosque. But,' Siddiq's voice dropped to a whisper, 'now you have to do one thing.' They had stopped by Hash's car. Siddiq tugged Hash's arm. 'You have to get ready for my guest.'

'When's he coming?'

Siddiq gave a pained smile, as though it was an embarrassing admission. 'Very soon but I don't have the exact details.'

MID-AFTERNOON - THURSDAY

There was a message flashing on the Arab BlackBerry when Hash got back to the house. He picked the phone up and read, 'Ok'. It had come through, with the same Libyan dialling code, at 12:30 while he'd been in the mosque with Siddiq. He dropped into a kitchen chair and gazed at it, his hands trembling with relief.

'Ok', Hash reflected, was short but huge; a cynical signal the bastards were pretending to feel his pain and cared enough to confirm Jim was alright. The spectrum of 'ok' was vast: at one end Jim was comfortable, fed, rested. 'Ok' at its worst meant battered, starved, terrified but still alive; to the Libyan Mukhabarat that would still qualify as 'ok'. It was also an acknowledgement they needed to keep communication going. Someone, some bastard from years ago, was throwing him a crumb to keep him in line. But 'ok', Hash reflected, was a hundred times better than 'Not ok'. Or worse, no answer at all.

He wondered if he should tell Siddiq about the Libyan connection, but he felt less sure of their relationship now. Sean, on the other hand, would need to know who they were dealing with. He'd be rocked, but it wouldn't throw him, as long as he still had the stomach for the game. Played correctly, kept out of sight and sober, Sean was his secret weapon. Hash felt a flicker of comfort, picked up the BlackBerry and tapped a question to the Libyan sender. 'What favourite name does Granny use?' Then he loaded Shamsa and his laptop into the Discovery, taking a wad of five thousand pounds with him. As before, he left the Arab phone.

The thought of wading through motorway traffic on his way back to Sparkbrook wearied him; he was plodding when he should have been galloping, he knew. He thought of Hakim. Something about his attitude, his confidence, arrogance even set alarm bells ringing although Siddiq obviously trusted him. And his own poking about the streets of Sparkbrook could potentially cause real problems, especially if the man was genuine about looking for Jim.

He was passing the housing estates near the chippy and diverted on impulse, parking discreetly away from the chippy, but close enough to see what was going on. He watched a trickle of customers build into a strong queue, the little team of two working hard to serve their clients, until it came to him that he'd been sitting there so long he'd effectively aborted the Sparkbrook vigil.

9

CHELTENHAM. MORNING – FRIDAY 6TH MARCH

After ducking out of the trip to Birmingham with his point-less vigil at the chippy, Hash had forced himself back home to take a hot bath and crash. Wide awake again by daybreak, and downstairs with a mug of tea, he was about to phone Siddiq when the front doorbell rang. The figure on the other side of the glass was female, but not bent over like Mrs Hamilton. Hash opened the door to a pretty face and a wide smile.

'Susan,' he said, his spirits lifting. 'Just when I thought you'd given up on me.' He extended his hand and held on to hers as he led her over the threshold.

'Sorry it's so early. I just thought I'd drop James's holiday work off.'

Hash was struggling to remember which part of the make-believe he'd spun her. 'Sorry,' he began. 'Late night, didn't get back in until the early hours.'

'Life in the fast lane?'

'I wish,' said Hash. 'Chasing someone who's giving me a headache.'

'A bit like me,' she responded. 'So, I won't stay long, then.'

Hash knew he was still being judged. The use of James, as opposed to Jim, Jimbo, Jimmy was the sound of the teacher's displeasure. It was something Jim had reported back from time to time when he and Miss Pine had clashed. Only his Mother called him James, and that was pure love. Tara had always insisted on James.

'On the contrary, you must stay. It would cheer me up. Unless you're still fed up with me?' He pointed towards the kitchen, but she hesitated.

'I've heard the dying granny story a hundred times. Just disappointed at it coming from you.'

'Grandfather with a stroke, and he is deteriorating,' Hash corrected gently. 'We really don't know how much longer he's got. And would you credit it,' he shook his head in disbelief, 'Jim's now down with some sort of virus, confined to bed on the farm.' He flicked on the kettle and pointed to a chair, 'So a cup of coffee and a chance to put it right with you is what I need.' Looking at her watch, she made a decision, nodded and put the bag of textbooks on the table. Hash made the coffee, watching out of the corner of his eye as she laid out the books and checked the bookmarks with her notes. He felt a sudden rush of emotion, hopefulness and something more, so much so that he had to look away She cared about his son, was going out of her way to help him.

He placed a steaming mug by the books. 'I'll take them over with me,' he said, and grinned. 'Jim will be so pleased...you can run but you can't hide.'

'How is he?'

'Exhausted. This virus is really hanging on, his grandmother tells me. She's talking about quarantine.'

'Really? Poor boy.'

He prised open a tin and held the contents out. 'Biscuit?' She took one. Shamsa came forward and nudged her thigh, hinting. She stroked the dog and talked to it softly.

They started to go through the assignments. Her closeness and the soft smell of her scent were a balm to him. Jim had once declared her, 'the best teacher, ever'. Hash watched her delicate finger as it traced across the open books and down the list.

The BlackBerry pinged a waiting SMS. 'Do you need to get that?' she asked.

'It can wait,' Hash lied.

'So, what does a boy like Jim get up to on a farm in Ireland?' Susan asked when the assignment checklist was done. She sat back too and picked up the mug in both hands.

'Well, he's doing his duty, for a start. He's the only grandchild they have.'

'No cousins?'

'None. Just one uncle, the black sheep of the family.'

'How come a Jordanian marries an Irish Catholic? How did you meet?'

'We were both phoning the Samaritans,' Hash said, 'and we got crossed lines.'

Susan absorbed this for a second. 'You're right, I'm being nosy.'

'I'm teasing,' Hash said. 'I was a sales rep in Ireland in the eighties, just out of Amman University, my first job was the North of Ireland. I met her at a party and,' he paused, smiling at the memory, 'I fell head over heels. When we decided to marry, all hell broke loose. They thought she was going to have to live in a Bedouin tent.'

Susan laughed. 'So, Jim's over there mucking out the stables?'

'A change from Play Station in Cheltenham,' Hash said. 'Fresh air, animals and a torrent of pocket money, of course.' He paused. 'A chance to sweet-talk his grandparents into splashing out on his current obsession.' He scrolled through the photographs on his phone and tapped on one of Jim and his Spitfire. 'His craze for the last three years, non-stop, ever since I gave him a kit one Christmas.' Hash flicked through a stream of photographs showing Jim with an array of models.

'Boys and their toys,' Susan commented. She pointed up

to the dresser where a photograph of Tara stood beside the old family portrait. 'I expect he still misses her?'

'Of course, and it breaks my heart. He thinks he's been cheated,' Hash said. 'He used to ask me if it was his fault, did he cause his mum's illness because he was bad or did something wrong.' Hash sipped his coffee. 'It takes him down every so often.'

She nodded. 'I've seen that at school.' There was silence between them. Susan broke it, saying softly, 'But you should be proud, you know, he's a remarkable kid.'

'Thanks to you, in many ways,' Hash said. 'He thinks the world of you. Maybe I should be taking him to Jordan more often as well. Introduce him to the language and all his aunts, uncles and cousins there.' He pointed to the old black and white group photo.

'Why don't you? I expect the tickets are expensive…'

'Oh, it's not the cost.' Hash shrugged. 'It's that other hazard,' he said, 'the Jordanian mother and her matchmaking.'

'Sounds interesting.'

'They wouldn't rest until I was married off. I hope you realise I'm still a catch, in Jordan at least. This place, my bank balance, the chance of a British passport, my good looks…'

'Your modesty….'

'Absolutely.' Hash offered the biscuits. 'And who'll be taking Susan Pine down the aisle?', and when she smiled, added, 'My father will make your father an offer of twenty camels.'

Her eyebrow arched, and she examined her biscuit. 'Look, Hash, I only came round to drop off some assignments.'

'Tell your father we'll raise it to twenty-five and he'll get free camel's milk for the rest of his life.'

'He'll probably just stick with the twenty camels, thanks.'

She got up and took her cup to the sink. 'So, back to reality.' She looked over her shoulder, smiling at Hash. 'There might be one more assignment and if I've time I'll whiz by on Sunday morning, and drop it in.'

As Hash opened the door, she hesitated on the step.

'Stay there,' Hash said. 'I need all the neighbours to see you.'

'See you at the debating society?'

'I'm looking forward to it'

'Me, too.' She gave a shy wave as she left.

'Be sure to tell your father.'

She put her hands over her ears as she walked back down the path.

Rushing back inside, he seized the Arab BlackBerry. The SMS, 'Dafe coming', sent a depth charge of adrenaline through him. He switched on the computer, waited a moment and then rang Jim's iPhone. There was no answer and the locating app offered nothing. If the guest was moving, then Jim was on the move, too. Or the five thousand pounds had swung it, and he'd been set free.

He sat, elbows on the table, eyes closed and thumbs kneading his temples, trying to think clearly, running all the possible scenarios again. Maybe Jim wasn't moving, and they still had to keep communications open. So far, the 'ok' was the only straw he'd been allowed to grasp. Siddiq and the hard little bastard at the mosque could, of course, both be in the game. And Siddiq... maybe twenty years of friendship and business partnership counted for nothing? Or did they have something on Siddiq, and his friend was doing his best. Maybe he'd gone out on a limb for him, taken a risk by involving Hakim, the bearded little fucker who'd accused him of alienating his child. He looked at his watch. He could make the midday Zuhr prayers if he hurried.

Shamsa came up to him and laid her muzzle on his knee. He stroked her ears. Maybe the dafe would unlock the mystery. Then, with an almost physical thump in his gut, he remembered the suicide vest sitting in its plastic skin. The bloody vest drove a coach and horses through the chance of any happy-ev-er-after scenario. The landline interrupted his thoughts with a call from the clerk to the justices reminding him he was on standby for any court sitting the coming Saturday morning. Bugger.

When he got to the mosque the prayers were already over, and a trickle of worshippers was leaving the building. Siddiq was the last of them. He tapped his watch at Hash, and said irritably, 'Now, soon.'

Hash's own patience was strained by fatigue and lack of sleep and he was equally short. 'Now? How soon? Where, and how many?'

'Is the place ready?' Siddiq asked.

'Of course. Where's Jim?' Hash countered.

Siddiq didn't answer.

'What news from your friend Hakim? The one I gave all the money to?' Hash persisted.

'He will do his best for you, Insh'Allah.' He offered an uneasy grin, somewhere between conspiratorial and embarrassed. 'Is the place... ok?'

'It's been ready for years. Everything's in place.'

Siddiq looked relieved and patted his shoulder. 'Good job, my friend.'

Walking back up Naunton Crescent, Hash could see old Mrs Hamilton standing outside her door, looking left and right. She caught sight of him a few seconds later and was waiting when he drew level.

'Hell of a noise,' she said. 'Again.'

Hash wasn't in the mood for guessing games. He could hear Shamsa barking on the other side of the door and he let her out. The dog rushed past and let rip with a series of barks.

'Hell of a noise,' the old lady repeated, pointing at the dog, 'Her, the madam.'

Hash said, 'Sorry about that, Mrs Hamilton. What was

the problem?'

'Your dog.' She always used the possessive when she was in a bad mood: your son, your car, now it was 'your dog'. 'Made so much racket I thought you were being burgled.'

'It all seems fine,' Hash said.

'Not twenty minutes ago it wasn't,' she said, arms folded, looking from Shamsa to Hash. 'I had to come out. But your visitors had given up.'

'What visitors?' Hash asked.

She looked at him, groping for the words. 'You know, those types. In a car,' she said. 'Went the wrong way up the one-way road, then parked. One of them knocked on your door.'

'A red car?'

'Think it was,' she said. 'Anyway, madam here,' Shamsa had returned from her patrol and was standing looking up at Hash, 'madam here started barking and wouldn't stop.' She reached over the low wall and patted Shamsa. 'Didn't like those two nasty men, did you?'

'Two men in a red car,' Hash said.

Mrs Hamilton considered the question for a few seconds then gave a quick nod. 'Dogs know, you know.'

'Know what?' Hash wanted to make her say it.

'They can smell it.'

'Curry?' he asked.

She shot a startled look at him. 'No, you silly sausage! They can smell fear.'

Inside and away from Mrs Hamilton, Hash went straight to the BlackBerry. No message. He called Jim's iPhone on his own mobile as he walked into the front room, checking the road from the bay windows. The ringtone purring in his ear was an astonishment. His heart thudded as he waited for an answer. Please God, let it be Jim. Instead, it went to message and Hash hesitated, almost paralysed, before blurting out 'Jim, this is Dad. If you get this message contact anyone, the police are looking for you, ask anyone for help, and come home.'

He switched his phone off and went to his laptop instead, keyed the locating app and waited. A few seconds later the screen showed a bookmark sprouting out of the West Midlands. His scalp began to crawl when he saw it was sitting on Cheltenham. Zooming in further, he pinpointed Jim's phone to a car park off the Bath Road.

It was two streets away. He could drive there in less than a minute, catch sight of him or call him again. Maybe Siddiq and Hakim had done something after all. Maybe Jim was with them, on his way home.

A change in light in the hallway flickered a shadow of movement and Hash caught it from where he was sitting in the kitchen. Shamsa must have picked up sounds inaudible to the human ear; she started a low growl. Ignoring it, Hash dialled Jim's phone again, leaning over to quieten the dog. But she shook him off and stood staring intently at the hallway. Hash rose, with the dialling tone still ringing in his ear, and peered into the hallway. There was a figure on the other side of the glass, and the ringtone was getting stronger, seemed to have an echo. He was hearing it through the door.

10

CHELTENHAM. AFTERNOON –
FRIDAY 6TH MARCH.

He outline on the other side of the glass shifted, searching for something in a pocket. The echoing ringtone stopped in the same instant as the purring on Hash's handset, and at that moment the shape behind the glass bent, reached forward and knocked on the door.

Hash hung onto the dog's collar and opened it. Standing in front of him was a tall, lean Asian, with a dark unkempt beard. He was wearing a baseball cap, cheap thin jacket and jeans, carrying a sports bag. He stood in silence, as though Hash would know what to do. He didn't hold out his hand or smile, instead he offered the Arabic greeting. 'Salaam-Alaikum.'

'Alaikum as'salaam,' Hash replied, extending his hand. The stranger's grip was strong, the calloused hand of a labourer. 'Kayf hallak?' Hash enquired, asking after his health.

The man responded with the universal Muslim gesture, touching his right hand to his heart, and gave the traditional reply, 'Alhamdulillah.' Thanks be to God.

'Can I help you, my friend?' Hash continued in Arabic. The

man's face went blank. Arabic clearly wasn't his native language then, even if he had some Koran Arabic. He tried the question again, in English, and saw a flash of frustration in the brown eyes.

The dafe fished in his pocket and held out an iPhone, like some gift or peace offering. Hash seized it, knowing instantly the phone was Jim's by its cover. He looked past the man's shoulders on either side, thinking Jim was behind him and the nightmare was over. Instead, he caught sight of Mrs Hamilton, watching from her window.

The stranger looked anxiously down at Shamsa who was still growling, then peered past Hash into the hallway. 'Dafe,' he said, his right thumb tapping his chest. 'Dafe.'

They were on public display, for heaven's sake. Hash stood back to let him into the house and his guest moved inside with clumsy haste. He kicked off his cheap, scuffed shoes as he squeezed past and Hash caught the whiff of airline cabins, a fusion of sweat, overcooked food and recycled air. The guest stood waiting in the hallway, his eyes flicking down to where the dog had retreated, still growling.

Hash hauled Shamsa through the kitchen, out into the little rear conservatory and left her there. He took the holdall, surprised by its lack of weight and dropped it by the stairs, pointing the guest into the sitting room. He went in but remained standing until Hash motioned for him to sit. 'Tea?' Hash asked. 'Chai?' The man's head bobbed at the universal word.

Hash flicked on the kettle. The man was no Libyan whom he could discuss the target with, or pump for information on Jim. With his spare, rangy frame and rough hands he had the look of a peasant, probably a Pakistani, recruited straight out of some poor village north of Peshawar, Hash thought, the surplus mouth in some sprawling tangle of relatives, singled out and sent to a madrassa to be groomed and then sold for martyrdom.

It struck Hash that, all along, he had never believed either

he or Jim was destined to wear the vest. He didn't know why he had taken that for granted. It was as though, with his background and training, he was always in the next tier up, one of those who 'facilitate', never one of the expendable pawns. A slender sense of relief began to warm through him as a piece of the jigsaw dropped into place. His mission was to assist the newcomer in his task; he'd need to be alive to do it, and that meant Jim would too. But when it was all over Libya would dispose of the witnesses, he knew. That was the way it worked.

Hash carried the tray to the sitting room and laid it on the coffee table. The man had barely moved, still upright and uncomfortable in an easy chair; maybe he'd have felt better sitting cross-legged on the carpet. Hash held the sugar bowl to the guest's mug of tea and counted in two spoonfuls of sugar. The rough, bearded face cracked enough to show pleasure. He took the mug muttering some words of prayer or thanks in Urdu, blew on the surface, sipped, and helped himself to two more spoonfuls.

Shamsa's barking had started again. He'd have to calm the dog down or he'd have Mrs H at the door every five minutes. They'd have to get used to each other, he decided, and fetched Shamsa. The guest stood up, alarmed and hastily backed away behind the chair, unleashing a torrent of anxiety. Too much too soon. Hash led her back into the kitchen and left her there, still growling a low rumble of suspicion.

He signalled "safe now" to his guest and got him seated again. Still no attempt to explain himself. It was a fair assumption, Hash decided, that he'd been systematically indoctrinated, crammed for his mission and then inserted before he could forget the details. Probably wouldn't even have been given his host's name, just told that he'd take care of everything once he got there, take care of him, set him up and send him on his way. Lockerbie flashed through his mind.

Hash made washing motions with his hands, and this

brought a nod. There was a large photograph of Jim on the wall at the bottom of the stairs, and Hash pointed at it. It had been taken a year or so earlier and showed Jim out in the open with one of his model aeroplanes. Hash pulled out the iPhone and mimed the connection between the phone and the boy. The dafe understood alright, looking from the photo to Hash and back, but there was no reaction; he shrugged his shoulders once, and again when Hash persisted.

He left the man upstairs and waited until the sound of water humming in the pipes could be heard before checking the hold-all, a cheap rip-off of the Manchester City brand with pockets at either end. He went through it quickly, first finding a folded prayer rug and a small Koran. Underneath was a pack of safety razors and some underwear with Urdu labels. He found a small packet of safety pins and a roll of what looked like electrical tape. The flush cranked upstairs and he put it all back, zipping the pockets just as the stairs began to creak. Hash made a gesture at the cooker through the kitchen doorway holding pinched fingers to his mouth and said, 'Food?'

The man nodded again but held up a finger. His sleeves were rolled up and he had taken his shoes and socks off. Droplets of water glistened on his arms and beard as he bent to his bag and took out the prayer rug and Koran, holding them up to Hash.

Hash took him back into the living room and pointed at a spot on the carpet, then drew an imaginary line from there, following it through the wall, into the distance, south-east across Leckhampton Hill out to the Channel, across Europe and all the way to Mecca. Visibly pleased, his guest lay the prayer rug down. The landline rang.

'Are you ready? The special guest has arrived,' Siddiq said, without any preamble.

'I know that. He's here, praying in my front room.'

'You have to come and meet me, now.' Siddiq's voice was urgent. 'Now.'

'And leave him here?' Maybe the angry, silent imam had kept his word. Could Siddiq have Jim with him, right now, if his delivery was only brokered on Hash housing the 'dafe' and looking after him for a few days?

'Meet me at the railway station,' Siddiq said.

The guest was back in the kitchen, his prayers done, looking purposeful. He opened his Koran at the flyleaf and tapped a large finger over a biro scrawl which read in Arabic, 'Friday 13th March 1500'. It couldn't be his guest's handwriting. He kept pointing to it and giving a thumbs-up. Hash was expected to respond, it was all part of the rehearsals. Next Friday, at three in the afternoon, something would happen, had to happen, and Hash, Jim and his suicidal guest were part of it.

Hash tapped the words and returned a thumbs-up. The checklist was being followed; first Jim's phone, now the written message which his host would be sure to understand. Hash mimed "Stay put" and "Food in half an hour" and left, taking the dog with him.

Siddiq's Mercedes was in the station car park. Dusk was falling, and the first spots of rain hit his face as he covered the short distance. The window came down smoothly to reveal Siddiq, grinning from ear to ear. 'Get in, my friend. Any minute now.' He was fidgeting, like a mischievous schoolboy. 'You have the place ready?'

There was the train, just pulled in, doors now easing open. Hash began to picture Jim coming up the steps from the platform, at exactly the place he'd last seen him.

'There,' Siddiq said, pointing. A melee of people, all ages and genders, was surging up from the platform, clustering under the awning of the station entrance away from the spattering rain. Some were looking for relatives, one or two lighting a cigarette, and others taking a moment to decide between bus and taxi. No sign of Jim yet.

'Can you see? Can you see?' Smiling more manically than

ever, he looked at Hash and winked.

Hash's eyes raked the thickening cluster of people under the narrow roof that fronted the station building.

'Get out and make a surprise for your guest.' Siddiq was beside himself. 'Make a surprise!' he urged.

Hash reached for the door lever. He still couldn't see Jim anywhere in the crowd, and he'd hardly be hanging back. He looked around the edges of the building. Could he have left by another exit?

Unable to contain himself any longer, Siddiq sprang from the car and gave a shy wave to someone in the crowd. A blonde woman broke away from the knot of people and came towards them, blocking Hash's view as he tried to look for Jim behind her.

Siddiq and the woman rushed towards each other. She was tall and slim, and beautiful, a head taller than Siddiq and as she wrapped her arms around him, crushing his head against her denim bosom, his expression changed to rapture. They hugged, kissed and hugged again before Siddiq introduced them.

'This is my best friend, Hash,' he said.

She held out a firm hand and looked at him. 'Hash.' She tried the name out. 'My name is Anna. Pleased to meet you.' She sounded East European and he guessed she was in her early thirties. Her eyes, strikingly blue and alert, lingered on Hash for a second.

'Mr Hash has an apartment for us. We should go there.'

Hash led the way out of the station, watching Siddiq's Mercedes in his rear-view mirror and wondered how he'd got it so wrong. Twice in one day he'd thought he was about to get Jim back, and twice his hopes had been crushed. He'd completely misread Siddiq's story. Anna was his secret guest and Hash had been roped in to setting them up in a love-nest. Now he knew why Siddiq hadn't registered the talk of his own guest and been so jumpy and nervous all this time. It had never been about Jim; the only possible conclusion was that Siddiq was oblivious to the whole set- up, the suicide vest, the money and the newly arrived dafe.

And now there was the further complication of providing a love nest for his friend in exactly the wrong place. He'd bought the maisonette in the late eighties, just after he'd been transferred from Ulster to Cheltenham, with the purchase price paid in Libyan cash, legalised through the chip shop and a laundrette. It became the Hash property formula, with the Libyan end providing the funds and Hash laundering them on his own initiative, an apparently reliable source of investment and income.

But this particular investment had always had a dual purpose. The maisonette's master bedroom upstairs overlooked the rear of Cheltenham's Government Communications Headquarters, GCHQ, Europe's biggest electronic spying station, with the garage butting up against the twelve-foot perimeter fence. In the old days, when he was playing it for real in the Gaddafi team, Hash had chosen and secured the perfect launch pad for a physical penetration of the huge complex.

As he gave the lovebirds a tour, he looked out of that window across the complex, now lit with harsh white light. The perimeter had acquired more sophisticated protection than men and dogs since then. That seemingly empty space would be seeded with sensors, watched day and night with cameras, both thermal and infrared. For a split second, Hash took a perverted professional pride in knowing he'd still be able to get someone over the fence and all its defences within a few minutes, even in the face of all the technological advances.

Siddiq wanted him gone, he could see that. Anna was upstairs, and the two men stood at the front door, Siddiq toying with the bunch of keys.

'You sure this is ok?'

'What about Jim?' Hash cut in. 'What news have you got for me?'

Siddiq shrugged. 'I will call that man.' He looked at Hash. 'If Jim is in Birmingham, then that man will find him.'

He looked back upstairs, smiled a guilty smile at Hash. 'You have to give it time, my friend.'

Hash thought about the fanatic in his front room and the ominous message he'd brought about Friday 13th and knew he had no time to give.

The two men were with him all the time now. "Protecting you, James," was what they said, "it's what your father wants." James. He hated that. His Mum called him James. She was the only one. Except for Miss Pine, of course, when she was ticking him off, but that was ok somehow. Not these two idiots. Not them.

One was a lot more friendly than the other. His name was Hamad, and he was always trying out jokes on him. He'd told Jim about the embarrassing pet name his grandmother still called him even though he'd stopped being a chubby-chops baby years ago, thought 'Lord Jim' was pretty cool in comparison. All pretty lame, but it was at least an attempt at being some sort of company he supposed. Today Hamad had brought his phone back, so he could show them his password. They wanted to contact his father, and did he have a message? 'Yes. I want to go home. Come and get me, Dad.' Hamad just laughed and said the same Arabic phrase his Dad had taught him, 'Insh'Allah', which basically meant 'Whatever.' Hamad kept saying he was much safer with them and that's the way his dad wanted it, that's what his dad had told them. Seemed this had to be the deal then, until Dad got whatever it was sorted and came for him. As far as he could see it was a crap deal, pretty much as shitty it could get for him. He hoped his Dad would hurry up and get his act together, before he lost it with these two fuckwits completely. And his marbles too for that matter. He lay back on the bed again, with his hands behind his head, and stared at the patterns in the dirty marks on the ceiling.

11

He'd had to go out to re-stock with basics and a few ready meals, but by the time he got back from the supermarket the dog had clearly disturbed the dafe's morning prayers and was still holding him at bay, growling her objections. Hash was forced to intervene and considered taking Shamsa with him for his next task but dropped the idea. There was no way of knowing where his meeting with Siddiq might lead.

Siddiq waved him to a booth, eyes twinkling, offering coffee.

'How's Anna?' asked Hash as he slid into his seat

'Quiet, my friend, quiet.' Siddiq dipped his head and held a forefinger to his lips, his grin broader than ever. 'Oh my God. Fantastic,' he whispered.

'You look exhausted! Tell me, who actually knows about her?'

'Nobody,' said Siddiq. 'That's why I asked you, my old friend.'

'How long's she staying?'

'Maybe a few months. Forever would be better,' Siddiq

said dreamily

'Difficult to keep these things quiet,' Hash said. 'A beautiful girl, stuck in a house on her own all day in a strange neighbourhood with a big Mercedes parked outside every night.' He watched Siddiq's face fall as he took it in. 'What news of Jim?'

'None from my side,' Siddiq said.

'When we sat in the mosque,' Hash said, 'with your friend Hakim. Does he really have connections? To the jihad types?'

'Of course not. He hates them,' Siddiq said, 'He hates them, just like we do. He's your best friend, better than me, for this business.' They waited until the coffee was placed in front of Hash and the waiter was out of earshot.

'Who's he working for?' Hash asked.

Siddiq put both his elbows on the table and clasped his hands as if in prayer. 'He is a business colleague. He runs the biggest taxi fleet in the south of Birmingham. Actually,' he dropped his voice 'he's a Pakistani and as a rule I don't have much time for them, but…' He canted his head from side to side, 'he's a very good Muslim, very straight. '

'He didn't seem to take to me much. Or care about Jim's situation'

'Maybe he thinks you're not a good Muslim. And he's very careful. He has enemies, people who hate him.'

'The jihadis?' Hash said.

Siddiq nodded. 'That's why he was hard with you. You're not the only father looking for a runaway, believe me, my friend. 'Siddiq leaned forward. 'All the mosques are different; some imams speak for Daesh, some for Al Qaeda, but only a few imams in Birmingham have the balls to speak out against all these rubbish people.'

'And he's one of the few?' Hash said. —

'Correct. Listen, maybe Hakim suspects you're not telling the whole story,' Siddiq said. 'It's not that difficult to see. I'm sure you're hiding something, and you know you can trust me.'

Hash could still see Siddiq's hand in Jim's disappearance: who else in Cheltenham was that close and knew their routine so well? His girlfriend as the 'dafe', and the unpleasant imam as the go-between? Had he got it all wrong? Maybe he was missing other obvious connections. Or perhaps this was part of a charade, a litmus test of Hash's resolve, protection of the guest sitting in his kitchen. He made his decision.

'A business deal went wrong, and some people are angry with me,' Hash said. 'Very angry, so they took Jim. I've got some money together, as much as they want.'

'Why Birmingham?' Siddiq asked.

'Because that's where Jim's phone was transmitting from, twice in the last few days.' Hash stared down at his coffee. 'Birmingham was the only clue I had. '

'If any Bangladeshis are involved, I will know soon,' Siddiq muttered. 'Pakistani gangs are more difficult, more time, but that's why you need Hakim'

Returning with the food, Hash began to prioritise. He would keep up communication with the kidnappers, cooperate for as long as it took to shake solid information from the branches. If Hakim proved to be as good as Siddiq believed, with all his eyes and ears in South Birmingham, it would make sense to throw the bomber's money in that direction. Sean, once settled in and briefed, would be kept in reserve for the final lethal strike. The odds were good they knew nothing about him. Partnership with Sean brought its own risks, of course, if he was in a bad way, but at the very least Hash could rely on him to watch his back while he did the fighting himself.

He knew, with Friday approaching, he should take the bomber on a recce of GCHQ as well as the maisonette and the garage, and somehow avoid being seen by Siddiq and Anna. That was a risk he'd have to take. Years earlier, Hash had assumed he would be pivotal in any attack on GCHQ. He was braced to receive advance warning via the letterbox, ordering him to ready the space and dig up the stashed weapons, prepare and launch the assault teams from the base he'd set up. In those days of course, he saw GCHQ as a justifiable target, the perfect concentration of enemy combatants. Today, he saw the futility of hitting a target hardened by sophisticated technology and reinforced concrete. The attack would guarantee international headlines but few people, if any, would get hurt Hash reckoned. It was a shred of cold comfort to help get him through the days ahead.

In twenty years, there'd been no message, no call for him, apart from that one: Lockerbie. The Provisional IRA's campaign in Ulster had unravelled and Gaddafi's crusades turned into lethal farce. Hash had watched the 2011 Libyan uprising on television and waited to be activated, expecting the old desert scorpion, Gaddafi, to have a sting in his tail. But the regime had collapsed faster than anyone could have predicted and Hash's masters in the Mukhabarat never pressed the button.

The Brits had held out the hand of friendship to him and he'd discovered he was amongst good people. He'd fallen in love, got married, then watched his sweetheart lose her battle with cancer and raised their small son as best he could without her. Like a freed slave, Hash had begun to hope. His new false life as a nationalised UK citizen and a successful businessman had become a solid and pleasurable reality. And then the tape on the bridge, the dead letter box, the knowledge of having been watched had told him he was utterly mistaken. And unknown hands had snatched Jim to guarantee his obedience.

No word from Dad, just another message passed on by Hog's Breath Hamad saying he was well but it was "too dangerous for him at the moment." What was that all about? He was being kept in the dark by these bastards, he knew he was. "No phones. Don't go near the windows," Hamad had said. "Or else," Grumpy Guts had added.

He wasn't sure where the woman was. She'd been kind, smiled when everyone else had been grim. And she smelt of perfume, had a softness that reminded him of Mum, maybe even Miss Pine on a good day. He had to admit in all this bloody mess he needed that. And to believe he was doing good for his Dad. They'd promised to take him out when it was safe. Maybe look for Dad, but "it all depended". On what? God, he was bored....

12

SATURDAY AFTERNOON

The prayer rug was lying on the sofa but there was no sign of the guest, so Hash called up the stairs and opened the food cartons hoping the good smells would entice him to come down. Shamsa came to him instead, limping slightly and pushing her muzzle into his hands. A small tear on her foreleg showed pink flesh where the skin was broken, and she began to lick it as Hash examined the wound. Poor thing, she must have picked it up on their morning walk, he thought.

No answer from upstairs. His guest clearly intended to spend most of his time in prayer and reflection on the imminence of the afterlife; maybe he was fasting. He called up the stairs again and this time got a mumbled response. While waiting he went to the garage to fetch the suitcase.

The man ate with his fingers, slowly at first, then with relish, tearing strips of naan and dipping them into the dishes. Not fasting then. When he'd finished, Hash cleared the table and hoisted the suicide vest onto it.

There was no reaction. It was as though confronting a suicide vest was perfectly natural, like meeting an old friend. He motioned for scissors. Hash brought them and watched as the man cut away the plastic. The smell of almonds, sweet and cloying, filled the room. He stood up and slipped the waistcoat easily over his head, pushing his arms through. Arms akimbo, he turned slightly left then right, as though he was a client in a Savile Row fitting room waiting for his tailor's unctuous approval. The canvas fabric was strained, its various pockets packed with flat brick shapes. There were at least three packs in the rear adding to the four in the front: his initial guess of twelve kilos of explosive was still good, Hash thought. If the dafe actually succeeded in getting inside the GCHQ buildings and cracked it all off, it'd be mayhem.

The bomber wriggled and shrugged in the vest, testing its fit. A short, coiled length of blue and black wires, sprouting free from the right armpit, indicated an initiation system. Hooking his right thumb into the coil, the man jerked the wire out of the lining a little way, well-rehearsed and perfectly calm. Hash could see the loops and cords at the rear by which the wearer could be laced into his vest, like a corset. It would be impossible to release them himself; he was trying on a garment that would soon, inescapably, blow him to pieces. His fingers probed into the right breast pocket, where Hash had felt the two cylinders, then pulled out a piece of folded paper, unfolded it, gave it a glance, and held it out to Hash. It was the same biro scrawl and the same message in Arabic: 'Friday 13th March 1500. Send confirmation.'

The precision of the timing was significant, and Hash wondered how many other vests might be positioned around the UK, all timed to go off at three the following Friday. Or was his man part of a sequence where one at a time they would detonate every hour, a Mexican wave of devastation? Pointing to himself and then to the man, he said in English and again in Arabic, 'We're going for a drive.' He pointed two fingers at his eyes, 'Check out the target.'

He got a half-nod of understanding. He tapped his watch on the number and held up five fingers,

'This evening.' He pointed to five o'clock on the kitchen clock. The bomber nodded and started to take off the vest.

The drive took them west through town, out to the edge of Cheltenham. As the huge, doughnut-shaped complex came into sight on their right-hand side, Hash said, 'Target,' and smacked his fist into his chest. 'Boom!' He could see the bomber making the connection between the ground view and the vest. With daylight fading, Hash turned off the main road and looped north to the back of the complex. He drove slowly, letting his guest see the layers of fences that protected it. He didn't want to give any sign that a reconnaissance was in progress, and his companion seemed to be following the process without too much difficulty. Bizarrely, Hash felt a moment of satisfaction as he remembered the various routes to mayhem he'd devised so many years earlier.

Parking up not far from the maisonette, where they had a view of the row of garages butting up against the main fence, he turned to the dafe.

'You'll go over. Best option.'

It was as if he was back in his time with the Mukhabarat, enthusiastically arguing the merits of under, through and over, depending on how many men they were sending.

He repeated, 'Over,' making diving movements with both hands.

'Ladders, six of them.' He held up six fingers. 'We put them against the first fence then haul up the second.'

There was no response.

'Over…using ladders…from there,' he repeated, pointing to the row of garages.

Siddiq's Mercedes was parked outside the house. They'd have to wait.

A little later, with dusk coming down fast, his companion stirred and reached for the door handle. Hash hit the central locking and shot a questioning look at him. The man held up his hands in the prayer position revealing a swollen patch on his right wrist, a raw graze with an inflamed red puncture mark. Hash shook his head.

'Not here.' He pointed around the genteel estate. 'Too many people watching. '

There was a flash of irritation at Hash's tone before he nodded vigorously and tugged at the door handle again.

'Maghreb.' he said urgently, the Arabic for evening prayer.

'Not okay,' Hash insisted. 'Not tonight, not here. Do it twice later, if you like, but not now.'

The man subsided, arms folded, his face a mask of fury, muttering something bad tempered in his own language. Half an hour later, when the sky had turned black and the yellow of the streetlamps changed the colour of their surroundings, Siddiq left the house. As the Mercedes glided away Hash called him.

'Where's Anna?'

'In the house.'

'Could you give her a call and say I need to check the boiler, just to be on the safe side? It's been some time since tenants were in. It won't take long. I'm in the area, so now would be good.'

'Okay,' Siddiq sounded doubtful. 'I'll tell her. '

When Anna opened the door, she was wearing tight denim jeans and a t-shirt showing off a slice of bare, toned midriff. Her blonde hair was artfully dishevelled.

'Did Siddiq call?' Hash asked.

'I know,' Her languid tone was full of ennui, 'the boiler. All of a sudden. Come in.' Arms folded, she sighed and stepped back to let them pass.

Her accent was definitely Eastern European. Not Polish, he thought, more likely further east, somewhere in the Balkans or Hungary. Hash caught her perfume as they stepped across the threshold.

'Won't take too long. Need to check upstairs,' said Hash, uncomfortably aware of the lameness of the excuse. 'I have my plumber.' He jerked a thumb over his shoulder at the Pakistani who held back, clearly mesmerised by Anna.

'Plumber... really?' She peered at the bomber, a sardonic expression on her face. 'Where's his tools?'

'In the car if we need them. We're looking at the thermostat and the boiler controls. '

'Whatever.' She wandered into the kitchen, reaching for a packet of cigarettes. 'Smoke?' She lit a cigarette. 'Coffee? Beer? It's all here.'

'We need to go upstairs, maybe into the attic, and into the garage.' said Hash, 'Just a safety check. A landlord thing.'

'Fine by me,' she said. 'As long as the water stays as hot as it was before you guys arrived to fix it. '

The bomber stood blocking the kitchen doorway, still staring at Anna, and Hash had to push him to the side to get past. She stared back with rising irritation, exhaling a stream of cigarette smoke. The bomber blinked first, but Anna kept her hostile gaze locked on the man until Hash pulled him away.

From the upstairs bedroom Hash pointed out across to the lights of GCHQ and the fences protecting it, their heights and their layers, trying to convey how little time he'd have once he had triggered the first alarm. The man's face showed comprehension but no glimmer of anxiety about the challenge he faced. He looked back at Hash, then at the double bed where Anna's clothes lay scattered, his eyes lingering on the female garments.

They found Anna in the kitchen, tapping out an SMS. 'That was quick,' she said without looking up.

'Thermostats are both fine,' Hash said. He moved past her and opened a cupboard. The bomber, back in the doorway resumed his staring. Hash looked at the boiler's display and closed the door.

'Your friend,' Anna said coolly, putting down her phone. 'I don't like the way he's staring at me. Unless he wants his ass kicked, don't bring him back. '

In the garage, Hash pointed to a stack of six ladders, making the bomber lift one up to confirm its lightness.

'Easy,' Hash said, pointing to the ceiling of the garage. 'On top.' He jabbed a thumb upwards. 'One in each arm. Then I follow. I put one across and you run over.'

He knew the man would never get the English and resorted to mime again, but he had the distinct feeling the only thing on the man's mind was Anna's underwear strewn across the bed. He stopped the briefing and mimed Anna's shape, cupping huge, imaginary breasts. For the first time, the man gave a broad smile and nodded his head enthusiastically.

'Later!' Hash pointed at his watch. 'Waiting for you. In Paradise, insh'Allah. '

'Insh'Allah,' the man grinned.

On their way back, they stopped off at Siddiq's main restaurant on the Bath Road. Hash had decided Siddiq should get a look at his guest. If Siddiq was involved maybe the shock would make him say something.

Siddiq wasn't there, but Hash decided they might as well take a booth and wait. He called one of the waiters over and eventually, trying different dialects, they worked out the dafe's choices from the menu. Watching his now hearty appetite and remembering his appreciation of Anna's curves, Hash wondered if he should try offering his guest some real temptation. It just might draw him off the straight and narrow path of jihad for a while and shake down a vital clue about Jim.

As soon as they got back, Hash had the bomber sit down and together they browsed the net. Starting at the chaste end of the spectrum, they looked at Pakistani brides first. The bomber's face lit up as they scrolled through a parade of demure Asian brides decked in opulent wedding outfits, gazing alluringly at the camera, appealing for a suitor. He was hooked, and Hash took the search to women with less and less clothing. Hash allowed the trawl to run for a few more minutes before he closed the lid abruptly. The man looked up, bewildered. Hash took a photograph of Jim off the wall and held it in front of him. They both looked at it, Hash repeating Jim's name over and over again, more and more loudly, and demanding in English and Arabic and Urdu, 'Where is my son?'

The man shrugged, no trace of sympathy on his face. Hash pulled notes from his wallet and laid them on the table, repeating the questions. He mimed Anna's voluptuous shape and when the man smiled, lifted the bomber's hand and placed it on the money. The man jerked his hand away, a flash of disgust wiping the smile from his face, shaking his wrist and massaging it. Annoyed at being asked to trade information for a woman or bothered by the wrist injury, it was hard to tell which.

13

MORNING – SUNDAY 8TH MARCH

Hash picked up the Arab BlackBerry and typed his message back to the Libyan number. 'Instruction confirmed Friday. Confirm name used by grandmother'.

He needed to get back to the racecourse and took Shamsa with him. Her limp hadn't improved with a night's rest, he noticed, as they walked on. Their usual route had been transformed into a massive, zoned parking area in preparation for the race meeting, but the letterbox had to be checked.

He picked Sean's number out on his phone.

'Tell me?' The Irishman's mock exasperation cheered Hash. 'You still on?'

'Any news of the lad?'

'I'm still waiting.' He'd reached the footbridge and could see there was no new tape: no mail.

'He's still in the Brum area, then?' Sean asked.

Hash turned back, heading for his vehicle. 'It was where the last phone signal came from.'

'So that's a plus?' Sean said.

'All I've got. Can you get down from Brum on your own?

I'll leave the keys, the address and some cash in the chippy. Same couple run it. They know you're coming. Put all your food and drink on tick and I'll cover it.'

'Am I not dossing in the usual place, then? No pun intended'

Hash smiled fleetingly. 'It's taken. You're in a different flat, much nicer.'

Sean was silent at the other end.

'Better to keep you off the radar for the moment, but it's nearby,' Hash said. 'Take a taxi from the station. Just call me when you're in town.' He whistled for Shamsa and headed for home.

The smell of frying eventually brought the dafe to the kitchen doorway, triggering a rumbling growl from Shamsa. The dog stood up, hackles raised, her muzzle a rictus of menace, and didn't stop growling until Hash cuffed her. Sidling into the kitchen, avoiding eye contact, the bomber sat down and began pushing omelette into his mouth. Hash refilled his tea and received a curt nod of thanks. A few minutes later the plate was near empty and the martyr looked at Hash with a roguish smile. He cupped his large hands to his chest and fluttered them downwards, outlining female curves.

Hash looked at him in disbelief. 'You're serious?'

The bomber, grinning broadly now, looked on as Hash thought it through. This was definitely breaking the rules, and not just for the martyr, but if there was a chance sex could drive a wedge between the bomber and his controllers, then Hash was happy to pimp for him he decided.

'This big?' Hash's hands described exaggerated bosoms, and for the first time they laughed together. The bomber guffawed with delight and repeated the pantomime.

'How many?' Hash held up his fingers, counting off. The bomber pushed back on his chair, waving a protesting single finger: one would be enough, thanks.

'Insh'Allah,' Hash told him, then tapped at his watch. 'Be

patient.' He went out to the rear porch and, rummaging in his coat, extracted a wad of fifties and returned in time to catch Shamsa standing on her bed, growling at the bomber again. He scolded her and shoved her back down firmly, waving the notes to the bomber and earning another smile and vigorous nodding.

'Wait,' Hash said, pointing to his watch. 'I'll come back soon.'

Eventually, he ran Siddiq to earth in a wholesale shop at the lower end of the High Street. He peeled off two hundred pounds in fifties.

'I'll do my best,' Siddiq said. 'You realise this is not my area.'

'Don't tell me you're embarrassed,' Hash said. 'One of your waiter lads will surely know a number to call. They're not all as strict about their religion as you, I bet. Or get one of your contacts to organise it? Quickly?'

'The big Pakistani, the one you took round to the maisonette, who is he?' Siddiq asked.

'He's part of my problem,' Hash said. 'I've got to keep him happy at all costs.'

'Anna told me about him,' said Siddiq.

'What did she say?'

'She said he was a creep.'

'He's their enforcer, I think,' Hash lied. 'No English. Maybe Hakim should see him?'

His mobile rang before he could go any further, and he saw 'Susan Pine' on the display. Waving an apology, he took the call. The voice at the other end was muffled but he could hear frantic cries for help. Susan was pleading, 'No! No!', and he could hear a man's voice raised in anger. He called her name and with rising horror heard, 'Hash, help! Help me!' The next sounds were muffled gasps from her and violent shouts from the man, then a dog barking furiously in the background. He knew at once where Susan was.

'Susan! I'm on my way!' The line went dead, and he looked up at Siddiq, appalled. 'She's being attacked.' Uselessly, he yelled 'Hold on, I'm on my way!' into the dead phone as he sprinted to the car.

A minute or two later, he redialled as he drove. To his relief she picked up straight away. 'Susan? Are you ok?'

The voice at the other end was hers, but it was barely audible. She was crying, harsh breathless sobs.

'Where are you? I'm coming right now…just tell me where you are?' He waited, straining to catch any sound.

'I'm ok.' Her voice was frail, muffled by her crying.

'Where are you…what's happening…tell me where you are.'

He was nearing the turn-off where a lane led to the rear of the college when a thought hit him like a thunderbolt. Maybe this was a stunt, set up by the same bastards who'd got Jim? He had to find her, get her to safety somewhere, anywhere.

'I'm okay. I'll be okay…' Susan's voice came over better, still out of breath and full of fear, but traffic noise told him she was on a street, walking too fast, hopefully to safety. She said something he couldn't make out before the line went dead again.

Slowing ahead of the opening to the lane, Hash caught sight of her ahead of him, half-running, half-walking. Relief burst over him; so far, she was safe. He heaved the steering wheel over, jammed on the brakes and pelted down the road towards her. She flinched at the sound of his pounding feet and turned, panic-stricken. She saw, and recognised, him but didn't stop moving. He overtook her and blocked her way. She walked into his arms, crying freely now, and he held her in silence for a few seconds.

'What happened?' Hash asked.

She steadied herself, swallowing, but as she tilted her face up to try to talk she started crying again. There was swelling on her face, as if from a punch, and her eyes were blotchy, her hair disarrayed. -

'Let's get you inside,' Hash whispered. 'Is this where you live? Which number are you?' He shook her shoulders gently to get a response. 'Are you hurt?'

She tried to speak but no words came out, and she swallowed hard.

'I just came to drop off some work for Jim,' she managed, still gasping for breath. She pushed a hand into her pocket and brought out a key then pointed it at one of the doors in the row, pulling herself away from Hash.

'That man, the one in your house...' She got the first words out but then stopped. Blinking and rubbing her eyes, she stared at Hash and tried again. 'That man, he...'

'What did he do to you?'

Hash felt sick. The bomber had seen him leave with the money in his hand, their session on the websites the previous evening had wound him up and right on cue Susan had knocked at the door, thinking only of helping Jim, and landed on his plate.

She unlocked her door and went in without looking back at Hash. He dashed forward, just getting a hand to the door before it closed.

'Susan! Are you sure you're alright? Please talk to me, tell me what happened.' He heard her sobbing again, felt her weight leaning hard against the door. 'Did he hurt you? Do you need a doctor?'

'I'm ok.' Her voice sounded weak and tired.

'Should I call the police?'

'Don't. I'm ok.'

He felt a despicable wave of relief at that answer but asked again, 'Are you sure?'

'Just leave me alone. Please, leave me alone.'

'Let me at least come back to check you're alright.'

She pushed the door harder without replying, and Hash heard the locks rattle.

14

The silence was absolute and menacing when he opened his own front door a few minutes later. Some catastrophe had happened here. The kitchen door was closed, and Shamsa should have been barking a frustrated welcome from behind it. He glanced into the sitting room as he strode past: empty, the Koran on the coffee table. Nothing untoward there.

He pushed open the kitchen door. A bald man looked back at him with fury in his eyes. On the table in front of him lay a pair of bloodied scissors and huge clumps of hair, hacked from his head. There were more tufts on the floor which was spattered with red dots. Hash stared at the chaos, struggling to make sense of it, as the bomber held up his right forearm. He started to shout, jabbing a finger at the blood dripping from arm. His words were incomprehensible, the menace in them unmistakable.

There was the sound of scratching from behind the rear porch. Hash ignored him and crossed to open the door. There was dead weight on the other side of it, and he had to push hard before it gave. Shamsa yelped with pain. Easing the door open more gently, he saw her lying half on the step and half on the grass, a large pool of blood beneath her, breathing feebly. She tried to raise her head and her tail thumped weakly as she recognised him. He knelt beside her, talking to her softly as he stroked her. His fingers felt warm and slick when he gently felt the back of her head. He held her up long enough to see punctures, stab wounds on her neck and chest. It could only have been the bomber.

Hash cursed. She needed to be on the vet's operating table this minute, but there'd be too many unanswerable questions. He couldn't possibly risk it. Shamsa would have to bleed out and die, right in front of him, please her master one last time by dying without fuss. He sat up against the porch wall and took the dog's head on his lap, stroking her flank, letting the torrent of anger boil up in his chest.

She struggled for a few seconds and he soothed her; her breath came in a choked cough and Hash felt tears rolling down his cheeks, dropping onto the dog's coat. He bent his face down to hers and kissed her eyes. They stayed closed and gradually her breathing slowed. For a few seconds, her rear legs kicked in powerful spasms as though she was accelerating across the meadow one last time after the old hare. Then she was still, and Hash knew she was past pain. Whispering a farewell from him and Jim he blessed her for her huge heart, her unconditional love, for completing their team unforgettably. He'd cuffed her for her defiance of the bomber, hadn't soothed her distress at the station when Jim had left without saying goodbye. Hash closed his eyes, holding her head, full of regret, trying to blank out for a moment the mess they were in.

The bomber appeared in the doorway and tapped Hash hard on the shoulder, gesturing at his injured arm. Hash jerked a thumb, ordering him back inside. 'You can wait in the kitchen, you stupid cunt!'

He stayed on the back step for some minutes longer, smoothing her silky ears and her soft muzzle where she liked to be tickled. He could hear the bastard moving around in the kitchen. God knows how he'd been occupying himself while

Hash was out, probably purifying, preparing for his approaching moment of martyrdom. Whatever, the appearance of Susan with her open smile, so soon after looking at all those available women online, would have been enough to bring on disaster. Hash guessed he'd jumped her straightaway and Susan had fought back, with Shamsa hurling herself to her defence.

He tipped his head back against the wall and contemplated the problems queuing up in front of him. Susan might well, in fact probably should, call the police or go to a doctor; he hated himself for thinking that shame and embarrassment might stop her, and that that might work in his favour. Shamsa could be explained away as a sudden collapse. Even old Mrs Hamilton could be persuaded the dog had had an inherited condition of some sort. He'd tell her the vet had said there was no alternative but to have her put down. He looked down at the dog's peaceful face and stroked her again. The blood drying on his hand made him realise how long he'd been sitting with her. He willed himself to act and, pushing Shamsa gently to one side, stood up.

Ignoring the bomber, who was still sitting in the kitchen in an almost trance-like state, Hash grabbed Shamsa's cushion bed and went back outside, unzipping the outer cover as he went. He dropped the sack of filling to one side, then lifted her into the outer cover. Carrying her in both arms to the garage, he laid her down gently and returned for the sack. He filled a bucket with hot water. Ten minutes of scrubbing the step, frantically working bleach over the bloodstains, removed every trace.

Back in the kitchen, he signed he was ready to look at the wound. Holding the injured forearm carefully, he saw a two-inch tear deep in the muscle; the area was swollen as well as caked with blood. Hash remembered the man's soreness the previous day, and the damage to Shamsa's leg. He realised now, too late, that the dog and the bomber had already clashed. The man needed a tetanus shot and stitches. He winced as Hash felt the flesh around the bites.

'You are a stupid bastard,' he said softly, looking at the bomber. His quiet voice did nothing to disguise the venom he felt, but Hash was beyond caring. 'You're a stupid, stupid bastard,' he repeated, 'and if you weren't going to kill yourself, I'd fucking do it myself.' The man could see enough in Hash's eyes for translation to be immaterial. They glared at each other.

'What other surprises have you got planned, you stupid, stupid cunt?'

The bomber looked away, grey with pain and anxiety, and Hash's gaze swept round the kitchen. There was a safety razor in the sink, and more tufts of hair on the floor around it where he'd used the razor to finish the scalp. The blood on the floor could be his, could be Shamsa's.

He laid the man's arm to one side and went to investigate his bathroom medicine cabinet. Back downstairs he washed out the sink then filled it again with warm water and plenty of Dettol. As he turned back to put bandages on the table, he heard the ping of an SMS message. He saw the bomber holding the Arab BlackBerry, attempting to type into it. In a spike of fury, Hash stepped over and tore the phone from the bomber's hands, making the man yelp in pain. There was a message waiting. He slipped the phone into his pocket, motioning the man to the sink full of water.

Hash held the damaged forearm in the warm water, while the man shifted from foot to foot in agony, directing a torrent of hate at Hash in his native tongue, stabbing a free finger at him. Hash longed to grasp it, twist it back until it broke.

Maybe Siddiq could produce a medic who'd be prepared to treat a man with a badly shaved head, shabby clothes and a seriously injured arm and not ask questions, he thought.

The bomber gestured at what had been Shamsa's corner. Hash looked across and saw more blood. Shamsa's or the bombers? A fist, hard and shocking, punched him on the shoulder. He recoiled and adrenaline surged as he turned. Wounded or not, in a physical struggle with this man he would lose. He stepped back and held up both hands in surrender. 'Later, later,' and he lowered his hands, palms downwards, murmuring, 'Calm down now, you have to calm down,' as he mimed wrapping the arm and injecting it to signify treatment.

The bomber's rage and contempt only seemed to intensify; he drew his good fist back, poised for another punch. Hash turned his shoulder to the coming blow and tried the calming gesture again. They were both breathing fast, and Hash could feel his own adrenaline pumping a mixture of panic and explosive anger.

Fist still raised, the man spat on the ground, unleashed another stream of venom and spat again, this time straight at Hash. Ignoring the gobbet of spit on his chest, Hash stepped back and deliberately walked away to switch on the kettle. He motioned to the man to sit, so that he could bind the wounded arm. It seemed to have an effect and the bomber dropped his fist. His eyes still full of hatred, he turned abruptly and went upstairs.

A wave of tiredness and emotion washed over Hash, and he leant heavily on the worktop, wishing he could talk to Tara, or Sean. Jim was gone, being held by bastards who knew how to inflict pain if they wanted to. Susan had been hurt, badly, maybe even raped. Shamsa was lying dead in the garage, her body stiffening. Nothing he'd learnt at Ben Gashir had prepared him for this degree of madness.

He fished the phone from his pocket and read the message, 'Lord Jim sends regards.' Someone at the Libyan end was on his side, or at least playing the game for the time being. Proof that Jim was alive. A dam of relief burst, and he started to cry again, short sobs of agony over his boy's appalling situation and self-pity at the chaotic position he found himself in.

He grabbed a broom and scooped clumps of hair into the

bin. Footsteps on the stairs told him the bomber was coming down again. He went straight into the sitting room and Hash heard murmuring as the praying started. He'd leave him to it. He took a cloth and bent down to get the blood spots off the floor; the sight of Shamsa's blood brought the prickle of tears back to his tired eyes. She'd stood her ground and paid the price, shaming him by instinctively doing her duty, keeping her pledge to protect her family.

Going into the rear porch for a mop, he passed the table where Shamsa's worldly belongings were kept: brush, tins of food, a box of biscuits and a coiled lead. The lead was made of a thick leather loop and a metre of strong chain; she had an endearing trick of carrying it to Hash when her walk was overdue. On impulse, Hash picked it up.

As snatches of mumbled prayer reached him from the sitting room, he twisted the leather hard around his right fist, his left hand taking the end of the chain and pulling it taut. The same compulsion moved him quietly through the kitchen to the sitting room doorway. He looked at the man sitting on his ankles, eyes closed, his head turning slowly to the left then to the right, following the ritual of prayer. If he was aware of Hash, he was taking no notice of him.

There was neutral daylight from outside. Nobody would be able to see in. Wrapping the chain end in his left hand, he edged noiselessly into the room. As the bomber bowed forward again, touching his head to the carpet Hash paused, his mouth dry, his heart thudding and then braced. A moment later the man sat back up, hands resting on his thighs.

Hash sprang forward, looped the chain over the man's head, rammed his right knee between his shoulder blades and hauled back. The bomber's body bucked, hands flying to his neck, and for a moment they were suspended by the opposing momentum. Then the bomber writhed, rolling forward and Hash had to go with him. All he had to do was keep his knee between those shoulder blades and his body weight on the chain.

They fell sideways onto the carpet. The man writhed and kicked back with his feet, his huge hands scrabbling to free his throat, his legs thrashing. Hash, breathing through clenched teeth, kept his arms hauling back. He could hear his victim gagging. His pent-up rage fuelled the pressure he was keeping on the man's throat.

The bomber tried reaching back, first clawing for Hash's arms, then scrabbling for the leg of the coffee table, but his wounded right arm must have been too weak to heft it, and instead of smashing it onto Hash, the hand lost its grip. Slowly he began to weaken, animal noises rasping from his crushed windpipe. Hash hauled back harder, arms aching, aware of his own breath coming in hisses, pushing further into the man's back, knowing he only had to hold the position. The bombers fingers fluttered. Convulsive spasms, just like Shamsa's own death throes, started to shake his frame. They subsided and stopped, but Hash still held on for two more minutes. Finally, with heart hammering, he let the chain go slack and the man's head lolled onto the carpet. Cautiously, still lying alongside, Hash flexed his wrists and fingers, seeing the white skin where the chain had cut the blood flow. He held his hands out and watched his fingers quiver with shock and adrenaline as they came back to life.

Dragging himself upright, Hash went to the bay window and closed the curtains. Looking down at the lifeless bomber, at the face with its half-open eyes, Hash despaired at ever getting Jim out of this. He kicked the inert form hard. How could his controllers at Ben Gashir, such sticklers for perfection, have chosen this brainless peasant to serve their purpose? As he was about to haul himself upstairs for a blanket, he noticed that the Koran, knocked off the coffee table during the struggle, lying open on the carpet. Two slips of coloured paper were lying beside it.

Righting the coffee table and stooping to pick up the Koran, Hash collected and examined them. He was looking at a pair of tickets printed with horses and holograms. Hash distinctly remembered paying for 'Any Day' tickets as part of the annual treat for Sean; this was always the deal, and it was always Hash's shout. The bomber in his hours alone in the house, like a thieving magpie attracted to shiny objects, must have spotted the tickets where they were kept in a crystal vase on the mantelpiece. Hash stepped across to return them to the vase and saw his own tickets there. He looked again at the pair in his hands. They showed a 'Friday Only' admission to next week's racing festival. Now he realised their significance; they were fresh tickets for Friday 13th March, Gold Cup Day, and they'd come in the bomber's Koran.

The martyr's lack of interest in GCHQ, his total indifference to the recce and all of Hash's attempts at briefings all instantly made sense too. No wonder he'd shown no fear at the challenge of breaching a site defended like the electronic equivalent of a mediaeval fortress. Hash had simply assumed the man was exceptionally stupid but the bomber, following the endlessly rehearsed procedures drummed into him somewhere in Pakistan, had been about to present the two tickets to Hash; they were the next item on the operational checklist. On Friday the 13th at three in the afternoon, the man in the Semtex vest was meant to be at the racecourse, right in amongst thousands of happy punters, immediately before the start of the Gold Cup.

His rush of horror was cut short by the doorbell. Still holding the tickets in his hand, he went to the door frame and peered into the hallway. Blue phosphorescence silhouetted a man's shape on the frosted glass of the front door. Choking back panic, he shut the sitting room door silently and, forcing himself to breathe as he pinned on a smile, opened up. A young police officer, still talking into his radio, had his eyes fixed on Hash. He finished his message and a disembodied voice crackled back an acknowledgement over the radio.

'Mr Hashmi, I believe?'

'Correct, Officer. What can I do for you?' Hash's eyes took in the periphery. Sure enough, Mrs Hamilton was on station behind her window, and some neighbours across the street had been lured to their doorways.

'Everything alright?' the officer asked.

'No, it's not,' Hash replied. 'I was in the middle of praying.'

The policeman shifted slightly, looking past Hash into the hallway. 'A member of the public has reported a disturbance.'

'Aah yes, that would be my next-door neighbour,' Hash sighed. Mrs Hamilton's face fell as the officer's gaze swung round to her.

'No, it wasn't, actually, sir. Another member of the public has complained about noise.'

'I'd have thought my neighbours would have come to me first,' said Hash, feigning disappointment.

'Maybe you weren't in, sir. Have you been away this morning, then?' The policeman had hooked his thumb into his uniform waistcoat.

'I was in court,' Hash lied. The policeman's eyebrow shot up. 'Catching up on some paperwork after yesterday's sitting,' Hash explained. 'And while I was away, I believe my son's teacher paid a call.' The policeman made a show of pulling out his notebook. 'A dog barking incessantly,' he read, 'in some distress. Does that sound right to you?'

'We have a new dog, a rescue, and she's nervous. Rather excitable, especially if I'm not here when someone comes to the door. She's still settling in.'

The policeman's walkie-talkie hissed with another transmission and Hash saw the car's lights blip twice. The policeman on his doorstep turned to check his colleague in the driver's seat, who gave a distinct shake of the head, drawing a finger across his throat.

'So, you're one of our magistrates,' the policeman said.

'Is that good or bad?' Hash ventured, smiling.

'I'm sure it's good, sir.' The policeman smiled back at him, and Hash hoped the neighbours could see their relaxed body language.

'We always take rescue dogs, and they always take time to settle.' He nodded across to Mrs Hamilton's door. 'I'll have to apologise to everyone. I was about to pray, it's prayer time for all good Muslims, but do come in and see for yourself,' Hash swept his arm towards the kitchen.

The police officer hovered, but another transmission killed any remaining interest. Stepping further back and looking up at the door to confirm the number, he said, 'Not today, sir, busy as hell. We'll leave it at that, then.' He cracked another smile, 'So, sir, see you in court sometime.'

Hamad had woken him up on Sunday night to ask a list of stupid questions. What were his hobbies, what was his favourite sport, his favourite food. He'd been pretty cheerful about it, hinted there was some plan in store to make life easier and more fun when it was not "too dangerous." Fine, but he wished he wouldn't stand so close. He seriously needed to use a toothbrush.

He'd had to explain Quadcopters to him because he could see he was having difficulty with the difference between model helicopter kits and the new quadcopters. He'd told him about the one in his suitcase and offered to demonstrate and seen Hog's Breath blinking when he'd gone into the necessity for good battery life, so he'd stepped in, taken the man's pen and drawn it all in pictures, the important stuff about the best models, the battery life, the cameras on board. He'd seemed pleased, really interested. If they were planning some treat, then best they get the right gear. Maybe Dad was getting through to them after all, making sure he got exactly what he wanted while he was stuck away from home.

15

LATE AFTERNOON – SUNDAY

Easing into a kitchen chair, Hash pulled out the Arab Black-Berry and reread the simple message. His eyes stayed on the words, willing them to tell him more than just that Jim was alive. Was he thinking of his father, wondering where he was, missing his home? Glancing up at the photographs on the dresser, he tried to summon reserves of strength and imagined Tara urging him on, telling him to gather his wits and pull himself together. Bella and the boy's grandfather across in Tyrone would be less polite about it, "Get the fuck on with it, you lazy Arab!" would be about right. His own mother would simply have hugged him, just as Tara would hug Jim, but both women were long gone and it was down to the men now. His father, who'd made him cut all ties with his Libyan family – "For your own good" were his parting words – would have been robust, but still with that twinkle in his eyes, and would probably have fallen back on a cryptic message borrowed from some old film, "You play till the final whistle, old boy." As much as he could have done with a shoulder to weep on, he was in too deep, far too deep to turn back now. Jim was alive and waiting for him to be the hero. He'd better get going then. Heaving himself to his feet, he glanced at the clock; at least he had a solution for Shamsa.

It was dark, dry and clear as Hash headed out past the race-course. He would have preferred it to be raining when he reached the municipal tip at Stoke Orchard, but his timing was perfect. Just ten minutes before it closed. He knew the staff were impatient, poised to close the gates, offices locked, champing at the bit to get home with their own cars running to heat up. None of them would be hovering at the big skips. Arrive a few minutes before closing time, and you could dump a nuclear warhead and maybe have an impatient employee help you throw it in. Pulling up at the big container marked 'non-recyclable', he got out, checking he was alone, no CCTV with a sightline and no member of staff in a hi-vis vest around. He tugged at the canvas dog bed, feeling Shamsa's weight inside, and swung her as gently as he could onto the edge of the container. He whispered a last goodbye, putting his forehead to her body through the fabric, smelling her familiar, sweet smell. Then he pushed her down the sloping metal shelf and let her slide into the maw of the huge container. The body thumped onto the steel floor.

Hash dialled Susan and waited. He had parked a few doors away from her flat, but saw no lights in any of the windows. After six rings the voice message came on and he said, 'Susan? It's me, Hash. I hope you're ok? It'd be a relief to see you, even just for a second if you feel up to it. If there's anything I can do, please, please talk to me.' He gave up and turned for home. He'd try again tomorrow.

'Your girlfriend was here,' Mrs Hamilton said, taking Hash by surprise as he slid his key into the lock.

'Mrs Hamilton,' he said, 'do you ever rest?' She stepped

forward from her porch and Hash faced her over the low wall. With her arms folded and from the way she looked up and down the street, he knew she wanted to talk.

'Bloody goings-on here,' she whispered, 'like Peyton Place. The police, your women...' She stopped in midstream. 'When Jim's away, eh?' She wagged a thin, crooked finger in admonishment.

Wondering if she'd been drinking and trying to stay polite, he said, 'Misunderstanding with a guest, someone I was doing a favour for. He's gone now, thank God.'

'How is Jim? Enjoying the country life?'

'Very much so,' Hash said, 'although it's not how he puts it when he can be bothered to ring. His granny and grandpa love having him.'

'Anyway,' Mrs Hamilton sniffed, 'that girlfriend of yours was here.'

'What girlfriend? Jim's schoolteacher came by this morning to deliver coursework for him.'

'Blonde, ponytail, five foot you know what,' the old lady smirked.

'You've lost me. Susan's dark-haired,' Hash said, wondering how she could have mixed Susan up with someone else.

'She could have been dark-haired once.' Mrs Hamilton was enjoying herself. 'Bottle blonde probably. Not what I would have called your type.'

Hash had had enough and broke the flow. 'You know Shamsa's ill? The vet's stuck her in hospital. I'm really worried she'll not pull through.' At this, the old lady's coy smile faded, and her hand shot to her mouth.

'What's the matter with her?'

'Some congenital condition. I took her in to the emergency place at the racecourse and they sent her down to the pet hospital in Bristol.'

'Poor girl,' the old lady said, looking shocked. 'Does Jim know?'

'I can't tell him until I know for sure.'

'Maybe better he doesn't know,' she said. 'He loves that dog.'

'It's been a long day, Mrs Hamilton,' he said. 'I'd invite you in for a nightcap, but I'd be asleep on the table in seconds.' The true depth of his fatigue hit him as he turned to open the door, knowing what was on the other side.

Hash stepped around the body and went to the curtains, making sure they were tight shut, allowing only the kitchen light to filter into the sitting room. His eyes adjusted to the half-darkness as he looked at the body lying on its side covered in the blanket he'd brought down earlier. He guessed he would be shifting twelve to thirteen stone of dead weight. He went through his tiny garden to the garage and, fumbling in the dark, gathered duct tape and cord.

He lashed the man's heels together, looping the cord several times to make a strong handle to pull on. Tugging two black bin liners over the shoulders, he taped the whole head at the throat: he didn't want any body fluids leaking out. Finally, with the arms roped to the side of the body and the head swaddled, he bent over and started walking backwards, pacing the route he'd have to drag the body over. Satisfied there was nothing to snag or tear at the corpse on the way, and only the briefest exposure to neighbourly eyes as he was crossing the lawn, he headed back in.

Bracing himself, he grasped the looped ankles, swung the body round on the floor and began hauling, relieved that it travelled smoothly on the surface of the kitchen floor. He paused to check once more at the rear porch before stepping out onto the lawn, tugging hard to get momentum. The man's head smacked onto the concrete slab as it dropped off the back step, making a sickening noise he had to hope no one had heard, but within a few seconds he was heaving the body into the garage and lining it up along one of the walls.

Red hot needles of water drilled down onto his head and shoulders as he stood in the shower a few minutes later, working soap onto his aching frame to break down the tension in his muscles and mind.

What he'd done to the bomber had opened a Pandora's box of troubles. As he towelled, he wondered if the bomber had any pre-agreed procedures to follow in the days prior to the attack, a checklist of tasks which, if left unfulfilled, would start alarm bells ringing somewhere. He desperately needed to sleep, he knew, but it was impossible to block out the shock and strain of the day.

He swallowed two sleeping pills, smelling their sharp herbal aroma, and lay on his bed, praying they'd work fast before his mind started churning again.

MONDAY 9TH MARCH

The ping of an SMS jerked him awake at nine the next morning, disorientated after his drugged sleep. He squinted at the phone; it was from Siddiq. A dog barked somewhere behind his house. Maybe someone was taking their dog for a walk and it had smelled the cadaver in his garage? How long before the body, lying stiff and cold out in the garage, would attract rats? The weather was chilly enough, at least from the evening through to mid-morning; he reckoned he had a few days in hand. Until Friday afternoon, in fact. After three pm on that day, when there was no massive detonation at the racecourse, someone somewhere, and with their hands round Jim's throat, would need an explanation.

Siddiq wanted to meet at the mosque. Quickly showered and shaved and hoping he looked his normal self, Hash walked to the school office, calling Susan's phone on the way. Still no answer; he wondered if she was in class. He needed to know she was

OK and then gauge her reactions. On the pretext of needing details for the debate, he learned from the headmaster's PA that Susan was off sick and would be away for a few days.

Bella called as he was back on the Bath Road. It was a balm to hear her strong voice, a small echo of normality.

'He's allowed up and about but no visitors,' Hash said. 'No pizza either. And they're serious about that.'

'I'd feed him a good dinner of bacon and spuds.'

'His absolute favourite,' Hash said.

'And you're full of shite, Mr Magistrate,' she retorted. Hash joined in her laughter and asked about his father-in-law.

'Aah, that old boy's always the same. Some days he's good and some days he's bad. You know how it is.'

Hash calculated he could make it to the mosque in fifteen minutes and ended the call as soon as he reasonably could, promising to keep her posted about Jim's recovery.

At prayers he saw Hakim, small and wiry, like a bearded elf, going through his devotions with a serene calm that Hash found irksome. The ceremony over, however, and mindful of showing respect, he was carefully deferential in his approach. He was subjected to another crushing handshake and a wordless scrutiny, Hakim's prayerful serenity replaced by suspicion.

'Salaams Haji,' Hash started, 'how is your family, your health?'

The man nodded, acknowledging the courtesies.

'Have you any news for me?' asked Hash

'Alhamdulillah, no news.'

Unsure whether the man was following the ritual or really had no information, he pressed on. 'About my son? Any news?'

Hakim's neutral expression did not change. 'Alhamdulillah, no news.'

'But you are looking?' Hash wanted to punch the sphinx-like face. 'Do you need more money?'

'Insh'Allah,' Hakim said quietly.

'So, how much?' Hash asked.

Hakim shook his head and with a look of irritation countered, 'Insh'Allah, I am looking.'

'Always,' the interruption came from Siddiq, 'always about money. But not today.' The Bangladeshi had crept up behind Hash, taking him by surprise. 'Today is not the day to be bothering the Haji. He is a very busy man.'

'But he is looking…?' Hash felt like a serf grovelling before his masters. 'And I do have more money.'

'Hakim will bring you good news, soon.' Siddiq took Hash's elbow, attempting to steer him away. 'Come, my friend, someone is waiting.' He waved Hash towards his car. 'Follow me.'

'Are you sure? I thought we had business here,' Hash said.

'Someone is waiting back at the house.'

Hash could tell that the maisonette had been given the feminine touch as soon as Siddiq opened the front door. The smell of dust on tired carpets and curtains had gone. Flowers in twin vases now decorated the sitting room. Anna and another woman were smoking in the rear garden, and Anna smiled and waved as she caught sight of Siddiq coming to the French window. Recognising Hash an instant later, she continued the greeting although her smile became a little more guarded. Hash watched her passing information quickly to her companion through a stream of exhaled cigarette smoke. The other woman, similar in height, was a clone of Anna: athletic, slim, blonde hair in a ponytail.

'You could be twins,' Hash said as he shook hands. The other girl, introduced as Daniela, seemed uncertain at the English and the laughter.

'But which is the younger one?' Siddiq made a pantomime wink, putting an arm around Anna's waist. 'Mine or yours?' Anna held her cigarette at arm's length as Siddiq pulled her to him. 'Come on, darling,' Siddiq whispered hoarsely, 'Don't be shy. Hash is my best friend.'

Daniela smiled at Hash, half in embarrassment at Siddiq's clumsiness, half in an appeal to kill the farce. Hash supposed he was getting a daytime look at the present Siddiq had sent last night and wondered what would have happened to this girl. Susan still hadn't responded to his messages.

'Coffee?' Anna broke away from Siddiq and went into the kitchen, dousing her cigarette at the tap, pointing at the kettle. Daniela was still in the garden, tapping at her phone.

'Or something stronger?' Siddiq said. 'Champagne? Brandy?'

'Coffee, thanks,' Hash said. 'This place is looking good, Anna. First time it's been so fresh in years.'

She shrugged off the compliment, 'Thanks, it didn't take long.'

'How long do you plan on staying?'

'Why do you want to know?'

'I can't decide how much rent to charge my wealthy friend. So stay as long as you like.'

'Sorry to hear about your son, James.' Hash was silent, taken aback that she knew about Jim and by her bluntness. How much had Siddiq told her?

'You've got to hope he'll come back soon,' she continued as water rushed into the kettle. Siddiq was sending a message on his phone, oblivious to the exchange.

'What else did he tell you?' Hash asked.

Anna, at the sink with her face turned away, picked mugs from the drying rack and replied slowly, 'He says the boy's lovely, he could do very well at school and he misses his mother.'

Siddiq's phone rang, and he heaved himself upright, a scowl darkening his cheerful features. Unleashing a torrent of Bengali, he moved out of the kitchen. Anna's eyes followed him then looked at Hash, her eyes rolling heavenwards. 'Always on the phone. Business, always business.'

'What did he say about my son?'

Anna considered for a few seconds. 'He's going through that teenager phase. You know.'

'Do you have kids?' Hash asked her.

She shook her head. 'Let's just say I had some bad luck where kids were concerned. But your son James,' she said, 'if he's in Birmingham, Siddiq will find him. So, everything's going to be fine.' She put a hand on Hash's arm. 'Siddiq knows people. He can fix things. Trust me.' She held up the coffee jar, tapping a spoon against it. 'Black, white, strong or weak?'

Daniela re-entered the kitchen, looking shyly at Anna and Hash.

'Where's that plumber of yours, the talkative guy?' Anna asked.

'He's gone,' Hash said. 'At least for the next few days. Is there a problem?' Anna had opened the fridge door, reaching in to free a container of milk.

'I don't know what it is,' she murmured into the cabinet. 'Maybe I need my thermostats looked at again.'

'I can do that easily, or we'll get him across to you,' Hash said.

'It was just a joke,' she said, holding the spoon over the open coffee jar, 'and anyway, maybe I will call you instead.'

Siddiq burst into the kitchen, his good spirits revived. 'So, let's go for lunch, a nice long lunch. What do you say?'

Anna put the coffee jar down. 'I'm making coffee now, darling. Do you want me to stop?'

Siddiq reached for her waist. 'They can have the coffee.' He jutted his chin at Daniela and Hash. 'You and me, we're going for lunch. But first my darling does something for me.' Hash saw a flash of irritation in Anna's eyes: she wasn't the sort of woman who took ham-fisted orders.

After they'd gone, Daniela stirred her coffee for a while and when the silence became too awkward pretended to be busy with her phone.

'Did he send you to my house yesterday?' Hash asked, wondering if she was the one Mrs Hamilton had seen.

She stopped texting and looked across at him.

'When? Yesterday? No. I was in Solihull, on a gig.'

'Gig?'

'You know, a gig. Dancing.'

'Why do you do it?'

She considered the question, still examining her phone. 'Pay the bills. Meet interesting people. That sort of thing.'

'How do you know Anna?'

'I don't. Just met her.'

'Where are you from?' At his persistence Daniela lapsed into a sing-song script. 'So, my name's Daniela, I'm from Lithuania and I'm studying to be a lawyer.' As an afterthought she added, 'I'm paying my own student fees.'

'Who's paying you now?'

She looked surprised. 'Now? That would be you.'

'Who told you where I live?'

'Don't worry,' she trilled. 'I'm discreet. Some clients are very shy. Okay by me.'

'And you never met Anna?'

She gave a bright smile and held up both hands, palms upwards. 'Anna who?'

'When you've finished your coffee,' Hash said, 'I'll take you to the station.'

16

Sean stood in the garage, taking his first look at the blanketed form.

'Jesus,' he muttered, digging his hands further into his coat pockets. 'Now I know it's for real.'

He lifted a foot to the dead man's shoulder and rocked the body. The knees had stiffened at a bent angle and the body would not roll over.

'How did you do it?' Sean kept his foot on the body while he pulled out a packet of cigarettes.

'Choked him with the dog lead,' Hash said. 'He was praying when I jumped on his back.'

'So much for the power of prayer.' Sean tugged out a cigarette. 'Best get him into a sleeping bag.' He lit up, looked through the garage door, then blew a steady stream of smoke across the chill. 'He'll not stink for a good few days.' He tapped the corpse with his foot.

'How do we get rid of him?' Hash asked. 'I put the dog in the council tip.'

'You're joking. Garden waste or non-recyclable?'

'The dog?'

'No,' Sean said, 'tossing this guy in a skip. Do you know what we really need?'

'Anything, tell me.'

'A fucking drink. Something strong, something to help me think.'

In the kitchen, Sean sat smoking while Hash rummaged. He put a bottle and two glasses on the kitchen table, 'Something special…we were going to celebrate your trip.'

'We still are, Darky. Aah, Crested Ten,' Sean murmured, looking at the label. Hash poured two generous measures.

'To Jim,' Hash raised his glass.

'To Jim,' Sean echoed quietly. 'And God help any bastard who gets in my way.'

They savoured their drinks in silence.

'What about this Susan girl of yours? Is it serious?' Sean said.

Hash shook his head, 'Romantically, after what happened? Hardly. The mere sight of me could trigger anything. Maybe she'll go to the police, maybe her parents will push her.' He held up his palms. 'Maybe she'll do nothing at all.'

'And this guy Hakim,' Sean asked. 'What's the score with him? He one of the good guys?'

'He runs a radio cab business in the Birmingham area, all Asian drivers, and he's an imam, you know, a sort of religious elder.'

'Protestant or Catholic?'

Hash smiled and sipped his whiskey. 'He tried to tell me Jim had run away to join ISIS, like one of those mad youngsters. He doesn't trust me, especially when I waved money at him.'

'Made it worse?'

'If he's a real imam he can give the money to an Islamic charity.'

'If he's not?'

'If there's more he might be tempted to help. Either way, I'm short of options.'

Sean said nothing for a few seconds. Then he pointed at the

vest Hash had carried in from the garage. 'What do we do on Friday after nothing goes bang at three o'clock?'

'I'm just hacking through each day. I haven't got that far yet,' Hash said.

THURSDAY 12TH MARCH

They'd agreed their only contact for the time being would be in the Guinness Village at the races; the crush of punters jostling for their pints was good cover. Tuesday's meeting, two days back, had allowed Hash to tell Sean, his voice raised above the hubbub of music and racing commentary, that there'd been nothing from Hakim or Siddiq, and nothing from Susan. Sean hinted he was working on someone who might move their package. Wednesday afternoon's meeting brought in the price from Sean's contact. The exchange was set for the following evening in the trade stand parking area where lorries and vans would be busy unloading fresh stock and moving out waste.

With Sean directing, Hash reversed the Discovery up to the back of a horse box. He could see Cork plates in the rear-view mirror, and Sean shaking hands with the driver. Within seconds the martyr, zipped into a sleeping bag, was carried into the truck. In a wordless exchange, Hash handed over two thick wads of notes to a tough, thickset man in a heavy tweed coat that smelled of beer and straw. He thumbed the corner of the wadded notes.

'Ten thousand, is it?' he said in a thick Southern Irish accent. 'You're sure, now, cos you've left me no time or light to count it.' He looked up, an eyebrow raised. 'Give me more warning next time. I can give a discount for groups, bring a bigger lorry.'

He and Sean burst into laughter and clasped each other in a bear hug. Hash was ignored. Then the man climbed up into the cab and fired the engine.

They watched the lorry reverse out, making a cautious turn

on the uneven ground.

'I don't think our friend's going to feel the bumps,' Sean said. 'Good riddance. One moment you're the farmyard cockerel, next minute you're a feather duster.'

The driver settled in his cab and flicked a salute at the two men before slipping the clutch.

Sean patted Hash on the back. 'One down, how many more to go?'

Hash was watching the horse box. 'What'll they do with him? Tip him over the side of the ferry?'

Sean pulled out a packet of rolling tobacco. 'My guess, he'll hit the food chain, be feeding the pigs somewhere in the arse end of Cork.'

'Ouch,' Hash said, grimacing. 'I heard from Susan,' he added.

'Good or bad?'

'Good, I think. This afternoon. She's asking me about the lecture.'

'What lecture?'

'I'd forgotten,' Hash said, 'I agreed to be in this school debate. It's her big deal and she asked me as a big favour. I was going to take her out to dinner afterwards.'

'Maybe your dinner date is back on.' Sean stopped pushing tobacco onto the skin and nudged Hash with his shoulder. 'How did she sound?'

'She sent an SMS, so I didn't speak to her. But at least she's communicating.'

'If she's sending you an SMS about a school debate, then her mind's not on that bastard.' Sean jutted his chin at the departing lorry. 'When's this debate?'

'Tomorrow afternoon.'

'Gold Cup Day. Bad timing, you'll miss the craic.' Sean licked the roll-up and held it up for examination.

'Maybe better for me not to be here tomorrow afternoon.'

Sean lit up, took the first drag, and blew a stream of smoke in the direction of the grandstand where there was a residual buzz of activity, punters making their way to their cars, some carrying drinks with them into the car park, some hanging onto each other for support. 'Lucky, bastards,' he breathed, 'enjoying themselves. They'd be gobsmacked if they knew two old gun-slingers from the Provos were watching their backs.'

The smell of sweet tobacco hit Hash's nostrils. 'I could do with one of those,' he murmured.

Sean ignored him.

'Remember some of the crazy ideas in the old days,' Sean plucked at a shred of tobacco stuck to his lip. 'The boys in Dublin thought about nailing this place, you know.'

'Must have been after my time.'

'Before your time, Darky,' Sean corrected, pointing over at the tented hospitality suites. 'The idea was ditched after the backlash over the Mountbatten thing in '79. I heard about it in the Kesh. We had lectures on stuff like that.' He smiled at Hash. 'The top brass wanted to take the old girl out. But then some of the Belfast big names, hands with experience, said no fucking way.' He spat on the ground and wiped his mouth. 'They said the Gold Cup was sort of a truce, off-limits, out of bounds. Know why?' Hash shook his head. 'The old Queen Mum,' Sean continued. 'The old doll used to walk around half-cut, shaking hands with Paddy. And Paddy bloody worshipped her. There would have been mayhem if one hair on her head had been touched.'

'And the ordinary folk, tomorrow, at three o'clock?' Hash nodded at the grandstand. 'Is it over? Do we warn them in case it isn't?'

'A phone call?' Sean suggested. 'The old anonymous tip-off?'

'They've probably had twenty of those already, just today,' Hash said. 'From pissed punters who've lost their money.'

Sean flicked his butt and watched the glowing tip shoot

into the darkness. 'How about we dump the suicide vest where the Brits will find it, make it easy for them? That would freak them out, the place would be crawling.'

Hash swung his door open and motioned to Sean to climb in on his side. Buckling himself in, about to switch the engine on, he said, 'We give them the vest we gain nothing. My priority is Jim and the bastards holding him.' He shook the steering wheel, 'Those good people out there can't be. And besides, we've just saved some of them even if they'll never know it'

'We're running short on time, mate.'

'I've got to keep the Libyan end on my side.'

'Well, you know the bastards,' Sean said, 'how their minds work.' He laughed at a sudden thought. 'But then you're one of them, so you bloody well should. Me? I'm just the technical guy.'

At the pub, when Sean had gone outside for a smoke, Hash tried Susan's number again and was surprised when she picked up after just a few rings. 'Susan,' he said softly, 'how are you? Is this a bad moment to call?'

Her voice had a tremble in it when she said, 'No, I'm fine. You know, getting on with things. How are you?'

'Frantic with worry about you, Susan.' He hunched his shoulders and jammed the phone to his ear to keep out the pub buzz. Sean came back, saw his concentration and went to the bar. When he returned with two fresh pints Hash was off the phone and had pushed back in his seat.

'Still love you?'

Hash blew out his cheeks. 'If only,' he exhaled. 'The bastard grabbed her and threw her around until the dog stepped in. She reckons she only got out because of Shamsa.'

'Is she going to the police?'

'I told her she should if she wanted to, and if she'd let me I would. And that the guy was being tracked by my contacts and I'd be wringing his neck.'

'Well,' Sean raised his pint, 'at least you didn't lie on that score.'

'I told her about the dog being put down too.' He contemplated his pint for a second then sipped. 'I really don't need her going to the cops…'

'Maybe she'll be too embarrassed,' Sean said. 'You read about these things.'

'She still wants me to do the debate. That takes me away from the races anyway.'

MORNING – FRIDAY 13TH MARCH

When Sean eventually answered his phone, his voice sounded slurred and thick with sleep. Hash interrupted his protests, urging him, 'Something warm that'll keep the rain off, your passport and maybe a small overnight bag.'

'That's all I brought with me in the first effing place,' Sean groaned. 'Jesus. I must be losing my touch. But there were three of them and I'd had a few scoops.'

Distracted by an image emerging from his printer, Hash wasn't listening. When the sheet of A4 was released, he laid it out on the desk, his eyes running over it, comparing it with three identical printouts, two for him and two for Sean. He silenced him, saying, 'I'm driving past you in two minutes, be ready.'

At the pick-up point, Sean's face was haggard and pale, the effects of a drinking session all too plain. He started to explain while he climbed in. 'I had a few more after you dropped me off, then I went for a fish supper. Then those boyos appeared. I didn't think you were serious.'

Hash thrust the four sheets of paper at him and jerked a thumb behind him. 'Thermos on the back seat.'

Sean's wariness gave way to astonishment as he looked at the pictures and Hash's grim smile. 'That's Jim. Bloody hell. How? When?'

'Siddiq,' Hash said. 'Eight o'clock this morning. It came through from Hakim and his boys.' He reached across and tapped the paper in Sean's hand. The sheet showed a grainy, coloured image of a scene in a park with a cluster of figures: one of them was a young lad in his teens, holding a toy helicopter. 'Must have been taken from a car. The driver was passing and thought he should snap it.'

'Top man. Fucking brilliant,' Sean said. 'But this wasn't taken this morning, was it?'

'Must have been yesterday afternoon before the light went. Maybe before, even.'

'Where the hell is this place?'

'Sparkbrook.'

'How do you know?'

'Siddiq, when he was telling me not to go there.'

'Which is why we're going there.'

Hash looked at Sean. 'Siddiq doesn't really get how serious this is.'

'You sure? Maybe he's smarter than he looks.'

Hash was silent, driving fast, hustling the cars in front, and within minutes the Discovery was running down the ramp north onto the M5. He relaxed just enough to jerk his thumb at the basket with the thermos and mugs on the back seat. Sean reached back and brought it forward. He poured a cup for each of them.

'Jesus, that's good,' Sean groaned after the first sip, 'I needed that. My bloody head hurts.'

Hash took his mug carefully, keeping his eye on the motorway.

'So, tell me. What happened?'

'They came in just before the place closed. The old Portuguese lad went white as a sheet and I recognised the guy with the tattoos on his neck.'

'Go on.' Hash was beginning to smile.

'I was waiting for my order, really peckish, like most gentlemen after a few gargles. And I don't mind other hungry people. It's when they get cheeky with it there's a problem.' He sipped again. 'And that's when things got interesting.'

Hash had accelerated hard to overtake a lorry and there was silence while Sean concentrated on keeping the liquid in his cup. When the lorry dropped behind them Hash glanced across. 'And…?'

'I gave them a lesson in good manners.'

'All of them? What about the manager? Was he involved?'

'He seemed happy to let me do the talking.'

'So, no cops?'

'Not that I know of, but you never know. Afterwards, maybe.'

Hash sipped from his cup. 'We've got enough to cope with without them.'

A motorway sign flashed past. Birmingham was still some thirty miles off.

Sean buzzed the window down and sucked in cold air. 'So, what's the plan now, Darky?

'Get there,' Hash said, 'park up, get out on foot. Hope to see them if they take him to play with his helicopter. We get close, and…'

'Nail them.' Sean made a hammering motion with his free hand.

'Grab Jim and run.'

'Run where? Back to the car, run to the cops?'

'Once you see we're out of the bastards' reach, you run like hell,' Hash said. 'I'll get a chunk of money across to you. Probably leave it with Bella for you to collect.'

'That would be just bloody all I need. I'm in enough shit with them as it is, without going to them to get money off them.'

'Yeah, but this is about Jim and by then they'll know you pulled the situation round for their grandson.'

'Won't make a blind bit of difference to them.' Sean massaged his temples with both hands. 'They disowned me, ever since that day.' He stopped, looked at Hash, seeing his nod of recognition, then out of the window. 'They turned their backs on me ages ago. Ten years in the Kesh and not one visit from my mother or my father.'

'Yes, but this is different,' Hash insisted. 'This is huge. You're making up for that stuff and I'll bloody well tell them what you've done.'

'What I've done.' Sean repeated quietly. 'That would be a bit premature.' He looked at the sheets on his lap. 'Jim's still skinny but he's taller. His friends look like minders.'

'Good you had a warm-up bout, then.'

Sean laughed. 'And here's me thinking that chippy thing was a coincidence. You set me up nicely, didn't you? Why the helicopter?'

'Quadcopter, drone or something. He's crazy about the things.'

'They gave him one to keep him occupied?' Sean said. 'Being nice to him?'

'Very considerate,' said Hash. 'But it might be his own. I think he packed it for his time on the farm with the old folks.'

Sean continued to study the photograph of Jim. 'How are we going to get close without Jim seeing one of us and giving the game away?'

'I don't know yet.'

'Maybe these guys have got guns. Any updates from Siddiq?' Sean asked. 'You know, like when the photo was taken, who took it?'

'I don't think we'll be doing too many interviews. Siddiq told me not to do anything, remember? Just confirm the photos are Jim. He says Hakim wants to get a clearer picture.'

'Was he serious?'

'Hakim's definitely the serious type.'

'Maybe he wants you to confirm, then he grabs Jim and ransoms him back to you. He knows you're good for cash.'

'I hear what you're thinking, but I don't think it fits with Hakim. Or Siddiq.'

'They've been clever enough so far.'

'It just doesn't sound like their style.'

'Well, you're the boss,' Sean sighed. 'You see the good in people. I come from the real world, mate.'

By the time they'd followed the M42 round the southern edge of Birmingham and hit the Stratford road it was nine forty-five and the rush hour was past its peak. The radio was interrupted by a traffic bulletin saying roads into Cheltenham were getting busy and wishing the punters a good day at the Gold Cup. Hash thumped the wheel and cursed.

'God, that bloody debate! I'll never make it now'

'Where do you need to be?' Sean asked. 'With Susan and a bunch of schoolkids, or up here trying to get Jim back? You're the one talking about priorities, so bloody well SMS her so we can both stay bloody focused.'

There was silence in the vehicle, until Sean looked at his watch.

'Ten o'clock. They could be up for breakfast or in the park after breakfast. How do you know the location?'

'I had to believe Siddiq, then I took it off Google,' Hash said. 'The two calls the night Jim was taken were made from around here, and I got a look at the area when I did my own stake-out. There's only one big park just a half-mile south of those streets. It's on the left as we're coming up now. Low red-brick wall running parallel with the pavement. You can see it in the picture.'

Sean looked down and examined the picture.

'So I Googled the whole Sparkbrook area this morning and,' Hash raised both hands off the steering wheel in prayer, 'this is my best shot.'

As the parade of shops on the left of the road gave way to

open ground, they stopped talking, looking both at the people on the pavements and deeper into the park. Mature trees, some planted in clumps, others on their own and some colonies of shrubbery broke up the landscape and their view. People were in the parkland in groups. All ages, some walking purposefully to work, others dawdling. Hash's slow driving provoked a horn blast from behind.

'Better we park up somewhere close,' Sean said, concentrating. 'I see an interesting bunch way out on the left.'

'Ok. We park, split and go for a walk, you to the top, me sticking around this end. What do you think?' Hash looked at Sean.

'Go for it,' he said.

Hash walked north along Stratford Road a short distance, past a Shell filling station, keeping to the right side of the road where the shops continued. He heard his phone ping with a message. Susan. He closed his eyes briefly and left it there. Thelma would just have to cope, and he'd deal with the fallout later.

Hash looked over the flow of traffic and into the park. He SMS'd Sean and got figure zero, nothing to report. If they were successful Sean wouldn't return, just fade away, reporting back to his probation officer as expected, and he and Jim would give him time to get away before going to the authorities themselves.

He watched a police car drive past slowly, its two occupants looking bored at being stuck in the snail's pace traffic. How quickly would they react if they caught sight of Sean and himself struggling with a group of men in broad daylight? He wondered if they carried weapons and how long paramedics would take to get onsite if a life-or-death struggle kicked off. Would they even up the numbers? Most likely stand off and call for backup, especially if Jim's minders pulled out weapons. Maybe the minders were martyrs too, with no fear of dying and only too happy to take some Kufar with them.

At half past eleven, Sean called, his voice electric with tension. 'Get the fuck over here,' he said, 'quickly but slowly!'

'Where?'

'Come into the park, way over! Use the trees to creep down towards me. You'll see what I see.' Hash was across the road and over the knee-high wall in seconds. He slowed down to as normal a pace as he could bear as soon as he was on the grass and cut across the park, head down, with his phone clamped to his ear to hide his anxiety. He thought he could hear a model engine whirring, not as loud as the Spitfire, but an engine nevertheless. He reached a tree and checked to his left and right, saw nothing in his immediate view and headed towards two trees a hundred and fifty yards away. Sean rang again. 'Hurry the fuck up! Something's happening. They're telling him to land the thing.'

'Stay on the line,' Hash said, his mouth dry. 'Keep talking. Can you see me?'

'Not yet. They're at the top end. He's just brought the thing to earth and they're all standing looking at it. One of them's on the phone, arms waving like crazy.'

'How's Jim?'

'Keep walking, stop fucking talking,' Sean hissed. 'I'm two fifty, maybe three hundred yards away. I can't do it on my own.'

Hash had begun to stride quickly, still looking down, glancing up and ahead every so often. Finally, he caught sight of two men and a youth standing together about two hundred yards distant. They were a tight group at the side of a road lined with parked cars. One of the men was opening a car door and pointing inside. He recognised Jim's diminutive shape instantly, his shoulders hunched, heartbreakingly obedient in front of the men. He was holding a quadcopter.

He wanted to yell at Jim, but the distance was against him. Any one of those men could intercept him, and the group was beginning to move.

'Doors open, one's just got in the driving seat, now Jim and the other. I think someone's onto me, Fuck!'

Hash could only watch as Jim disappeared into the car and the door closed.

'Bloody hell! We're too fucking late…' Sean's voice trailed off. 'Black car, moving now. I'm crossing the road in front of them.'

'Can you stop them?'

Hash caught a glimpse of Sean on the kerb, letting cars pass. He saw a flow of cars, one of them a black saloon swinging into the northbound flow on Stratford Road. He watched it go and within seconds it was swallowed up, fading into the mass of vehicles.

Sean was strangely elated when they both met at the Discovery. 'Jesus!' He held up his thumb and forefinger. 'This close! Your man drove bloody past me, nearly knocked me over. But he looked ok to me.' Sean patted Hash on the back. 'He looked ok, fit. A bit underfed, but ok.'

Hash smacked a fist into his palm in despair, 'Not bloody close enough. Did you get a photo of them?'

Sean had just stuck a cigarette between his lips and stopped in the act of lighting up and clicked his fingers.

'I wish I'd thought of that.' He held the lighter to the tip and Hash watched the glow. 'No bloody photos,' he said, coughing as he exhaled. 'Would a video do?' He dragged on the cigarette a few times then dropped the cigarette, crushing it underfoot. 'Want to see?'

The camera had wobbled, unsteady with Sean's rapid movement, but the lens zoomed in on a black BMW saloon approaching the camera. There was traffic noise in the background and through the front windscreen Hash saw two men, suited, both dark-haired, their smooth faces showing concern and purpose.

'Arabs,' Hash said as the camera showed the car's side windows sweeping past. In the rear seat, looking down at the quadcopter on his lap, sat Jim. The camera saw the BMW disappearing, its rear plates immediately blocked by the vehicles following.

'Jim!' Hash put his hands to his eyes. Sean had to pause the video and wait for a few minutes.

'Fuck it,' Hash shouted. 'We were so bloody close.'

'A bloody sight closer than we were yesterday,' Sean growled, 'And we didn't get clocked by them, so there's still tomorrow.'

'Play it again,' Hash said.

On the fourth rerun Hash told Sean to freeze the video. 'Try to zoom in on that,' Hash tapped the screen. 'The stuff behind the windscreen.'

'They've had a meal,' Sean muttered. 'Chicken Hut. A newspaper, what language?'

'Arabic,' Hash said. 'Zoom in on that sign.'

'A big letter M,' Sean said, 'like one of those passes you get on the ferry to hang on your mirror.'

'Member's enclosure,' Hash said.

'Don't follow.'

'Member's enclosure at the races.' He looked at his watch. 'It's one o'clock now. They're going to the races.'

'Taking Jim to the races? Can only be the Gold Cup, then. They're going to hand him over, leave him there after the big bang.'

'And when there isn't a big bang? What do they do with Jim?'

'Have you not told Libya?' Sean asked.

'No, and I never bring that phone,' Hash said. 'It stays at home in case someone's tracking it.' He held up his watch. 'An hour to get to Cheltenham. The roads'll be reasonably clear now. Most of the punters are already there.'

'One of them was talking on the phone,' Sean said as they nosed back down the Stratford Road. 'Maybe taking a message.'

'But Jim did look ok, didn't he?'

'Considering what he's going through,' Sean said, 'he looks

in good shape. Someone's got to be looking after him. Aaah, bloody hell.' He hit his thigh. 'I should have just reached out and ripped open the door.'

At two-thirty, after dropping Sean off at the racecourse, Hash was sending an SMS to the Libyan number: 'Dafe disappeared. Took all funds. Left equipment. Advise.' At two-fifty-five he was walking through the turnstile on the western entrance to the racecourse and watching the huge screen showing horses and jockeys leaving the ring across to his right. Where would the bomber have been told to position himself? Perhaps in amongst the crush of people overlooking the ring, but that crowd was thinning fast, already following the horses down to the track.

The screen flicked to the starting- gate where the first of the jockeys were circling their mounts. Hash tried to imagine what sort of a figure the tall, gaunt bomber would have cut in amongst the racegoers. Maybe he would have gone into the crowded stands, or maybe up the stairs to meet his Arab contacts for one last briefing. There was a good chance Jim was somewhere around there. If he could just catch a glimpse of him, there'd be no hanging back this time.

The big race started, to deafening approval from the grandstand. Hash concentrated on the crowds, trying to spot anyone out of place, anyone not caught up in the excitement. Within minutes it was over, racegoers beginning to celebrate, hugging and cheering, heading for the booths to cash in their winnings. Hash's eyes carried on raking the crowd for any sight of the two men and Jim.

The vibration of an SMS against his thigh distracted him. Still scanning the crowd, he took out the phone, expecting it to be Sean reporting in. Instead, it was the clerk to the justices confirming the bail hearing for the following morning. The time on the SMS was three minutes past three and the deadline was past.

Standing not far from him was the headmaster in tweed and suede brogues, a pair of expensive-looking binoculars slung over his shoulder. Hash raised his hand to catch his attention and offer his apologies and an explanation of some sort, but the man was already walking away, studiously ignoring him. Susan would surely be informed; but then why wasn't the hypocrite at his own debate?

Swallowing hard, he moved down the slope and headed through the throngs of punters towards the tented village of bars and boutiques. His phone rang and Siddiq's name appeared on the screen.

'Where are you, my friend? At the racecourse?'

'Of course.'

'All day?'

'Since this morning.' Hash heard discussion at the other end, as though Siddiq was conferring with somebody else.

'Not in Birmingham?' A muffled exchange took place at the other end before Siddiq came back with, 'Mr Hakim says you are a liar.'

'What do you mean?'

'Mr Hakim says he saw you, has a photograph of you. I am looking at it now. You are in Birmingham. I will send it to you.'

'I was in Birmingham, but that was much earlier.'

'Mr Hakim says you have made a big mistake. You are a stupid man who does not care about his son.'

'I can explain this,' Hash began, but was cut off by Siddiq delivering the rest of the message, '…and your son will die because of your stupidity.'

Sean listened to Hash's update in silence, rolling a cigarette, leaning against the vehicle. 'And you lose me tomorrow, Darky,' he said. 'The licence business, remember?'

'Do you think Jim was ever going to be handed over here after the bang?' Hash asked. 'He could've been dumped here and made his way home easily enough.'

Sean lit the cigarette, inhaled and examined it before exhaling a stream of blue smoke. 'Some hope. D'you think they're going to buy your story about the guy running away?'

Together they watched the emptying racecourse. Then Sean said, 'Aah well. Maybe they'll try again, save Jim for another go.'

He was exhausted, and bitterly disappointed. And the day had started so well. They'd promised he would be back with his father if everything went right, but it all went wrong and now he was back in this bloody prison. Hamad had been ok about it being a fuck-up but Grumpy Guts, the other guy, had been a pig, even took away his food before he could eat any of it, the bastard. Hamad had sneaked back in with it later though. He was a good guy, really. Sometimes they even talked about normal things. Like when he asked about the Irish granny and how she ran the farm.

Then the woman had been back and told him there were still some problems for his Dad, so he'd have to stay put for a bit longer, keep safe with them. She said his Dad had passed a message.

Apparently, he had to be patient and play the game. As if that helped. Christ, he was fed up with the fucking 'game'.

Stupid bloody game. But she said it was helping Dad. How for Christ's sake? Although when they'd tested his quadcopter the woman told him there was a good chance they could use it to look for his Dad, or maybe look for the people who were chasing his Dad, so that was good, he supposed. Pity he hadn't downloaded the footage though. He wanted another look. There was something about that bloke walking in the park who'd looked up at the machine...

'The main thing,' the woman had said, 'is we're all on the same side, trying to help your Dad and he wouldn't want you to stick your neck out.' Yeah, right. Never mind his neck, what he needed was to get his whole bloody body out of here. And soon. Best get some sleep though. And probably best not to rock the boat for his Dad. Wherever it was bloody going.

17

CHELTENHAM, SATURDAY - 14TH MARCH

Hash was joined by the same magistrates as before. It was possible the clerk intended to rub in the folly of their previous decision. The Chairman gave a weak smile as Hash entered the retiring room, a greeting without conviction, probably still stewing over the Harrow faux pas. The female medical professional, sour-faced champion of the beleaguered, said nothing, trying to look busy. They waited in silence until the clerk called them into court.

A policeman stood in the dock handcuffed to the defendant as the three magistrates took their seats. Before them sat the same legal aid counsel, and at the back the same reporter from the *Gloucestershire Echo*. Déjà vu, in fact.

The man in the dock had a heavily bruised face, both eyes swollen, and lips still crusted with blood. His neck was in a brace and his right arm, in plaster, was held by a white sling. His left arm hung free but with a large dressing over the whole hand. He tried to direct a fingertip to one of his clogged nostrils but couldn't quite reach it for the pain.

Citing the defendant's failure to comply with bail reporting conditions, the clerk gave the floor to the legal aid counsel who rose, attempting a show of regret.

'My client will not contest the fact that he missed his reporting obligations. As your Worships can clearly see, he has suffered a brutal assault which occurred before his curfew on Thursday evening. The police have agreed to share CCTV evidence of the attack on my client. If it pleases your Worships…'

He pointed to a television screen in the well of the court and Hash found himself looking at the scene inside his own chippy. There was the wide window with a central door, the familiar drinks fridge with a table next to it where a solitary customer sat, baseball-hatted and crouched over a newspaper. In the foreground, the round-shouldered Portuguese stirred the serving bins. Hash watched the big main door being pushed open hard, startling the seated man. Three men walked up to the counter. One of the trio made his way to the drinks fridge and immediately started tossing drinks to his friends, at the same time stuffing bottles into his pockets. The obscene hand gestures meant there was no need for a soundtrack.

'My client,' the counsel paused the video, pointing at the tattooed ringleader on the screen then across to the man in the dock, 'readily concedes his behaviour and that of his friends was unacceptable and is happy to compensate the proprietor in full.'

He pressed the play button and the screen jerked into action revealing the owner remonstrating with the leader. The customer in the baseball cap stood up and moved to the counter to fetch his serving, elbowing past the men. As he turned back, one of them smacked a hand underneath the wrapped chips sending the food into the air, then swung a punch at him. 'Again, your Worships, my client fully agrees that this was deplorable behaviour.'

The next few seconds of tape showed the three thugs crowding round the man, jabbing at him, one of them flipping his hat off. Hash saw Sean step back, arms akimbo, then carefully take his reading glasses off, putting them into a pocket. The Portuguese was waving his hands at the door, ordering them all to leave. In that brief instant Sean landed a punch on the tattooed man's face, sending him reeling against the drinks fridge. The court audience gasped at the speed and saw Sean step across and reach down for the man's throat. The victim, unable to break the one-handed grip, found himself being dragged through the doorway and out of the camera's reach. His two mates, cans in hand, looked at each other and went out after them. The camera now showed only the Portuguese proprietor, hands clasped on his head, flinching repeatedly as, one after the other, punched rag doll figures reeled and jerked back against the steamed-up window of the chippy.

'My client,' the counsel began, as he signalled the orderly to switch off the screen, 'failed to meet his bail conditions because he was in the General Hospital overnight, a matter put beyond his control due to the nature of his injuries, injuries so severe that at one point the surgeons feared for his life. The wounds are consistent with grievous bodily harm and I have informed the police. And asked them,' he held up a USB stick, 'to find the person who carried out this assault.' He paused, gripping his lapels. 'My client stands ready to atone for his mistakes but in respect of bail, your Worships, my argument remains that he is not a risk.' Hash watched the reporter scribbling, the beginning of a grin on his face. The female winger looked on, stony-faced.

Siddiq gestured to a booth at the far end of the restaurant and followed him a few seconds later. He eased onto the seat, sighing as he held his hand out in greeting.

'Are you ok?' Hash asked. 'Something wrong?' His friend looked tired and distracted.

He focused on Hash and sighed again. 'Very sad.'

'Look,' Hash began, 'I cannot thank Hakim enough. But he

gave me an opportunity to take Jim back. I couldn't waste that chance.'

Siddiq leaned his head forward onto his hands and began to massage his temples. When he stopped, he opened tired eyes and looked at Hash. 'Mr Hakim is very angry with me for bringing you and your trouble to him.'

'Does he still have any contact with Jim? How can I make the situation right with Hakim?'

'Look at this picture.' Siddiq pulled out his phone and flipped a finger across the screen, selecting the image and offering it to Hash. It showed him in the doorway on Stratford Road when he'd received Susan's call. He saw his own face, phone jammed to his ear. 'Hakim took this photo.'

Hash pushed back against the seat, handing the phone back. 'Where is he now? Can I speak with him?'

'He is too busy for you. He's too busy for me as well.'

'I can give the mosque more money.' Hash reached inside his jacket. 'How much?'

'He told me he saw your son with other people and your son was happy, playing games. He said your son has new friends.' Hash thought of the video, the two Arabs behind the windscreen and the executive car.

'What sort of friends? Boys his own age? Girls?'

'He did not say.'

'Then let me see photos of these friends and photos of Jim being happy with them.'

Siddiq shrugged his shoulders. 'Who knows what is true?' He snapped his fingers at one of his staff.

'Do you trust Hakim? Is he really helping me? Or is he holding Jim, trying to get money from me?' Siddiq rubbed at his tired eyes again as Hash continued, 'He isn't right about Jim and his new friends.'

Siddiq interrupted him. 'Mr Hakim says he found Jim, like you requested. And he told you to keep away until he had finished his part.' He silenced Hash who was about to interrupt. 'Because you do not understand the Asian community around here. Hakim is the expert. Nobody better than him.'

'That's why I…'

Siddiq silenced him as a waiter brought coffee and set it down. 'He told me he sent his drivers to look and they found your son with the people from the bad mosque.' He held up an admonishing finger to Hash. 'Bad people ruling this area. No police interest. British police do not protect.'

'Tell Hakim I was there to do good. I have a video of these so-called friends. Tell him,' Hash tapped his chest, 'tell him I insist on apologising in person, face to face, father to father. I will tell him I know Jim is with very bad people who are not his friends. Promise to do this for me.' He watched his friend digest the message and turn it over in his head. Then, with an almost imperceptible dip of his head, Siddiq indicated he would pass on the message.

'I will ask. Maybe the answer is yes, maybe no. I will ask.' He sat back, exhausted.

'Are you ok, Siddiq?'

'No, not okay.' He toyed with his phone, pushing it around the table surface.

'How's Anna? Is she not keeping you busy enough?'

'She's gone.' Siddiq's face crumpled as though he was about to cry. 'Gone away, to somewhere else.'

'When?'

'Last night.' Siddiq prodded at his phone. 'Yesterday she came back from all day shopping. Then she's on her phone, in her language but not nice words, I know…then boom! She's calling me names. My God, so angry, such terrible names, I did not know this Anna before.'

'Is she coming back?'

'So angry,' Siddiq continued, rubbing his eyes. 'And then she says she wants to marry me! Oh my God! When I tell her impossible,' he flicked both hands open, 'bang, explosion, terrible. Shouting, throwing things, hitting me…'

'Any damage?'

'Thank God no, I am alright. I loved her, so much. I thought she loved me.'

'I think you loved her body.'

'She liked you,' Siddiq said. 'She said you were an English gentleman, not an Arab, but like Johnny English.' He smiled weakly and pushed his phone away. 'Well, maybe she will come back. And if she doesn't, there'll be another out there. So many sexy women just waiting for a rich, handsome, young Bangladeshi tycoon.'

Hash shot Siddiq a sardonic look. 'How quickly you recover, my good friend.'

Settling in for the drive to Birmingham Airport, Sean clipped himself in. 'I can't believe they let the bastard walk,' he said.

'Believe me,' Hash said, 'the guy could barely stand. You're famous. Wonder if we should put it on YouTube.' He chuckled. 'And you're front page in the Echo. "Punch-up in chippy. Thug gets battered."'

'Nice one.'

'A really grainy photo, luckily,' Hash added.

'I saw the camera up on the wall,' Sean said. 'That's why I dragged him out. Funny thing with me and surveillance cameras.' He tapped out a cigarette. 'Mind if I burn one? Years on the streets, setting stuff up,' Sean continued, 'then years in the Kesh. Fucking cameras everywhere in that place.' He lit up. 'I'm probably on at least three street cameras outside but the light was bad and then the distance factor, and I had my cap back on.'

'Gustavo says you've got free fish and chips for life,' Hash said. 'He told the police they're looking for a Polish builder who comes from Gloucester. Good job there was no soundtrack.'

'Every cloud,' Sean murmured. 'Maybe it's better I'm off the streets for a bit.'

'Can't tell you how much shit I'm having to eat with that guy Hakim. He thinks I'm a liar and an idiot.'

'Do you think he's involved, knows the whole thing, playing both sides?'

'You videoed two Arabs,' Hash said. 'Arabs are Arabs and Asians…'

'Are Asians.' Sean finished the sentence. 'So what?'

'They don't like each other too much. If we saw Arabs with Jim, then they'll be run by other Arabs. I'm thinking maybe they're on the Asian turf under sufferance, some sort of arrangement.'

'And you think Hakim is the Asian arrangement?'

Hash looked over at his companion. 'He's an obvious place to start. He seems to be a big noise and he'll have his area and his reputation. And his competition, of course. But then, maybe he's a genuine good guy trying to tell me to keep out of his way.'

'That's what you want to believe, he's really a good guy?'

'He seems to be more concerned with doing the job I asked him to do.'

'Don't mind me,' Sean said, 'it's the cynic in me.'

'By the way, Siddiq's been dumped by his blonde nymphomaniac.'

'Jesus. I take it you congratulated him on his luck,' said Sean, grinning.

'He was heartbroken,' Hash said. 'But briefly.' He looked across and was surprised to see Sean's eyes closed, his face contorted. 'You ok? Want me to stop?'

Sean waved the offer away. 'Just a twinge,' he said. 'Get them from time to time.'

'Where?'

'In the chest.' He thumped himself gently. 'Have to bump start the lungs these days, you know.'

'Maybe you overdid it in the chippy,' Hash said.

'I've had a few tests,' Sean said.

'What tests?'

'I had a whole battery of them before I came over,' Sean said. 'Things stuck up me, down me. Stuff sucked out, pumped in and swallowed a ton of shit for them to X-ray.'

He held up his packet of cigarettes, 'Started smoking Gallaher's Plain as soon as I could steal them from the old boy. Been puffing ever since. You don't need the brains of an archbishop to work it out.'

'Is it bad?'

'That's what they'll be telling me when I go to see them, if I can be bothered.'

'What do you mean?'

'Maybe I don't want to know.' Sean took another drink. 'Just carry on in my own sweet way and take my punishment when it's due.' He looked evenly at Hash. 'Prioritise, that's what you like to say.'

'Well then, your health has to come first.'

'Jim comes first,' Sean said. 'I had my chances long ago and I screwed it all up.'

'Yes, but if you need treatment you've got to have it,' Hash said.

'Let's change the subject. What news from our friends in Libya?'

'Silent as the bloody grave. I can practically hear their minds ticking. Like I said, I told them their candidate disappeared. I'm standing by for the next order.'

'What do you think they'll do?'

'Fuck knows. They'll have a big, long think, no immediate panic reaction. That gives us time.' He looked at Sean. 'Get yourself sorted out and come back.'

'What happens if Hakim sees Jim again?'

'Maybe we get him to take us in.'

'What if they're armed, these Arabs?' Sean asked.

'They will be. And so will we.'

SUNDAY 15TH MARCH

Hakim watched the video in silence. Hash let the scene play once through. On the second showing, he froze the screen, tapping on Jim's face. 'Sayyid Hakim,' he said, careful to be respectful, 'that is my son. I cannot thank you enough for getting me this close to rescuing him. Surely you cannot be angry that I tried.'

Hakim made no response, his eyes on Jim's face.

'I took your photo and made the connection to this part of Birmingham. It was easy. Maybe if your drivers let me go with them next time.' Hash was pleading now. 'Or maybe I stay closer than Cheltenham and they fetch me as soon as they see Jim.'

Hakim shook his head, still saying nothing. Hash tried again. 'Where's the harm? If your men had got through to me sooner, as soon as the photo was confirmed, then maybe we could have succeeded.'

'Succeeded?' Hakim spoke at last, his beard quivering with anger. 'You are a fool and you do not understand what success is. Success for you is when you take your son home after he ran away. This is not success for me.'

'I don't understand,' Hash began, but Hakim's fist banged down on the table.

'This is clear, that you do not understand,' he spat. 'You Arab people, all the same. Lazy, stupid, throwing big money around, giving orders.' His finger trembled as it pointed at Hash. 'You want us to clean up your mess. You bring it to our area, to poison our happy community. We have schools, mosques, business, clinics and then,' he stabbed in Hash's direction, 'we get the Arabs, like a cancer to our system. These people say it's Jihad, say it in the mosques, but these people are not Muslims and do not know true Jihad.' He looked across at Siddiq for agreement. 'Then the trouble starts, and where are the Arabs? They run away,' he answered his own question. 'They run away, and they leave their shit behind. Tell me, Sayyid Hashmi,' Hakim mocked, 'where you come from, in Saudi, did you have Pakistani slaves to clean up your shit?'

'I come from Jordan,' Hash lied. 'My family is not wealthy. I've never been to Saudi. You can ask Siddiq how I made my money, how I do business.' He gestured to his friend. 'He can speak for me, knows I work hard and knows I am not a bad man.' Hash held his hands up to Hakim. 'I hate these clowns in Daesh, Al Qaeda. I would kill them myself if I could.'

'You think you can ask my help with your money,' Hakim snapped his fingers. 'Just like that. Bring your problem, make it my problem. When you're gone and it's still my problem, then what will you do for me?'

'Tell me what you want me to do, Sayyid Hakim, tell me and I'll do my best.'

'I gave you my orders to stay away and let me do the job, but you pushed in when I had only a little information. Your action could have killed your son. We saw you easily when you came here yesterday.' He pointed the same finger at Hash. 'My drivers, they have a photo of you as well as your son. You want to know why?' Hash waited. 'Because I tell them you will do something stupid, frighten the Arabs. And make them do something stupid.'

'I was doing what any father would do,' Hash protested.

'By getting in the way, you are making more problems for my men.' But Hakim's voice was losing its bite. 'My men have the face of your son, they found them, they found the mosque and now they want to get the location where he is staying.' He eased back on his chair at last. 'This takes time and patience, and they are busy men, self-employed.' He tapped the table. 'Losing taxi customers by doing this task.'

'For sure. I'll pay them for their time,' Hash said.

'I will come to you when I have the full picture. Then I will hand it over to you, so you can pretend you did it all.'

'I don't follow,' Hash said.

'You can tell the police how you,' he stabbed at Hash again, 'and only you, found your son. I do not need police, immigration or other Arabs looking for me.'

'That is why I went there yesterday,' Hash interrupted again, 'to do the job and get my son away, not to cause you trouble.'

'You are an Arab, with money, who wants everything quickly. You are trouble. You can kill your son if you wish, but don't involve me anymore.' Hakim resumed his sphinx-like persona. 'Show me the video again.'

Hash played the clip once more and Hakim made him repeat it. 'Not enough information,' he concluded.

'What is missing?'

'In the video,' said Hakim with laboured patience, 'how many men with your camera?'

'Two men, Arabs, and my son. In a BMW, and they must be going to the Racing Festival in Cheltenham. It's the only one happening. They had some food from Chicken Hut and my son has a toy helicopter on his lap.'

'Is there a third man?'

'He's in the back seat, beside my son.'

'Are you sure?'

'He must be.'

'No, he's not.' In the silence that followed Hash ran the video again and watched the BMW sweep past, followed by two cars obscuring its plates.

'So, Mr Hashmi, my next question. Who is beside your son?' He folded both his hands on the table and waited. Hash groped for an answer but came up with a helpless shrug.

'There is a lady sitting beside your son, making sure he does not try to jump out.'

'A woman?'

'Yes, a woman.' Hakim had dropped the ironic courtesy. 'Your son is being looked after by two men and sometimes a woman. There is a mosque where they sometimes go with your son, but not with the woman. But so far, the house they keep the boy in is the missing part of the jigsaw.'

'I had no idea...' Hash murmured.

'An unknown woman,' Hakim continued, 'but she's the one in charge. The others, including your son, are all afraid of her. Mr Hashmi, tell me, have you ever seen Arabs afraid of a woman?' A flicker of satisfaction played on Hakim's face. 'I think you can agree with me, now, that if you had not been so lucky on this occasion then things could have gone much worse for your son?'

Hash had no words, so Hakim continued. 'We agreed to do this for you, as one Muslim to another, one father to another, to use your words. Then I asked to be left alone. You broke your word. So now, what am I to do?'

It was a small consolation that Sean's presence had not been mentioned: he was still below Hakim's radar. 'Please don't give up on us,' he replied. 'We can't rescue Jim without you and your men. But this woman, who is she? Have you got a photograph of her?'

Hakim's finger was instantly in the air. 'Any interference and we cancel what we are doing for you.'

'But a description at least,' Hash pleaded, 'for me to work on.'

'Most times she's in a burqa with full niqab and not even we can get a clue. But one exception was this day. She dressed in Western clothes.'

18

PLASMA HOTEL, TRIPOLI, LIBYA. SUNDAY 29TH MARCH

Frequent power cuts had made regular electricity and air conditioning a dream for most of Tripoli's inhabitants. With the remorseless temperature rises of late March and the humidity keeping pace, only the offshore breezes staved off total misery. Plasma Hotel on the Omar al Mukhtar road was an oasis, struggling to maintain pre-Revolution standards of luxury. It owed its survival to the need for a central, neutral location where players from all factions could meet with discretion, and without the risk of being murdered.

Two men, one an elderly, white-haired, elegant figure of some seventy-five years, the other his younger aide, had arrived early to prepare for such a meeting. The pair, both wearing stylish suits, inspected the rooms they had hired, enjoying the cool air. The aide set aside his jacket and got to work checking for hidden eavesdropping devices with practised ease. As members of Libyan Intelligence, the Mukhabarat, it was a task both men had performed many times earlier in their careers. Search completed, they sat on the overstuffed sofa and called room service for refreshments.

'Have we got this under control?' the older man asked as they settled in to wait.

'We've given him a "laissez-passer" and an armed escort to bring him in,' the aide responded, 'and to get him out of the city afterwards, back to Daesh lines.'

'And the agenda?' the older man said.

His aide extracted a notebook, opened it, and squinted at his jottings. He looked from the pages to his boss. 'Last communiqué was two days ago. Plus, a full report brought out by the letterbox team,' he listed. 'We have our man's side of the story. The retard of a martyr lost his nerve, ran away with the money, left the bombs behind. Given the sort of people we're dealing with,' he tapped the side of his head, 'cuckoo, brainless, it could be true enough.'

'The man had a change of heart, wanted to live. He couldn't have been that stupid. Do we believe our man?'

'Our man sensed a problem when the Daesh player started showing signs of stress, maybe questioning his motivation after seeing life in England. The guy started demanding things he shouldn't have. Drink, women....' The aide shrugged.

The elder dismissed the rationale. 'That's all very well but I'm about to be asked about our damage control measure. Details, please.'

'Our man has put out feelers to his contacts in the Asian community. They run the asylum racket in that part of England. The thinking is that the defector surfaces somewhere on their radar and then we get him back.'

'And if that doesn't work? I'll be asked that.'

'Then our agent says the police will get to him sooner or later.'

'Let's hope it's later. Why did they send someone like that?' the old man asked, looking at his watch.

'Our man's good to go again.' The aide continued. 'Asking

us what to do, now the school holiday's coming to an end.'

'Aah, the boy,' the older gentleman said. 'Lord Jim. Was that from Kipling, or Conrad?' he thought aloud in English.

'It's what his grandparents call him,' the aide said.

'How is that young man?'

'The team keep him healthy and busy, but of course he asks for his father.'

'How do they keep a fifteen-year-old occupied?'

'He has a hobby, toy aircraft. Apparently, he prefers them to friends.'

The older man considered this. 'Good. Is he a clever boy?'

'It seems so.'

'The whole damned operation should have been over by now, of course,' the older man said. 'He should already be back with his father.'

The doorbell went; his aide went to the door and took the small tray from the waiter. When he carried it back to his boss, the old man said, 'Why the hell did they change the target at the last minute? Complete madness.'

'Amateurs. Although our team said it came as no surprise to the Daesh woman on the day,' the aide said, twisting the cap on a plastic bottle and pouring two glasses of cold water. 'She must have had a prearranged schedule with her bomber. They both knew what was going on. Cheltenham reports the man showed no interest in GCHQ from the start.'

'I can understand them, up to a point,' the old man said quietly.

'It's how operations fall apart,' the aide said, 'when you start throwing amateurs into the mix.'

The old man took the glass and then shook his head as if try-ing to order unruly thought processes. 'We're stuck. We can't go back or go forward until our ISIS clients,' he nodded towards the door as if expecting their guest to enter, 'our Daesh friends, decide what they want us to do next.'

'We're good to go at the UK end. No compromise yet.'

'Why have they put a woman on the ground?' the old man asked. 'Given their attitude to women,it's unusual, isn't it?'

The aide shrugged again. 'Ask him when he gets here. Our team say she's a really tough bitch, a psycho, not much of a mother figure.'

'Where are they now?'

'Safe house in the Midlands, under our control. That's our side of the deal.'

'Just keep the boy safe and the father's hopes alive.' He waved a thin hand out across the rooftopsof Tripoli. 'It always comes down to one thing. Family.'

They waited. Half an hour into a game of Italian football, the reception clerk rang to say their guest was on his way up. The aide immediately ordered refreshments and went to the door, holding it open to keep watch. The lift disgorged its only passenger. A short, slim man emerged dressed in jeans and scuffed brown leather shoes, a waistcoat over his plain white shirt, one of the multi-pocketed variety favoured by aid workers and journalists. In his mid- thirties, he was a few years younger than the aide with the shaved head and long, unkempt beard of a zealot; there was a central smudge of darkened skin above his brow from constantly resting his forehead on the ground whilst at prayer.

He was conducting an animated conversation on his phone as he advanced into the room and pointedly ignored the aide's greetings. Instead, and without making eye contact, he offered a limp hand to both his hosts. He sat where directed, still talking and took out a set of amber prayer beads, flicking them through his fingers. When he finally put the phone down, the older man began the polite, soothing ritual that precedes every Arab meeting: enquiries about health, family and news, addressing their visitor as 'Sayyid Director'.

The ISIS man, still looking at his phone, irritably cut him

off. 'Just tell me what happened.'

The old man, already tense despite his outward sangfroid, stiffened with annoyance at the abruptness.

The visitor compounded his breach of etiquette with, 'We supplied our agents, you promised to deliver them to the target, but nothing happened and my side,' he held up his phone, 'needs an explanation.' He sat back, playing with the beads, watching the two men opposite. 'A lot of promises, and now nothing.' He cupped his free hand to his ear insolently. 'An explanation please?'

'You will get it, of course,' the older man said, 'but they might not like it.' He paused, maintaining his mask of politeness. 'The first thing you can say is that we,' he tapped his striped tie and pointed to his aide, 'were working on an agreed target for you but you switched, at the last moment and without informing us.'

The guest said nothing.

The older man continued. 'We were under the impression we were working with professionals,' he held the guest's gaze coolly, 'but it seems that was naïve of us. Your side,' he jabbed a finger at the man's phone, 'doesn't know much about the complexity of this game, which is why you came to us in the first place.'

The guest listened as the old man continued. 'We offered you an insight into our network, and a demonstration as a gesture of our goodwill in the deal. But how were we to know the first person you would send in would be an idiot?'

The aide hid a smile, noting the Daesh man's growing discomfort. 'A man who,' the older man continued, flicking an imaginary piece of lint from his shirt, 'has now snatched the money and gone missing in the West of Britain. Perhaps you don't have anyone better. Of all the problems we anticipated,' he shook his head in mock bewilderment, 'we did not see this one coming.'

The guest raised a hand, stalling the speaker and took up his phone, concentrating on an incoming message. After a few seconds he put the phone on the table and looked up again, waiting.

'All your man had to do was sit back, enjoy the ride to the target and then blow himself to pieces,' the older man resumed. 'Instead, he appears to get a taste for alcohol and discovers that sex with Kufar women is much better than it is with goats.' He pointed at the phone in the guest's hand. 'Changing the target at the last moment without telling your partners is an appalling breach of all the rules. Only amateurs do it.' He leaned back in his seat. 'That's the explanation. Under normal circumstances we would be the ones demanding clarification. And an apology.'

The guest was smiling, pleased at having riled his hosts. 'Who told you all that?' He looked at his prayer beads as he spoke. 'This bullshit about our man running away. Your man on the ground? Maybe your man on the ground is a liar, trying to cover his own lazy backside.'

'Our man has a pedigree of excellence. I've known him for years, directed him in operations in Ireland before I transferred him to the UK to build the file on the GCHQ target, the one we'd agreed to hand to you on a plate. But,' he held his hand up, 'I recognise your point, which is why, as you know, we keep his son as a guarantee.'

'The absconder will have his family punished as well if it's true,' the Daesh man offered. 'They will forfeit their blood payment.'

'Hardly the same,' the aide said. 'The son is a guarantee of compliance, not a punishment. Unless things go wrong.'

'They did go wrong.'

'Because you switched the target. No fault on our side,' the aide said.

'Enough, gentlemen,' the older man interrupted. 'Can we please get back to the proposal, make a deal for the provision of services.' He pointed at the guest's phone. 'Forgive me, but I have to ask. Am I speaking to the right person, here?'

'You're speaking to the Director of European Operations,' the guest answered coldly, 'and I am the right person.'

'Then you knew all along,' the aide insisted. 'We agreed on a high-profile target for the demonstration of our capability. Wasn't GCHQ good enough?'

'Maybe your choice of target was too easy,' the Daesh man said.

'It could only look easy to amateurs,' the aide muttered.

The guest shrugged off the counterpunch, 'Our privilege,' he said. 'We changed the target at the last minute because you Mukhabarat are singing from yesterday's song sheet. Our choice would have been much more sensational, more dead Kufar in the newspapers. Even if we had told you, what real difference would it have made to your man? He's just the taxi driver.'

'Maybe so,' the aide conceded, 'But without us knowing, with no authenticating procedures in place...' He paused. 'Our agents do not switch targets, just like that.' He snapped his fingers. 'That's not how it works.'

'That is how it works if we're doing business,' the Daesh man said.

'Are we still doing business?' the older man asked.

'Have you got another client out there somewhere?'

'Your side needs to understand. We're now running two operations for you and the meter's ticking. Your martyr is running around the West Midlands with an erection and too much money. He doesn't speak English so he's almost certainly dependent on third parties by now for food, shelter, all the essentials. And that's before he splashes out on prostitutes.' He paused, holding his glass out for more water. 'We have to get our man on his track fast and shut him down before the others get to him.'

'The others?'

'The Kufar, the enemy,' the aide said, his tone ironic. 'Unfortunately for all of us, none of them are amateurs. The British police, immigration authorities, MI5, MI6, and then there's the asylum industry in that particular area.'

'How long will it take you to find him?'

'We need to give our man time. He's tapping into his contacts.'

'What'll you do if you find him?' the ISIS Director asked.

'When we find him,' the old man said, 'he'll disappear. But he'll spend his last hours wishing he had stuck to the plan and gone to paradise the easy way.'

The doorbell brought the aide to his feet to allow a waiter in with refreshments. Plates of sliced fruit were placed on the coffee table; the waiter set small glass tumblers in front of each man and began to pour sweet red tea from a silver jug. There was silence until he had finished and left. The guest murmured a blessing on the food and took his pick from the plate.

Speaking in more congenial tones, the older man resumed. 'That target had been prepared for years, you know. Weapons were in place and it would have been a guaranteed success in terms of showcasing Daesh's ability to strike deeply and surgically. It would have impressed the world.' He held his tea glass up. 'But you're the client and if you want a different target, better you tell us and we work on it together.' He put down his empty glass. 'Tell your side that when we see all the arrangements are still in place, we're still in business with you. We have the system, the agent and the support. All of it still in position, uncompromised. It all belongs to you afterwards, of course. We hand it over intact. That's still the deal on the table.'

The guest digested the words, saying nothing, playing with his beads.

The older man made his final pitch. 'Either we stick to GCHQ, and go again, or we go for a target we all agree on.' He held up a finger. 'One you will really like. Either way, as a gesture of our continued goodwill, we will send one of our own martyrs on this new mission, one we choose, who will do the job, play to the final whistle, so to speak.'

The Daesh man's eyes became more alert, switching from one suited man to the other. 'All of which sounds too good and means you want more money.'

The old man replied evenly, 'You switched from a military target to a mass attack at a famous venue. Cheltenham Racecourse. I see your thinking now that we've talked.' His hands balanced the options. 'Government infrastructure, their cyber hub, versus mass civilian deaths and a very soft target, members of the establishment present, the British royalty?'

The Daesh man interrupted, 'How much?'

'We want double,' the old man said. 'One target, done properly, taking out a member of the royal family as well as hundreds of Kufar, is worth double. If your team,' his tone softened, 'had done their homework on Cheltenham they would have known their chances of a senior royal being at the Cheltenham races on that day were minimal and their chance of getting a martyr right alongside were zero. They could have pulled off an attack of sorts, but that would have been our last chance gone.' He leaned forward in his chair. 'We know the systems in England. Double the money gets you a member of the royal family.'

'Who? The Queen?'

'We don't know, yet. We haven't seen the court diary or the invitation lists. Yet. If you agree, then we will choose the time and the place. Your side fits in with the plan. We'll only get one clear shot.'

'Gaddafi's men,' the guest said softly. 'Now you're all businessmen.'

The old man inclined his head, leaning forward. 'We set up these networks to combat Libya's enemies. It took years, cost tens of millions. We lost good people and still,' he tapped the table, 'still we've got good people in place. The Americans, the Russians and the British haven't brought us down. Gaddafi's gone' his voice slowed, 'and they're your enemies now, aren't they? We're still in the game and we can run the biggest attack the world has ever seen, just for you, my friend. Don't tell me you're not interested.'

'I budgeted five million dollars,' the guest said.

'Ten is small change to your bankers in the Caliphate. Look at what you're getting. You want us to pull this off for you, you want it to shock the world and make history?'

The Daesh man said nothing.

'Your silence tells me you're interested.' The older man put the tips of his fingers together and contemplated his visitor.

'We need to insure it.'

'That sounds like a condition,' said the aide.

'Conditions,' the guest said. 'You want my support and this,' he pointed at his phone, 'is a European operation. Here's how it'll work. You'll insert your martyr, but my team leader takes over and because I'm not happy with the lies from Cheltenham, the boy comes under my direct control.'

'It will slow things down,' the aide objected.

'It's the only deal on the table,' the Daesh man said.

'And the target?' the older man asked. 'Can we at least agree on that?'

'As you propose, we target British royalty at a public event to ensure mass casualties.' The two Mukhabarat men waited. 'And I will want to check your martyr,' the guest said, standing up, signalling the meeting was over. 'My team leader will need to induct him. Send him across to us in Sirte. I'll have my personal escort ensure he gets through. We'll put him through our system.'

'Your system?' the aide asked.

'Briefing on the target environment, but not the actual target. We'll run him through our acclimatisation phase.'

'Acclimatisation,' the aide snorted.

'And the last donkey actually passed all that?' The older man said.

'Once I've transferred the funds, you'll see it my way,' the

Daesh man responded.

'And we'll need to see whoever you're sending in as commander,' the aide fought back. 'Check his cover, get him to fit in, make sure he's not a classmate of our missing friend.'

'You'll find she has all the papers and cover she needs,' the Director said.

TRIPOLI OUTSKIRTS. SATURDAY 4TH APRIL

The instructors ordered the exhausted men to form a three-sided square with the open side against the camp headquarters hut, then bellowed at them to start jogging on the spot. The men chanted as they obeyed, hands thrust forward, arms outstretched, knees pumping to the barked cadence of the chief instructor, himself soaked in perspiration. Poised directly above them like an executioner's sword, the sun burned their exposed, perspiring and bruised flesh. Tortured lungs could only breathe in dust and hot air and, knowing the hour of midday prayer must be near, the longing shared by all the men was to hear the static crackling from the mosque loudspeakers. Midday prayers meant shade, water, and relief. Abruptly, suspiciously early, the chief instructor brought the drill to an end.

He walked down the first rank, selecting one man by tapping him on the shoulder and jerking a thumb behind him towards the square of bleached sand. He moved along the next rank without selecting anyone, then turned up the third rank and made another selection. By the time he reached the end of the line he had two men facing each other in the centre of the sandy square. His barked order saw them taking up a stance, ready for unarmed combat. He turned towards the Portakabin HQ where a tired air-conditioner hummed and clattered, pumping frigid air at the two Mukhabarat inside. They watched, through windows speckled with dust and fly spots, as the spectacle unfolded. The white-haired man stood, supported by a walking stick, his innate elegance undisturbed by the heat and dust. He was smoking and observing the scene with thoughtful interest. His aide, wearing his suit with less comfort, looked intently at the two men on the square and made notes of comparison in a folder. The chief instructor nodded at the window, assuming authority to proceed.

Turning to his charges, the chief shouted 'Bousaif!'. Neither of the two moved but a third, in the second rank, stiffened to attention. The use of a name was unusual; it hinted at respect, a commodity sparingly bestowed in the Special Forces camp. They were universally known as 'brothers' and addressed each other as 'my brother'. The only exception was the chief instructor who was simply 'Chief'. The man answering to Bousaif, medium-height, stocky with broad shoulders and a shaven head, now stepped forward and the chief ordered the men to fight, two to one, against him. The ranks burst into roars of support as the teamed pair, exchanging glances, stalked warily towards Bousaif, their boots scuffing up sand as they moved.

He waited, crouched in a posture both defensive and confident, rolling his shoulders to loosen them; his hands, held high like a boxer's, opened and closed ready to grapple. His legs were bent and braced apart. His crouch made him appear much shorter than either of his adversaries who now separated, circling to take him from two sides. Bousaif waited for a few seconds before retreating quickly towards the nearest rank of cheering men, using them as a wall to keep his assailants from getting behind him.

As one of the pair came close, Bousaif went for him, barrelling him and turning him into the line, tumbling him in the confusion and landing on him knees first, flinging sand and grit in his face, and jabbing punches at his eyes and throat as he tried to protect himself. Bousaif jerked upright onto his feet, then drove two merciless kicks into the man's ribs. If the watching Mukhabarat men heard the howl of pain, they showed no sympathy. Spinning away from the prostrate figure, sensing his companion had to be only inches away, he lashed out with a sweeping punch, just missing his man. The ranks roared and cheered his fighting instinct as he skipped into the centre of the square and waited. The first man stayed down, shaking his face clear of sand, hands holding damaged ribs.

His teammate took his eyes off his opponent long enough to glance across and realise there would be no help from his mate. Bousaif crabbed towards him, reaching out to snag him in a powerful hold. The man found his retreat blocked by a wall of yelling onlookers who thrust him back. There was a blur of movement as the two men closed, and an audible snap as Bousaif's forehead made contact with his opponent's face. With gasps from the onlookers, he folded. Bousaif stood over him, poised to deliver the killer kicks, frozen by a command.

As a modicum of recognition to the victor, the chief walked over and took Bousaif's right hand, raising it to the onlookers in the Portakabin, to the cheers of the rows of spectators. At that moment, the loudspeaker on the roof began to crackle with the call to prayer and the chief gave the orders releasing the men to their devotions.

Entering the Portakabin, he greeted the two men and stood to attention. 'Bousaif,' he announced, 'awaits your orders.'

'Tell him he grows his hair and shaves his beard from now on,' the aide said.

'English?' the older man asked.

'His papers say he has good English and French, sir,' said the aide looking at his folder. 'We'll get that tested.'

His boss nodded, still pensive, smoke rising from his cigarette. 'Where has he served?'

Glancing at the folder again to check, the aide said, 'Cut his teeth in Algeria, moved on to counter-intelligence in Europe...'

'Where exactly?'

'Rome first, then Vienna. He ran with a surveillance team in Southern Europe, keeping an eye on our problems.'

'Aah,' the older man murmured, irony in his tone, 'enemies of our beloved homeland.' He jabbed his walking stick at the distance outside the window. 'Most recent operation?'

'Iraq, with a team in Basra, operating against the Shia.'

Satisfied, the older man switched tack. 'That will please our Daesh friends. His degree?'

'Political Science at Tripoli.'

The older man thought for a few seconds before pointing to the now empty parade ground. 'How religious?'

'He's a good Muslim.'

'Have him ready,' said the old man. 'I'll send someone for him.'

EVENING – MONDAY 6TH APRIL

The summons from the chief came after Maghreb prayers.

'Salaams, Bousaif. How are you? Well, insh'Allah.'

Bousaif responded with a cautious, 'Well, thanks be to God. How can I help you?'

The chief pulled a packet of cigarettes from his pocket and lit up. 'Go and get ready. You leave in five minutes. Do not tell any of your companions.'

Within minutes, well before the chief had finished his cigarette, Bousaif returned carrying a sports bag. The instructor took it and, still smoking, trailed his free hand through the modest contents. His expression changed from boredom to interest as he extracted a small plastic photograph album. He held it up and then steadied it on the table, to flick through each of the pages, looking at each image, smiling when he recognised the man standing in front of him. He puzzled briefly at one image, an old black and white of a family group.

'My family,' Bousaif explained.

The chief grunted, dropped the album into the sports bag and handed it back to Bousaif. He ordered him to follow, pushing the door open with his foot and flicking the glowing butt into the dark.

He set off across the sandy square with Bousaif in tow. They walked in silence out to the brightly lit chain link fence and its imposing double gate. An armed guard keyed the padlock, swung one of the heavy gates back and watched as the chief led Bousaif out. A Mercedes saloon waiting in the darkness came to life as the driver switched on the engine and, with only sidelights on, purred across the compacted sand towards them. The driver emerged, greeting the chief quietly, with a smile and an embrace. Taking Bousaif's bag, he introduced himself as 'Manager' and pointed him to the passenger's seat.

Bousaif felt a tap on the shoulder as he was about to duck into the car. Turning, he was surprised to find himself embraced. 'May God go with you, my brother,' said the chief

He settled back in his seat, enjoying the smell of leather and hiss of air conditioning, hearing locks click and, as the vehicle began to roll, took a last look at his compound. He watched the chief walking back, silhouetted by the fence lights, the sports bag slung on his shoulder. He'd suspected some trick like this and smiled as he felt for the family photograph he'd slipped out of the little album earlier. His talisman and only reminder of another life lay against his skin. It was too dark to check it, but the feel of its glossy surface gave him strength.

They'd picked up an escort within minutes of the Mercedes pulling clear of the camp and setting course for the lights of Tripoli. Two crewed pickup trucks with machine guns mounted followed behind, driving without lights. The Manager beside him chuckled quietly. 'You're a VIP now.'

Many hours later, with dawn breaking, Bousaif woke. The swaying and jerking of the vehicle had stopped and a conversation was taking place outside; they'd reached the perimeter check-point of a military base. Ghardabiya Airbase proclaimed itself from a bullet-pocked wall. That meant Sirte, and Daesh territory.

The airport infrastructure was familiar enough: a terminal building, control tower and hangars, all damaged by war. Walls had been splashed by rockets and stitched by machine gun fire, plate glass was missing from windows and vehicle wreckage of all sorts, both military and civilian, was scattered around. The Mercedes crunched across the debris and nosed between cargo sheds, passing the hulks of jets and helicopters, mostly casualties of the fighting stretched out along the tarmac. One aircraft in civilian livery, twin-engine with its propellers turning, was in the process of taxiing from the runway to a berth amongst its derelict companions.

The car drew up at the crash-rescue station, a single-storey blockhouse with three fire tenders lined up on parade. A figure appeared in the doorway of the fire station, greeted the Manager with a wordless thumbs-up and pointed round the side. The Mercedes moved on in that direction, halting in front of a cluster of Portakabins. Both men got out now, walking the stiffness out of their legs. The Manager led his charge into the small complex and began a tour, pointing out dining room, classroom and briefing room before opening a door and bidding him enter his own room. He pointed at fresh clothes on the comfortable bed and sandals underneath, telling Bousaif to change and drop his old clothes in the basket, 'for burning.' Gesturing to the shower, he invited him to join the team in the garden for breakfast after he had washed and prayed and left.

Bousaif sat on the bed, amazed at its softness and fresh smell. The room was like a hotel suite. He lifted the clothes off the bed. His new clothes were tracksuit bottoms and a Chelsea football shirt.

After a long shower, Bousaif emerged from his room, self-conscious in the sports strip. He'd become so used to being marched in a squad that making his own way, in his own time, felt strange.

The noise of conversation led him to the rear of the complex where a small oasis had been coaxed from the sandy soil. Bougainvillea walled the square in mixtures of pink and white blossom. Four well-trimmed date palms marked the corners and tied to them, at about fifteen feet, hung a canopy of cam-ouflage netting. A garland of light bulbs on a cable had been strung diagonally across the square under the netting; an elec-tric mosquito killer with three purple-lit bars hung off one corner. It snapped and crackled as insects committed suicide. There was a brick barbecue stand at one edge accompanied by a bar, complete with beer pumps and bar stools. Four strangers seated at a wooden trestle table stopped in mid-conversation to look at Bousaif.

The Manager was standing behind the bar preparing a tray of food. He looked up with a broad smile and pointed to the trestle table where three men and a woman now stood ready to greet him. Bousaif was unused to such courtesy after the long weeks of grinding in the Special Forces camp, and the presence of a woman took him aback for a moment. She was dressed in the traditional black burqa, her hands covered by long, black gloves, and a niqab over her face which left only her eyes vis-ible. Two of the men wore the football strip and tracksuit uni-form, and the third was dressed in slightly less casual European clothes.

He heard his name announced by the Manager, who indi-cated the group, saying, 'We all speak English from now on. This is the Director.'

The man in European clothes nodded. He was slim, with a thin, straggly beard in contrast to his expensive open-necked shirt. The limp hand he offered to Bousaif was decorated with a Rolex and smelled of cologne. He sat down immediately after the handshake and fished out his phone and prayer beads. 'Director of European Operations, he's our boss,' the Manager explained. The man barely glanced up, already checking his messages.

'These two gentlemen are ManCity and Gunner.' The Manager pronounced the nicknames carefully in English. 'Their job is to instruct you in the ways of the British while you are here.'

The two men presented themselves, hands outstretched. ManCity was slightly built, with Asian looks, and the Gunner had a mix of Caucasian and African in him. They studied Bousaif warily. He guessed they were in their mid-twenties, much younger than him. The Gunner said, 'Alright mate?' as he shook hands.

'Umm Ali,' the Manager indicated the woman, 'is your team commander for the mission. She's just back from England, here especially to meet you.' The woman had sat down straight away and remained seated, not bothering to offer a handshake but dipping her head in acknowledgement. On the twin-engine plane that had been taxiing to its berth when they arrived, Bousaif thought. He was aware of scrutiny from all of them. The woman's pale blue eyes, framed by the black material, stayed on Bousaif longest until she seemed to lose interest and turned her gaze instead to the Manager. He hurried back behind the bar and soon laid a tray of bread, honey and boiled eggs on the table before disappearing into the kitchen. The Gunner offered a cigarette. Bousaif declined.

'At least he doesn't smoke, like you two,' the Director said, looking up from his phone, his manicured hands theatrically wafting the smoke away.

Bousaif sat, as he'd been told, and waited.

'Where did you learn your English?' the Director demanded.

'The basics from school, some at university,' Bousaif said.

The Director was unimpressed; Umm Ali said nothing.

The Gunner chipped in nervously, 'No problem, mate. A little's good enough to work with.' He glanced at ManCity for support. 'As long as you've got grammar, happy days innit. We'll work on the vocabulary the next four weeks.'

Bousaif made the obvious deduction about the length of his

stay in this small slice of Paradise.

Keen not to be left out, ManCity added, 'So our job's to get you sound for moving around in England. We'll work with whatever you got, don't you worry.' He pointed at the Gunner. 'We've both lived in England. In fact,' he seemed encouraged by the thought, and sat a bit taller, 'in case you didn't already catch on, we're British.'

'We were British,' the Gunner corrected. 'We volunteered for the Jihad, did our bit on the front line, but we've got important skills, see? So now we help with the acclimatisation programme.'

The Director interrupted. 'They will school you on every-day British talk, habits, politics, likes and dislikes.' He wrapped the beads around his index finger. 'They will talk about every-day things you will not know about. And you will specifically concentrate on horse-racing. The emphasis is on blending into a particular scenario.'

'Not standing out or drawing attention because you're a stranger,' ManCity repeated sternly. 'Could give yourself and the whole mission away.'

'When you're new in Britain it's easy to make mistakes and get noticed, innit,' Gunner butted in nervously, not wanting to miss the chance to impress the Director. 'The Kufar get right nosy if you don't watch your step, especially the women.'

'Before we deploy you,' the Director nodded towards the woman, 'she will approve or disapprove you. Only then will you be moved into Britain for the mission.'

'When do I learn my mission?' Bousaif asked.

'When I'm ready to tell you about it.' Umm Ali spoke for the first time. Her voice was monotone, the accent from some-where in Europe. Studying Bousaif with an intensity that made him uncomfortable, she added, 'The last Shaheed scheduled for this mission disappeared just after we moved him into the English safe house.'

'We think he got demotivated.' The Gunner sounded

defensive. 'With us, here in the camp,' he gestured around the enclosure, 'he was strong, committed, y'know. But he must've got corrupted by the temptations of Kufar life in England.'

'That's what we mean about vulnerability,' ManCity said. 'He lost the plot.'

'See what I mean about Kufar women?' Gunner tried some levity. 'He was badly handled on the ground,' the Director observed, looking up from his phone. 'He was struggling to acclimatise, and he could not communicate.'

'He was a thick as shit idiot and whoever passed him fit for his mission was an ass,' Umm Ali said. ManCity and the Gunner squirmed as she continued, stabbing a gloved finger at the Director who was pointedly looking back down at his phone, 'and you gave him more money than his entire village had ever seen in their lives.' Her accent was making her hard for Bousaif to place; maybe Bosnian, definitely a Muslim but not an Arab. She jerked a thumb over her shoulder. 'So, he did what any self-respecting Afghan would do. Obeyed his natural instincts, grabbed the money and disappeared.'

'His village won't be seeing the martyr's bounty,' the Gunner said.

'Sayyid Bousaif,' the Director silenced them, 'the mission will go again, with you as Shaheed and against a significant British target. We will succeed.'

'Insh'Allah,' Bousaif said, 'if God wills.'

'You know what Shaheed means?' the Director asked.

'Of course,' Bousaif said.

'It means you don't need a return ticket when you leave here, mate,' ManCity said.

'Lucky bastard.' The Gunner tried more levity.

'Which brings us back to our Afghan friend,' Umm Ali said. 'He's on the run somewhere in England, he knows the target. Who's solving that problem?'

'He knew the target,' the Director corrected. 'The mission's changed now.'

'He's still a problem for me,' Umm Ali said.

'They're looking for him,' the Director sighed. 'We've been through this. It can't hold us up.'

'Who exactly is looking?'

'The Mukhabarat. Their guy, the one who's been in England for years. His controllers say he's got all his contacts on high alert, out looking. There's a good chance of catching him on the underground asylum network.'

'And we believe that?' Umm Ali snorted.

'We've got his son as a guarantee,' the Director said. 'You're taking him over, then,' he said, 'to be sure of it.'

The Manager returned with flasks of sweet tea and coffee and brought some relief from the growing tension round the table. Bousaif stayed on the side-line, content to enjoy the rare pleasure of an unhurried meal. He listened to the nervous chatter of his football shirted instructors and tried not to watch Umm Ali as she pushed food under her veil.

'Are you guys sponsored, or something?' she asked. 'Etihad, Emirates? I knew Daesh had some heavy-hitting backers, but not this big. What's next?' She turned to the Director, 'The Caliphate hosts the World Cup?'

He smiled for the first time, and came back with, 'How soon do you go? I'm not sure how much more of this I can take. Haven't you got Kufar throats to slit, somewhere?'

'I've only just flown in. Can I finish breakfast first?' Umm Ali countered.

19

CHELTENHAM. TUESDAY 14TH APRIL

'Hello, Hash.' The soft voice made him spin round.

'Susan! How are you? It's good to see you.'

'I missed Jim amongst the known suspects in class. What've you done with him?' Her voice was entirely neutral.

'Yes,' Hash said. 'It's been a really strange holiday.' He pointed across the street to a corner café. 'Time for a coffee?'

'I'm heading for the shops, getting some essentials in,' she said. 'I haven't got long. Tell me about Jim. Is he better? Has he recovered from that virus?'

'He's fine,' Hash said. 'He spent more time than he bargained for in Ireland. His granny kept him hostage until he fattened up.' Susan's expression didn't change, and he was pretty sure it was the look she gave fibbing students.

'He's in Jordan now,' he said, as if confessing, and compounded the lies. 'The Jordanian granny had to get involved too when she heard Jim was sick. And there's family money involved, Jim's inheritance. To a great extent, my hands are tied. But he's at an amazing place, international, with most of the curriculum in English. It wasn't an easy decision'

'How long for?' Susan asked. 'Will they understand Jim,

over there?'

'Susan, bless you for asking,' Hash said. 'He's got a thousand cousins in the same place. It's swarming with Hashmi and Al Hashem,' he said. 'Nobody will get the chance to pick on him.' He changed tack. 'Are you OK, Susan? I've been so damned worried about you. That nightmare experience. I felt dreadful, somehow responsible. Can we talk about it or,' he held his hands up, 'is it still too awful to even think about?'

'I'm putting it in the "too difficult" tray for now. I'm not at all sure how much I can handle,' she answered. 'We made the best of the debate, in the end. You had more fun at the races, I'm sure. I hope you won?'

'I couldn't have won, Susan,' Hash said. 'What I did, I fear, is lose a precious friend instead.'

She looked away, and then at her watch. 'I've got to get my bits and pieces and make it back before the bell goes.'

'I'm so sorry, Susan. About everything. Can I give Jim your regards?'

She softened at that. 'Tell him he owes me the course work I sent.'

TEN DAYS LATER

'They've got me under the bloody doctor,' Sean rasped, hamming up his Belfast twang. 'Got me on all kinds of pills. Pills for this, pills for that.'

'Are you drinking?'

'I haven't had a scoop for days.'

'Your liver'll be in shock then. How soon can you come over?'

'Are the Constabulary still after me, or has the trail gone cold?'

'Cold as the grave.'

'Anything from Jim? Anything at all from that wee Lord?'

'Nothing bad, if you know what I mean,' said Hash. 'They

let him pass a message now and then. It's driving me crazy he's still out of my reach.'

'Our friend disappearing and not leaving a forwarding address. They should be bothered about that. No questions from them?'

'None. And he was the only player as far as I can see. Nothing went bang anywhere else that day or since.' On the other end of the line Sean's coughing made Hash hold the phone away from his ear. 'I can smell them down the phone.'

'Gallaher's,' Sean spluttered, 'free on the National Health, over here. What's the word with your mates?'

'The taxi guy's on hold. He's gone on the Hajj.'

'The what?'

'It's a pilgrimage they all have to do, once in their life. I think this guy's been a few times. He can afford it.'

'Sounds a bundle of laughs. When's he back?'

'Could be as much as two, three weeks. But as soon as he is, we pile on the pressure. Jim must

be in a hell of a state by now. He's living in a nightmare., God knows what they're telling him, but he

must be beside himself with worry. Scared too. And then I imagine him getting angry, and them

getting physical…'

'Can't imagine what I'll do when I get my hands on the bastards. Life, probably,' Sean said. 'What about your mate, the one whose girl just dumped him? Is he on this pilgrimage too?'

'He's here, still on standby. I'm pretty sure he's got my back. How are Bella and the Badger?'

'Just the same,' Sean said. 'It's the bitterness keeps them going.'

'Did you go and see them, tell them about Jim and everything?' There was silence at the other end, as though Sean was deciding what to answer. Eventually he said, 'They couldn't really take it in. They say we're both crazy, but they'll always blame me first.'

'Poor old Bella,' said Hash.

'Yeah, right. She told me I'll burn in hell. I can feel the heat already.'

'Do they know you're sick?'

'I wouldn't give her the satisfaction. She'd fold her arms and tell me 'serves you right and you're no son of mine.' I don't need that at this moment.'

'You need to be here then. We can do this together. What can I do to help?'

'Do the chemo for me…old chap?

It's been almost six weeks. They tell me all the time Dad's sending his love, but every time I ask how long I'm going to be stuck here, I just get, 'As long as it takes,' from Grumpy Guts. Or 'Soon, James, soon,' from Hamad. I don't think I can do this much longer. I miss home. I miss Dad. And Shamsa… even Mrs Hamilton, a bit. There's nothing to do, nothing, and this place is so rubbish. The woman came in yesterday though. That was ok, although the two twits always get weird and jumpy when she's around. She's always nice to me. I think it's a bit of an act though, the 'caring' thing. She did bring news of Dad, said he was overseas, and she might have to go and meet him, didn't say where or how long. It's driving me mad, not knowing anything. She said she had a special message from him. 'James has to be strong, he can help us all by staying strong and keeping his fingers crossed and we will win in the end.' What does that even mean? Win what? And it didn't really sound much like Dad. Plus, he never calls me James, not even when he's dishing out a bollocking. The one good thing she said was, her and Dad agreed I could get a new quad-copter, top spec, camera…blank cheque. That did sound like Dad. Made me smile. And she smiled too, for the first time in ages. She waggled her finger at me, and said in her 'funny'

voice, 'James gets no free lunch, has to practise with that cop-
ter thing. Daddy's orders.' Which didn't sound like him at all.
And then she left.

CHELTENHAM RACECOURSE.
THURSDAY 7TH MAY

Without Jim or Shamsa for company, and because the letter
box system was still live, Hash had taken up jogging as his new
reason for appearing on the racecourse. The ground rule was
never to compromise another team by disturbing them at the
letter box. The key to survival, drummed in at Ben Gashir with
ample graphic examples of failure, was to maintain the integ-
rity of the cell system: nobody must know about the other,
no names, no sightings, no details. Any clumsy overlap of
cars or persons at the letterbox was deemed a penetration and
carried a death sentence enforced by the compromised team
itself. Darkness belonged to faceless postmasters and daylight
belonged to Hash.

On this blustery morning Hash sat waiting, switching up
the blower to keep the windows from misting up, wondering how he was going to explain Shamsa's death to Jim. He'd
considered various scenarios, perhaps an accident, or maybe a
terminal illness, before remembering that before he could be
having the conversation with Jim at all, this nightmare would
have to be over. He gave himself a shake and stepped out of the
car.

As he jogged across the wet grass towards the footbridge, he
noted he was sharing the whole area with only four other cars,
two well across to the right and two closer to his route. He soon
passed alongside the first, a Renault car-van hybrid, a sort of
palace for dogs, fitted with a pet partition for two.

The other car on his immediate route was a BMW hatch-
back in an expensive looking shade of metallic blue. The windows were steamed up and the engine running, with wispy

exhaust trailing, to keep whoever was inside warm. He covered the ground quickly and was at the bridge and over it, taking care to miss the mud but still able to see there was no tape to indicate an incoming message. He cut out across the meadow, feeling the bite of the incline as he leaned forward, pumping just that bit harder to keep the speed constant. He had to admit he was beginning to enjoy the enforced exercise, a bonus in the current chaos of his life.

He followed the route he'd always taken with Shamsa and Jim and headed out to the foot of Cleeve Hill before turning back. He ran slowly. Jogging wasn't sprinting, thank heavens, he told himself. Two hundred metres off the footbridge he heard shrill yelping and barking. He slowed to a walk as the barking increased and a puppy, a Weimaraner, burst into view, running with a lead trailing from its collar.

It saw him at the same time and veered towards him, running hard, hurling itself at his knees. Tail wagging furiously, the pup was clearly enjoying its day. Its owner followed behind, looking flustered and calling it back with a wail of frustration. Hash caught the lead and then knelt, one knee in the muddy grass to pet the animal, instinctively gathering it up and hugging it. Hash looked up as the owner reached him, relief written all over her pretty, fresh face and saw a pair of blue eyes gazing down at him, with strands of blonde hair escaping from her grey wool beanie.

'Hope you don't mind,' Hash said. 'He started it. He wanted to say hello.'

'Thank God. This dog is driving me mad, always running away from me. I am always chasing.' She was quite happy to let him pet the dog. 'It runs too much,' she said. A European accent, but not one Hash could easily define.

'He's beautiful. How old?'

'This dog.' She thought about it. 'I think four, five months. It's not my dog, my boss's dog. His name is Bruno.'

'And what's the dog's name?' Hash asked.

The woman blinked. 'No. The dog's name is Bruno.' Then, catching Hash's smile, she laughed. 'English bastard.'

'Sorry?' Hash said, startled.

'My boss. English bastard.' She smiled back at Hash.

'Touché,' he said. 'That was good. I used to have one.' He stroked Bruno's muzzle and tickled his ribs. The pup loved it, squirming, nipping Hash's fingers.

'You used to have bastard English boss or ugly little dog?'

'No. I used to have one of these.' It was Hash's turn to laugh.

'You had one of these ugly dogs,' she said, in no hurry to leave. She looked up as a light drizzle started. 'First dog, now English weather.'

'My lovely dog,' Hash said. 'This Bruno is going to be big and beautiful.'

'I was joking,' she said. Hash looked up at her. Her delicate fingers tucked the wisps of hair inside her hat then dug in a pocket. He saw her red nails flick at a packet of cigarettes as she lit up and exhaled a pleasurable stream of smoke. 'Where is your dog?' She looked around her.

'She's gone. I don't have her anymore.' Hash could feel salt stinging his eyes and he concentrated on stroking Bruno. She waited, not saying anything, and Hash stood up and held Bruno's lead out to her.

'You miss him?' she asked. For a moment, Hash couldn't answer. 'I miss her,' he managed eventually.

'But now you share Bruno?' she said brightly. 'I come here sometimes.' She pointed at the car park. 'He sends me.'

'He's waiting in the car and you do the dog walking in the rain?' Hash smiled. 'Good arrangement.'

'I take his car,' she said, 'when I am working. I come lunch-time, mainly. Today is extra punishment.' She indicated her mud-spattered trainers and jeans. She took Bruno's lead and tugged it sharply, making Bruno yelp in protest. Hash felt an urge to take the dog back and show her how easy it was to train a pup.

'I come here nearly every lunchtime to jog,' he replied, and couldn't believe he was lying.

'Next time you see my BMW, you jog with Bruno and I sit in my car?'

'That's win-win for me.'

'How much you charge?'

'For Bruno, hmm, that's tricky.' Hash reached down to pat the pup. 'The special rate for Bruno,' he paused, watching her expression, 'is free.'

She digested this while finishing her cigarette and flicking it away. 'This is great,' she replied. 'That's the car.' She pointed through the trees. 'When you see it here, then Bruno is wait-ing.'

Hash held out his hand. 'I'm Tariq Hashmi. Everyone calls me Hash.'

'Eva,' she said. 'Lucky to meet you.'

'I'm the lucky one, now I've met Bruno,' he said. They walked to her car and he watched Bruno leap inside, his muddy paws leaving tracks on the leather.

'Ooow!' Eva wailed. 'Shit! Look at the mess in my boss's car.' He waved at the BMW as it pulled away and turned towards the exit. Her hand shot out, a fresh cigarette between the fin-gers, and waved back. He was still smiling when he got back into his vehicle.

SIRTE, LIBYA. TUESDAY 20TH MAY

The Director and Umm Ali's unannounced arrival in the early evening, brought unease to the small camp. Like students caught idling, the Gunner and ManCity went overboard in their welcome. The coolness of the Director's response, and the pointed silence from Umm Ali, merely increased the tension.

Bousaif kept quiet; only the Manager seemedunfazed. Tapping his watch, like a schoolmaster bringing a class to heel, he called them together for Maghreb prayers.

Seated opposite him after prayers, Umm Ali acknowledged Bousaif's growth of black hair. He heard, 'Good,' through her veil.

'Passport,' the Director demanded.

Bousaif handed over a worn Lebanese passport.

'Easy stuff first,' the Director continued, opening the pages. 'Date and place of birth?'

Bousaif gave his real date of birth, 5th May 1985, and his birth-place as Tripoli, Lebanon. Close to the truth; his real birthplace was Tripoli, Libya.

'Religion, education, profession and recent travel?' the Director continued.

'Christian, political science at CNAM in my home city,' Bousaif responded. 'Joined the family stonemasonry business when I left university. Internships with Greek and Italian partners. I've been to Cyprus recently. I had a girlfriend there.'

Why Christian?' the Director asked, and Bousaif hesitated.

'One less Kufar when you press the tit, innit,' ManCity offered.

Nobody laughed. The Director held the passport to Umm Ali who shook her head dismissively. A clattering of trays and pots sounded from the kitchen where the Manager was busy. In the soft warmth of the evening only the random crack and snap from the insect killer broke the silence.

'Continue,' the Director said, putting the passport down and picking up his prayer beads.

'I've got a Schengen visa that allows me to visit and stay in UK for a Technical English course at a language school, in Cheltenham. I'm stopping over in Germany, in Munich, for football games.'

'Why is he hanging around in Munich?' the Director interrupted.

'I'll call him in when I'm ready,' Umm Ali said.

'When?''I'll know when I know,' she said. 'Until then he's better off waiting in Europe, not small town UK.'

'Yes, but I have other teams running operations in Europe,' the Director said. 'What if he gets caught in some police round-up?'

'So, tell me which cities he can hang around in, then,' she said.

'I've got tickets for games in Berlin and Paris too,' said Bousaif.

'How do you communicate with her?' the Director asked.

'I transmit on ManCity's Facebook, and I receive on Gunner's Facebook.'

'When you get to Britain, what do you say to the immigration people?'

'Show them the invitation letter from the language school.'

The Director turned his head to Umm Ali. 'Your turn.'

'Horse racing,' she stated. 'Have these two clowns briefed you well on horse racing in Britain?'

Bousaif gave her a rundown on the forthcoming racing events the royal family might be expected to attend. The instructors had steered him through the various venues, he said, with the help of their websites. Umm Ali said nothing.

'So, it seems Bousaif is ready.' The Director said. He studied him. 'Your holiday had to end sometime. You've had time to adjust, mentally prepare for the mission. Are you ready to take it through to the end?

'Insh'Allah I am ready to do this.'

'Martyr's speech?'

'Already filmed it,' ManCity said.

'What about the martyr's bounty?' Umm Ali asked.

'One million US dollars to his father,' the Director answered.

The Gunner and ManCity sat back in their seats, exchanging glances. 'I'd blow myself up twice for that sort of money,' the Gunner breathed.

'Epsom or Ascot?' The Director looked at the woman.

Bousaif realised he was hearing the locations of his targets for the first time and wondered why the Director was discussing them in front of the two instructors, a serious breach of security, although it didn't seem to alarm Umm Ali.

'One or the other. It depends,' she said.

'On what?'

'On the boy, how soon we can get him competent with the new drone we've given him. The Epsom Derby is the first big opportunity. It runs over the fifth and sixth of June. Ascot is seventeenth to twentieth June.'

'There may be more chance of the royal family being at Ascot,' the Director said. 'I'm getting the Mukhabarat to check the court diaries through their embassy. We won't know until nearer the time.'

The Director grew uncharacteristically animated. 'Bousaif, your mission will be the biggest attack ever in the history of jihad. Of the world. We'll have the boy filming it with his flying camera.'

'What do I do with the boy and the father?' Umm Ali asked.

'We return the kid to his dad, and everyone goes home,' the Director said.

'You're not serious?'

'What do you think?

ManCity and the Gunner looked down at their empty plates, shifting uncomfortably. They too knew a cardinal rule had just been broken.

'Sayyid Bousaif is leaving very soon,' Umm Ali broke the silence, pointing to the two British instructors, 'You two, Posh and Becks, you need to say goodbye now.'

The Gunner and ManCity rose and came around to Bousaif's side of the table. Bousaif stood up and they hugged him in turn, murmuring 'God go with you.'

'I wish it was me instead of you, my brother,' added the Gunner.

Just as they turned away, Umm Ali, who had been observing the two men as they moved off, called them back, waving them to resume their seats.

'Just got one last little issue,' she began. 'The last mission went wrong because of...' she paused for thought, '...probably a number of things. And we're still trying to find the other guy you two trained.' Her voice was ice. 'We need to be sure Bousaif hasn't picked up a virus here.' She pointed a gloved finger, first at ManCity, then to the Gunner, from one to the other and back again, like a metronome.

'Bousaif needs to tell me which of you two gave him a message for someone in Britain.' Both went pale. The Gunner tried to speak but her hand silenced him. 'The question is for Bousaif.'

The Director moved back on the bench. The Manager, leaning forward with a fresh tray, put it down and stepped back. Bousaif felt sweat pricking his face.

'Which one?' Umm Ali repeated. The metronome stopped as her hand dipped into her bag and came out with a pistol, a small-calibre automatic with a silencer.

'Which one?' Umm Ali's voice was low and grating. Bousaif watched as she picked up the pistol, handling it effortlessly, slipping out the magazine and thumbing the bullets, testing the spring. Even the Director recoiled and Bousaif realised she was still talking to him, pointing the weapon at his chest. 'I'm not a patient person, Bousaif,' she said ramming the magazine back in and racking the slide, driving a bullet into the chamber.

'They both did,' Bousaif said.

'Aaah,' she sighed, 'now that's an interesting call.'

She handed the weapon to him. As he grasped it, she guided the barrel to point at the two men opposite him. 'I think you know what's required.'

20

CHELTENHAM, MIDDAY THURSDAY 28TH MAY

Hash was hard pressed to concentrate in court, fretting that the case might drag past the midday break and stop him being in time to meet up with Bruno, and Eva. He hadn't seen either of them for days and he found he was missing her. His days felt like a waking nightmare, with constant thoughts of Jim and the Libyans, the crazy bomber, the fear of discovery, Sean's diagnosis, Susan's anger with him and God only knew what was coming next. It was relentless, and Eva's relaxed company, her sunny, quirky outlook on life, were something he found he increasingly looked forward to.

The defendant in the dock was trying to look confident. Over the years, as his own taste had become more refined, Hash had become absurdly fixated on the difference between flashiness and elegance. The fleshy balding middle-aged man standing before the Bench wore a black suit with a thick pinstripe and a pink shirt with a broad, pale yellow silk tie. As he raised his hand to straighten it, a gold bracelet hung at his fat wrist. Instinctively, Hash knew he would be finding this man guilty.

The charge of fraud was pronounced, the defendant pleaded

'not guilty', and the floor was given to the defending counsel. The picture of a hard-working independent financial adviser soon emerged, that of an experienced, savvy hunter in the jungle of investment whose clients stood ready to attest to his skills. Finally, the point was made that the defendants' clients had all been exhaustively briefed about investments going down as well as up and had all signed a disclaimer absolving their man in the case of such downswings. The counsel compared the number of those complaints with the apparently vast number of those who were perfectly satisfied, adding that the losers were managing their lives competently in all other respects.

In the retiring room, during the break, the chairwoman, a friendly retired schoolteacher, poured coffee for Hash, murmuring, 'I can see how this will go.'

'Let me guess,' Hash said. 'They knew what they were doing, they just got their fingers burned for being a bit too greedy.'

'So tough luck,' she said.

The other winger, a businessman, chipped in from his seat at the table. 'These people spend their working lives building up savings, often quite big pots of cash. And the banks pay next to nothing these days, so our chum in the dock can always finds someone eager to listen to him.'

'They listen,' the chairwoman said, 'they think he'll see them right, and they sign up.'

'Maybe there was a cooling-off period?' Hash said.

'Undoubtedly,' the other member of the trio said, 'but don't underestimate greed, theirs or his, and he's smart. I'd guarantee he has a practised bit of spin to get past that and make sure of his massive upfront commission.'

'What's the worst he could get for this?' Hash asked.

'We can slap him on the wrist and let him go,' the chairwoman said. 'Tell him not to do it again.'

'They've given him money, he's taken his fees. Whether

he gets a slapped wrist or a fine, they'll never get their money back,' the other winger said.

The clerk saved the situation, and Hash's rendezvous, by steering the decision to the Crown Court. As he left the court-house his phone came to life with an hour old SMS from Eva: 'am late r u still there'.

'On my way,' he replied.

Reaching the court's car park, he caught sight of the freshly bailed conman and a young woman, hugging each other and kissing passionately.

'Probably not his daughter then,' he thought, raising an eye-brow.

The conman, making a major show of it, handed keys to the girl, pointed to his car and waved her away. Hash watched her get into the silver Audi estate. The rear window had a 'Help for Heroes' sticker on the left edge and a 'Keep Calm and Carry On Hunting' sticker on the right.

Hash's phone vibrated as he strode away; a new message from Eva. 'Cannot make it now. Sorry.'

He stopped short, disappointed and disheartened; he'd been counting on their walk with Bruno, and spending time with her, to lift his spirits. His phone buzzed again, and he answered it before it had even sounded a second time, but it was Siddiq's voice he heard.

'Good news, my friend, you will be so happy,' said Siddiq, full of childlike excitement.

Hash was instantly wary. 'Don't tell me.'

'Yes! Anna's coming back.'

'When?'

'Very soon. It's so wonderful,' Siddiq was beside himself. 'She's coming from London. She can't wait to be with me again. She misses me too much.'

'I'm happy for you.'

'Is the place still OK?

'Well, I've had to replace the bed.'

Siddiq went silent, and Hash quickly put him out of his misery. 'Of course, everything's okay, it's all yours.'

'Good, good,' said Siddiq, relieved. 'Are you in Cheltenham?'

His high spirits were beginning to grate. 'Yes, why?'

'Sayyid Hakim is back. He wants to speak with you.'

'Has he got something for me? Anything at all?'

'You should be at the mosque tomorrow. Be ready.'

The maisonette still smelled of Anna's scent and she had left it tidier than he could have managed. He took the bunch of red roses and bottle of champagne he'd brought with him up to the master bedroom and looked out across to the brightly lit expanse of GCHQ, surveying the old target. It was just too much of a coincidence, he thought; Anna was back in the game and Hakim, either nemesis or ally, wanted to see him. Below him, the row of garages stood peacefully, deserted by their owners. His eyes swept up and down, double checking, and he decided it was dark enough.

Parking the Discovery as close as possible to the garage, he stepped out and eased up the door, closing it quickly behind him, and flicked the light switch. To his left, bathed in the glare of the strip light, lay the stack of aluminium ladders. He checked the door was completely down, sealing him in, and started to shift the ladders one by one to the far side. Once he'd moved them all, he kicked at the length of carpet they'd lain on for years. The corner flap began to lift and he reached down with both hands and pulled, slowly shifting the whole strip to expose a thick sheet of plywood a foot across and three feet long lying flush to the cement floor. The wood had a loop of plastic cord at one corner and Hash hooked a finger into it and began to lift. It came up easily to reveal an even layer of fine gravel. Kneeling by the exposed trench he scooped away handfuls of gravel. It was still dry after all these years.

He stopped, listened. There was a car engine purring outside. He was sweating, he realised, his heart thumping. Doors opening, voices, adults mixed with children; a family back home, parking up for the night. Sniffing and scratching at the garage door told him he'd been detected by their dog. Her voice tired and irritated, a woman called 'Fenton' to heel. The sniffing escalated to a growl with paws scrabbling at the door. The owner grew angry and Hash, holding himself perfectly still, listened to the tussle as the animal was put on a leash and dragged away. He waited until their own garage door had slammed and their footsteps receded, then released his breath and dug quickly until he could feel the canvas bag. He recalled the modus operandi back then: the assault team couldn't waste time digging up a deep cache, or loading magazines, while sitting comfortably in the garage. A steady, quiet approach would have been a luxury so, to be on the safe side, Hash had planned for the police coming hard on their heels, maybe tipped off, probably armed. His team would have hit the garage at the gallop, one pair pulling out the ladders with the other pair hauling up the kitbag and sharing out the weapons. The two men going over would have been ready to cross the fence, weapons loaded, within less than a minute. The remaining pair would have kept the police at bay, drawing fire, throwing the grenades, making it as noisy as possible, buying enough time for their comrades to get across the first fences and start shooting their way into the complex.

Testing the weight of the contents and guessing at fifteen kilos, he heaved it upright, hearing metallic clunks as the contents settled and adjusted. He got his left arm under the bundle, and swung it onto his shoulder, waiting for a few seconds to settle his nerves and hearing before he flicked off the light and hoisted the garage door back up again.

MORNING – FRIDAY 29TH MAY

Hakim was seated in the mosque kitchen. The crushing handshake and the silent, cynical appraisal had the instant effect of making him more annoyed than apprehensive.

'Salaam-Alaikum, Sayyid Hakim. How is your family, how was the Hajj?'

'Umra Haj,' Hakim corrected sharply. 'Maybe one day you will take your son.'

'Insh'Allah,' Hash said. 'With your help, everything is possible.'

Siddiq, his face beaming with pleasure, placed cups of coffee before them.

'Thank you, my friend,' said Hash

'Have a look at these,' Hakim interrupted, 'and tell me what you see.' He pulled his phone from a pocket and flicked through images until he found what he was looking for. 'You still haven't heard from him?' The question was more like an assumption.

'I have not heard from him,' Hash said grimly.

'Have a look at this one.' Hash was looking at Jim's bruised, face. The photo had been taken from a low angle and a table edge obscured most of it. But it was clearly the same long-haired Jim, injured, frightened and shocked, staring at a plate of food.

'He's been in an accident?' Hash said.

'He's been beaten.' Hakim let the information sink in. 'This was taken at a restaurant two days ago.'

'What? Why are they beating him?' Hash gasped. 'Why?'

'They are training him. When he does good, he gets taken for nice food. When he does bad, he gets punished, maybe no food.'

'Animals,' Siddiq growled.

'Training? For what?' Hash said, 'I'll kill the bastards!'

'Arab bastards,' Hakim corrected.

'So, you believe me now. You believe these people are holding my son and he has not gone to the Jihad.'

'I believe some of what you say,' Hakim nodded. 'I'm never sure.'

'You mean I'm still a liar to you?' Hash sat back in his chair and looked at Hakim. 'What do I have to do to convince you my son is a prisoner of these people and I just want him back? You've found him, you can see they're harming him.' Hash held out his hands. 'So why don't you help me get him back?'

'You want me to hand all this over to the British police?' Hakim held the phone up to Hash. 'Would you prefer that?' Hash didn't answer. 'I thought not. I am helping you because,' Hakim pointed at Siddiq, 'I have been asked, and as a Muslim it is my duty. Maybe also now I see the danger these people bring.'

'Who are they?' Hash asked.

'Mr Hashmi,' Hakim said, 'don't play games with me. You know these people, maybe better than me. You must have upset them very much.'

'I have told Siddiq about the business disaster, but I swear I do not,' and Hash emphasised the words, 'repeat not, know who these people are. But I will kill them and go to prison if that's what it takes to get my son away from them.'

'I know this type of Arab well, from the jihad in Afghanistan against the Russians,' Hakim said, 'when I was a boy like your son and first saw wealthy Arabs playing at jihad. These men do not care about the Holy Koran. They are not good Muslims, they are rubbish.'

'I'm an Arab,' Hash said, 'and proud of it. But these people are a disgrace to me and my race.'

Hakim was silent.

'Sayyid Hakim,' Hash tried again. 'Why are they training my son?'

'We don't know, yet. In the beginning it looked like play, to keep him occupied. Now they make him practise often, more like they're making him train.'

'Did your people see them beating him?'

'No, but they see them shouting at him, pushing him, especially when the woman in the burqa is there.'

'The woman from before, in March?'

'Probably the same.' Hakim nodded. 'We see her now and then.'

Hash sat forward. 'I thank you from the bottom of my heart. Can't you just let me get close and then take over? Please?'

'What do you mean, take over?' Hakim was exasperated. 'You have not been listening to me. You cannot possibly take over what I do. Your son and maybe you yourself stay alive because I do not let you take over.' He tapped the image of Jim's bruised face looking from the screen.

'This could have been a dead boy.'

Siddiq cut in. 'Hakim is trying to find out who in the area is supporting these people, who is hiding them, which imams are giving help.'

'I cannot let you blunder about and leave a mess I can't clean up,' Hakim said. 'I will be living here long after you've gone home with your son.'

'Does your team know where they are keeping Jim?' Hash said.

'They did in the beginning. Not now.'

'So, they change their location?' Hash said.

'Wouldn't you?'

'How do I know? I'm not one of these bastards,' Hash said.

Hakim's face cracked a sardonic smile. 'Of course you're not.'

They'd got angry and then hit him. Hard. It had all been about the new quadcopter. A Mavic, one of the latest and best, with that cool tracking camera . It was the gift she'd talked about before, from Dad the woman said, when she handed it over. And then she'd said "He must have spent a fortune on it and guess what?! You're going to use it to find your Dad.", as if he was some idiot five-year-old. He was getting seriously pissed off with her. Then something had got up the Chief Bastard' s nose, probably when he told him, "It doesn't work without my iPhone, dickhead," or maybe when he'd told him to get his greasy hands off the machine. The woman had turned really nasty then and yelled at all of them. She'd shaken him, too, and then of course the Bastard in Chief had gone one better and whacked him in the face. Christ it hurt. He'd cried a bit, actually, but it was just the shock; he wasn't that tragic. That was when she really lost her shit, turned nastier than anyone ever, like some sort of underworld harpy on steroids. She'd screamed 'How the fuck can we take him out looking like this!' And then she'd sat with him, playing the good guy all over again, 'Your Dad will be ok soon, that's the news we're getting, that's what he said to pass on to you. Meanwhile he says for you to play the game and stay cool. Do you think you can do that for him?' Yeah right. Not for much longer I can't. I won't either. Sod the lot of them. Not Dad though. What does he really want? Does he even know I'm here?

21

SATURDAY, 30TH MAY

Hash looked at the BlackBerry the moment he woke from a fitful sleep. He'd asked for a new picture of Jim, this time with that day's newspaper. It was a challenging demand, he knew; they'd have to decide whether to engage in mind games with a desperate father. There was no answer to his SMS.

He gazed at his drawn face in the mirror and splashed cold water on it. He thought about Jim, his weeks away from home, God knew in what circumstances by now. He longed to hold his poor, damaged boy and tell him, "Never, never again." He was almost paralysed by his fear for him, but a promise was a promise. He'd better get going.

Mrs Hamilton was waiting for his door to open, apparently having a sixth sense for his anxiety to be about his business.

'Going somewhere nice on this beautiful day?' she asked from her doorway. She caught sight of the wicker hamper Hash held delicately in front of him as he walked down the path to his car. 'Goodness, Fortnum & Mason,' she said mischievously. 'Can mean only one thing…'

'Good morning, Mrs Hamilton,' Hash cut her off. 'I called

you so many times, but you were engaged, so I had to go with my second choice.'

'Oh yes, Hash,' she said, 'my diary's chock-a-block these days. Where are you taking her?'

'I don't know yet.'

'Which one is it this time?' She hovered on the threshold. 'The dark one from the school or that blonde with the ponytail? Never saw you do all this stuff for Tara.' She closed the door leaving Hash feeling stung, and thoroughly wrong footed.

At the sight of the BMW down in the parking zone, he took a few seconds to check his appearance and make sure he was smiling naturally before pulling up alongside. Eva emerged, first a foot in trainers, then an elegant denim-clad leg. Hash could hear her shouting at the pup in the backseat barking at the sight of Hash. She stood up, dressed in pale blue denim jeans and a Bomber jacket. 'Say hello to the lady first,' she said, with a warm smile. 'Lady first, dog second.'

'You look great, but it's only a picnic,' Hash said, pecking her on the cheek. 'We'll be sitting in a field, not on a boulevard.'

'Oh...' she sounded crestfallen, and Hash hurried to put things right.

'You look fantastic, I wish it was a boulevard after all.' He had to defend himself against Bruno's welcoming assault. Crouching down, ruffling the dog's ears, he said, 'But we're going to be up on Crickley Hill. It's only ten minutes away. A surprise! Follow me in your car. I'll take this guy, he can jump all over my seats instead of yours.'

'No walking, no cow shit, no mud,' she pointed down at her jeans and trainers. 'You and the dog can walk, but not me.'

'Deal,' Hash said, 'I'll walk the dog before we have our food. All you have to do is relax and enjoy the English countryside.'

She inspected the spread as Hash unpacked the hamper and laid it out on the tailgate.

'Better than any restaurant,' she said.

He poured a glass of wine and held it out to the west, pointing at a shadowy outline way in the distance. 'That's Hay Bluff, sixty miles away. Clear as anything, not a cloud in the sky.' But when he clinked glasses with her, he felt a stab of guilt; old Mrs Hamilton's barb had bitten deep. What was he doing, what had he been thinking for heaven's sake? This extravagant picnic should be for Susan if anyone at all. And was Mrs H right? Had he ever actually done anything like this for Tara? He felt a cheap bastard, laying on this performance for someone he barely knew. He caught Eva looking at him, sensing something was not right.

'A picnic like this really makes me happy,' she trilled. Hash knew she was playing her part, repaying his efforts, and it only made him feel worse. He thought of having Jim on his right, Tara on his left and Shamsa running around them. He felt empty and false. Eva was having none of it.

'Yes, please, Mr Hash,' she said, thrusting her empty glass at him. He filled it and she held it up to him, waiting for him to lift his. 'Cheers!'

Just then her phone rang and, as she examined it, Hash was surprised to see how quickly her expression changed to anger. She spoke quickly in a Slavic language, hissing into the phone, clenching her fist.

'My boss,' she said, simply when she had finished. 'Bastard.'

'You speak to your boss like that? Remind me not to upset you.' Hash said. But by then the storm had passed, her face had softened again, the phone had been returned to her jeans pocket and her merry smile was back in place.

'Only when he doesn't do what I tell him to do,' she said, grinning up at him. 'Now I have to give him instructions. Enjoy your walk with Bruno but keep it quick; I'm getting hungry.'

She eased into one of the folding chairs and was instantly absorbed with her phone, fingers flicking across its keyboard. Hash took the hint and whistled for Bruno.

22

CHELTENHAM, SUNDAY 31ST MAY

The SMS waiting for him on the Arab phone when he got back to the house had simply asked, 'Ready?'

Siddiq's call came as he was heading for the garden shed to retrieve the kitbag from its hiding place. 'Come over, my friend,' he insisted. 'Anna is always talking too much about you.'

Hash accepted, trying to work out Anna's reasoning as he dumped the kitbag on the kitchen table.

Years ago, in the full spate of revolutionary ardour, he'd put in a request for everything he'd need to support a team getting over the GCHQ fence. Now, opening the bag, he was struck by the naivety of those times and the stark simplicity of his list. He pulled out two folding butt AK47s and six empty magazines. Next, a bundle of grease-stained cloth wrapping two Tokarev pistols each with its magazine. A pair of British Army old-style 36 Mills grenades were tied in the sleeve torn off a shirt and the other sleeve contained the ammunition for the AKs and the pistols. Finally, wrapped in two chequered blue police tabards, the two sets of car number plates he'd also asked for. Surveying it all, neatly arranged on the kitchen table, he was rather impressed by his thought processes back in the day. He had in front of him the makings of a fighting approach, or withdrawal using stolen cars. There wasn't enough ammunition for a prolonged firefight, but there would have been a hell of a noise and some real damage done once they were inside the wire. He counted the bullets into a plastic tub and doused the whole lot with WD40. Then he sprayed the four weapons and tested the mechanisms until they worked smoothly.

Wiping the oil off his hands, he decided to ring Sean.

'What's it like with you?' Sean's voice was strained. No banter, no attempt to wind him up.

'Great weather over here today,' Hash said.

'Pissing with rain over here, as usual. And I'm in dock,' Sean said, choking off a cough. 'Got outpatient treatment tomorrow. What's new?'

'Does that take long?' Hash asked.

'I'm fine, thanks, actually. Good of you to inquire.'

'That's more like it, mate.'

'Oh shit,' Sean said. 'It's mate, is it?'

'And I preferred it when you were a cantankerous bastard,' Hash said. 'We've got another visitor coming. It feels like a rerun of the last one.

'Or another racecourse,' Sean said.

'The next big one is Epsom, the Derby, next weekend.'

'I can't make it that soon,' Sean said. 'Like I said, chemo leaves me wrecked for a few days, weak as a kitten, and then they sit me down and read the tea leaves.'

'Shit,' Hash said.

'Shit about my lung cancer? Or shit about me not coming across?'

'Both.' Hash was quiet for a few seconds then said, 'They've been hitting him. I saw the photo. Hakim's boys got one.'

'You sure it wasn't his boys who did it?'

'He seemed angry about it.'

'Christ.' Sean's voice was hoarse. 'No need to twist my arm. I'll come when I can, soon as I'm fit enough.'

'Can I do anything for you?' Hash asked. 'Do you need a cash injection?'

'About the only injections that don't hurt,' Sean said. 'But no thanks. Don't know what I'd do with the stuff anyhow.'

Anna stood up unhurriedly before she greeted Hash, reminding him of their last encounter and her languid appraisal of him then. And how dangerously attractive she could make herself; she was   calculating and manipulative, he thought, and used all her charms. Now she kissed him full on the lips then held him at arm's length, contemplating him sympathetically while Siddiq looked on, jealous and surely hurt.

She nailed Hash with the question he least wanted to hear. 'How's your son? Is he in contact, is everything alright?'

He looked across to Siddiq, with a raised eyebrow, irritated, unsure how much he'd told her. 'He's ok,' he began. 'Once his troubles were pretty much behind us, we found a place for him in Jordan at an international school.'

'Troubles? I thought it was just adolescent problems. Did you go to the police, what did they do? Useless, probably.' Her expression was somewhere between pity and tolerance, clearly thinking him incompetent.

'Adolescent problems are always trouble,' Hash managed before she could go any further.

'No mother to guide him, that's the problem. You poor thing, Hash,' and she pointed at Siddiq. 'He's been worried sick, so have I.'

Hash heard himself saying how touched he was by everyone's concern.

'So who's looking after him?' Anna persisted.

Hash ended the interrogation. 'How are you, Anna? It's good to see you back.' He looked at Siddiq who was beaming with pleasure again. 'We missed you.'

'It depends on him.' She shot a coy look at Siddiq. 'He's the boss.'

'Really?' Hash said with a smile. 'I sometimes think that's you.'

'Aah,' she said, 'you are a good judge of character but why do you say 'sometimes' and not just 'all the time'? I keep him jealous, too. It's good for him!' She blew a kiss at Siddiq then winked at Hash. 'Men…' She sighed, pleased with her performance. 'Tell me, how's your plumber friend?'

'Him? Oh, he's gone, ages ago.'

'Trying to make it in stand-up? I could see he had talent.'

'Drinks, everyone,' Siddiq interrupted from the kitchen. 'Time to relax. Hash, my friend.' He held out the bottle of champagne for him to open and went for glasses. Hash eased off the cork.

'Hash knows all about horse racing, darling,' he called to Anna. 'He goes all the time to the races. Maybe he knows.' 'Knows what?' Hash was concentrating on pouring a glass. 'What do you need to know?'

'When is the next big race in Cheltenham?' Anna asked.

'Months away.'

'That's no good, darling,' Anna pouted. 'I want to go in summertime, wear my best outfit, get dressed up like the rich people do.'

'There's the Derby at Epsom. It's famous,' Hash said, pouring the third glass. 'The Queen always goes.'

'The Queen? Really?' Anna looked at Siddiq, eyes wide. 'Did you hear that, darling?'

Hash said, 'It wouldn't be the Derby without her.' Holding up his glass, he toasted, 'The Queen!' and Siddiq and Anna both murmured, 'The Queen.' They sipped the champagne in appreciative silence.

'So, will I see the Queen if I go to Epsom?'

'See her from a distance or close up?' Hash asked. 'You have to be in The Queen's Stand to rub shoulders with royalty. That's where the action is, but you can still see her with binoculars from outside.'

'That's no good.' Anna pouted at Siddiq. 'I want to be right beside her, rubbing shoulders with royalty, like Hash says.'

'Hash will arrange tickets for this place.' Siddiq looked at his friend hopefully. 'He knows this procedure.'

'Which day?' Hash said. 'There are two, Friday and Saturday. The Friday is when all the beautiful ladies get to show off their outfits.'

'That's a good day for you, darling,' Siddiq said. 'You will be the most beautiful of all.'

'Whichever day the Queen will be there,' Anna cut in.

'They don't necessarily say which day she's coming on,' Hash protested.

'Can't you find out?' Anna said.

'Maybe see which days her horses are running,' Hash offered. 'She presents the prize after the big race, the Derby.'

'Darling,' Anna purred at Siddiq, reaching over to stroke his arm. 'What do you think? I want to have fun this time, go out, see places, not just stay hidden here waiting for you to visit.'

'Of course you do, my lovebird.' Siddiq drew her hand to his lips. 'Of course you do.'

'And maybe Hash will take me if you don't want to go.'

Siddiq followed Hash out to his car as he left.

'You can arrange this thing, my friend?' Siddiq asked. He knew he'd been overselling Hash's powers.

'You've only given me a few days,' Hash replied. 'And you want the most expensive tickets. It's better you go on the last two days, to be sure to see The Queen.'

'But you can do it, can't you? She can get crazy when she doesn't get what she wants. I have to keep her happy.'

'What is Hakim doing for me?' Hash countered. 'I need to hear from him. Then the tickets for Friday and Saturday will happen.'

Siddiq took the ultimatum calmly. 'Hakim has more sympathy now,' he said. 'This is different from before.'

'Because of the beating?' Hash asked.

'There is a connection.' Siddiq nodded. 'A long time ago,' Siddiq waved to where his Mercedes stood, 'before all the business, Hakim was a mujahid fighting Al Qaeda on the border. The Taliban took his brother prisoner. Then shot him.'

'Hell,' Hash said softly. 'Poor man.'

'The point is,' Siddiq said, 'that was not the Taliban way. They should have ransomed the brother like they normally did. You know the practice of hostage taking; it has rules, part commercial and part family thing. This time there were Arabs with the Taliban, and Al Qaeda disregarded the rules. Afterwards, Hakim found out they had given the orders.'

He looked at Hash. 'This brother was the same age as Jim.'

CHELTENHAM. MONDAY 1ST JUNE

Eva had phoned early in the morning to say her employer had unforeseen travel commitments imminent, involving her, but not the dog. He had asked her to arrange kennels, but she had suggested her friend as dog sitter. The boss was happy to pay a fee. Hash waived the fee.

'This is win-win.' She smiled, pausing in the doorway as Bruno barrelled past. She held out her hands to Hash and he gave her a chaste kiss on the cheek. The pup came back to check on the delay.

'Maybe you keep the damned dog forever,' Eva said. 'Maybe Jim will like him.'

Intrigued by the smells of Shamsa, and eager to investigate the nooks and crannies of a new house, the pup galloped through the rooms and then upstairs, coming down seconds later to claim Shamsa's bed in the kitchen.

'Your wife.' Eva looked up at the photo on the dresser shelf. 'You never told me she was so beautiful. And your son. He's a good-looking boy.'

'She still is beautiful,' he said.

'Does he miss her?' She pointed at a picture of Jim posing with his Spitfire.

'Sometimes,' Hash said. 'We both do.'

'So why did you send him away to Jordan?'

'Cheltenham can get pretty small and there was some family money in the pot. It was a chance to meet my folks and his cousins and learn some Arabic. I'll bring him back for sixth form and university.'

Eva seemed fascinated by every detail in the house. She looked around, peering at every object in the room. 'This is a man's world. No sign of a woman here,' she murmured when Hash brought her a glass of wine.

'It was hard to have too much of Tara around at first,' Hash said. 'But as Jim grew, we began to get used to doing things our own way, I suppose.'

'Sad,' Eva said. 'How long has she been dead?'

'She passed away twelve years ago.'

'Since then, no girlfriend?'

'Too difficult,' Hash answered. 'I didn't want any other person in this space. I wanted to prove I could do everything, be mother and father. Maybe it was easier because Jim was a boy and needed a man's influence.'

'No grandmother, no grandfather closer than Jordan?'

'There's a grandmother in Ireland, and a grandfather, but he's very frail now. She's great though.'

'So sad,' Eva said, softly. She looked up at him and put a gentle hand on his arm, adding 'I'm sorry. I didn't mean to upset you. I know how you must feel'

'Do you?'

'Yes,' she said. 'I've lost people close to me too, a long time ago. It still hurts.'

'You do understand then,' said Hash. 'Thank you. I really appreciate you telling me, but I'm sorry you've known that sadness too.'

Then he smiled at her, and raised his glass, saying, 'But listen, it's a beautiful day and we're getting maudlin. My father would be saying "Brace up, you two" if he could hear us! So, tell me about this business trip you're going on. Anywhere exciting?'

The doorbell rang at around nine-thirty in the evening and this time it was Bruno, not Shamsa, who gave tongue at the silhouette on the other side of the glass. The sheer bulk of the figure behind the glass told Hash it was the visitor he was dreading. Bruno's sharp yapping, as if warning him there was real danger present, made him think about his armoury. There was one Kalashnikov, a pistol and a grenade stashed in a daysack bag under the stairs and a matching pair, also hidden, in the back porch. But he had not loaded magazines and cursed himself inwardly, knowing what Sean would have said. The man on the other side of the door began to fidget, sensing he was being observed.

Hash opened it to find himself looking at a much younger man, a few inches shorter than himself but broader with a strong, open face. There was a wary, alert expression on the face which softened as Hash offered his hand and gave the traditional, 'Salaam-Alaikum'. The new arrival joined in with the ritual greetings, his accent telling Hash he was an ethnic Arab from North Africa, Palestinian or an Egyptian, maybe a Tunisian or Libyan. He stood back and ushered the man past into the main hallway. Bruno remained cautiously out of range in the kitchen as Hash took the man's bag, noticing the Manchester City logo. He took him straight upstairs to his room and pointed out the direction of Mecca before telling him to come back down for refreshments when he was ready.

In the kitchen, the two men began assessing each other. Hash had nothing to lose by introducing himself, and his guest readily gave his name as Bousaif.

'Tea, coffee?' Hash said, flicking on the kettle. Hash took fresh mint leaves from the fridge and held them up, 'Mint tea is easy, or English tea. I could try Turkish coffee? And you must be hungry. How about food? We can get a takeaway, or I can cook, but maybe they warned you about that. If the Kufar don't get you, Tariq's cooking will,' Hash said, as he dropped a pair of takeaway fly-ers onto the table.

Bousaif smiled, and leant down towards the pup, holding out his hand to make friends, gently encouraging him to come forward. Hash wanted to ask him about Jim there and then, about what the hell was going on. Instead, he dropped the mint leaves into a cafetière and poured hot water over them. Push-ing a sugar bowl towards his guest and placing the jug and two glasses on the table, he gestured 'Welcome.' The young man nodded his appreciation.

'Make your choice.' Hash tapped the menu and smiled at Bousaif. 'I call, then they deliver. Just like back home in Trip-oli.'

'You come from Tripoli?' he asked.

'Born and bred.'

'Me, too.' Bousaif stirred his tea, pressing at the mint leaves. He looked down at the menu and decided. 'Margherita for me.'

'Good choice. I'll join you.' He dialled the takeaway and placed the order. 'Thirty minutes,' he said to Bousaif. 'Feel free to pray whenever you need.'

Bousaif held up his glass and took another sip, enjoying the tea.

'It's Epsom, definitely,' Hash told Sean. 'They've sacked

the first plan, by the sound of it. This guy's just pulled out his ticket for The Queen's Stand on Derby Day.'

'When's that?' Sean said.

'This Saturday, the big race is at four-thirty. He doesn't even want to do a recce.'

'He'll be going for HM, then. Maybe I should get something on at the bookies while the odds are good,' Sean said.

'He can't hope to get her, but just being close and getting fifty dead and a hundred injured will do,' Hash said.

'It'll be horrific,' Sean said.

'That's exactly what they're going for.'

'The sick bastards,' Sean said. 'So, four and a half days to go. What do you do now?'

'Help him,' Hash said, 'or else. Can you get over?' He could hear Sean swallowing and spitting. 'I need you, mate.'

'Whenever you call me "mate", I know you've got plans that involve getting me killed. It's all part of your unique charm, Darky.'

'Come on,' Hash said, 'you know what I mean.'

'It's no go. You'll have to do it by yourself. Maybe Siddiq and your other mate will step up.'

'Shit,' Hash muttered.

23

TUESDAY 2ND JUNE

He kept his Koran and prayer beads to hand; Hash and Bruno were woken by the murmur of Bousaif at prayer in the early morning, but he'd kept to his room until he was called. He went to the sitting room and began channel-hopping until he found a football game. Hash had never had time for football...they'd missed that on his syllabus at Ben Gashir... and regretted not being able to talk of clubs, players and recent matches. It would have been a way to find common ground but contriving a sudden clumsy interest right now would jar. None-theless, at breakfast Bousaif, with his occasional questions and alert eyes, was practically a chatterbox in contrast to the mute Pakistani, and Bruno's irreverent curiosity proved a great success. The pup had stolen one of Bousaif's trainers while he was praying the previous evening, and he'd been far more amused than put out. They found each other entertaining, and after they'd eaten Bousaif had ventured into the garden, lobbing a ball for the pup to fetch.

Like Eva, he lingered over the photo gallery in the hallway and on the kitchen dresser when they came back in. Hash saw how he peered at the Libyan family photo, a smile playing on his face. 'My family,' Hash ventured. 'Tripoli, in the eighties. Before you were born, I expect.'

'I was just born by then,' Bousaif protested mildly. Hash pointed out his father, mother, sisters and nephew. Bousaif took in each name and seemed to get pleasure from the connection to his home city.

'I haven't been home in years,' Hash said. 'When I was deployed, they didn't tell me it would be forever. Someone at Ben Gashir said to look forward, never back. Now I know what he meant.'

'Allah Kareem,' Bousaif murmured. 'God is good. They could have sent you to Africa.'

'You were at Ben Gashir?' Hash probed.

Bousaif looked away from the photograph and met Hash's inquiry with a shake of his head, leaving Hash wondering if it was a denial, or he just a reminder that he couldn't answer those questions. He felt a flash of irritation at being fobbed off so dismissively and pointed at the photograph of Jim holding his Spitfire. 'My son, fifteen years old. Do you know where he is?' When Bousaif offered the same lazy head shake, Hash snapped, 'The bastards beat him!'

Bousaif's eyes widened, and hardened.

Hash's mobile phone ring broke the impasse. It was Eva.

'I could visit you today,' she told him. 'See Bruno, make sure he is OK.'

'That would be great,' Hash started, 'but he's fine and he's going to be out with me all day. I'll be looking at two buildings I might be buying. There'll be hospitality and all that stuff.' He heard her sigh and offered, 'How about we meet on the racecourse later if there's still time?'

'Not so much fun,' she said. 'Are you trying to keep me away, Mr Hash?'

'You could always come with us, spend the day going round building sites. You'd look great in one of those yellow vests,' he teased.

'As if,' laughed Eva. 'Ok, I'll call you later when you're

done with big business'

Hash rang off and looked at Bousaif. 'Sorry. A friend of mine. I don't want her coming here while you're in the house. Safer for everyone.' Bousaif nodded but said nothing. 'If she does appear, we tell her you're a student, just arrived, looking for more permanent accommodation.'

'A language student,' Bousaif said, 'studying English in Cheltenham.'

'I know the school, actually,' Hash said, 'in Rodney Road, always full of Saudis and Qataris. We see them in the mosque.' He paused, struck by a thought. 'Do you want to come to the mosque? It's small and friendly. There are good people there.'

Bousaif shook his head. 'Better to stay away from it. Friendly people ask questions, want to offer hospitality. Better if I keep away.'

'You're probably right' said Hash and, deciding to try another tack, stood up and fetched a framed portrait of Jim with his first model aircraft. 'I get upset when I think about my son,' he said, apologetically. 'He's missing, and he's young. He'll be very frightened.' He sat down, pulling his chair round to Bousaif's side. 'He'll be sixteen next birthday, but he hardly remembers his mother.'

'He looks a good boy. You should be proud.'

'I'm going to kill them, maybe get killed as well, but they will pay with their lives,' Hash said quietly, his eyes still on the photograph. 'I'll kill anyone who tries to get in my way.'

Bousaif looked at him evenly. 'I hear what you say. But you don't frighten me, my brother. I have my mission.'

THURSDAY 4TH JUNE

Meeting Eva on the racecourse later in the day cheered him up. They walked Bruno together, keeping step and talking easily.

'So, this son of yours, Jim,' she began thoughtfully, 'who

only calls when he needs money. When did you last speak to him?'

The question caught Hash off guard. 'Ages ago.'

'And did you tell him you loved him?' Hash didn't answer.

'Did he tell you he loved you?'

'He asked for money. Boys and their dads don't talk about emotions very often, you know.'

'They think only girls use words like "I love you, Dad",' said Eva. 'If I had to tell Jim something from his father, what would it be? Come on,' she pressed, 'you have to say it.'

'I'd tell him I love him. Very much,' Hash said quietly.

Bruno darted forward to investigate the bramble thickets lining the railway embankment and splash happily in the stream.

Eva pulled out her phone, looked at it and hissed a quiet curse. 'My damn boss.' She held the device up to Hash. 'He needs me for a meeting.'

'Right now?'

'Not now, half an hour ago!' she grimaced. 'Always tells me too late.' She looked to the noise of splashing and told Hash, 'Please, you and Bruno have fun. I've got to get back.'

She gave him a quick hug then turned, waving back at him as she made her way to the car.

The blinking light on the Arab BlackBerry was the first thing he noticed as he entered the kitchen. The photograph had come through while he and Bruno were out. Jim was wearing a baseball cap, staring at the camera and holding up an Arab-language newspaper. It was at least a gesture from the Mukhabarat, to keep hope alive.

Hash immediately emailed the image to his own phone and within minutes had it on his computer, zooming in on every detail. The newspaper was the Sharq al Awsat printed in the UK and only a few days old. Jim was holding the paper so that only his middle fingers were visible, pointing up in a v sign.

The peak of the cap, pulled low, kept the boy's face in shadow but Hash could still see blue and yellow tinges around his eye and cheekbone. He spent a long time examining Jim's blank, strained expression, getting angrier and more distressed by the minute. His boy looked haggard, worn out. He'd get some grim satisfaction out of showing the image to Hakim later, he thought.

EPSOM. SATURDAY 6TH JUNE – MORNING

Before they left, he'd watched Bousaif standing in the kitchen coolly checking the suicide vest, even asking for his help to test the fit, just as comfortable with it as his Pakistani predecessor. This man, who was hours away from detonating twelve kilograms of explosives and creating international mayhem, now sat calmly watching the English countryside slip past as they drove to the racecourse. They'd set off early to be sure of getting a closer parking place, one where Bousaif could get a clear view of the Queen's Stand. Hash wound the window down to flush out the smell from the vest. Somewhere down the eastbound M4, Bousaif had broken the silence to ask Hash not to leave until after the explosion. Hash had considered the simple last request, searching his father's repertoire for a suitable reply to a last wish from a dangerous doomed lunatic. His reply in cut-glass English, 'Of course. My dear boy, why ever not?' was met with a half-smile from Bousaif, who may have missed the irony but was content to be understood.

'I have a request too,' Hash said, 'My son, Jim. Have a look at this picture, it's a good one.' He juggled the wheel and his mobile, finding the shot of Jim. He held it across for Bousaif to see. 'This boy, my son,' he began. 'He didn't deserve to be involved, didn't deserve to be beaten. The people who did this are pigs and have no values. Are the people who did this good Muslims?'

Bousaif looked at the image and slowly shook his head.

Hash pressed the advantage. 'Now that the mission's running and there's no turning back, will you as a brother Libyan, help me? You believe in family'

Bousaif switched his gaze back to the landscape. 'What can I do?'

'Do you know where he is now, how I can get to him?'

Bousaif looked across at Hash steadily. 'You will see him, insh'Allah.'

'But when, my brother?'

'If you are a true Muslim and he is, too, then you will meet him.'

Hash shook his head. 'He's just a boy. I worry about him now, about his health, his mind. Do you have any information? Anything at all?'

Bousaif considered for a moment, then shook his head. 'None.'

'Can you understand? Is it right, that a child is held hostage? Are you a father yourself?'

But Bousaif had hoisted up a drawbridge of silence. His eyes were fixed on the passing countryside, and Hash gave up.

At the racecourse they followed the signs to the public parking, getting as close as they could to the grandstand. They parked at the end of a row of already empty cars. Hash eased his seat into a reclining position, motioning Bousaif to do the same, then pulled a plastic shopping bag forward from the rear seat and placed bottles of water, some fruit and biscuits on the dashboard.

The Derby, scheduled to run at around four-thirty, was more than six hours away, time they'd be spending trapped in the car together. They watched the car park fill up. Racegoers in their finery extracted themselves from their vehicles and set off for the members' enclosures. The less expensively dressed walked to the gates. Hash hadn't expected a funfair to be operating on the other side of the fence, obscuring the last hundred or so metres of the racetrack, and was surprised to see the rides in full swing this early. The smell of frying onions wafted over on the gentle breeze and from midday onwards groups began to come back for picnics around the boots of their estate cars. He watched as they laid out their wooden tables, placed champagne in ice buckets and laid out sumptuous banquets under the bluest of skies. These were good people, the British at leisure. He could not resist turning to Bousaif, who was also watching them, and commenting, 'Filthy kufar.'

If Bousaif understood that irony too, he didn't show it. Instead, hoisting Bruno onto his lap, he smoothed the pup's soft fur and closed his eyes.

Hash dozed alongside them, waking intermittently as the rise and fall of cheering and tannoyed announcements charted progress towards the big race. Eventually, at three-thirty, Hash pointed to the clock on the dashboard. Bousaif sat up and, rubbing his face with his hands, whispered a short prayer to himself. He got out of the vehicle and went to the rear door. Hash joined him and pulled the boot open. Inside, still in the roll-on suitcase, was the vest. Quickly, and with Hash keeping watch across the sea of cars, Bousaif pulled the waistcoat out of the case and laid it on the tailgate. Looking around, Hash checked they were completely alone and unobserved. Bousaif's fingers flicked across the garment, more thoroughly now than he had done in the kitchen a few hours earlier, pulling back Velcro tabs, satisfying himself once more that all was as it should be. He paid meticulous attention to the power pack, an old school but fool-proof combination of a pair of connected cylindrical alkaline batteries. Hash watched him hesitate as he contemplated the two objects which would send the lethal charge of electricity to the detonator. He reached into the breast pocket of the waistcoat and pulled out a roll of black wire which he uncoiled. Hash looked at the plastic syringe where it ended and the crude plastic collar which kept the plunger top from closing flush with the cylinder. Red electrical tape, a single strand, easy to tear off, kept it from moving. This was the safety catch and when Bousaif was ready he would just rip it off, flick away the collar and press the plunger home. Hardly sophisticated stuff, everyday bits and pieces, but then it's genius lay precisely in its simplicity.

Bousaif let the lead dangle as he lifted the waistcoat and shrugged himself into it. He felt for the straps to tighten it to his body, holding on to the swinging lead and pointed at the Barbour jacket they'd bought earlier in the week. He was overdressed for such a warm day, even though the sun had gone well past its highest point. They'd agreed the risk from that was minimal. Most people would be too busy jostling for position to watch the big race to care, and anyway overdressed foreigners at Epsom were not unusual. Bousaif pulled on the coat cautiously, holding the lead in his right hand and threading that arm first through the sleeve. Once it was through, he let the plunger swing free and pulled on the rest of the jacket.

In the distance, loudspeakers were beginning to heighten the atmosphere, drumming up excitement. The commentator kept up a stream of race statistics, facts and figures, the runners and the odds. Hash looked at Bousaif as he pulled on a tweed cap. There was sweat on the man's face and Hash momentarily imagined clubbing him down, killing him just as he had killed the Pakistani before Cheltenham. Bousaif presented himself for inspection, as if seeking Hash's approval. They shook hands.

'May God forgive you,' Hash said.

'May God return your son, my brother,' Bousaif said before turning and walking towards the nearest gate. He'd be entering as the race started, Hash calculated, when there wouldn't be anybody in the queue. The assistant on the turnstile would practically pull him through so he could concentrate on the race himself, probably. Standing on the rear bumper to watch his man, he let him cover two hundred yards and cross the road before he began to follow him. There was just the chance the Libyan group would gather for a last-minute brief before Bousaif made his final approach. Hash moved cautiously, preparing to duck behind a car if he was seen.

Up ahead he saw a sign for the Lonsdale Enclosure and caught sight of one of the punters stumbling; a woman, tipsy or trying to walk too fast in a dress that was too tight. Something about her was familiar. She grabbed at the shoulder of her companion, an elegantly dressed man, who obligingly put his arm around her waist. Her wide, pink hat had slipped to one side and she took it off, shaking out her hair and looking around as if embarrassed. He was looking at Anna. Within seconds she and her escort were through the turnstile and walking away in animated conversation. Hash crossed the road to keep them in sight. Anna's presence was suspicious enough for him to momentarily consider buying a ticket from a tout and following her in. Then he realised the move could get him trapped in any security clampdown. Instead, he headed back to his vehicle.

As he walked, he called Siddiq. 'Are you at Epsom?'

'Sorry, my friend,' Siddiq said. 'Anna had a last-minute business appointment. Something in London, so we didn't go.'

'Did she take the tickets I sent you?'

'I don't know, maybe, she left this morning. But listen, I have heard from Hakim. It's not good news,' Siddiq said. 'His team followed them out of Birmingham but lost them somewhere. Maybe the drivers can tell us later.'

'Later's no good.'

'He's looking for you.'

'Give him my number, I'm away from home but I need to hear anything, anything at all, from Hakim.' Hash rang off and strode back to the Discovery. He wouldn't be hanging around. In the background, the voice on the loudspeaker was getting more tense and frantic with a non-stop flow of last-minute informa-tion about the runners and riders. Hash looked at his watch: four twenty- five. Jim and his minders were off the map, last seen heading south out of Birmingham, linking up with Anna maybe. Perhaps Hakim's men had sighted the woman in west-ern dress and would report in soon. This was why she was lying to Siddiq.

The 2015 Derby started to a massive, surging release of tension. A tumult of cheering welled out from the stands and over the tannoy. Hash felt his mouth go dry: this was a short and furious race. He braced himself, wondering if Bousaif was elbowing his way to the front of the rails, maybe looking back up at the stand to glimpse the British Queen and then clam-bering over the rails to get closer? Hash knew he wouldn't be able to get near her, but twelve kilos of high explosive would vaporise anyone in the vortex and blow out a storm of shattered debris.

The carnage would be indescribable. Hundreds of cam-eras would capture it and replay it forever: first a strange figure scrambling over the barriers, then a pulse of shockwave, then the flash and that massive, final thundercrack detonation. The dryness turned to nausea and he reached for a bottle of water to sluice out his throat.

He heard the excitement as the commentator yelled into the microphone, reeling off a stream of names and numbers in a hysterical crescendo. He hunched his shoulders, ready for the blast. He felt the earth trembling beneath his feet and a rumbling, rushing sound from across the road to his left. The drumming of hooves pounding the turf was like an approaching avalanche, and he imagined the tornado of colour and strain-ing flanks thundering past heading for the roaring, packed grandstand. The commentator, now shrieking with excitement, babbled the names of the leaders and in one last climactic gasp the name of the winner. Hash just managed to catch the name 'Golden Horn' before a massive explosion crashed over everything.

24

EPSOM. AFTERNOON - 6TH JUNE

It was a crashing wave of pure jubilation, a primal roar of celebration and it lasted for a full five seconds before dying away to let the commentator take up again. For a moment Hash wondered if the bomb could have detonated only to be drowned out by the crowd, but he would have felt the shock and seen the smoke. Bousaif had stayed his hand and was choosing a better moment. He imagined him burrowing through the crowd working towards the paddock, getting to the rail to set up for The Queen at the prize-giving ceremony. There was still buzzing excitement in the commentator's voice as he repeated facts, timings and names. Hash imagined him keeping an eye on the prize-giving dais, an attendant beside him talking to royal officials, monitoring The Queen's progress, getting the timing right. He guessed Bousaif was in position. The red tape would have been torn away and the thumb and index finger twisting at the plastic collar on the plunger. He wondered if he would yell 'Allahu Akbar' as he closed the plunger in his fist.

His phone rang. It was Sean. 'Any news?'

'Could happen at any moment,' Hash said. 'The bastard's out

there, still going for it. It's out of our hands.'

Sean said, 'I can come over soon.'

Hash wasn't listening, his eyes were trying to process new information to his tired mind.

'Are you listening?' Sean's voice was positive, cheerful even. 'Are you listening, Darky? Say something.'

Hash tore his eyes away from what was coming and concentrated on the phone, 'Can't talk. SMS me.'

He closed the call and stood up. Bousaif, walking fast, threading through the rows of parked cars, was speeding towards the Discovery. He saw Hash and circled his finger in the air, signalling, 'Let's get moving.'

Hash jumped in, switching on the engine. Bousaif kept heading towards the car but didn't turn into the row where the Discovery was parked. Instead, he moved past, jerking his head to Hash, urging him to catch him on the move. Hash reversed the vehicle onto the exit route, passing alongside Bousaif who wrenched the door open and threw himself in.

Hash could see he was pouring with sweat and breathing hard. He sat, staring ahead, his eyes wide with shock and fear. Bruno immediately leapt for his friend.

'What happened?'

'Nothing.'

'Don't let that bloody dog set anything off!' Hash pointed at Bousaif's right arm, held stiffly across his body, 'Is it still live?'

Hash could see from the way Bousaif held himself that something was badly wrong. He guessed the crude red tape safety collar was lying on the ground somewhere near the Queen's Stand, which meant a vest full of primed explosive was waiting for a voluntary or accidental trigger from Bousaif's clenched, dripping fist.

'Batteries dead?' Hash asked. 'Do you want me to fix it?' He got no answer, and said slowly and clearly, 'If it's live, either you fix it, or you let me fix it.'

There was still no reaction from Bousaif who sat staring ahead. Hash leaned across and crashed his open palm on the dashboard making Bousaif jump at the impact. The Discovery seemed to have pulled itself into a lay-by.

'Let me fix it! Now!' Hash yelled.

'Ok,' Bousaif whispered, melting with fatigue.

Hash could see he was shaking. 'Hold your arm out to me. Don't do anything else, and for God's sake keep your fingers off the syringe.'

PLASMA HOTEL, TRIPOLI. 7TH JUNE.

'You go first.'

The older man pushed back in his seat, indicating with a motion of his hand that the ISIS Director of European Operations had the floor. The meeting was in the same suite, with the same players and the same atmosphere of simmering acrimony. The refreshments carried in earlier lay untouched, but the aide poured tea into long glasses. Outside in the street the temperature stood at forty-five degrees centigrade with eighty percent humidity. In the room, the ageing air conditioning system did nothing to cool the anger and the mutual suspicion.

'You explain…' the Director began, only to be immediately silenced by an abruptly raised hand.

'No,' the older man said quietly, 'we followed instructions. Better you explain!'

'Our plan was frustrated at the last moment by a technicality,' the Director stated. 'Your man did not read the situation in advance.'

'Men in his position live a precarious life and do not have the luxury of always reading situations in advance. We should have been looking at a huge success.' He pointed to the CNN newsreader on the TV screen. 'Look. Nothing to celebrate.'

'We're doing damage control. Again,' the aide added. 'Our man does not think Bousaif was compromised or followed.'

'We gave you our best man at this end and tied him up with our man in the UK,' the older man said. 'The rest was up to your team commander.'

'It appears there was a problem with access to the particular area of the racecourse,' the aide added. 'We're hearing the operator could not get in because he wasn't wearing the correct dress.'

The older man looked out of the window, pointing east to Sirte. 'What do you actually do, over there in Ghardabiya? Surely your acclimatisation training is better than this?'

'We were using British brothers who know the British customs.'

'Then they should have known the correct dress codes.'

The Director was stung. 'We also had a technical problem and we're still checking on it.' He picked up his tea glass and drank, then settled back into his seat. 'The boy.'

The older man contemplated the ISIS man. 'Don't tell me, the boy ran away.'

'He lost control of the drone with the camera.'

'Lost it completely? So, we supply another.'

'He got it to a thousand feet, we had it steady and really clear video on the camera. Then he lost control.'

'What happened?'

'The winds changed. At that height, they were too strong. They took the machine away with them.'

'You need a more powerful machine,' the old man said. 'How did you clean it up?'

'The machine has a default setting which commands it to drop and hover at about four feet. We got to it first.'

'So, it was nothing to do with the dress code,' the aide said.

'A combination of the two. And bad luck,' the Daesh Director said.

The older man nodded. 'From our side, the mission is still intact. Do you agree?'

'The plan is still good,' the Director agreed.

'We have a fallback option, of course,' the aide said. 'The next big horse racing event is Ascot.' He checked the date on his watch, 'It's only ten days away.'

'What about the boy?' the old man asked. 'You need to keep him positive. He needs to want to keep doing all this.'

'We will handle it our way,' the Director said.

'You need to assist me, here. What do we pass on to the father?'

The ISIS Director fingered his prayer beads for a few seconds. 'Leave it as it stands. You've got the father working to save his son,' he said. 'We're doing the reverse. The boy's being told he's doing all this to save his father.'

25

CHELTENHAM. 9TH JUNE

Hash was shocked to see how much bulk his friend had lost from his frame when Sean emerged at Arrivals. Instead of his usual easy athletic prowl he trudged wearily towards him, carrying his overnight case as though it weighed a ton.

'Mind if I burn one?' Sean asked as he clipped on his seat belt.

'If you must,' Hash said.

Sean patted his scalp. His hair had thinned drastically. 'What do you think of my new look?'

Hash smiled at him. 'I could get you a wig.'

'An Afro?' Sean lit up and inhaled with relish. He breathed out a slow stream of smoke, and Hash buzzed down the window, flushing out the fumes. 'Don't give me that Holy Joe shit,' Sean said. 'Been cooped up at no-smoking since I hit Aldergrove four hours ago. You have no idea how good this tastes.'

'Our new friend bottled it at Epsom,' Hash said. 'He seemed fine on the journey, all martyr-like and resolute. I got him vested up and pointed in the right direction.' Sean's wracking cough stopped him.

He watched Sean pitch forward, veins bulging in his neck

as he fought for breath. When the spasm had passed, he wiped a fleck of spittle from his lips and looked across. 'That,' he croaked, 'would have killed a Prod.'

'I saw Anna there, too.'

'Siddiq's bunny boiler?'

'But not with Siddiq. He told me she was in London at a meeting. She's got to be involved.'

'What happened?'

'Nothing. The big race, nothing, then the prize-giving, still nothing, no big bang, no flying bodies. The next thing I see is our man galloping back towards me,' Hash pointed at Sean's seat. 'I get him on board and he's in a trance, white as a sheet.'

'What was his problem?'

'He got held up at the turnstile by some attendant. Etiquette. The dress code or something, he said. 'I hadn't even noticed. Must be losing my touch.'

'Living to fight another day.'

'Hakim's come up with an address,' Hash said. 'Brilliant effort.'

'Or another set-up.'

'I'm getting Hakim on board, bit by bit,' Hash said. 'He was in the mujahideen, fighting Al Qaeda, at Tora Bora. Remember, after 9/11?'

'I remember 9/11.'

'His little brother was executed on the orders of some Arab fighters. They would have been Al Qaeda.' Sean wound the window down and jettisoned the cigarette butt. 'That's why he hates all Arabs.'

'So, it's not just you then.' Sean grinned.

'Jim and the kid brother were the same age. He saw how Jim was standing up to the pain, taking it on the chin. There's a photo.' Hash reached for his mobile, juggling it and the steering wheel to scroll through his pictures. 'Here.' He passed the phone across to Sean who examined it, a scowl spreading across his face.

'Bastards,' he whispered.

Sean climbed the flat's stairs slowly. He moved like an old man.

'Something to please you in that cupboard.' Hash pointed to the drinks cabinet. 'Take a look. It's vintage, one I've been saving for a very special occasion. Got to be at least thirty years old.'

Sean walked over to it and stooped to look inside. 'My absolute favourite,' he exclaimed, with real pleasure on his face. 'You remembered, you old devil.'

'Take it out,' Hash said. 'You know you want to.'

'Really? I can?'

Hashed waved him on. 'Knock yourself out.'

Sean ducked down again to the cabinet and carefully drew out the Kalashnikov, holding it at arm's length, turning it over, admiring it. 'Mint condition for thirty years,' he whispered.

'There's something extra,' Hash said, 'deeper in, at the back.'

'More?' Sean was incredulous. 'A magazine too? You sly dog. Nothing looks better on a Kalashnikov than a loaded magazine.'

'Look again, deeper in,' Hash said.

Sean bent down again, looked and stood up. 'Would you bloody well stop!' He gasped in mock delight, reaching in to retrieve a sleek, black Tokarev. Holding it up to the light, turning the weapon in his hand, slipping out the magazine, racking the mechanism. 'I'm assuming you do actually have the ammo.'

'Limited, but enough.'

Sean fitted the magazine, held the pistol to his forehead and squeezed the trigger, blinking at the metallic click, 'Ouch!'

'Please,' Hash said. 'No party tricks. Maybe save them for later.'

Back at the house, Bousaif emerged from his room and came downstairs in response to Hash's quiet but insistent call. He looked drawn and pale, as though his summer tan was wearing off; the trauma of near death at Epsom was very obviously taking its toll. Bruno, alert and always eager for attention, left Hash's side and went to Bousaif, nipping at his outstretched hand.

'Are you ok?' Hash asked.

'I am tired,' Bousaif said. 'I was sleeping. Someone came looking for you.'

'Who?'

'A woman came.' Bousaif slumped on a kitchen chair, looking at the kettle. 'Asking for you. She said she is your friend. Eva, some name like that.'

'What did she want?'

Bousaif shrugged it off as though it was trivial, 'To say hello, talk with you.' He tickled Bruno's neck. 'Nothing special. She says this is her dog.' Bousaif put on a puzzled look. 'I told her this is your dog. She wanted to take Bruno, but he wouldn't go with her.'

'He belongs to her boss,' Hash explained. 'The deal is I look after Bruno because she's not a dog lover.' They both watched Bruno enjoying Bousaif's attention. 'What did you tell her?'

'I am a language student, you are my host. I'm waiting to get my course paid, then I start soon.'

'Did you tell her where you come from?'

'Are you crazy?'

'Sorry I missed you,' Hash said, stepping into the garden to take the call. 'I got caught up in business, made me late, dammit. You came round?'

'Yes, to see you and check on Bruno. I met your student, he's a very nice boy. He's teaching Bruno tricks. We talked a bit. He said he's from Lebanon but he's getting used to English weather.'

'Did he? I wasn't expecting you. I could have got back in time if you'd called. Do you need Bruno back, or something?'

'Nothing to worry about, but maybe I should get the dog back to my Boss. Tomorrow will do. I'll come and pick him up. Tell me a time.'

'No, don't worry, I'll bring him to you. We could meet on the racecourse,' Hash countered. He didn't need her to get involved with Bousaif again.

Back inside, he found Bousaif watching football. 'You said you didn't tell her where you were from,' he said.

Bousaif looked startled at the question, and Hash's abrupt tone. He shrugged and held up his hands, 'I didn't.'

'Then how does she know you're from Lebanon?'

'I don't know. I didn't tell her anything except the language school story.'

Hash walked away before it became a confrontation. Maybe he'd misunderstood, maybe the stress of Epsom had got to them both.

26

CHELTENHAM. WEDNESDAY 10TH JUNE – MORNING

Their morning rendezvous, Sean looked pale and was clearly in pain, easing himself into the Discovery carefully. The smell of tobacco hung about him, but there was no trace of alcohol. He spent the first few seconds coughing into a handkerchief, then cleared his throat.

'Where did they go?' he said.

'Hakim's saying they upped and left Sparkbrook in the evening. They went separately, Jim and the woman in the red Citroën and the two men in the BMW. But they linked up at some garage on the A34 and went on down the M40 as a pair. He thinks they've gone to ground in Earls Court.'

Sean said, 'That's not near Ascot.'

'But it's on the right side of London. Same distance as from Brum to Cheltenham Races.'

'We need another vehicle, running around in your old Discovery won't do.'

'I'm working on it,' Hash said. 'Hakim's waiting to see me at the mosque. Want to come?'

'You have to be circumcised to go into one of those things, don't you?' Sean said. 'I'll pass, thanks.'

'I've got a task for you, mate.'

'That bloody word again.'

'I'll drop you off with this little bugger.' He jerked a thumb at Bruno in the back. 'Take him for a nice walk but keep your phone camera handy. I'll tell you what you're waiting for. But it'll be pretty obvious.'

Sean watched Hash grinning to himself and scowled, unimpressed. 'I assume this is all really necessary?'

'I don't think you'll be disappointed.'

Leaving Sean attached to Bruno and looking unconvinced, Hash pulled out of the car park on Birdlip Hill and made his way back into town. He'd already called Thelma earlier that morning, giving her a few business updates and putting her in charge while he went to London for a short business trip. She was as unfazed as ever.

Hakim was smiling for the first time Hash could remember. Siddiq hovered, about to say something, but Hakim sent him to bring tea. When the door had closed, Hakim gestured to a chair and they sat.

'They are in Earls Court,' he began. 'And don't ask me for the address yet.'

'If you lose them, I've got no hope of finding Jim in London.'

'Go on,' Hakim said.

'I think you know who these people are,' Hash continued. 'They're an Al Qaeda cell and they're planning a mass attack at one of the big horse racing meetings, and soon. I think it's Ascot.

We stopped them attacking Cheltenham. Then they went for Epsom but called it off at the last moment.'

Hash saw Hakim flinch.

'Who's we?'

'I'll come to that.' Hash tried to dodge the question. 'Ascot is world famous. It's only days away, and The Queen will be sure to attend. These bastards are using my son. They need him for some…'

'They need you,' Hakim interrupted, jabbing a finger at him. 'These people are using you! Yes, they have your son. But first, it is you. Who are you? Why are they using you?'

'I am no friend of Al Qaeda, Daesh, the Brotherhood, or any of those lunatics,' Hash said. 'And you have to believe me.' Hash wished Siddiq was at hand to support him. 'I have a past life, one I am ashamed of. I thought I had escaped from it, left it in a room and closed the door, just as you did in the mujahideen. But I didn't close it properly.' He matched Hakim's gaze. 'And now the past has slipped out to follow me and call in a debt. They,' he pointed out of the window, 'the men and the woman you have found with my son, are the devils from that room. I despise them and I hate them, but they have my son.'

'They are Arabs, for sure.' It was also the first time Hash could recall Hakim agreeing with him. 'Maybe Al Qaeda, maybe Daesh.' Hakim flipped a hand back and forth. 'We are not sure yet. We have seen where they get their support, which mosques, which imams.' He fixed his eyes on Hash. 'If you are an outcast from their organisation then I cannot help you anymore.'

'I am an Arab and I'm proud of that. I'm not the best Muslim, but I'm better than the scum who have my son,' Hash said urgently. 'What I know about Al Qaeda fills me with shame that they share my religion.'

Hakim looked at him, in frosty silence. 'Give me your word,' he said at last.

'I swear it.' Hash held his hand to Hakim. There was a further silence as Hakim considered the value of Hash's word. Then he reached across and shook hands with him.

'Look at this picture.' Hash unfolded a sheet of A4 and laid it in front of Hakim and Siddiq. They leaned forward to look at Jim holding the newspaper.

'The boy's fingers…' Hakim was chuckling now. 'He's showing defiance, this boy, this young man.' Siddiq had joined them, holding a tray with three mugs of tea. They looked at the picture, then round at Hash to congratulate him on his feisty son but he'd turned away, suddenly overcome, trying to hide his despair. They waited.

'May God help him to stay strong,' Siddiq said.

'May God give the father some of his son's courage,' Hakim added.

'Let me know when I can go in and rescue my son. Soon, before they change addresses.' Hash wiped his hand across his eyes. 'I will go in and stop them, or I'll die in the attempt. You can help me save my son and hundreds of innocent people.'

'You will do all this by yourself? You have nobody to help you?'

'If I must, Sayyid Hakim. How can I best explain?' Hash looked at them. 'I said the door was not properly closed and maybe, because I am desperate now, I have to slip back into that room myself for a while.'

'Is that why you offered me a weapon?'

'Yes.'

Hakim eased back in the chair. 'My promise to your son is this. I will do as you ask. As soon as I have the address, and only,' he held up his hand, 'when I am ready. When all my men are out of the way, I will pass it to you. But,' and again he stopped Hash interrupting with a finger, 'I will not take the weapon you are offering me, and I did not even hear this offer. And if,' he pointed at Hash's chest, 'Insh'Allah you are successful, and you rescue your son then we will meet again, and we will be happy together.' He looked harder at Hash. 'But no killing! This country took me in when I was poor. The British gave me the hand of friendship when I had no friends. They taught me to play with a straight bat. So, my friend, I tell you now; if anyone is killed, I will go to the police.'

AFTERNOON

Sean was grinning from ear to ear when Hash rolled to a halt. He took a last drag on his cigarette and flicked the butt away as the window buzzed down.

'You were right about the views,' Sean said. He waved out across towards Gloucester and May Hill. 'Gorgeous sights!'

'And the wildlife?' Hash asked. 'As interesting as I promised?'

Hash got out to hoist Bruno on board and held the door for Sean. Getting comfortable, Sean breathed out. 'I'm amazed at the birdlife up here. Must be something in the air.'

'Did you see the tits?'

'Bruno was traumatised by what he saw,' Sean said.

'Let me see, then,' Hash said.

'Hang on, you old pervert.' Sean pulled out his phone. 'Oh shit,' he said, shaking it. 'The bloody thing's died on me.' He looked up at Hash. 'Can you bloody well believe that?'

'Pull the other one,' Hash laughed.

'Are you sitting comfortably?' Sean said. 'Then we'll begin.' The screen steadied as a view of the woodland and parking area came into focus. The lens zoomed in on a silver Audi estate with the familiar Help for Heroes and Carry On Hunting stickers in the rear window. He saw the conman climb out from the driver's seat and the pretty girlfriend from the car park emerge from the other side. They embraced against the back of the vehicle, enjoying long minutes of kissing.

'My God, you got bloody close.'

'By the time they got started you could have marched a brass band past and they wouldn't have noticed.'

Back in the flat they started packing the weapons and Sean's few belongings.

'The problem with that woman, Anna or whatever she's called,' Sean observed as Hash picked up his ringing phone, 'is she's too tough for your mate.' He looked into his small suitcase, tossing in items of clothing, 'Do we actually know who she is, where she comes from?'

Hash's phone bleeped. 'It's Thelma,' he said. 'Sorry,' and turned away to take the call.

Sean listened as he lapsed into business jargon. 'We're borrowing five hundred k…Remind me how much we're borrowing at?... That's too kind of them…no, we don't really have much choice. Tell the vendor's agent we're good to go at a million and not a penny more…Gotta go…yes…thanks, Thelm.'

Sean held up his glass of whiskey and breathed in the scent of the liquid. 'I'll drink to that.'

Hash had finished the call and was back in the real world. He saw Sean grinning at him.

'What?'

'I can't believe you, Darky.'

'What?'

'Fucking tycoon, you. Fucking magistrate too. Your boy at a private school, the pink shirts and posh suits, the signet ring. What happened to wee Darky off that fucking boat, shitting himself, frozen?'

'Still the same Darky,' Hash said.

'You've done well, pal, fair play to you.'

'Have I though? Really?' Hash said. 'I thought I'd outrun them, outlived Gaddafi and all his madness.'

'How the hell did they keep such close tabs on you all these years?'

'The team running my letter box,' Hash sipped his whiskey. 'The only logical answer. They've shadowed my life, our life. Kept the line open to Tripoli. Compromise the box and they kill me or Jim. Or Tara if she'd been alive.' He snapped his fingers. 'They left me alone for years, and then they brought me out of hibernation.' He was lost in his train of thought. 'They would have known Jim from the racecourse and his models, the dogs, our whole life.' He looked at Sean and drained his tumbler. 'Another one?' He poured generously without waiting for an answer. 'Jim gets snatched, and all of a sudden my devout friend has a man-eater on his hands, running him ragged.' He sighed. 'The bomber, a woman in a burqa…' His arm swept across the gleaming Kalashnikovs. 'And now this stuff. I'm back to square one, except now Jim's caught up in it too. It's play the game or die.'

'She sounds like a psycho,' Sean said, 'the type who owns you just because you happened to shag her once. She knew about Jim, didn't she?'

'Siddiq told her.'

'She appeared out of the blue. Dumped your mate after the Gold Cup, then reappears at the Derby. Are you joining the dots?'

'I am, but Siddiq brought Hakim.'

'How do you know for sure?'

'I don't,' Hash conceded.

'Is she the one in the red car and in the burqa?'

'That makes her the one who hit Jim,' Hash said.

'And that makes it personal.' Sean picked up one of the AK-47s and took off the magazine. He checked the rounds, pressing them down on the magazine. 'This spring's good, even after all these years.'

'Insh' Allah,' Hash said.

'And I'm still good after all these years.' Sean winked at Hash, lifting his glass. 'Sláinte, Darky.'

He fitted the magazine back on and wrapped the first weapon in a towel. He held up the Tokarev next, assessing it. 'Ugly thing, isn't it?'

He wrapped the pistol and picked up the first grenade, trying to unscrew the base plug and grunting with the effort. 'Gummed tight after all the time underground. Got a pair of pliers?'

Hash fetched the pliers and watched as Sean wrestled the

base plugs off and laid out the innards of the two grenades. 'If they work at all, it's pull, throw and get the head down, two seconds, maybe three.' He started to reassemble them. 'Look.' He held up the pliers. 'I'll pinch the end of the pins, so they pull easier. Give them a dab of oil, too.'

'Your time in the Kesh wasn't wasted, I see.'

'Always happy to do your dirty work, Hash, you know me.'

He slid the grenades into the Jameson whiskey tube. Hash heard them clunk on top of each other. 'Although, give credit where credit is due, you did actually manage to kill that Paki all by yourself. No, wait, Susan and the dog tired him out first. You just finished him off.'

'So, how are Bella and the Badger? Did you go and see them?'

'I bloody knew that was coming next,' Sean slumped in the kitchen chair and took out his cigarettes.

'How did it go?'

'Not very well. They don't want to see me, there's nothing more to say, nothing we can do.'

'They know you're ill, don't they?'

'You told them, not me.' Sean took out a cigarette and lit up, exhaling, his eyes following the stream of blue smoke. 'A judgement from God, were her words. The old boy didn't get it at first. Then he did his usual, started to cry and she tells me I've put him under the stress. All my fault. So, then I leave and drive all the way back to Belfast. I was only there for fifteen minutes but I got a cup of tea.'

'Christ,' Hash whispered. 'I'm so sorry.'

'Don't be, I know how my mother feels. When I look at myself in the morning, I hate me too.'

'I'm sorry, Sean.'

'What's it they say about sympathy?' Sean smiled at Hash. 'You'll find it in the dictionary, somewhere between shit and syphilis.'

'You told them you're doing this for Jim, their wee Lord, didn't you? I told you to.'

'Can't remember if I did or not.' Sean drew on his cigarette.

'Bullshit,' Hash said. 'I wanted them to know.'

'Yeah, I think you told them that, too. Thanks for trying. Look, Darky,' Sean put his glass down and leaned towards his friend. 'The thing about our game.' He stabbed a nicotine-stained finger at the wrapped AK-47. 'You can join but you can never leave.' He eased back. 'You've done well, Darky. You're the only one I know who got away with his mind in one piece, in the nick of time.'

'But I didn't get away. Maybe I've had better luck than you, Sean,' Hash said. 'I certainly had the better deal, until now anyway.'

'I never regretted joining,' Sean said, 'and in the same circumstances I'd do it all over again but,' and he looked away, out of the window, 'when you get blood on your hands it never quite washes off, does it?'

'We were in a war,' Hash said.

'Innocent blood.' Sean continued staring at Hash for a few seconds, then stubbed his cigarette out.

'We're doing this for innocent Jim,' Hash said. 'Your nephew, your sister Tara's son, their grandson,' he added gently, 'so that you can do the most that's humanly possible to set things right.' Sean sat, elbows on the table, head in hands. Hash saw a tremor in the hands, his knuckles whitening as they kneaded his eyebrows and forehead.

'You've got this chance,' Hash said softly. 'We pull it off and we can walk away our heads held high. If we fail, at least we'll have done more than most people would have even dared,' he said. 'That's what you're bringing to this whole thing, Sean,' he added. 'I couldn't do any of this without you. People like you don't come along every day. You're here for a purpose.'

EVENING

'There he goes,' Sean said. 'Just got in. Starting her up.'

'Jump in then. Let's go.'

Sean led Bruno across the grass to where Hash had the Discovery idling and hoisted the pup into the cargo area. They let the silver Audi move into the light evening traffic then tracked it, following the tell-tale stickers in the rear window.

'Not steering for town,' Hash muttered. They had talked the plan through painstakingly but were both tense now they were playing it for real. Hash kept the Audi in sight for a few hundred yards, then began closing in on it. He wasn't sure how soon the driver would turn off in the direction of a client or his girlfriend, and he knew he had to force the pace. By the time they'd reached the traffic lights at the junction with the High Street, Hash was directly behind the silver car. It headed across the junction at College Road only to be held up by a pedestrian crossing with the lights on red

'Now,' Sean urged.

Hash slipped the clutch on the Discovery and it lurched forward to hit the rear of the Audi. It was a perfectly judged bump, hard enough to shock, but no real damage. Both men saw the driver's bald head bounce back, then shake in anger and disbelief.

'You've really pissed him off now,' Sean said, grinning. He slipped out of the passenger seat and made for the Audi.

Hash pulled out and slowly overtook the car, coming to a stop a few parking spaces ahead. The drivers queuing behind began to filter past, gawping as they went, the first few amused, the remainder only interested in getting past.

Sean went to the window and waved passers-by on, to keep other witnesses away. 'I saw it,' he told the driver. 'I saw it all, no problems, mate.'

'You should have,' the bald driver said, 'you were in the fucking car. Is that other guy blind or something? And he's not supposed to drive off. That's leaving the scene of an accident, that is.'

'You're right, mate,' Sean said, 'blind as a bat. Wasn't paying attention, his fault. He says he's coming over as soon as he parks.'

'Tossers!' the man hissed. 'You've been drinking, haven't you?'

'Just a few, mate. It'll be alright,' Sean said. 'Are you ok, my friend? No cuts and bruises?'

'Probably got whiplash,' he said, rubbing his neck. 'That was a hell of a bump.'

'Not much damage though,' Sean said. 'Just a wee bump, not even a scratch.'

As he got out to inspect his rear bumper, Hash caught up with him. 'Sorry, my friend, all my fault,' he began. 'You stopped a bit too soon, that bloody pedestrian crossing. I just wasn't quick enough, dammit.'

The man looked up from the bumper inspection, too angry to focus on Hash's face. 'That's a body job for sure. Could be an insurance write-off.'

'No problem, my friend. My fault, blame me. I'll pay. Just let me have your bank account details and I'll transfer the money.'

'Doesn't quite work like that here,' he said, his eyes coming to rest on Hash for the first time. In the background, Sean was still waving on the traffic. 'In this country we take insurance details.'

'I understand.' Hash gave him a wide smile. 'But I'm about to travel, emigrate in fact, and the paper trail might never get to me. Better I settle with you now. With cash.'

'You've either been drinking, or you're not insured.'

'I am, actually,' said Hash, 'but it's better we settle in cash.'

'Or both.' His eyes narrowed as he continued to rub his neck. 'You're definitely not insured,' he said. 'Fuck…' he exclaimed. 'So, tell me why don't I just call the police?

'Can we settle it now?' Hash's smile was becoming more fixed, and his voice took on a pleading tone. 'How much?' he asked.

'It's my living, that car.' He pointed at the bumper. 'Don't know what you do for a living, mate, but I work from that.'

'Whatever is reasonable,' Hash said. 'I can pay.'

'You people,' he said sardonically. 'Money solves everything, doesn't it? I don't suppose you've got two thousand in cash on you?'

'I can get it, no problem. But we'll have to go and get it together'

He looked at him, then back at his bumper. Hash leaned in and said, 'The cash deal means now, my friend, right now. My mate will jump in with you, and you just follow me up to the Bath Road car park where the banks are.'

The man looked at Sean and then back to Hash who was gesturing the way ahead. 'Ok,' he said.

Five minutes later they were parked and all three in the Discovery to continue the negotiation, Sean seated in the back, silent. The bald man had ratcheted the price up to three thousand pounds and was visibly happy about Hash caving in so easily.

'I'll get the rest of the money now,' Hash said, opening the door. 'Give me ten minutes.'

In the Discovery there was silence for a moment or two before he spoke. 'Your mate's quite a fan of hard cash. Wealthy, I suppose?'

"Just your average millionaire who likes to keep a low profile,' Sean said.

'Driving this heap of junk, done over a hundred thousand. I'm not impressed. How'd he make his money, then?"

'Property mainly. Bit of this, bit of that.'

'That's my line, too,' the Audi man started, but his phone rang a grandiose fanfare and he put it to his ear. Sean heard a woman's voice asking questions. 'Sorry love' he answered. 'Not going to make it. Why? Some bloody idiot pranged me, that's why.' Having Sean behind him didn't inhibit him. 'Yes, a pair of idiots who've been drinking. Damage? You mean to me? Thanks for your concern.' He laughed. 'Yeah, I'm fine but the car's practically a write-off. We're sorting it now. Catch you later.' He put the phone back in his jacket pocket. Hash was approaching the car.

'What's your mate's name then?' he asked.

'Didn't he tell you?' Sean said.

'No.'

'Well, then.'

'Well, what?'

'Maybe he wants to keep names out of it,' Sean said

'My neck hurts,' the man said, reaching up to rub his fleshy neck.

'Do you want the cash or not?'

Sean's tone jarred and the man craned round to look at his face. 'You taking the piss?'

Hash was climbing into the driver's seat. He passed an envelope over and switched on the ignition. 'We're a bit short. Been round four of those 'hole in the wall' machines.'

Their companion opened the envelope to see the notes and was soon too busy checking them to feel the Discovery moving.

As the vehicle exited the car park, he held up a note, 'It's five hundred short,' he said.

Hash looked over, reassuringly. 'I just said that, my friend. We're going to get it, right now.'

'What about my car?'

'We'll be back in ten minutes.'

He was silent for a few seconds more until he saw Hash was driving south, out of town. 'There's no bank out here,' he said, 'you're going the wrong way.'

'Relax, my friend, it's a different bank.' Hash waved a free hand at him. 'Soon be there.' The man went doubtfully silent again, looking down at the wad of notes. 'Unless you want to give me a discount?' Hash said.

'Hang on, fifty-pound notes out of the hole in the wall... you 'aving a laugh? This a con?'

'When do I get to beat the shit out of this arsehole?' Sean growled.

As the man turned, incredulous, Sean slapped him hard in the face with an open hand. The shocking sound of the impact filled the cabin. Sean looped a leather belt over his head and pulled tight. As his head jerked back his hands instinctively rose to his neck and the belt, but Sean's weight was against him and he found his head jammed against the headrest. His fingers pulled at the belt and his voice came in choking gasps. The envelope of cash slid off his lap.

'I want complete silence, shithead. Otherwise,' and he dug his fingers into his victim's crimson neck, fingers probing for his throat, 'whiplash will be the least of your worries.' He slapped the man's face again. Hash kept quiet, staring ahead as they drove up Leckhampton Hill.

Sean said, 'I'm going to let you go as long as you promise to stay fucking silent, completely silent. Got me?'

Their passenger nodded and held his hands up in submission. Sean slackened the belt, leaving white marks on the reddened skin. The man began to breathe more easily, but his head stayed tight to the headrest, his body frozen and shoulders hunched in case another blow came from behind.

'The bad news, my friend,' Hash said slowly, distracted by traffic at a roundabout, 'is the last five hundred may take some time after all.'

'But you said…' he started before his voice was choked off by Sean jerking the belt back.

'Completely silent, shithead,' Sean said. 'Didn't you hear me the first fucking time?'

The Discovery parked at the far end of the Air Balloon car park. Anyone nearby would see three men sitting comfortably, having a chat.

'But there's good news.' Hash turned, watching him fight for breath, his head jammed against the headrest. 'The good news will be if you and I can do a deal, come to an agreement where everyone is happy.'

He signalled to Sean to release the pressure and they watched the man lean forward, gagging for air. Hash clicked his fingers and Sean hauled back, slamming his head back against the headrest. Hash looked at the second hand of his watch and then at the man's bulging eyes.

'We can go on all day.' Hash held up his hands, palms open. 'It's up to you, my friend, but time is precious.'

'Let me kill him,' Sean said. 'Please.'

'Not if our friend is prepared to help. Give him air, please.' The belt slackened, and his throat sucked in air. When he had recovered, Sean took the belt away. The man rubbed his neck, staring wildly at Hash and flinching as Sean shifted behind him.

'Shall we take a quick look at something we saw?' Hash let Sean reach forward between them, holding up his phone. The video began to run, showing the silver Audi parked on Birdlip Hill and the conman getting out, smiling as his girlfriend came around for a long embrace.

'Your girlfriend,' Hash took out a sheaf of printed images, is probably a secret you want to keep.' He placed the images on the man's lap one by one. He looked down at them then across as Hash continued. 'Embarrassing if your wife sees any of this, embarrassing for your girlfriend too. We can post it on their Facebook and I've got your email.'

'Who are you? What do you want?' the conman said in a small, frightened voice.

'You're a fucking thief,' Sean said.

'I don't know what you're talking about.'

'Silence,' Sean growled, making as if to replace the belt. Hash leaned over and tapped the man on the knee. 'My friend behind you is not patient.' He made a show of looking at his watch. 'As time runs his temper gets worse.' On cue, Sean slapped him hard. His victim's head flicked sideways, and his eyes fixed on Hash. 'Hang on…I know you…seen you some-where…'

Sean caught the flash of alarm on Hash's face in the mirror, and slapped him again, harder.   'They all look the same to you, don't they…All darkies look alike to you, don't they,' he hissed.

'I didn't mean it like that,' he tried to point at Hash, 'He…'

'No offence taken,' Hash said, dismissing the moment with a shrug, 'a misunderstanding.'

'Only offence here is your thieving,' Sean growled, 'thiev-ing money from pensioners.' He punched him with a full fist. 'Thieving,' another punch, 'bastard.' The conman was sobbing in pain.

'Stop that, please,' Hash remonstrated. 'Calm down every-one, I think we can do a deal, as friends, can't we?' Hash asked, offering his hand.

'What are you talking about?' He looked at Hash's hand. 'What deal? My car?' The right side of his face was red, and he was breathing hard.

'Are you a thieving bastard?' Sean's fist hung poised in front of the man's face. 'Did you take money from pensioners? Spend it on cars and whores?' Sean's hand rammed into the man's crotch, grabbing at his genitals. 'Old people's life savings?'

He screamed, and Sean slapped him in the mouth. 'Stop crying, you fat, fucking shite.'

'Yes, your car,' Hash said.

'Take it,' he sobbed.

Sean leant forward. 'We've already got it, you stupid fat fucker,' he snarled into his ear.

'Then what do you want? Just leave me alone.'

'We want to give it back, my friend.' Hash spoke in slow confidential tones. 'Just borrow it for a few days, then give it back to you.'

'I don't understand,' he began and was immediately choked

by Sean hauling back. Sean pulled at the scrabbling fingers, catching one and wrenching it back on itself. He gagged in pain.

'I just want to borrow your car,' Hash said. 'It's that simple.' He put his face close to the man's and signalled Sean to ease off the pressure. 'When I've finished with your car, I'll leave it, with some more money under the seat.' The man nodded, eyes still bulging, sweat pouring off his forehead.

'Do you understand, now?' Sean said.

When the man nodded again, Sean released the belt.

'We take your car, we use it, we leave it with some money in it,' Hash said. 'Car hire. Simple.'

'What will you tell your wife?' Sean hissed. He hesitated. Sean slapped him. 'You'll tell her it's in the garage, being fixed.' He struggled to get away from the next blow. 'Sit still! What'll you tell your girlfriend when she gets horny and calls you for a shag?' Sean's fist was poised.

'I'll tell her it's in the garage...' His voice came in gulps.

'How long's it in the garage for?' Sean asked. He didn't see Sean's fist as it came around from the left of the headrest. 'Until we fucking say so,' Sean answered. The man rocked away from the blow and his head began to droop. Hash shook him to get his concentration. 'We're going to let you go home now.'

'You're not going to the police, are you?' Sean coached.

'Please don't involve the police,' Hash added. 'It would be awkward because...'

'Because you're thieving scum,' Sean spat into his ear, 'and I'll find you.'

'Because we're in a business agreement that you are lending us the car.' Hash retrieved the fallen envelope and dropped it together with the sheaf of photographs into the man's lap. 'You should keep these safe,' he said. He patted his knee again. 'Not for long, just a short while. We'll let you know when and where to pick up your car and,' he tapped the envelope, 'some more of this.'

'Where are the keys?' Sean asked.

'Yes, your keys, please.' Hash held up a restraining hand as Sean raised his fist again. 'Now, where shall we drop you?'

Hash said goodbye to Sean at midnight.

'You should get to London in a couple of hours,' he said.

Sean looked up from the dashboard. 'Never driven one of these. Bet those two had a lot of fun in it mind. God, would you look at all these dials. All I need is the cigarette lighter'.

'Where will you rest up?'

'Maybe doss in the car for tonight, then any place that takes cash. I'll get out to Ascot tomorrow and look it over.'

'Got everything you need? Cash, weapons, plates?'

Sean patted the little suitcase beside him on the passenger's seat. 'All in here, ready to go.'

27

THURSDAY JUNE 11TH

Eva looked down at the sandwiches Hash had unwrapped and laid on the tailgate. 'The problem is the dog,' Eva said, looking down at the sandwiches Hash had unwrapped and laid on the tailgate. Bruno tried to leap up to get them and she swatted him away. Hash heard the pup squeak in pain and saw him retreat, his tail tucked. She held up a sandwich, examining it.

'The problem is your boss,' Hash said.

'He's going away again, and he wants me to come with him.' She sipped coffee from a paper cup.

'The problem is your boss,' Hash repeated. 'It sounds as though he doesn't even want the dog.'

'I don't want the dog, he doesn't want the dog. Now he likes horses. He changes his mind the whole time.'

'I can't help you exercise his horses,' Hash waved his hand at the racecourse, 'but you're in the right place.'

She smiled at his attempt to lighten the moment. 'Bloody horses. We have to go to Ascot next weekend,' she sighed, 'Every day. Can you believe it?'

'Ascot? Horse racing? That's not this weekend, it's next weekend,' Hash corrected.

'Whatever,' Eva shrugged. 'Too soon anyway.'

'Don't go,' Hash said.

'Why not? It's my job.'

'It's not safe,' Hash blurted. 'Please don't go. Make an excuse.'

'It's Ascot, England. Not Ascot, Gaza Strip.'

'Say you're sick,' Hash said. 'Really. Don't go.'

'I can't be sick all week. He needs me to show off to his business friends.'

'Who are these people?'

'Arabs.' She snorted, then clapped a hand over her mouth. 'Not nice Arabs like you.' She pinched his arm.

'Where are they from?'

'Here and there,' she said airily. 'Qatar, Saudi. All those places.' She waved her hand. 'My boss wants oil business. They don't look at the horses, though. They look at the girls.' She clucked her tongue at him. 'This is my job. Big hat, short skirt. He says some of the English ladies, they look like horses. This is why I am needed.'

Hash watched Bruno in pursuit of somebody else's whippet. There was a play-fight and a chase across the meadow, with the whippet showing Bruno what speed was about. Eva called but he was too far away to hear or care, waiting to catch his playmate as he swooped past.

'How's James, Lord Jim? Did you tell him?'

Hash brought his attention back to Eva. 'Tell him what?'

'You miss him?'

'Of course. But he's with his grandparents and they're good for him. I hope I'll see him soon, maybe I'll visit him in Jordan or bring him back here for some of the holidays.'

'Does he call you?'

'Not very often. He's a teenager.'

'I know,' she mimicked, 'he only calls when he needs money.

Do you think he would like me?'

'I'm sure he would.'

Her phone buzzed, and she wriggled to get it from her hip pocket. She looked at an SMS, her lips moving as she concentrated on the text. 'Bloody boss. Time to go home. Bring the bloody dog back.'

'So soon? We've only just got here.' Hash gave up trying to save the day and whistled. The sound reached Bruno who turned instantly to check, then came running to them.

Her phone buzzed again and she studied it intently, her brow furrowed, then suddenly pitched forward as Bruno rammed into her legs. The phone fell, and coffee splashed across her white jeans. Hash caught her as she staggered but she shook him off.

'Fucking dog,' Eva hissed, her face white with anger. She lashed out with her foot, catching the pup in the ribs. Bruno squealed in pain and darted away with Eva screaming, 'Fuck off, dog!'

'He didn't mean anything,' he said, watching Bruno who was now some yards away, trembling and licking his injured side ribs. 'You've hurt him, Eva. It wasn't his fault.' It was the first time he'd felt at odds, and uneasy, with her. He leaned down to pick up her phone which had fallen under the tailgate.

'I'll kill it!' She glared at the pup. 'Look at these stains on my jeans. What the fuck am I going to do now?'

Hash was only dimly aware of her exasperation; he'd picked up her phone and was checking the screen for damage. Amongst the list of calls with their numbers alongside, a Libyan dialling code stared at him. Bruno was yelping, turning on himself, limping but too frightened to come back.

Eva snatched the phone back. 'Maybe my boss heard that,' she groaned. 'I just don't like dogs. Hash, please, do something.'

Hash picked up a piece of food and walked slowly towards Bruno who retreated, keeping his distance, panting. Eventually

Hash tempted him to take the morsel and comforted the pup, then scooped him up and brought him back to the vehicle.

'Sorry, Hash...I feel terrible,' Eva said, 'look at me. What a mess.' She watched Hash feed the dog another piece of meat from the sandwich. 'I have to go. So sorry, Hash,' she said again, standing, plucking at her stained jeans. 'Pressure from my boss and this Ascot thing. Men always looking at me, you know?'

'Some of us are gentlemen. . I've heard Libyans are nice too. Have you ever met any Libyans?'

They were standing at her car and she ducked down to check her appearance in the wing mirror. 'My boss doesn't have any Libyan clients, so I wouldn't know about that.'

Hakim was waiting at the mosque, and this time he looked concerned.

'I have the address. Two men, your son, but not, so far, the woman. We don't know where she is.' He tugged at his beard, thinking. 'She comes and she leaves, sometimes with one of the men. Always with the burqa.'

'Can you give me the address?' Hash asked. 'Then I can go as soon as possible.'

'Too risky,' Hakim said quietly. 'Too risky.'

'You promised.'

'I know exactly what I promised.'

'Sayyid Hakim, I am running out of time. They may move. They are going to Ascot Racecourse.' Maybe they will change their accommodation again.'

'How do you know?'

'Not one hundred percent sure, but probably.'

'Why Ascot?'

'Ascot Racecourse,' Hash corrected. 'It's the logical place. They've been training for a racecourse, and they're looking for the Queen as a target.'

'Are you sure?'

'It's a pattern they set and they're following it. Remember Cheltenham Races in March? Well, this is even bigger, and there's a greater chance of the Queen being present.'

'You have someone helping you, I assume?'

'Just two of us,' Hash said.

'But you are carrying weapons?'

'We will only use them if we've no choice. You know who these people are.'

Hakim sat back on the chair to look up at the calendar. 'Why would they be in London almost a week before Ascot? Why leave their safe network in Birmingham?'

Hash followed his gaze. 'Maybe they want to set up and prepare, give themselves more time. Who knows what else they have planned for that day?'

Hakim looked back to Hash. 'I am not confident about your predictions,' he said.

'Just give me the address and we'll hit the target as soon as possible. Maybe tonight, tomorrow morning.'

'This friend of yours.' Hakim switched tack. 'Does he come from that same dark room you were in all those years ago?'

'Yes.'

'So, he's a terrorist, too?'

'Were you a terrorist in Afghanistan, or a freedom fighter?'

Hakim did not answer for a while. 'Maybe I let you have the information and maybe you win.' He tilted his head left then right. 'Or maybe it's a disaster.' He looked at the calendar again. 'Or maybe I keep my team on the task and bring you in at the last moment. You will not get much time,' Hakim said, 'so be ready when I call.' He patted his pocket, pulling out a notebook. 'Take down these numbers and give me yours. From now on we can work together.'

'Sayyid Hakim, I don't know how to begin to thank you,' Hash began. 'Can I make a donation to the mosque, this one or yours?

Or both?'

Hakim stopped him. 'We prayed for your son in our mosque and in this one, too.' His eyes swept the bleak kitchen. 'Strangers, but good Muslims, prayed for his deliverance. To thank those strangers, just bring your son to pray beside them…that would be enough.'

'I've been thinking about it, too,' Sean said later. 'I'm not convinced yet. Yes, it's early for Ascot, but they could just be making double sure of their ground before the security steps up. That way they can come in and go to their exact positions.'

'I'm with you,' Hash said. 'Hopefully you'll see them, or we'll at least get a bearing on them if Hakim's boys give us a tip-off.' Hash heard Sean's coughing at the other end of the phone. 'They know about you now, and they know that we're carrying too.'

'Fuck me,' Sean exclaimed. 'Did they have a pair of pliers on your crown jewels? So, we're working with them, now?'

'They'll hand over to us as soon as they have the location and can get clear.'

'How do you know they won't ambush us or rat us out?'

'I don't. But I'm trusting them. We don't have too many choices.'

LATER

Unable to sleep in the early hours, and with the endgame approaching so fast, Hash left his bedroom and crept downstairs. As he walked past the kitchen he flicked on the light, waking Bruno who yawned but stayed put. He retrieved the Jameson whiskey tube with the two grenades. Emptying the contents carefully, he took a pair of kitchen scissors and, stacking the grenades one on top of the other, matched the cardboard tube against them. Measuring where the safety rings on the pins would touch the tubing cardboard, he cut two coin-sized holes in the flank then covered the grenades in bubble wrap and eased them back into the tube so that they sat, one on top of the other, rings exposed to view. He tied two inches of wire to each ring so he could ease the pins out and arm the bombs, and then contemplated his final statement to the Mukhabarat. When the time came, as Hash knew it would, whoever emptied the letter box, the human link between him and the rest of the cell, would be blown to bits.

28

CHELTENHAM. MORNING
- FRIDAY 12TH JUNE

B ousaif and Bruno watched the ritual polishing of his brogues.

'Old shoes, well-kept, are a sign of good breeding,' Hash said.

'Or you throw old shoes away because they're a sign that you can't afford new ones?' Bousaif responded.

Hash caught a last glimpse of the pup putting both paws on Bousaif's knees, cadging scraps off his breakfast plate, as he closed the front door.

The court assembled at nine in the morning. Hash was sitting with an elderly magistrate he didn't know, similarly disappointed at being handed a tedious morning of traffic offences. There'd been no update from Sean since last night, and reluctantly he switched the phone to silent. They made it through three cases before coffee break, by which time there were two new messages on his phone. The first, from Sean at nine-thirty, simply reported in; nothing doing so far in the Ascot area. The second, sent at ten o'clock, was from one of Hakim's numbers and gave him the address of a building in London's Philbeach

Gardens, in SW5. Hash just had time to pass this to Sean before he had to shut the phone down again. Heart thumping as he resumed his seat in court, he knew at least that Sean was on his way to the target. He became dimly aware of his colleague saying that the next case might be livelier, with the defendant there in person to contest the charge. The clerk escorted a young woman to the dock where she stood, her expression somewhere between determined and nervous. There was something familiar about her, and Hash began to feel uneasy. The charge was driving without due care and attention, and she pleaded guilty. His colleague asked what she had to say in her defence.

'I'm a carer and I can't do my job without a car,' she began, as Hash studied her with a growing feeling of discomfort. 'I look after my mother and father. They both need regular medical help,' she stated, and added, 'round the clock.'

'And this care can't be provided by anyone else but you?'

The young woman shook her head. 'We live out in the country and I'm the breadwinner, too.'

Hash was staring at her, his suspicion becoming acute. She'd been coached and was sticking to her script. 'I'm their lifeline.'

The magistrate beside him scribbled 'Any questions?' on a scrap of paper and passed it to Hash, who shook his head.

'You knew the importance of the car,' his companion began. 'Your licence is your lifeline, as you so eloquently put it. So why would you risk it by speeding excessively?'

Hash was barely listening, aware of someone new entering the court. The woman's face looked across and broke into a smile of relief. 'My partner,' she explained. 'In case I lose my licence.'

'Maybe your partner can help with the driving?'

'He doesn't live with me. And he hasn't got a car.'

Hash wasn't looking at the woman or concentrating on his colleague's line of questioning. He was looking at the bald conman. There was a moment of mutual recognition and the man sat down, barely glancing at his girlfriend, his mouth an

'O' of surprise as he stared at Hash. Then his head went down, and he was texting furiously.

All Hash could do was sit it out as his colleague went through the ritual questions of who else was available to care for the parents and whether there was a neighbour, bus service or alternative form of transport for prescriptions to be delivered should a ban be imposed. As his colleague turned to Hash for his final decision, the public door opened for a second time and the legal aid counsel slipped in, taking a seat beside the con-man.

'We find you guilty of the offence,' the colleague announced. 'You are to be banned from driving for two weeks. You will now hand your licence to the clerk.'

They rose and left the court. Hash could feel the con-man and his counsel watching him every step of the way. He couldn't get away until midday; opening up his phone, he saw he had missed calls from both Sean and Hakim.

'Where the fuck've you been?' said Sean. 'I've been ringing like crazy.'

'Change the plates on the car,' Hash said.

'What the fuck are you talking about? I'm nowhere near the car, I'm on foot. I left the car in Philbeach Gardens.'

'On the street?'

'In a hotel car park. What's the sudden panic? Want me to do it in broad daylight?'

'Change the plates as soon as possible, or your car's done for. Long story. Just do it.'

'I'm on foot, following them out of Green Park tube station.'

'As soon as you can then.'

'Thanks to your new friend, we've got our eyes on the whole group.'

'The woman, too?'

'All except the woman,' Sean said. 'You need to get here.'

Hash was walking fast, passing the front entrance of the

Ladies' College, beginning to feel out of breath.

'They're going into this big park beside the tube station,' Sean continued. 'Two men, Jim and the bloody drone thing.'

'Are you sure the woman isn't with them?'

'No sign of her.'

'What's the place look like?'

'One of those townhouse places, big porch, pillars, railings. Typical B and B place. I haven't been inside.'

'Be careful,' Hash said. 'Don't get too close.'

'They were outside, piling Jim into the building, then they walked out half an hour later, as if they were going for a stroll.'

'I'm on my way.'

'What'll you do with the new candidate?'

'I'll have to bring him. There's no other option.'

Hash was outside the Rotunda, thinking a taxi could get him home faster. The conman would have blown the whistle for sure by now and the appearance of that legal aid bastard meant it was game over. A miracle was pretty much out of the question, and the realisation struck him hard that their life in Cheltenham was history, probably for good. He prayed Sean's threats of violence were still vivid enough to stall the man for a bit longer.

The taxi dropped him at the junction on Thirlestaine Road and Naunton Lane, leaving him just a short burst of walking to get him home. Rounding the corner into Naunton Crescent he saw blue lights flashing. It was an ambulance, not the police car he was half expecting, but parked close to his house with a paramedic hauling a wheelchair from the back. As he arrived, he saw another supporting Mrs Hamilton. She was deathly pale, her eyes failing to focus on the gallery of interested passers-by. As the medics settled her into the chair, she raised a fragile arm to Hash. 'Is that you?' she croaked.

'Mrs Hamilton, what on earth's happened?' Hash asked.

'Fell off a ladder trying to reach something, silly fool.' She beckoned him forward. 'Do me a favour…water my plants.'

'Of course,' Hash lied, knowing it would be impossible. 'How long do you think…'

Her sly expression stopped him, her old self surfacing through the pain. 'They might keep me in,' she whispered. 'Bloody hope so. I could do with the rest and the free food. How's Jim?'

One of the medics started to turn the wheelchair so they could get her into the ambulance. She looked uncertainly at the vehicle, then over her shoulder at Hash as the chair was wheeled past him.

'She'll be fine with us,' the medic told Hash.

Bousaif had been watching from the hallway, staying back from the door. He looked past Hash to where the ambulance crew was closing the door. 'What was the problem?' he asked.

'Never mind, they say she'll be fine. Get your things ready. We're leaving.'

'The dog,' Bousaif said, and Hash saw blood on his arms as he pointed to Bruno, who was lying on his bed, his flanks heaving as he struggled for breath. 'We were playing. Now he's sick.' Hash went to Bruno and the pup's tail started to thump. Gently he lifted the dog and saw a deep gash on his side. There was blood over the dog's coat, but it was drying.

'We were playing,' Bousaif said. 'In the garden, playing with the ball in the garden.' Bruno was reaching out a paw, trying to get from Bousaif to Hash and Hash took him. They went into the kitchen and looked at the tear in the dog's soft skin. 'A nail sticking through the fence?' Bousaif offered.

'Not your fault. Pack your stuff, we're leaving,' Hash repeated.

Bousaif started in surprise. 'Why?'

'If we stay there is no mission. So, we're leaving.'

'Bruno?'

'We leave the dog with food and water.'

'It is sick, in pain, maybe it will die?'

'Better you kill it then, and we dump it. Stop wasting time.'

Bousaif bent down and stroked the pup. 'I will not do this.'

'You're going to kill humans in a few days, lots of them. Why should one dog be a problem?'

'Please,' Bousaif said. 'Take care of the dog first and...' His words stopped.

'And what?' Hash snapped. 'You help me with my son?'

While Bousaif was upstairs, Hash settled Bruno and called the vet to set up an emergency appointment. He heard Bousaif moving upstairs and went to the stair cupboard to drag out the sports bag with his share of the weapons, unzipping the bag for a quick visual check and making sure the Jameson cylinder was set on top of the rest. Then he dashed to the garage for the suicide vest. Bousaif came downstairs holding his bag, looking down the hall to the front door, as though the police were already waiting. Hash contemplated the Arab BlackBerry and the choice between cutting off messages or taking it and giving away his next locations. He put it in his pocket, shouting to Bousaif to pick up Bruno and carry him to the car.

The receptionist at the vet's surgery took the pup away for an assessment. The clock on the waiting room wall read one-fifteen and the people he had queue-jumped were looking on with disapproval. He went outside and returned Hakim's call.

'You got the place?' Hakim's calm voice gave Hash a surge of confidence. He made him repeat the address. 'And you've got the numbers of my men? Are you on the way?'

'Just leaving.' Hash looked at his watch. 'I could be there in two hours.'

'Don't rush it,' Hakim said. 'No Hollywood stuff.' Hash

could see the receptionist waving at him through the window. 'Call my team when you get there,' Hakim said. 'Check with them before you do anything.'

The girl facing him over the reception counter looked both embarrassed and anxious. 'So, I just have to ask this.' She hesitated. 'Is the dog yours?'

'No, he belongs to my girlfriend and I'm dog-sitting.'

The girl's anxiety remained, 'Umm...that's ok, then,' she said. 'The vet says the tear is minor and we can glue it. He'll need one of those cones though.' She smiled hesitantly at Hash, 'But we might have to do an X-ray.'

'Why?'

'The vet says there's a good chance one, maybe two, ribs are broken. We must have the owner's consent before we go any further. Is there any chance we can speak to her?'

Hash looked at his watch, then pulled out his phone and dialled Eva. Waiting for her to answer, he gave the receptionist a reassuring smile. 'Actually, it's a bit more complicated,' he said. 'The dog belongs to her boss and she delegated the dog-sitting to me.' He could hear her phone still ringing. 'Not answering,' he said to the receptionist. 'Is the treatment urgent?'

'Well, in an emergency we'll just go ahead, if you're willing to pay the costs...'

'Whatever it takes,' he said. 'I'll pay.'

They were interrupted by the phone on her the desk. Apologising, she picked up and he watched her expression flit from concentration, through bewilderment to surprise, with her eyes checking him. She covered the receiver with her hand and looked at Hash. 'We've actually got the owner, from the microchip database. One of my colleagues is trying to call on her landline.'

Poleaxed, Hash let the significance of those words sink in. His brain spun like the wheels on a one-armed bandit jacked into action, then stopping one by one to ring up three heaps of dog shit. The dog had a past, of course, but Eva had never mentioned the owner was a woman. She had always talked about her boss in the male sense. While he was standing at the counter faking a relaxed smile, he felt as though he was far out on a frozen lake, way too far out, with the ice cracking underneath his feet. The weight of a microchip in Bruno's neck was going to sink him.

Before he could do anything, the girl said brightly, 'This happens all the time. Sometimes the old owners don't pass on the news of a sale, so the system doesn't get updated. But she's a breeder, and she shouldn't have missed that.' The internal phone rang and again she picked up. Hash saw her colleague had done the maths and had come up with a different answer to hers, essentially the same as Hash's fruit machine.

'So, we've got a bit of a problem,' she said, covering the receiver and lowering her voice. Hash leaned forward. 'The owner says the dog was stolen some months ago. In this case, the procedure is we have to keep the animal until...'

'The real owner can come and collect it,' Hash finished her sentence, feeling the eyes of the waiting room boring into his back. 'What a mess.' He held up his phone, trying to stay relaxed. 'Really embarrassing. Nothing from my girlfriend, wait till she finds out. Will Bruno get treated, now? I'm happy to pay if that helps.'

'That's good of you, but the owner has authorised the treatment. Can we ask you for a few details? Won't take a minute of your time.'

'Where's Bruno?' Bousaif asked as Hash climbed in. Hash ignored the question, strapping in and switching on, watching carefully as he reversed out onto the road. 'Where is Bruno?'

'No more Bruno. Bruno is safe, and we won't see him again. You ready to go?' He looked at Bousaif and repeated, 'You ready?'

'Insh'Allah.'

Hash's mind was churning. His exit from the vet surgery had been fine, not too abrupt, just a show of polite confusion and a getaway from the place while they were still wondering what to do. They would put it down to embarrassment on his part rather than anything shady. But the fact of Bruno's theft had set other details clicking into place. And the bald conman held a key card; it was better to expect the worst. The police might well follow up on Bruno too, now that he was remanded in the vet's custody. He needed to talk to Sean, find out what he'd seen.

'Where are we going?' Bousaif asked.

'As far away from Cheltenham as possible, West London. The police are getting interested in me, and that's bad for you.' Hash drove to the racecourse, nosing the Discovery close to a bramble hedge.

'What are we doing?' Bousaif asked.

'You're changing these plates,' Hash said, handing over a set and a screwdriver, adding, 'You'll have covered that at Ben Gashir.'

Bousaif shrugged and took the equipment. Hash lifted the Jameson whiskey tube out of his bag and walked down to the footbridge. While he waited to see who was around, he fished out the Arab BlackBerry. He'd already made his decision, no longer worried it might be betraying his location, and tapped an SMS telling Tripoli he was on the move with Bousaif and they needed to clear the letter box. He opened the tube, took out the tape and replaced it with the BlackBerry. Glancing around to confirm he was alone and Bousaif was still working on the plates, he ducked under the wire heading for the culvert. Pausing to catch his breath, ignoring his soaked feet, he looked at the protruding wires for a few seconds. Gently he drew both pins from the grenades, knowing the levers would be held by the side of the tube. Then he pushed the whole tube into the aperture and shoved it in by a few inches. He stepped away, checked around him, dropped the pins into the stream and edged back to the footbridge. He tied three rings of green electricians' tape to one of the uprights. As he smudged the green freshness with muddy water, he pondered the savage justice he was preparing. It was right here, at this very spot, that his tormentors had chosen to wreck his life. And it was here, by their own methods, he would have his revenge.

'Where am I?' Hash answered Sean's question. 'I'm watching my guest change a set of plates. Have you done yours, yet?'

Sean ignored the question. 'The group's in Green Park,' he said, 'and it's full of Arabs, kids playing football, women in burqas, picnics, you name it half of Dubai's here. But they're here too and I'm watching them. Jim's been playing with that quadcopter all afternoon.'

'Where am I taking my guest tonight?' Hash asked. 'We'll be in London around six, latest seven.'

'Got to keep him with us,' Sean said. 'He's a trigger and if we lose him God knows what could happen.'

'Where are you staying?'

'Little hotel right here in Philbeach Gardens. It's perfect for what we need. Cash deal. I'll text you the address. You can park at the back.'

'Can you get rooms for me and my friend?'

'Will do. The place is only 300 yards from their B and B, my window overlooks the street.'

'If we get this right, we can take the bastards down tonight and be away, leave this bugger to his own devices,' Hash said.

Hash briefed Bousaif as they left the racecourse. 'Unless you've got any better ideas Cheltenham is over, finished, never coming back.' He drew a finger across his throat. 'The police will be looking for us here, so we'll hide amongst Arab tourists in London.'

He looked at Bousaif for a reaction but got none. 'We need to be close to your target in Ascot but not on top of it.' Hash looked across at him again, and said, 'West London is best.'

'What about the mission?' Bousaif said a little later as they drove out onto the Evesham Road.

'What about my son? You promised.'

'He will be ok, insh'Allah.'

'I'll kill anyone who harms him,' Hash said. 'Even you, Bousaif.'

'I know. You told me.'

'Your mission is close, next weekend at Ascot. When will you tell me about my son?'

Bousaif did not respond, and Hash pressed him, 'So I have seven days to hide you and then I find my son.'

Bousaif looked at him. 'Seven days? Where's the vest?'

'I've got it in the back,' he jerked a thumb behind him.

They reached West London as the evening rush hour was subsiding but still busy enough to slow Hash to a stop-start crawl as they worked their way across from White City to the small hotel. He left Bousaif in his room and immediately dived back into the flood of heavy traffic on Warwick Road. He soon made it across Cromwell Road and up to the calm of Holland Park where Sean was waiting, smoking as usual.

'What have you done with him?'

'I left him in his room with plenty of food, watching football on the telly.'

'From what I saw,' Sean said, losing interest in Bousaif, 'they were practising. The men were putting Jim through some drills with the quadcopter, zipping up and hovering then dropping.' His nicotine-stained finger described the swooping and hanging, the cigarette leaving a thin trail of smoke.

'And the woman,' Hash said. 'Did you see her?'

'Not at first,' Sean said. 'She came by later, gave them a bollocking and left. When I followed them, it was only the two men and Jim. That's roughly when you phoned.' He looked at his watch, frowned and made a dismissive gesture. 'Roughly, but I don't remember exactly. They were down by The Mall by then and that's when she got out of a taxi.'

'What did she look like?' Hash said.

'I was hanging back, but from that distance it could well have been your Anna, by the look of her.' He looked quizzically at Hash for a reaction, then added, 'No burqa or black gown but she was fit and blond and she was the boss, no mistake about it.'

'Slim, athletic?' Hash prompted, and Sean said again, 'Tidy figure but she was bossing them all around.' He shook his head. 'I thought I'd get closer, but it was one of those weird moments when you know someone's onto you.' Hash watched Sean focussing his thoughts. 'I was about two hundred yards away, just about to swing up the phone to get a shot of the group, when her eyes locked onto me, pinned me to the bloody tree.'

'What did you do?'

'You get someone looking at you like that, and it sends a steel blade through you. The animal that senses a threat before it actually sees it.' He examined a stained fingernail, 'I've been there, mate.' He flipped an imaginary coin in the air. 'Heads, they come straight at you, guns, knives, sticks. Tails, if you're lucky, they fuck off, hoping you'll forget them. Sound like your Anna?'

Hash let the question hang. 'The place they've got Jim. Is it an easy place?'

'What are you planning?'

'Whatever you suggest, mate.'

Sean winced. 'We'll wait for them to come out in the open. We can watch from my window and then run like hell to our vehicle. They can only drive out one way and they'll probably get slowed turning onto Warwick Road.'

'Ok, that's what we'll do. Hang on a minute. Got to SMS Siddiq.' Hash took a few seconds to type the message.

'It gets worse,' Hash said. 'The dog.'

'What about the bloody dog?'

'It wasn't hers. It was stolen all along.' Hash knuckled his forehead. 'I was taken for a complete ride all the way, a witless fool. Never saw it coming. She was the one, all the time.'

'Anna?'

'There's something I've been keeping from you, mate. A new friend, a woman. She's been around for a bit.'

'Susan?'

'No. The exact opposite,' Hash said. 'Nowhere near as lovely as Susan. Someone else.' He leaned back in the seat and groaned. 'What an idiot, what a total fucking idiot.' He thumped himself hard in the chest. 'Eva, she calls herself. She appeared after Cheltenham, after you'd gone.'

Sean said nothing, lighting another cigarette, watching his friend.

Hash said, 'From the start, in the car park with the pup. She must have planned the whole thing. She reeled me in, and I went for it. She even came to the house, chatting away, all cosy, asking about Tara and Jim. Had me completely fooled. I thought I'd found someone I could really open up to, had a really lucky break for once. I looked forward to seeing her, for God's sake' He snapped his fingers. 'That was most likely to brief our friend upstairs. He must have known who she was all along, the bastard.'

Hash was aware he was talking to himself, working back through Eva's trail of deception.   Sean smoked, watched him rubbing his forehead. 'She was the one beating Jim, then sweet-talking me about the message I would send my son. And I never told her he was called Lord Jim. She would have got that when I asked them for the nickname his granny used. Dammit! All the time she had a gun at his head.'

'This is the woman in the burqa,' Sean attempted. 'The one I saw today, I mean.'

'She's Al Qaeda, or ISIS, it doesn't matter anymore.' His phone chirped an incoming message. 'What matters is...' He broke off and looked at his phone, then held it to Sean. 'Tell me what you see.'

'I see your mate, Siddiq, and his bit of stuff.'

'Anna. What time was it sent?'

'A minute ago.'

'From Cheltenham? Probably,' Hash answered his own question. 'Siddiq does Gloucester or Birmingham but never London, and she would have had to drive like hell to have made it from the West End all the way back to the Bath Road in time for this.' He held the screen up and showed Sean the image of two smiling people sitting in a booth in a restaurant. 'That wasn't Anna at The Mall, getting out of the taxi.' Hash closed his eyes. 'I've been miles off target. She's good,' he said, 'really, dangerously good. But,' Hash thought on, 'she's not the one who stole the dog. She just planned it, needed something to get my attention. Whoever stole the dog knew about the breed but not about our microchip system...that must have been a new letter box crew, fresh out from Libya, for sure.' He turned to Sean, 'Little Bruno gets a kicking, and it blows their game apart.'

'So, can we assume she doesn't know you've sussed her?' said Sean. 'She came to the house, briefed the bomber and they're carrying on, as planned?'

'I suppose so.'

'Then let's play this cool,' Sean said. 'Don't let on to your man. Let them think they're ahead of us.'

Hash opened his eyes. 'Give me one of those.'

'They'll kill you,' Sean mimicked, offering the open pack.

Hash took a cigarette, turning it end to end, examining it before he put it to his lips. He flicked his thumb at Sean for a light. 'Have one yourself,' he said to Sean. 'You're going to need it. This is a complicated one. It's about a complete idiot who can look at the hand in front of his face and still not know what it is.' Sean held the lighter and watched Hash draw in the tobacco.

'Like a pro,' Sean said.

'I'm a bloody amateur,' Hash said, his eyes remaining closed. 'From the beginning?'

'Tell me back at the hotel,' Sean said. 'We need to check your friend. And we need to set up.'

Taking it in turns, they watched through the night. The view from the side of the bay window allowed them to look down the curving street to the stucco-fronted, pillared entrance where Sean had seen the group enter and leave during the day. Now, in the small hours, the whole street was still. An occasional car passed slowly by the front of the hotel, then turned out of sight towards Warwick Road. A night owl pedestrian made his way past, and the movement roused Hash's weary senses. Sean's breath came in rapid, sawing gasps as he slept, his diseased lungs working like ancient bellows in some old smoky forge. When a man's young, Hash reflected, sleep's taken for granted, an inexhaustible reservoir of vigour. Watching his friend so restless on the bed, ravaged by illness, mumbling occasional incoherent words, he saw how sleep had become a precious thing, the pool finite. He decided to spare Sean his next watch and take the vigil through to the morning.

He looked at the weapons Sean had stripped, cleaned and reassembled earlier. They had talked about Jim, then Tara. The subject of Eva soon resurfaced.

'That's why you never told me about Eva,' Sean had said. 'In case you felt bad about Tara?'

'Because I knew you'd be upset and angry. We were getting close, and I felt really good with her. I began to think I might be ready to move on, leave Tara behind, put her and the memories with the photos into a drawer and close it.'

'Were you?' Sean had asked quietly. Hash had taken a moment before answering, and the silence made Sean look up from wiping the pistol in his hand.

'You don't move on, ever,' Hash had said.

'Did you love my sister?'

'I still do,' Hash said. 'She'll always be there.' He had tapped his heart.

'That's all I needed to know,' Sean had said.

Jim sat cross legged on the bed, wide awake, head tipped back against the wall, lips pursed, staring at the ceiling. So, tomorrow was the big test, the final challenge. If he had to, he'd fly the drone, get it right this time and get back to his Dad that way. But he didn't trust one of these goons, not even Hamad or the Woman with No Name who'd started off all sweetness and light. Cruella de Ville more like. She'd turned out to be worst of the lot of them. They were all saying the long wait was over now. Too right it was. His Dad was going to be there, they'd told him today. And if he was, all he had to do was spot him in the crowd and he'd be off like a bloody ballistic missile, drone or no effing drone.

Hash locked his brain onto the frighteningly simple rescue plan, looking for improvements. Just thinking it through made his palms go clammy. At the first sight of Jim exiting the porch onto the street, they would react. They were guessing movement could only happen after a late breakfast, when the weather forecast would offer them an opportunity to practise. They would probably call up their driver and head for Ascot, or maybe the London park. It made sense to Hash that they would stay in plain sight amongst other tourists rather than move to a racecourse car park where someone might notice an Arab group. When the move from the porch to the car was building, he or Sean, with their police tabards over their jackets, would burst from the hotel one taking the silver Audi and the other running down towards the Bed and Breakfast. They would block them there. Once on the street, the police vests would buy them a few seconds and the weapons would do the rest.

No matter how hard he tried, the events in Cheltenham kept intruding. Hash was mortified, more so as he thought how easily he'd been duped, how willingly he'd let Eva insinuate herself into his life. Anna had been so easy to suspect; she'd been in all the wrong places at all the right times. Good-looking, interested in Jim, flirting to make Siddiq jealous: in reality, she'd been guilty of no more than being human. Then there was Mrs Hamilton's watchfulness and a blonde visitor knocking on his door when the first bomber was lying dead in the front room; this pattern repeating itself when in fact it was Eva who'd come round to meet with Bousaif. It had been so easy to point the finger of suspicion at Anna, all the way up to Epsom, when he'd seen her two-timing Siddiq, and beyond. There was no excuse...

Groaning from the bed pulled him up short as Sean began to stir. The rumble in his congested lungs built up to a series of hacking coughs. He hauled himself up, swallowing phlegm and grabbing for the glass by his bed, stared blearily at Hash, then looked around the room. 'So, it's not a dream, then. What time is it?'

'Just on six, been light for a bit,' said Hash, switching on the mini kettle.

'Shit,' Sean lay back, rubbing his face. 'You were supposed to wake me.'

'You were sleeping so soundly I didn't have the heart.'

'Bollocks. You fell asleep yourself.'

He made Sean a cup of sweet tea and watched him grimace at the taste before he said, 'I'll get dressed in a minute and take over.'

'Take your time.'

'Anything going on out there?' Sean nodded to the bay window.

'Quiet all night, the occasional car, someone on foot now and then. Nothing in or out of the place itself.' Sean swung his legs off the bed and sat up.

'Are you ready for this?' He held the mug to the glistening black metal of the Kalashnikovs. 'We're getting close and it's going to get rough. We've been there before, Darky, you and me.'

'We shouldn't rush it.'

'Maybe you should just let me do it all. That's what I'm here for. You bring the car and let me do the shooting?'

'I'm fine,' Hash held up a hand. 'I'm ready.'

'What's this bollocks about not rushing, then?' Sean snapped. 'We're here. It's happening. Is this you talking or is it Hakim?'

Before he could answer Sean stood up and went towards the bathroom door. Turning to Hash, he stopped, tapped his temple with an index finger. 'You've got to be ready up here, mate, up here,' he tapped again, 'if you're going to back me up out there.'

Hash listened to the sound of running water and looked back down the road. Sean emerged.

'Our friend upstairs,' he began. 'He's not as keen as he ought to be? No praying the whole time, you know, psyching himself up? You said he almost went to pieces at Epsom. Has he talked about Ascot at all? Shown any interest?'

'Not really,' Hash considered. 'But he was the same before Epsom, cool and indifferent on the surface. Ascot's still some time away.'

'And the first bomber, wasn't interested in GCHQ, right?'

'Right.'

'Something's not right.' Sean picked up the mug and looked at the dregs gloomily. 'I'm going out the back for a smoke.'

At eight-thirty they flipped a coin for who would go down

to breakfast. Hash won and left to collect Bousaif and head down to the basement restaurant. He found him strangely on edge and sensed he wanted to talk. He'd started in Arabic, but Hash told him to switch to English. He barely touched his food, sipping coffee, darting glances at the other guests.

'What's the problem?' Hash asked quietly. 'Dreaming about Paradise?'

'No dreams. No sleep.'

'Go back and rest. I'll call for you in an hour and we can go out for a bit, if you want.'

Bousaif sucked in a sharp breath and shook his head irritably.

'Think of my son, then,' Hash said. 'Maybe he hasn't slept either. Or eaten.'

Silenced, Bousaif sat staring at his half-eaten breakfast. Eventually, he asked if he could take a coffee to his room. They walked back up the stairs, and as he entered his room Bousaif said, 'I am sorry for your son.'

The snib on the lock clicked as the door closed. Hash went back to Sean and took over the watch.

By now the city was coming alive and the rush hour traffic hummed and throbbed out on Warwick Road. Hash toyed with the TV remote and found a news channel, switching the volume to low, hoping he could listen rather than watch and wondering if Sean would approve of anything less than total vigilance. The announcer's voice faded out on a report about increased numbers of tourists expected and the traffic diversions for the Queen's Birthday Parade. At that moment, his mobile rang. Sean's voice was muted but urgent.

'Am I going mad?'

'Tell me,' Hash said.

'Your car alarm's going. Get the fuck down there and deal with it.'

Hash was met in the courtyard by the receptionist who had come out to see the fuss. They looked at the broken side window. She held her hands to her ears, even after Hash had switched the alarm off.

'Oh dear, sir, I'm so sorry. Has anything been taken?'

Hash moved cautiously around the Discovery. 'I don't think so,' he lied.

'Shall I call the police?' the girl asked.

'Not just yet,' Hash hedged. 'I don't think they've taken anything.' He moved to the rear, crouched and looked through window. The suitcase with the suicide vest was missing. He straightened up, looked at the receptionist with a puzzled look. 'I don't get it,' he said. 'They must have seen something but then run off without it. This car's so old there's nothing worth pinching. No need for the police. Waste of their time. This is an insurance job.'

'Yes, but don't you need a crime number for a claim?'

'I'll take care of it, thanks.' With that, she returned to her office leaving Hash looking up at the windows in case anyone was observing. He took the stairs two at a time and found Sean in their room, grim-faced.

'Fucking good job,' he hissed. 'Your man, the candidate. What's he look like? Five feet five, broad shoulders, fit-looking guy, jeans and trainers?'

'That's right,' Hash nodded. 'Brown jacket?'

'Yes.'

'Carrying a roll-on suitcase,' Sean stabbed a finger at the window, pointing towards the porch. 'He's just run down there, and they've gone.'

Hash felt the strength go from his legs and he sat heavily on the bed. 'Gone?'

'Good work, the smart little bastard,' Sean spat. 'Picked his moment, set the distraction and nicked his vest back, all in one hit. Now they've all fucked off. God only knows where.'

'It's happening,' Hash said, squeezing his eyes shut. 'It's

happening, now! Not Ascot, it's now.'

'Where the fuck is it happening?' Sean said. 'We're stranded here, all dressed up and we don't know where to go. I saw Jim get pushed into a car and then your friend runs up and away they went.'

'I know where it's happening.' Hash dug in his pocket for his mobile. He hushed Sean's swearing, putting a finger to his lips, whispering, 'Hakim.'

Hakim answered on the third ring, offering a cautious 'Hello?' Then 'Sayyid Hakim. Are your boys still on the ground?'

'They should be. Why?'

'We've lost them. They're definitely doing the attack today, this morning and it's in the Green Park area of London. If your boys are in our area, then they're looking for two vehicles. Wait…' He looked at Sean who gave him the details. Hash relayed, 'A blue BMW and a black Mercedes. My son is in the blue BMW with the blonde woman and one man. Two men in the follow-up black Mercedes.'

'Where are they going?'

'The target is the Queen's Birthday Parade. The Trooping of the Colour.' Hash saw Sean's head snap back as the penny dropped. 'It starts at Buckingham Palace in,' he looked at his watch, 'half an hour, at ten-thirty.'

With Sean at the wheel of the silver Audi they sped out of the car park, halting at the junction to avoid an oncoming car. Sean hissed at Hash to stay back in his seat when he saw it was the police, waiting to turn into the hotel car park.

'There goes the Discovery,' Hash said. He looked at his watch. 'Five past ten.'

Fifteen minutes later, Hakim rang.

'They are on Cromwell Road heading for Knightsbridge. Two cars as you describe.' Hash could hear him talking to one of his drivers. Hakim updated, 'Hyde Park Corner, wait. Wait, Piccadilly Underpass.' The phone went dead.

'This could be the mother of all set ups,' Sean said.

'Got no option now. Step on it, Sean,' Hash said. 'We can still catch them. Green Park was where they were practising. That's where they'll do it. When the Queen's leaving the Palace, or when she comes back down the same route.'

Hakim's call came through three minutes later. 'They've stopped in Mayfair. All getting out, the two cars. Woman and boy getting out of one...Green Park tube station. Now crossing the road.' His voice carried on a staccato interrogation of his driver. 'Second group, two men also crossing at the same place.'

'Can any of your men follow on foot?' Hash pressed. 'We're only a couple of minutes behind them.'

'Insh'Allah,' Hakim said, continuing a rapid series of orders.

Hash waited for him to finish. 'We're parking up now. We'll be at Green Park tube in two minutes.'

29

Dumping the Audi in Half Moon Street, Hash and Sean crossed Piccadilly at a run, dodging traffic as they went. Sean dropped back to let Hash take the lead as they approached the tube station. The crowd on the pavement was a mix of people. Some waiting for a tour bus, others entering and leaving the station. As Hash looked about, wondering how he was going to recognise his contact, he felt a hand on his elbow and spun round to see Hakim.

'Follow me.'

He guided Hash until they were halfway between the tube station and The Mall. He came to a sudden halt and pointed down The Mall. A crowd fringed the wide avenue; knots of sightseers were drifting towards Buckingham Palace. Drumbeats, insistent and rhythmic, carried across the air, drawing people towards them. Hash scoured the throng for Jim and the group. A couple of Asian tourists, map spread and held outstretched, paused beside them, orientating themselves. Hakim shoved past them, still pointing. 'There…look!' until Hash dipped his head to look along the man's arm, over his pointing finger. He saw a group that was static, not drawn along by the lure of the music. A slim, blonde woman in jeans and black leather bomber jacket stood close to Jim who was unslinging a bulky daysack. There were two men beside them, both looking around, hands clamping phones to their ears.

Hash tore his eyes off them and turned, urgently beckoning Sean in. 'Got them.' Sean advanced as bidden and nodded to Hakim. The two looked at each other without curiosity or animosity. Neither spoke nor wanted an introduction. Hakim's eyes took in the bulkiness of Sean's parka then flickered over Hash's jacket. Hash was sweating in his Barbour and the pistol bulged in his pocket.

'Over there?' Sean squinted through the trees, following Hash's gaze.

Hash pulled out his phone and dialled. 'Watch,' he said. For a few seconds, the drumbeats took over as the wind blew their thudding cadence across the park. Hash's phone began its call over the speaker. 'Watch her now!'

The blonde woman in the distance felt her phone vibrate or heard it, and her hand shot to the back of her jeans. She jerked the phone out of her pocket with her left hand and examined it. Her right hand went straight to Jim's shoulder and Hash killed the call. They saw her whirl round, first left then right, glaring, searching, instinct telling her she was being watched.

'Christ,' Sean said, 'that's her.'

She said something frantically to the two men and pushed Jim to his knees.

'And that's him,' Hash said. 'About a hundred yards to their left, brown jacket, all on his own, very bulky.'

'Remember your promise,' Hakim interrupted, 'remember what I asked from you about guns. I meant what I said. I am handing over to you now.'

Sean froze, caught between the urgency of their situation and the intensity of Hakim's words.

Hash said, 'I have to do this my way. Let your conscience as a father direct you. Whatever happens, there will be a package, addressed to you, waiting at the mosque in Cheltenham. It comes with my deepest gratitude.'

'May Allah go with you, my friend,' Hakim said.

Hash could see Bousaif clearly, isolated and hanging back, and felt a brief pang of pity for this young man, dressed for his death, with the plunger threaded down his right sleeve. He would be sweating with heat and fear, just like at Epsom.

'Let's do it,' Sean urged. 'I'll take the bomber. You go for Jim.'

A trumpet fanfare signalled movement from the area of the Palace and the sound of hooves and drums mingled with a ripple of cheering and applause from the crowds. Hash guessed the first of the royal carriages was passing through the huge metal gates and turning into The Mall.

'The quadcopter's running but not hovering.'

'Can you see any police?'

'Only on the edge of the crowd. There's no sign of anyone back in the trees.'

Hash spotted Bousaif's change of direction. 'He's walking to the left, trying to get some lead on the first carriages.'

'For fuck's sake,' Sean grunted. 'Now or never.'

'Can you do it without shooting?'

'I'll batter him to death with this.' He slapped the bulge under his shoulder. 'Anything. Just say the word'

Hash's mouth had gone dry. He struggled to breathe out the words, 'Good luck.'

He saw Sean break into a trot and started to run himself, caution abandoned, sprinting towards Jim and Eva. All he had to do was call Jim, yell at him to lie down. He cut the distance to one hundred and fifty yards. Eva had her back to him, her phone to her ear. She was watching Bousaif's progress, her free hand holding Jim's shoulder. He was back on his feet, hands on the controls, eyes following the quadcopter. It rose and hovered above the pair. She could trigger the vest from her phone at any second if Bousaif lost his nerve.

Cheering had started in the crowd nearest the Palace gates, swelling in volume as the sightseers realised The Queen's coach was on its way out of the entrance. A rising rattle of drumbeats, jingling harnesses and the clopping of hooves filled the trees. Hash's eyes momentarily swung to a group of men spilling from a Park Service van, rear doors open, bulky men in green coveralls, one of them with an Alsatian in tow, ignoring the parade. The whistling revs of the quadcopter drew his eyes back and upwards. The machine screamed as it gained height swiftly, gliding away in the direction of The Mall. It had already reached the top of the tree canopy as it carried its camera to a hover above the royal procession. Hash stopped dead and drew his pistol, steadying himself. To his left, he saw Sean crashing into Bousaif, kicking, raining punches onto his head and face. Few in the crowd were looking backwards, all eyes were fixed on the procession.

Eva's phone hand dropped in shock as she saw Bousaif go down. Looking around for her backup, she saw Hash, yards away, stalking forward, his pistol held in front of him.

'Let go of him or I'll shoot you dead!' he shouted. 'Jim, run! Now! Run!'

Eva's face showed recognition but no surprise as she hauled Jim round in front of her. Her hand went for her pocket and came out with a small black pistol. Jim's face was chalk white, his mouth open in shock.

Hash felt a kicking blow from behind and staggered, falling forwards. All his breath left him as he hit the baked earth. Someone was on his back scrabbling for his hands. He fought back, kicking and trying to work his pistol from under his body. Eva was still holding Jim tightly to her, walking backwards, her pistol pointing at Jim's head. In his breath-starved fog, Hash saw her forearm rising in protection as a blur of brown hit her. Crushing pain surged through his whole body.

30

He opened his eyes. He could make out a nurse and, sitting at the end of his bed in an unfamiliar room, a familiar boy. Long hair, pursed lips and a sardonic grin. The pain from the light was too great, and he shut them again. He thought he felt a hand touching his, and when he reopened them the apparition was still perched, like a bird of prey waiting to strike.

'Jim...thank God...you're ok.'

'Yup, still here Dad,' it said. 'Hiding with you for safety.' Hash, fighting through the fuzziness, struggled to reach out to him, but his arms were leaden.

'I took one for you, Dad, it was hell.'

'Bastards, what did they do...are they still after us?'

'They aren't...she is.' Jim's smile widened at Hash's confusion.

'Mrs H. You let her plants die, apparently. She had a go at me...so you owe me. I only got away because Grandfather said I had to come and see you.'

'Grandfather?' Hash croaked. 'He's over from Ireland... can't be...unless I'm dying.'

'Grandfather,' the boy confirmed. 'And you're not dying.'

Hash struggled to sit up, but the nurse restrained him, and he felt a plastic straw touch his lips. He took a sip of sweet juice. 'You mean Grandad and Granny?' he rasped.

Jim lent forward and took his hand gently as he said, 'Dad, you need to keep up. I told you all this already. Not Bella and Badger. Grandfather. The other one. Your Dad, the one from Jordan. Anyway, before he went back, he took me home to get some clean clothes, and he rescued me from Mrs H while he was at it.'

Helped by the nurse, Hash managed to pull himself up further.

'How did I get here?' he demanded.

'You've had a nasty fall but you're OK,' she said. 'You're nice and safe and getting better every day.'

Hash lay back and looked at his son. 'What's with the long hair?'

Jim smiled at him. 'Well done, Dad, that's more like it. They wouldn't let me go anywhere, not even to get a haircut.'

'Who?'

'That woman and her two mates, the ones who were supposed to be looking after me and finding you. Anyway, Grandfather asked me to give you this. It's a present, he said. Not much of one, really. He asked to borrow it when he saw it in the kitchen.' Faces swam into focus, staring from the old black and white family snap.

'He's written all the names on the back,' Jim said.

Hash looked and saw neat handwriting in Arabic, listing names he already knew; his mother and father, both sisters. His baby nephew's name had been crossed out, and the name "Bousaif" written beside it in inverted commas.

'Bousaif is the baby in that photo. My nephew,' Hash whispered. He could feel the fog of painkillers swirling back. Bousaif, in on the whole thing, a plant, no wonder he was friendly, no wonder he flunked Epsom. A hell of a family reunion that would have been. His vision started to blur, and he struggled to stay with it...

'You have to tell your grandfather...'

'Which one?' Hash crooked a finger, and the boy's face came down to his. 'The new one?'

'Tell your grandfather, yes, my father.' He tried again, and Jim leaned in to hear him better. 'Tell him...' He tried to swallow and the nurse held the straw to his lips again.

'You'll have to speak up, Dad. I can't hear you.' He bent until his ear was against Hash's lips.

'It's urgent. You've got to tell him,' he whispered. 'I rigged the letter box...green tape... the racecourse, at the bridge.'

'Dad, what letter box? What are you on about?' Hash shook his head, gasping at the pain, and fell back on the pillow.

The nurse stepped forward. 'That's enough. He needs to rest.'

TRIPOLI

The older man looked at the aerial photographs, as one by one the aide slid them in front of his boss.

'It might appear on Google Earth soon, everyone will see it,' he said.

'When you thank the Brits, tell them I enjoyed the live footage. When did the strike go in? UK time.'

The aide nodded. 'That would have been 10:15 UK time on the 13th.'

'So, no last-minute transmissions or contact between them and the lunatics at the Queen's parade. And how many killed by the strike?' the old man asked.

'The last count, according to the Manager, was around a hundred dead and as many wounded.'

'What a wonderful result,' the old man said. 'A job lot. And that ghastly Director? Hopefully also blown to pieces with all of his horrific protégés?'

'The Manager said it was timed to perfection, they were all at some ceremony when the strike happened. The director would have been taking that ceremony.'

'My son, how is he coming on? And my grandson, young Lord Jim?'

'Your son is still recovering, and your grandson is with him, he's doing well too. Not back at school yet. That teacher he told you about is being a great help.'

He snapped his fingers, 'I'm forgetting things…did you send a team to clear that letterbox?'

'The new team at the embassy did it. They weren't happy taking out the grenade with no pin in it.'

'It's why they get extra pay. Tell them there are vacancies in Yemen'

'As for Tariq, our liaison officer says it will be house arrest with privileges. More or less his regular life, but with weekly check-in conditions. There's a memorandum of understanding which freezes legal action indefinitely until all parties can take the circumstances into consideration'

'A good compromise, very British. I suspect they'll want much more than that, now they know what we can offer. The flight to UK, when is it?

'Take off in two hours. And we arrive Northolt, midday local time.'

'Absolutely blinding, old boy,' the old man said contentedly in his cut glass English. 'Now, I need you to find my old tailor in Savile Row.' He snapped his fingers, and tapped his brow, 'That's it, Welsh & Jefferies. Find out if they're still in business and book me in for a fitting. Then we need some fun. I'll take my sons and grandson for a treat. Book tickets for any decent cricket match. Start with Lords or the Oval. You'll need to check the fixtures.'

'Cricket' the aide murmured, scribbling diligently on his notepad and simultaneously working on a plausible excuse for missing that particular treat.

ALDERGROVE AIRPORT.
NORTHERN IRELAND

On his way out of Arrivals at Aldergrove, because he was in no hurry, Sean's attention was hijacked by a news monitor and a strapline showing Royal Ascot. The Queen in a pastel outfit, binoculars in hand and eyes alight with excitement, watched as one of her four-legged hopefuls powered across the Ascot turf. The camera panned to the horses strung out, with the leader well clear of the other runners pushing hard for the line.

A tap on the shoulder and a whispered 'Excuse me, sir' brought him spinning round to face two policemen. 'Would you mind coming with us?' It wasn't an invitation. He looked back at the screen to see a jubilant jockey standing up in the stirrups, waving to an ecstatic crowd.

'Did you have money on that one?' one of them asked. Sean said nothing, just held out his fists, one over the other in a public show of submission, and the trio moved off.

Seconds later, inside the warren of airport corridors, a door opened and a stout middle-aged man in a dark suit wearing a badge round his neck intercepted them, waving the two uniformed men away with a, 'Leave us lads. We'll need a wee minute or two to ourselves.'

Except for the basic furniture of a desk, and two chairs, the office was bare. The man in the suit pointed to one of the chairs and Sean sat.

The suit stayed upright, looking down at Sean, then held up two fingers. 'Two, isn't it?' he said. Without waiting for a response, he stepped back and tugged the door open, yelling into thin air. 'Dying of thirst here! Bring us two mugs of decent tea with two sugars!' Winking at Sean, smug that he'd called it correctly, he peeled off his jacket and draped it over the spare chair. Sean watched his handler sourly, unsure if he'd ever liked him; his false cheeriness in the sordid game had always rankled.

'We expected you earlier. What happened? You get lost?' The man loosened his tie and started to roll up his sleeves.

'Mind if I smoke?' Sean said.

'Just you set yourself on fire, Sean, old mate.' He finished rolling up his sleeves, went to the door again and yelled out, 'And an ashtray!'

Somewhere a female voice responded and with a cheery smile the man pulled over his chair and sat. Sean lit his cigarette and inhaled, his eyes closing with pleasure.

'Good to be back, is it?' the suit asked. 'Been missing the rain?'

The door opened and a young lady brought in a tray, off-loading two steaming mugs, the ashtray and a plate of biscuits. The handler pushed the ashtray over, then lifted a mug and placed it in front of his guest.

Sean blew on the surface before savouring the brew. 'Nectar,' he said. 'Always better at home.'

'It's the water,' his companion said easing back, contemplating him. 'You alright, Sean? I've seen you looking better.'

'You'd be looking a bit rough if you'd had a police baton up your arse for the last few days.'

'Bollocks. We told them to take care of you. Stop your moaning.' He raised his own mug to Sean and held it in salute. 'You did great. Everyone's chuffed with the way you handled it.'

He jutted his chin out of the window to the green hills in the distance. 'Those jokers up at Castlereagh almost shat themselves at how close to the wire we took it. We had more plain-clothes people strolling about there than tourists, by the way. That Gurkha couple with the map,' he flapped his hand, 'don't even ask how we got them. She tasered your mate then her chum took him out. Almost overdid it, I'm hearing.' Sean raised a weak smile, reaching for one of the biscuits. 'You hungry? Want something brought in from the restaurant?'

Sean waved his cigarette. 'Tea and a smoke'll do just right, thanks.'

'You did a number on the lad with the vest.'

'He fought like hell. Must be losing my touch.'

'No harm done. We've got him isolated. He's fine, mate, you don't have to worry about that bugger.'

'I wasn't worried about him. Just sorry I couldn't kill him.'

'Suicide vest saves bomber...they'd probably print that in the Star. Just as well you didn't mind, because he's a guest of Her Majesty, now. One of the police dogs caught the psycho woman. Our team was stacked up in the Parks van, waiting for you. They clocked you and your mate as you went past, and they already had eyes on her and the wee lad. Should have seen that old dog take her out.' He let Sean savour his cigarette for a few seconds. 'They found all sorts on her, drugs, a pistol, a stack of cash. The Brits have gone all coy about her, she'll be gold-dust to the spooks now. An investment,' he snorted.

'Meaning?' Sean arched an eyebrow.

'Meaning, no publicity, they'll turn her, tag her and release her back into the wild.'

'Sounds familiar to me,' Sean rasped, coughing into his sleeve. 'I was an investment, then, was I?'

The handler smiled. 'She's Bosnian, her family slaughtered by Serb paramilitaries and her kept on for amusement, gang-raped by the bastards. Somehow, she got away, got herself recruited by the ragheads. Found her way into ISIS. Fully qualified head banger.' He shuddered at the thought, adding, 'Your mate Darky's a poor judge of women. She'd make the bunny boiler in that film look like Mother Teresa. That wee lad Jim wouldn't have stood a chance.'

He smiled at Sean. 'You know there's a pardon in this for you,' he said, 'full and final, slate wiped clean, all-singing all-dancing tea with The Queen sort of pardon.' He waited for Sean's response. 'Are you listening, Sean? You're a free man.'

Sean said, 'Free from what?' He took a last long drag before crushing the cigarette into the ashtray.

'You're free to retire, slip away, get a new start. We'll fix you a pension, enough to keep you in silk stockings and suspenders in the style you've always wanted. Or,' he balanced one uplifted palm beside the other, 'if you're bored, we'll get you a job. We can fix anything you want. You can be a barman in Majorca by next week if that takes your fancy. Just say the word.'

'Thanks, but no.' Sean started to say something more, but fell silent.

'Tell me then?' the handler said. 'We'll get you a medal, the press'll love it. How about,' and he made inverted commas in the air, 'Provo hero saves Queen from ISIS fanatics, collects top gong, Liam Neeson considering the part?'

Sean looked up from his cup, put it down, and held his fingers up too. 'Or how about, IRA supergrass gets in the way of ISIS, accidentally saves the British Queen, given Brit gong as a death sentence. Gets gunned down at Aldergrove, Neeson shits himself, turns role down?' He managed a gravelly chuckle as he picked up the mug, nodding at the man opposite. 'Fucking spot on, you got that right enough.' He took a sip.

Looking dejected, his companion folded his hands and rested them on the table. 'Ok, then, so maybe Daniel Day-Lewis'll take the part.'

'I'm dying,' Sean said, tapping his watch. 'Matter of time. I had it coming.'

'I'm sorry to hear that. But we're all dying, likely my turn next.'

'It's my mind,' Sean burst out.

He put both hands to his head, thumbs kneading his temples. 'It's playing hell with me. I keep seeing that wee lad's face.' He stubbed his cigarette out and immediately lit another.

'Look,' the man opposite said, suddenly gentle. 'You did the crimes, and you did your time. You, of all people, paid. You've paid your debt a hundred times over, man. Not many can say they've saved the Queen and, my friend, you're not the only one wrecked by the Troubles. Thirty years of waste and countless peoples' lives ruined. For what?'

Sean's head was down, his shoulders heaving. 'I think about it every day and night,' he gasped., 'Every fucking day and night'. The handler kept silent, watching.

'That kid,' Sean said at last. 'That poor wee kid.'

'Darky's kid?' the man opposite said softly. 'You saved his backside. He's back with his dad where he belongs. You, Sean Barr, his uncle, you saved him, got him back to his dad in one piece. Cue standing ovation, beers all round. Liam Neeson reconsiders the part.'

'No. The kid,' Sean whispered urgently, looking up, tears on his cheeks. 'My neighbour's kid, the tout's wee lad.' Sean's breath came in gulps, and he started coughing. The handler reached behind into his jacket pocket.   Sean got his coughing under control and wiped his eyes with the heel of his hand, taking a deep shuddering breath. 'He knew me, I was his fuck-ing neighbour. He thought I'd come to save him. God, his eyes when he realised what I was going to do. Those eyes begging me not to do it. I took that innocent kid's little life.'

The handler reached over and held his shoulder. He slipped a hip flask in front of Sean and flipped off the cap.

'Take a shot ....' He watched Sean take a pull from the flask, then took one himself. 'Poteen's the nearest thing to treatment for PTSD we've got in Ulster.' Sean managed a weak smile.

The man leaned in. 'We were in a war,' he said. 'You did what you thought was your duty. Innocent people got hurt on all sides. That wee boy was caught in the crossfire. He was going to die, and you put him out of his misery.'

Sean began to sob again, harder than before.

'Darky couldn't pull the trigger. Didn't have the balls. You told me that. The wee lad would have been in terrible pain. You've paid for it, Sean. Over the years you've saved hundreds of lives. At the end of the day, when the scores are tallied up, you're a hero.'

'At the end of the day,' Sean said fiercely, recovering a little and looking up at the man opposite, 'I'm just another fucking tout, is all.' He reached for the flask. 'The only thing I want in this world is to see that young lad again, alive and smiling. But that's not going to happen. I've been living in Hell ever since that day, and my old mother's bang on when she says that's where I'll burn when my time comes.'

**NINE
ELMS**

Nine Elms Books offers an interesting list of fiction and
non-fiction books.

Visit our website
www.nineelmsbooks.co.uk
Contact: *info@nineelmsbooks.co.uk*

INTO THE FIRE

One photograph can change a nation

By Philip Trotter

Philip Trotter's debut novel is an exhilarating and original take on the Vietnam theme, exploring less familiar aspects of the country's painful history through the generation-defining image of the Burning Monk.

Saigon, 1963. With the tensions of war starting to swirl, rookie photographer Ned Rivers lands in South Vietnam, hungry for the iconic shot that will make his name.

But a shocking and violent act of protest by a local Buddhist monk quickly draws Ned's focus from the battlefields and the Viet Cong. Behind the front pages, a different conflict is churning – political, religious, and cultural – which threatens to tear this fragile nation even further apart.

As Ned learns more about the Buddhist community's suffering at the hands of the state, his journalistic detachment becomes harder to justify. New friendships turn to solidarity and action, leaving him open to the government's wrath.

President Diem sends out his ruthless attack dog Colonel Tung to manage the interfering journalist. Meanwhile, Diem faces mounting criticism from his American allies as their stake in Vietnam deepens. With political pressures at home driving US policy, the regime seems increasingly like a liability.

For Ned, caught at the centre of this international chessboard, the adventure becomes too real. With friendships, love and a career in balance, can he hope to protect it all from the conspiracy of violence, arrest and war that surrounds him?

Paperback: Price: £7.99
e-book: Price: £3.99

THIS CHANGED EVERYTHING
The Truth is Dangerous
By David Palin

This Changed Everything is a dark psychological thriller has more surprising twists and turns than the wild Cornish road on which newly pregnant Claire Treloggan suffers a sinister and voyeuristic sexual assault.

The fallout puts a strain on her stale marriage to Richard, as does the presence of Detective Chief Inspector Ben Logan – an enigmatic police officer who has risen quickly through the ranks despite the problems he struggles to control and hide, not least of which is the prosopagnosia which renders him incapable of recognising faces.

In *This Changed Everything* author David Palin weaves together the stories of two very damaged people – Claire and Logan. Each has a hidden agenda, there is no room for compromise, and both are being pushed towards a cliff edge below which their personal demons await them.

Paperback Price: £7.99
eBook Price:£3.99

THE ARMISTICE KILLER

Heroes Aren't Always Heroic
By David Palin

Philip This is author David Palin's second dark psychological thriller involving the unsettled, and unsettling, Inspector Logan.

The plot of *The Armistice Killer* is as intriguing as the characters who stalk its pages all the way from Cornwall to Afghanistan.

The bizarre and brutal murder of a military hero – retired RSM Tom Wright – sets in motion a complex investigation headed by the troubled Inspector Logan. The detective's prosopagnosia – facial recognition blindness – is almost the least of his problems as his overlapping inner demons and desires threaten his professional competence.

But it's not only faces that confuse Logan as he struggles to read the minds and motives of a compelling, dysfunctional cast of characters, where nobody is quite what they seem, including the murdered soldier himself. Yet Logan's flashes of intuitive genius likewise constantly unsettle those who would remain faceless.

Can Logan and his deputy Pascoe keep on the trail of blood as it leads their investigation up more dark alleys – most of them blind, and some of them heading into their own disturbed pasts?

The Armistice Killer's parade of clues, red herrings, lies and deceits will keep the reader guessing to the last page.

Paperback Price: £7.99
eBook Price: £2.99

HANGMAN
A Simple Game... Deadly Consequences
By Simon Rae

Six little dashes. One empty gallows. Fancy a game?

This most simple of children's games involves the temporarily suspended Inspector Dalliance on his third, and most intriguing yet, murder mystery. There's all to play for if lives are to be saved... even his own.

Driving home one night from his mother's funeral, Chief Inspector Dalliance suddenly finds himself embroiled once more in a new string of murders – and a dangerous, cynical game targeting the lowest, the most vulnerable, and the most desperate.

His own life unravelling around him, Dalliance is cast out of the investigation under the guise of compassionate leave. But as the case grows increasingly personal, he strikes out on his own to solve the sinister riddle, with or without official sanction.

With the victims chosen from the voiceless, invisible underclass, and human life seemingly valued at nothing, local feuds and professional politics begin to take precedence. Perhaps only Dalliance, with so little left to lose, can take on the Hangman and win.

The first two intriguing Inspector Dalliance books are – *Bodyline* and *The Pill Box Murders*.

ENGLISH CRIME MYSTERIES IN THE BEST TRADITION OF MIDSOMER MURDERS

Paperback Price: £7.99

eBook Price: £3.99